Age of Darkness

Brandon Chen

To my grandma, who taught me that no dream is unachievable and with enough work anything is possible.

CONTENTS

I want to thank all of the friends and family who have supported me along my journey. Without you, I would not be where I am today.

1. THE BOY

The boy was dazed. The world seemed to spin, turning his peripheral vision into a hazy white mess as he hit the tiled school floor. A fresh red bruise, the result of a powerful punch, bloomed on his cheek, and the young boy grunted, his breath heavy. Long, spiky black hair fell over his face, shadowing his dark brown eyes. He was only fourteen, yet this harsh treatment was normal for him. Salty blood gathered in his mouth, and he realized that he had bitten his tongue when he had fallen.

His name was Keimaro, and he abhorred every part of his dull, abusive life. Each day was the same, dragging on and on with his tormentors and the townsfolk always putting him down for no particular reason, as if he were some kind of monster.

Even his own father—of whom he wasn't exactly fond—ignored him. In fact, whenever he came home with a bloodied nose, a split lip, or a bruised cheek, his so-called father pretended not to see anything. It was as if his injuries didn't matter at all.

Nevertheless, Keimaro was forced to face the cruelty of his harassers, and their punishment was brutal. He would've run away from this terrible village, but something stood between him and his freedom. Surrounding the village was a massive force field—a giant invisible bubble encasing the entire village of Bakaara. It allowed nothing to come in and nothing to leave. He had heard rumors that it had been placed there a couple of weeks before Keimaro was born and that it was originally meant to contain him. Though, he knew that those were merely lies. The village elders had set up the force field as a giant ward to prevent beasts from invading and killing the inhabitants of the village.

Outside of the village was the Forbidden Forest, where dangerous beasts dwelled in silence, waiting for night. Then, they would slither out from the shadows and hunt, eager to break through the wards. Few had ever seen these beasts before, but there were rumors of shadow beasts that fed on the flesh of human children. Again, those were only rumors. The forests' enormous trees, that stretched to the very clouds, dwelled in the distance, creaking and groaning at night. Sometimes it seemed as if the forest itself were alive, trying to reach for the village. However, the force field had been up for fourteen years. There was no reason for it to come down.

The force field was comparable to a jail cell—at least, for Keimaro, it was. He felt confined, like a caged animal, incapable of seeing the world. What was the point in educating himself if he wasn't even allowed to leave? Besides, staying in the village seemed like suicide. Everyone hated him. He didn't even know why, and he found no valid reason for the disrespect that he received from those around him. He had learned to adjust to this, but he simply felt segregated as an individual. Isolated. Hated.

Keimaro pushed himself up from the dusty ground, brushing grit from his cheek with the back of his hand as he sniffed back tears. He was grasping his diaphragm, which had taken several blows from the boys at his school, trying to refill his lungs with air. He glanced at the teacher, who had simply watched the spectacle without stirring to stop the bullies from attacking him. Instead, the teacher gazed at the scene before her with profound interest, her arms folded as if she were actually enjoying the display.

Burning hatred coursed through Keimaro's heat-filled veins, and his heart pounded with a burst of adrenaline that sent energy channeling through him. Keimaro's lip was bleeding, and he exhaled audibly, his ribs aching. The pain dragged out, and his injuries pulsated, creating a sort of mismatched rhythm of pain. He didn't know why they hated him or why they always beat him up. All he knew was that they did it every single day.

He turned around and glared at the main bully with a look of pure hatred in his eyes. His name was Buu, and he had curly brown hair and glistening blue eyes that resembled the color of the morning sky. The ladies loved him, though Keimaro didn't understand why. He was the one who led the assault on Keimaro each day. Oh, how he detested this boy. He couldn't even count the number of times that he'd imagined driving his fist solidly into Buu's gorgeous face. But, would that solve anything? His anger, his hatred all boiled down to the fact that Buu existed. Having such strong negative feelings was sometimes disconcerting, but it was unavoidable. These feelings had built up over many years of abuse. He was sick of it!

Keimaro suddenly sprinted forward, his fist clenched tightly as he rotated his body, hatred throbbing in his heart. Buu turned around just as Keimaro's fist shot forward, his knuckles smashing solidly into the bully's cheek. A crack resounded as the boy's body twisted. His legs left the ground, and his body went airborne, spinning wildly. He slapped hard against the tiled floor with an unnatural thud and was left motionless.

Keimaro's fist burned from the impact of his punch. He shook it animatedly, as if the rapid movement of air would cool it. His heart raced as the teacher stared at him in absolute shock. "I-I...."

What was he supposed to say? That this boy deserved it? As if anyone would believe him. They were all against him. Every last one of them. He looked at the other boys that gathered around the body of Buu. He heard whispering amongst the girls.

A bead of sweat formed on his brow, and he took a few steps backward toward the door, their words echoing loudly in his ears. Outsider, freak, monster! He spun around and broke into a sprint, racing out of the door. He could hear the boys scampering after him, but he wasn't worried about being caught—he knew that he could easily outrun anyone in the village. He bit his lip, trying to keep from crying, but he could already feel the tears coming as he sprinted off.

The young boy dashed along the dirt path that led to the marketplace, the more industrial part of Bakaara, leaving the rural area where the school was placed. The tall, dull wooden buildings towered off in the distance, but Keimaro wasn't going in that direction. Instead, he broke off from the dirt path and plunged into the lush green plain that bordered it. The right side led to the farms, the left to the border. Keimaro took a left.

The boys had stopped behind him and were watching him from the edge of the dirt road. They leaned forward and placed their hands on their knees, gasping for air, either completely out of shape or simply exhausted from the long run. No one dared follow him away from the path of the village. The kids had been taught—at an extremely young age—that traveling outside of the village would result in someone's death. The force field didn't just prevent monsters from coming in; it also prevented humans from entering or leaving. Bakaara was a self-sufficient village and had all of its resources nearby within the magic walls. They had no need for outside resources and always had everything that they needed.

Bakaara was an independent speck on the continent, surrounded by the empires of Sparta, Athens, and Faar. All three of these empires were massive and fought each other for domination over the entire continent. Each of the empires could send a simple squad to Bakaara and would probably still be able to wipe out the entire village without any problems at all. But the shield was what truly stood as the only reason Bakaara hadn't already been conquered, dominated, and wiped out. Bakaara itself wasn't an empire. It was far too small. It was a simple, neutral village that had not been dominated by any of the human empires. Yet.

Something that Keimaro had always wondered was how it was that certain small critters were able to squeeze in and get through the force field. The other villagers thought that the animals were simply breeding on village grounds, so they never really questioned where the critters came from. Nevertheless,

Keimaro was curious. In Bakaara, they never feasted on huge animals unless they were bred. Typically, there would be small animals like squirrels, wild boars, or prairie dogs that roamed about. One day when Keimaro was twelve, he saw a small, unrecognizable critter. It was an interesting orange squirrel with miniature antlers that poked from the top of its head. It scampered about, running in the direction of the force field. Intrigued by its exotic antlers, Keimaro stalked the foreign creature, making sure to keep his distance. However, as he tried to follow the small squirrel, he finally hit a wall. The force field. Upon striking the barrier, a surge of energy exploded into Keimaro's body—not enough to harm him, but enough to deflect him backwards. The young boy had been absolutely confused, wondering how it was that the squirrel surpassed this barrier and was out there striding across the free fields outside Bakaara. After many attempts of trial and error, Keimaro finally poked his foot through an open hole in the force field. It took hours, but he finally found it, a place to fit through the barrier and escape. After attempting to escape through different parts of the force field, he realized that the squirrel had found the only crack in the barrier. And that was his only key out.

The young boy, drenched in sweat, slowed to a jog as he reached the force field. Keimaro threw himself through the weak spot in the barrier and walked out of the village without a sound. He was outside of the perimeters and knew that he should've been scared. However, he wasn't. Not one bit. He wouldn't have cared if a massive monster came and mauled him—or swallowed him up, for that matter. No one would miss him. No one. His mother and younger sister were the only exceptions. Definitely not his father, though.

"Now, this is quite a surprise," a voice said from behind Keimaro.

Keimaro blinked as he slowed to a stop and turned to see another young boy standing there behind him. All that stood between the two of them was the invisible wall. The boy had flowing, dark-brown hair and blue eyes that were like sapphires. His hands were in the pockets of his baggy, ripped pants, and his brown shirt had some soot on it. His name was Yata, and he was the most intimidating boy in the entire village. He was known for picking fights with everyone, even the teachers. It took five guards to restrain him, and he was sent to jail on a daily basis— only to get bailed out by the leader of the village himself, who was forced to support Yata since he had been orphaned. No one really knew why he picked fights with everyone, including the bullies of the village, but he was similar to an untamable beast. No matter what the authority, he would fight for whatever he believed in or wanted.

"Tch," Keimaro muttered, looking Yata directly in the eye. His hands were balled into fists at his side, and he raised his head high as he spoke to the boy. "And what do you want?"

Yata raised an eyebrow at Keimaro's attitude and whistled, "Oi. Aren't you a bit aggressive? Didn't seem that way only a moment ago. Think you can act so tough because you're near the border of the village, huh? Just because you landed your first punch on a kid at school?" He cracked his knuckles and pulled back his fist with a smirk on his face. "Well, I'll show you the difference between your punch and mine!"

His fist rocketed forward and slammed solidly into the force field. The transparent wall seemed to absorb the punch. There was a ripple in the shield for a moment before a surge of invisible force smashed into Yata and sent the boy flying backward through the air. Time slowed for the boy as he felt his body thrown off of his feet, his eyes widening as he slammed heavily into the grass, the field cushioning his fall. The boy blinked a few times, looking at the blue sky in a daze, not sure what had just happened.

After a few seconds, he pushed himself up slightly into a sitting position and gulped back his fury. "That...." His eyes went from the disappearing ripples to the boy and back to the force field. "You're beyond the barrier?"

Keimaro's heart was pounding a bit from shock. However, a part of him just wanted to burst out laughing at the sight of Yata being knocked back like that. He smiled lightly, noticing that he had the upper hand against Yata. He knew, though, that he couldn't piss off Yata too badly; otherwise, when he came back into the force field, his life would be over. But a part of him also wanted to share his knowledge. Even though this was the most intimidating boy in the entire village, Keimaro felt willing to share his discovery with someone. Anyone. As long as he wasn't alone. "Eager to see how I got out of here?"

Yata nodded his head curiously. "How did you do it?"

Keimaro pointed to the weak spot in the force field in front of him and stuck his foot through with a chuckle. "It's just a little hole in the wall. I don't know if there's any more, but this was the only one that I found. You wouldn't understand how long it took for me to find this hole."

"You spent time looking for it?" Yata said with a laugh as he crawled underneath the force field and popped his head up on the open side of the world. Fresh air. It was brilliant. "Why would you do that?"

"I'll explain later," Keimaro said simply and stuck out his hand toward the boy before him. "My name is Keimaro Hayashi. It's a pleasure to meet you." *Not really.*

"I'm Yata," the other boy said and grasped his hand gently with a nod as he began to walk with his new acquaintance across the lush green plains that had yet to be touched by human feet. All of this freedom, it was all for them.

***

About a mile from the village was a large apple tree that stood perched upon a hill. It was high and overlooked the village in the distance. The night had taken its place in the sky, and the stars were twinkling down upon the tree and the two young boys who were lying underneath it. Their arms were folded behind their heads, and their bodies were relaxed—more relaxed than they had ever been within the confines of the force field. Keimaro sucked in a deep breath of cold air, not caring about the cool temperature. This was really the first time that he had spent time with another boy his age—or another human his age at all.

He looked over at Yata and knew that the two of them were much alike. Their seclusion from the rest of the kids their age was out of their control. They were both isolated from society, but it always seemed there was nothing they could do about it.

"So, tell me, Kei," Yata said gently, looking up at the gleaming stars that shone in the dark sky above them. "What has got you wanting to leave the barriers? I always saw you as the type of kid that paid attention to his studies. I didn't think you were the adventurous type. You were always so quiet."

"Yeah," Keimaro said with a shrug. "I suppose you could say that there was no one really to talk to. People seem to judge me before they even say a word to me. I could waltz up to a complete stranger, and they would act as if they were completely disgusted with me. I don't particularly know why, or what I've ever done to them. My father doesn't really care about me either. The only people in this entire village that I've felt some type of affection from have been my mother and my little sister, Mai. Other than them, this village can go to hell. They want to keep us trapped inside of some tight barrier, thinking that we'll accept that we are on this planet only to survive," he muttered, beginning to pluck blades of grass from the ground. "There's no way that I'll accept that. I'm here on this planet so that I can experience things and live life to its fullest. Life is short. So, why in the hell do we need to spend our lives sitting inside of a barrier, trapped like livestock? Why do we learn about the outside world in school when we will never be able to see it for ourselves?

"I don't want to be trapped in this village like a prisoner. I want to experience new things. I want to meet new people. I want to eat new foods, see new places, and do all kinds of new things! Staying in one place—where it is hell for me, anyway—is pointless. I'm not even sure what I would do if I hadn't found the small gap in the barrier. To be brutally honest, I might actually be dead by now. The bullying only gets worse, and it's only a matter of time before they beat me to death. When those idiots hit me, no one cares. The teachers let the kids off with a small warning. It's as if I am an animal, another type of species. I see the way they look at me. They all treat me like an outsider.

And I'm sick of it."

Yata remained silent during Keimaro's long rant, and the silence stretched afterward, dragging out in the night. "I get you," he said suddenly, and Keimaro turned to him with a look of surprise.

"You do?"

"Yeah, there was a time when I was like you," Yata said. "You see, my father was quite the murderer. He killed one of the elders of the village in an attempt to try and escape the barrier— just as you have. As a result, my father was captured and hanged before my eyes. I was only five. At such a young age, I wasn't really sure what to think about his dangling body. I cried. I don't really know why, though. He had never been there for me and had always beaten me when I messed up. He wasn't an ideal father. But my mother was the closest person I had. I loved her so much. And the government of the village … these elders…." His hands clenched into tightened fists as he suddenly let out a low, anger-filled growl. "They took my mother away because she was married to and therefore associated with my father. They hanged her as well." Yata gulped, blinking a few times. "They would've hanged me as well if I hadn't been so young. They hanged my mother, the one person I had. She died there right before my eyes as I watched the life choked from her body. And as I saw her corpse dangling there, her feet inches from the ground, I wondered … why? Why did my mother deserve to be punished for something my father had done?

"It was at that moment that I finally realized the reality of it all. That these elders of ours aren't the gods that we think them to be. They cower in their homes, hidden deep in the village with those damn armed guards. I swore I would finish what my father started and kill them all." Yata sucked in a deep breath and exhaled deeply. "But I suppose I won't need to, if we have found a way to get out of this hell-hole."

"So, is that why you always pick fights with everyone? Even against guys like Buu. Because you hate the elders and the village?" Keimaro asked, raising an eyebrow at him. He hadn't

9

expected for Yata to open up so easily, but he also saw that the two of them both wanted freedom from this village. He wanted to see the world while Yata wanted to escape the cruelty of the elders. It was about time that he had found someone who shared his ambitions.

"And the fact that they piss me off," Yata muttered, shrugging lightly. "Fighting has always been a way to express myself. If anyone messes with me, I don't mind treating them like a punching bag. My father taught me to be tough, you know."

"So, why did your father … uh…?"

"Kill the elder?" Yata finished Keimaro's sentence without even a change in emotion. He wasn't angry. He wasn't depressed. His expression was simply neutral as he looked up at the stars. "There was a rumor that if all the elders died, then the barrier would collapse. He killed one elder, betting everything on that rumor. Quite the brutal guy, huh? I never said that I liked my old man. He was a very violent person, and he ruined any chances that he had at getting out of Bakaara.

"I'm sick of looking around and seeing the same stupid crap everywhere! I'm glad to have left the village. Even touching this tree … is enough to make me smile." Yata leaned backward and reached out with his hand, gently running his index finger along the rough bark of the apple tree.

Keimaro nodded his head gently at Yata's words. He knew what he was feeling. He knew all about being trapped like an animal. "What's the point in anything if we just waste time sitting there in those walls? The world out there is vast, Yata," he said and swallowed lightly, concerned by the vehemence in Yata's voice. "But there's no rush to leave yet. We aren't ready. We would probably die as soon as we entered the Forbidden Forest. We need to get stronger before we decide to go out there."

"The Forbidden Forest," Yata scoffed, as he ran his hand through his hair and shook his head in disbelief. "To think that a freaking obstacle such as a forest could be keeping us from our freedom. The elders are afraid of some monsters in the trees, huh? That's why they're keeping up this force field."

Keimaro blinked when he suddenly heard shuffling and spun around to see a young girl with long brown hair and blue eyes, blinking at him. "W-What?" He was about to yelp when Yata clamped his hand over his mouth. "Mm!" His words were muffled, and his heart was pounding. Who the hell was this person?

Yata kept his hand on Keimaro's moving mouth for a moment and examined the young girl up and down before slowly lowering his hand and placing a finger to his lips. The girl was wearing a rather fancy blue dress made of a type of silk that he had never seen before. However, the seams of the dress looked as if they were slightly ripped, and the bottom rims looked as if they were splashed in mud. A red sash was wrapped tightly around her waist and tied perfectly in front. Her long brown hair reached down past her shoulders, something quite unusual amongst girls in their village. There were a few scratches on her knees, and she squinted her eyes against exhaustion as she fought to stay conscious. She was around Keimaro and Yata's age, only fourteen.

"Who are you?" Keimaro whispered to the girl, who stumbled toward them as if she were inebriated.

Keimaro looked down at her feet, caked in mud, and saw that they were bloody from blisters and cuts from walking barefoot a reasonable distance. He saw the girl reaching up toward the branch of the apple tree for a gleaming, shiny apple. As she reached, she fell and Keimaro immediately sprang forward, catching her in his arms. He grunted, feeling her weight bearing upon him, and made sure to stabilize her in his arms before reaching up and plucking the fruit from the branch above and gently handing it to her. She held the apple tightly and took a deep bite into it, closing her eyes and savoring its sweet flavor. It was as if she were in some type of trance, lost in her own little world.

"Kei, look," Yata said in a serious tone, looking off into the distance at a rising smoke that was drifting off from the Forbidden Forest into the dark night sky. Something was on fire in the distance. "I'm assuming that other humans caused that fire. Someone is nearby, and this girl is one of them."

"Yeah," Keimaro said, allowing the girl in his arms to continue munching on the apple. "Her clothes are so different from what we have in Bakaara. She must be from somewhere else. What do we do about her?"

"I don't know!" Yata exclaimed, scratching the back of his neck. "We could take her back to the village. She seems tired and beaten up from having walked so far. Either way, if we leave her out here, she is going to get killed by the beasts in the Forbidden Forest. They'll smell her blood."

"Are you serious?" Keimaro said, incredulous. "Bring her back? We can't do that! Where is she going to stay? Like I said, her clothes are too foreign! We don't even know who she is. She could be a spy for all we know. If she knows the way into the village, everyone could be in danger!"

"You seriously think a girl our age is going to be a freaking spy, Kei?" Yata snarled just as a roar split the night sky and shook the earth to its very foundation. Both of their eyes widened in shock and disbelief at the sheer amplitude of the sound. They stood rooted to the spot, staring at each other in fear. In all the fourteen years that they had lived within the force field, not once had they heard a single sound of a beast. The only evidence of monsters had been minor tremors in the earth. With the ground rumbling beneath their feet, they now knew what caused the tremors.

Keimaro placed one arm on the girl's back and his other underneath her knees and lifted her up into his arms, wincing at her weight. His eyes locked onto a beast that burst from the trees—a black, scaled tiger with a long slender tail that had a spiked circular mace-like shape at the end. The mace-tail dragged through the dirt with ease. The tiger-beast's eyes were dark like the hue of the night, and it bore its sharp teeth at Keimaro, who stared at the pointy daggers in fright. *Those things could probably rip through the hardest of armors.*

"What is that? What do we do?" he gasped, his heart beginning to pound furiously against his chest as panic struck him. He blinked when he felt the weight of the girl bearing down upon him more. She was unconscious. *Perfect.*

"You're fast at running, aren't you?" Yata yelled, beginning to sprint down the lush green hill and back toward the force field. "We need to get the hell out of here! Let's go!"

Keimaro snapped back to reality and spun around, running as fast as he could while holding the girl. Ordinarily, he would've been much faster than Yata, but with the extra weight, he was lagging behind. He grunted as he heard the tiger growling behind him. He knew looking back would only cause more fear in his heart, slowing him down. Keimaro panted, accelerating as his breath began to grow heavier. The roar of the monster grew louder, and the pounding of its paws on the ground was coming closer. He turned his head slightly and in his peripheral vision caught sight of a pounce. He yelped and spun himself to the side. He gasped in shock as the tiger landed directly where he had been only moments before, smashing into the dirt. *I could've died there*, was the first and only thought that hit him. He continued running and saw that Yata had already slid underneath the force field and was waiting for him on the other side.

Keimaro held the girl tighter and his eyes were locked onto the tiny slit in the force field as the tiger began to dash after him once more. *Oh god, oh god, I don't want to die*, he thought. Death was an end to every single dream he'd ever had! He couldn't die now. Not after meeting his first friend. Not after this new goal that he had set for himself. Not after everything!

He pushed off of the ground and leapt high with the girl in his arms, his legs flailing clumsily through the air. The tiger swiped at the exact same moment and scraped the bottom of his legs, ripping his pants. However, Keimaro had jumped high enough to avoid getting his legs lacerated entirely. He landed heavily and got low, sliding underneath the force field as the tiger pounced up into the air and slammed into the force field at full speed. There was an electrical noise that buzzed before the tiger roared, being thrown backward by a massive amount of force. The creature slammed heavily into the dirt and rolled a few times before slowly raising its head. Its eyes changed into a demonic red and locked onto Keimaro, snarling loudly, as if pledging vengeance, before turning from the force field and dashing back into the direction from which it came.

Yata was at Keimaro's side and was examining him to make sure that he wasn't hurt. "Holy crap, Kei! You scared me!" he exclaimed, out of breath. "After a commotion like that, the guards are bound to come somewhere around here. We'd better get going. I'll take the girl with me since I live alone. Hopefully when she wakes up, she can answer some questions. Come over first thing tomorrow morning, okay?"

"Yeah, sounds good," Keimaro said, still sitting on the ground.

"You okay?"

"Yeah, of course."

"You seem like you're still in one piece," Yata said. He finally spotted the scrape from the tiger's swipe and frowned. "That's a nasty cut you've got there. We don't know anything about that creature. I suggest you find out if that's poison because…. I mean, you'll need to get it treated if it is."

"If I was poisoned, how would I explain to the doctor how I was infected with such a poison?" Keimaro muttered, slowly pushing himself to his feet. His leg erupted in pain, and he almost toppled over. Luckily, he hopped a foot and steadied himself, shaking his head in disbelief. He turned to look over his shoulder at the area where the creature had been only minutes before. His heart was beating rapidly against his chest, and he gulped. "What the hell was that thing?"

"I don't know," Yata muttered. "That's one of the reasons why we aren't ready to leave the village yet, I guess. We'll be fine. We just need to train ourselves to be stronger in case we encounter one of those things whenever we do decide to leave the village." He lifted the girl over his shoulder casually and nodded with a reassuring smile at Keimaro. "Go on; go home. The longer we stay out here, the higher the chance of someone finding us with the girl. Come over first thing tomorrow."

"Got it," Keimaro said and turned from Yata, beginning to walk his normal way home. A part of him wanted to rush after his new friend so that he wouldn't be alone anymore, but he knew that right now he had to get home. It was getting late. Turning back to look at the direction that the beast had run in, Keimaro exhaled. He was alive; that was good. And something else had happened. Something exciting. Every day had been the same within the small village of Bakaara, but tomorrow was going to be different. He rubbed the back of his neck in disbelief and sighed. Man, how were they going to keep this girl a secret? Everyone in the village already knew each other. They would need to make up a story—and even so, her clothes were unrecognizable. Someone would clearly find out that she is foreigner. He ran a hand through his hair as he walked through the village. Since night had fallen upon Bakaara, it seemed that hardly anyone was in the streets. It was common for families to spend time with each other at nighttime, except for a few of the guards who would switch shifts.

The market square's center was surrounded by many different wooden buildings that had been built—and rebuilt—from the original wood that had inhabited the land, since no one could leave for more resources. Keimaro walked on the tiled ground past merchants' tents and caravans filled with fruits and vegetables from the farms. These were locked for the night and packed away to keep them safe from thieves. Though, not many people had the guts to steal. The village itself only had a population of around ten thousand. That might've seemed like a lot for a small village, but everyone was spread out over vast fields of farmland. Bakaara was mostly a farm-driven society, with the villagers surviving off of grown foods. There was only one area on the entirety of Bakaara's grounds that somewhat resembled a city, and that was located in the center of all of Bakaara. The land, however, was nothing in comparison to how vast the empires were. Bakaara was nothing but a speck in comparison to a kingdom like Athens.

15

Keimaro continued walking past the markets toward the long, stretching farmlands that filled the rest of Bakaara. Finally, he locked his eyes onto his house, a small cottage in the distance in the center of a reasonable amount of farmland. The crops had already begun to grow, filling their yard and towering over Keimaro.

Keimaro walked up the path and opened the door slowly to find his mother, father, and younger sister sitting at the dinner table. He broke the silence with his footsteps and plopped in a chair silently, exchanging glares with his father. He looked down and saw beans, rice, and corn on his plate. There was never any meat because the amount of animals they bred was limited. Meat was considered a luxury that was eaten only on special occasions. But Keimaro knew that the elders probably had meat every single night.

"Dinner is ready, Kei!" Mai, his four-year-old sister, exclaimed. She had shorter black hair like Keimaro with small, gleaming dark eyes. She sat upon her mother's lap with a bright smile on her face, as if she were having the time of her life. She waved her spoon about cutely until their mother calmed her down by guiding her hand to the food.

"Where have you been?" his father asked, his eyes on his food as he began to spoon some corn into his mouth. His black beard had been trimmed to stubble. His blue eyes flickered across the table at Keimaro's mother, and he cleared his throat. "You've been coming home later than usual these past couple of weeks."

"I went out for a walk."

"Where to?"

"Since when is it any of your business where I walk to?"

"Since I became your father," his father snapped loudly, turning his head abruptly to his son. "Now, when I ask you where you were, you'll tell me. Were you doing something suspicious, Kei?"

"Why would I have any reason to do something suspicious?" Keimaro muttered, running a hand through his hair as he sighed. "There's nothing to do in this damned village anyway."

"Where did that come from?" his father said, raising an eyebrow.

Keimaro shrugged and shoved some peas into his mouth, chewing slowly before finally swallowing hard. He began to speak without making eye contact with his father. "Father, will you teach me how to fight with a sword?"

Silence reigned at the table. The only sounds were the crackling and popping from the fireplace. When Keimaro peeked from the corner of his eye, he saw his father frowning at him. The older man put his fork down on the wooden table and scoffed. "I've already been teaching you how to defend yourself with your fists. Why would you need to learn with a sword?"

"I was walking around the perimeter of the barrier today," Keimaro said simply, "and I saw a beast outside of the barrier. I knew that he couldn't get in, but I was still afraid. I couldn't move. I simply watched as the beast bashed into the barrier over and over again...."

"What the hell were you doing at the barrier?"

Keimaro ignored his father's words and continued with his fake story. "It made me think, what would I do if the barrier weren't there? Would I run, only to be hunted down again? This barrier won't be here forever, father! Don't you understand that? If I don't learn how to fight, then I will never be able to face the horrors of the world! Whether it be another mage that takes down this barrier himself or some psychotic fool that assassinates all of the elders of the village, the barrier will eventually come down!" He slammed his hand on the table and glared at his father with a look filled with confidence. "Do you simply expect for me to sit here and watch my family's life be put in jeopardy when those monsters finally do break in? When it comes down to it, nothing is going to protect us except ourselves. You can't place all your faith in the damn invisible shield that surrounds us! Everyone in this village looks around blindly and accepts life in this miserable, isolated, piece-of-crap land that we own. Hasn't anyone else wanted to see the outside? The barrier will come down someday, father. When it does, wouldn't you want me to be able to defend myself against the cruelty of the world?"

"The barrier is here so that we can be isolated from the cruelty that is the world," his father snapped, shaking his head in disbelief. "You have no idea what's out there, Kei! If the barrier ever broke down … you would die no matter what. Even if I taught you how to fight—"

"Then you'd prefer me to just accept my death rather than fight back against the forces that would take my life?" Keimaro snapped.

His father was silent for a moment and closed his eyes, massaging his temples as he tried to calm down. "I refuse to teach you a useless technique that will only get you into trouble and, even worse, give you another way to hurt yourself. Leave me to eat in peace. At least allow me that luxury in my own home."

Keimaro ignored that last comment and continued to shovel food into his mouth forcefully before he finally picked up his plate and brought it to the sink. He washed the dishes that night in solitude, before finally walking upstairs to his room. He heard his mother urging Mai to take a bath, but the young girl kept complaining, saying that she would do it in the morning. Keimaro smiled.

He passed by his younger sister, who was sitting outside her room with her arms wrapped around her knees. She was pouting after having the miniature argument with her mother, but her eyes glistened when she saw Keimaro. The older brother squatted down in front of her to pat her head. "Hey, Mai. How was your day today, hm?" he asked with a warm smile.

Mai was rubbing an eye with her fist, completely exhausted.

She looked as if she were ready to fall asleep right on the spot. "It was good. I aced my test at school today! The teacher said I was the brightest in the class," she said with a yawn.

Keimaro lifted Mai into the air and held her in his arms as he began to walk to her room. "Is that so? Well, you'd better get a good night's rest, okay, Mai? Keep doing well in school. And don't fight with Mom. She's just doing what's best for you," he said with a smile as he placed Mai down in her bed and pulled the blankets over her. He watched Mai snuggle up with a teddy bear that Keimaro had bought her for her birthday. It was made from leftover scraps of resources that the village hadn't used. It wasn't the best present, but she cherished it like it was the greatest thing she had ever received. Keimaro didn't know if what he had said at the dinner table was true, but if the monsters really ever did break in, then he would never forgive himself if he didn't have the power to protect Mai. He watched as Mai fell asleep within a minute and turned his head to the hallway as he heard the floor creak behind him.

"Kei, I want to speak to you," his father said from the doorway.

Keimaro stood up straight and walked to the hallway, closing Mai's door silently before turning to address his father.

Before he could speak, his father said, "Your teacher told me about your little incident at school today. What do you think you were doing? Fighting with Buu again? Why would you do that? I thought that we agreed that you shouldn't fight."

"Yeah?" Keimaro muttered, not meeting his father's eyes. "So, I should just let him beat me every single time that I go to school? Are you so oblivious that you don't even notice the bruises and beatings that I receive every day? Or is it that you're like the rest of the idiotic adults of this village and don't care if I get beaten every day and teased? You wouldn't even care if I died, I bet."

His father stared at him with a look of shock and disbelief. One hand balled up into a tight fist at his side as he put the other hand on the wall with a snarl. "Look, Keimaro—"

"Look what? It's true. Not to mention, if I learn to fight, I won't just be able to protect Mai, I will be able to defend myself against the evils that exist within this stupid cage that we live in," Keimaro growled, looking into his father's eyes with a convinced glare. "I know that you adopted me as a child, father, but that gives you no right to treat me the way you do. That gives you no reason to accept the fact that your own son was almost beaten to death today. Are you going to look the other way again? Or are you actually going to do something? The teachers all turn the other way as if nothing happened. There is no authority. There is no one that will stop these bullies from harming me. So, it's either that you prevent these bullies from harming me, or I'll do it myself. Teach me how to defend myself."

His father stood there and closed his eyes. There was nothing for him to say. He was unable to tell Keimaro why the bullies were harming him. He was powerless in this situation. "I'll teach you. My style of combat is unique. It is unlike any style in the globe. I explored much of this world back in my day before the wards around the village were put up. But, my fighting style is very difficult. No one else has mastered its speed and accuracy. Don't expect to be able to protect yourself in a month or even six months. It'll take a year merely to grasp the concept of my style. Perhaps two years to begin to master the way of the sword, and that is only if you train every single day with maximum effort."

"You know I would do anything to obtain the strength to protect Mai and me," Keimaro said.

"Then we begin tomorrow," his father said simply before walking past him in the hallway. He left Keimaro standing there alone, watching the shadows dance around the candles on the wall.

Keimaro inhaled a deep breath as he walked to his room, which was practically empty except for a bed, his wardrobe against the wall on the left side of the room, and a large chest on the right side of the room. The chest had been simply lying there for many years, and Keimaro couldn't remember a single day when he hadn't seen that chest in his room. However, he had never opened the chest. The only one with the key was his father, and he had it wrapped around his neck like a necklace at all times. It sometimes made Keimaro curious as to what was inside of it, but, knowing his father, the chest would be complicated and impossible to pick—and stealing the key from his own father definitely wasn't a solution.

He sat on the edge of the bed, his eyes locked onto the keyhole of the chest, listening to the silence of the night. He ran a hand through his messy black hair and exhaled a deep breath. His father had always told him that he would know what was inside of the chest when he was ready.

When would he be ready?

The question was always lingering in his mind, and he shook his head as if to clear it. He kicked off his shoes and threw himself onto his mattress, bouncing a bit before settling in. He lay still and sat looking at the blank ceiling, while a streak of moonlight shone in through the window of his house. He folded his arms behind his head and looked out the window at the gleaming stars in the sky, remembering the sight that he had seen earlier in the day with Yata. A year, huh? That's the amount of time it would take to escape this place. Maybe even longer. Would Yata be able to wait that long? Keimaro didn't even know if he wanted to wait that long.

There was a whole world out there, and he was stuck inside of a cottage, behind a barrier—like a coward. He closed his eyes, noticing that he had called himself the worst of insults that he could think of. Cowards ran from something when they could turn and face it themselves. Cowardice. Keimaro hated the concept, but knew that it existed in him. He thought it was horrid and absolutely ridiculous that some stories told of soldiers who would go to war and ended up fleeing. It was cowards who sat there and watched their friends die. Keimaro didn't ever want to be like that. That was why he had asked his father to teach him how to fight. It would have an all-around benefit. He would be able to protect Mai, protect himself, and finally obtain the strength he needed to leave the village. He remembered when speaking to his father that he had only said he would protect Mai.

If the beasts broke in through the wards, would he not try to protect his mother and father? He honestly didn't know. His mother was always kind to him, and he would love to protect her. But his father. He always looked the other direction. A person could slice off Keimaro's leg, and his father probably wouldn't even blink an eye or be worried about whether Keimaro was okay. He would probably just ask his son what he wanted for supper and then cook the opposite of what he had answered. It was actually a surprise that his father had agreed to teach him. Perhaps it was the speech that he had made earlier.

He wondered what Yata would act like the next day and who that foreign girl was. That sense of mystery that glistened around her made him all the more curious of her origins. He also wondered if Yata would continue being his friend and whether or not he was okay with waiting a year to leave the village. Should he spend his time to master the way of the sword rather than just learning to protect himself? Which would be more beneficial to him in the long run?

Keimaro closed his eyes, allowing the feeling of overwhelming thoughts to surge through his head. He had made his first friend, a mysterious girl was lying in Yata's house, they had seen a beast earlier today, he would be training swordplay tomorrow … it was all so much. Such a day out of the norm, he couldn't help but smile to himself. Something exciting was coming in his path of life. He could feel it. When it was coming, he didn't know, but he supposed that was the excitement of it and the excitement of life as a whole. It was a thrill that one couldn't obtain while living behind the walls of the magical shield. It was one that could be caused only by outside forces.

The girl.

2. THIRD MUSKETEER

Keimaro grabbed his bag he used for school and put some materials into it for later that morning. He stuffed a few apples into it, along with some of his mom's clothes. All this hassle, just for the mysterious girl. Not that he minded. In fact, that girl was all that he was thinking about. Not in an obsessive way, but he was rather curious. He wanted to know where she came from. He wanted to know everything about the outside world. Was it different than Bakaara? Well, of course it was, but he was sure that the technology must be more advanced! In fact, Bakaara was probably incredibly behind the other empires technologically since it was a small and isolated village with no contact with any outside sources.

He folded the clothing neatly and placed it into the bag, blinking a few times as the realization of how awkward it was to be taking clothes out of his mother's wardrobe hit him. *At least I won't have to be here again*, he thought. Unfortunately, he turned around only to find himself face to face with his mother, who gave the bag in his hands a knowing look. Keimaro could feel the heat rising to his cheeks as he stammered, "W-Wait! I can explain. I need the clothes for … an acting project! That I'm doing for school, yeah, an acting project. Umm … a girl that I know needs some more old-fashioned clothes so—"

23

"So, you're saying I'm old-fashioned?"

"No, no, no!" Keimaro waved his hands before him, his face flushing red. To his relief, his mother giggled—he knew that she was just teasing him. He hated when she did that, teased him. But, to be honest, it definitely wasn't as bad as when someone else did it. When other people did anything to embarrass him or make him look bad, he always felt a certain resentment toward them. He hated being frowned upon.

"I'm sure you have a good use for all of that," his mother said with a warm smile. "It's not like I need these clothes right now. Just make sure you return them. I trust you'll be using it for the right reasons." She paused before continuing, "You know, if you ever feel like you're a little more feminine … you can always tell—"

"No!" Keimaro exclaimed, his face red with embarrassment. He groaned loudly. "It's not that I'm feminine!"

"Of course not," his mother said with a sly wink and a chuckle, sitting down on her bed and patting the space beside her. "Kei, come and talk with me just for a moment?"

Keimaro sighed reluctantly and sat down beside his mother, looking into her eyes as he kept the brown bag on his lap in a rather uncomfortable position and shrugged. "What is it?"

"You shouldn't be so angry at your father all of the time."

Here we go again. "It's not my fault he doesn't care," Keimaro jumped in.

"It isn't his fault either."

"Isn't it? Does he have no control over his own feelings?" Keimaro said, rolling his eyes dramatically. He scoffed, feeling rather annoyed at the nature of this conversation. He hated talking about his father, the man who always abandoned him in his time of need. "The old man chooses to always look the other way instead of acting. He's a coward."

"Think what you want, but keep your thoughts to yourself," his mother said in a gentle tone. "If you get your father extremely mad, you never know what's going to happen. Just … try to be a little more caring, okay? He's the one who raised you, after all. He was a little reluctant when we decided to adopt you and Mai. I know for a fact that he doesn't regret our decision. Your father and I are just trying to take care of you two. Just try and behave, please? For me?"

A few minutes later, Keimaro had left his house and was walking in the morning light, tossing an apple lightly into the air and swiftly catching it in his hand. A cool wind blew, ruffling the paper bag as he held it and also blowing his clothing. The blades of grass in the field swayed as if they were all dancing in unison. Yata's cottage soon came into clear view. It was an isolated building away from most of the village in the middle of a field. There was a stone well beside the small cottage; a wooden bucket set beside it along with a lot of rope. Smoke was drifting off from the chimney, signaling that Yata was indeed home. Excitement and positive energy radiated from his body as he smiled to himself, eager to meet the girl.

He scratched his neck and took a bite of his apple as he approached the cottage. He felt the sweet juice run down his throat as he rapped loudly on the door, watching as it swung open. He jumped with surprise when he saw Yata raising a metal bat high into the air, nearly ready to smash his skull open.

"Eh?" Yata said with a surprised expression and then relaxed, lowering his bat. "Oh, it's you."

"What were you planning on doing with that?" Keimaro said, his face pale. "That's used to play a children's sport, not kill me."

"I planned on smashing someone's skull in," he replied without hesitation.

"Why would you do that?"

"No one can find out about her!"

25

"You're being a bit paranoid, aren't you?" Keimaro muttered, tossing an apple to him as he walked through the doorway into the next room. He found the girl sitting upright on a bed, leaning back against a pillow. He blinked for a moment, not realizing how beautiful the girl was until that moment. Her long brown hair flowed down past her shoulders and extended toward the small of her back. Her eyes were an enchanting royal blue that scanned him—similar to the way he was examining her. Keimaro felt his face growing hot as he looked at her and gulped. "Has she talked yet?"

"No," Yata muttered with a sigh, shrugging as he sat on his bed. He bounced on it before leaning back and crossing his arms behind his head. "Did you bring her something to eat?"

Keimaro nodded and reached into his bag. He pulled out an apple and walked over to the girl, offering it to her. He watched as she grasped the apple as delicately as she would a young child and blinked a few times while looking at it. Then she took a small, experimental bite, sinking her teeth into the fruit. A piece of the skin ended up on the corner of her lips as well as specks of juice, but it didn't matter. A small smile stretched across her face, and she began to take larger and faster bites into the juicy apple. Keimaro also pulled out a loaf of bread and handed it to her, watching her devour the food as if she hadn't eaten in days. "She seems pretty hungry."

"Yeah," Yata said with a resigned sigh. "Hey, are you ready to talk yet?"

"You really don't know how to talk to girls, do you?" Keimaro muttered and sat down beside the girl with a reassuring smile. To be quite honest, neither did he, but he figured that maybe talking to Mai would suffice as some practice in talking to females. "Hey, I'm Keimaro, and that's my friend, Yata. We are the two boys who saved you from the monster on the hilltops last night, remember?" *Smooth.*

The girl looked at him as if he were a foreign being and nodded lightly upon finishing the apple. She placed the core on the table beside her and then folded her hands neatly across her lap. "My name is Aika," she said in a soft, innocent voice. "I … umm … I'm the princess from the empire of Faar. I was kidnapped by Spartans and was taken through a forest. In the forest … it was extremely dark. There were odd creatures everywhere. The Spartan soldiers, as you probably already knew, are well-known for their melee combat. They were able to fend off many of the vicious beasts that came to devour us. However, every time blood was shed, stronger and larger beasts came in a brutal attempt to slaughter us all. A small troop of soldiers tried to escort me. They burned the carriage as a decoy to lure the beasts away. The large, black tiger-like creature slaughtered the rest of the escorts and chased me. That's when I found the two of you, simply lying underneath an apple tree upon a hill. Might I ask what you were doing there, next to such a dangerous place?"

Keimaro was first surprised that this girl was even speaking their language. Well, he had read somewhere that all humans spoke a common language in this continent. Her accent was different, but it made her all the more attractive to Keimaro. Wait, this girl that they happened to meet outside of the barrier was actually the princess of one of the largest three empires on the continent? That wasn't good. They had an extremely important person living inside of their barrier! It would only mean that the Faar Empire would target Bakaara, jeopardizing the safety of the citizens.

"Uh…." Keimaro also wasn't particularly sure how to answer Aika's question. What were they doing out there? It was somewhat hard to explain, especially to an outsider who wouldn't understand the feeling of being isolated from the world and trapped within the barriers.

"We were simply gazing at the stars," Yata intervened, clearing his throat in an attempt to change the subject. "Either way, it's going to be rough if you want to get home, princess. It could take some time, actually, but you're welcome to stay here for the time being. We just need to figure out a way for you to fit in with everyone else."

Aika blinked a few times in confusion, not sure whether or not to be scared of her current situation. "Where exactly am I?"

"You're in the small village of Bakaara," Keimaro said with a sigh, finding no reason to hide the name of their village from her.

"Bakaara? But isn't there a ward that isolates—?"

"Yeah," Keimaro said with a sly smile. "You're lucky you met two boys who found out how to bypass the magical wards. But that also means that if the beasts find out how to get inside the barriers, we would all be dead. So, let's keep it a secret. I've got some clothing that will probably fit you, Aika, but your proper posture and all of that princess stuff has got to go," he said, realizing how proper and neat the princess was even sitting on the bed.

Aika watched as Keimaro reached into his bag. He pulled out a few folds of clothes and tossed them onto the bed beside her. "I'm going to become a peasant for a few days?"

"A few days?" Keimaro said with a chuckle. "It's going to be a while before you're able to leave this village. I also don't appreciate the term *peasant* either. Your vocabulary is probably going to have to change. Yata and I have a dream to leave the village one day and explore the world. When we do obtain the ability and strength to leave and escort ourselves through the forest barrier between the Faar Empire and Bakaara's grounds, we'll take you. Then you'll see your empire and home again, but that won't be for a while, understood? For now, you'll just have to lay low. Otherwise, they'll have you executed and have Yata and me in chains. The elders don't want any of the townsfolk meeting an alien from the outside world." Though, that was a bit of a lie. In reality, Keimaro and Yata would be the ones executed and the princess would be held hostage so the king wouldn't barge into Bakaara and slaughter everyone. At least, that was the more realistic outcome.

Nevertheless, Aika nodded her head in understanding, her heart beginning to race with excitement at the mere thought of pretending to be one of the townsfolk. It was like switching lifestyles. Being a princess, she had always gotten what she wanted and lived with the luxuries of life. However, she was never able to meet anyone or speak to anyone. Now that she was a commoner, she was officially able to speak to anyone she pleased. It was exciting to know that she could now live a life outside of politics. The two boys before her seemed like two adventurous young men with aspirations that suited them and even matched hers. She also longed to see the world beyond the walls of her citadel. This was her chance.

"What's it like to be a princess?" Keimaro asked curiously, leaning against a wall.

"Well," Aika looked at nothing in particular and pouted, rather surprised by the question, "it's hard to explain, I suppose … since I'm not quite sure what peasant life is like yet! But I suppose I could explain to some extent. I could consider it somewhat like a cell. Everything you do is monitored. Everything you say is recorded. You have to watch your tongue; otherwise, you ruin the family name, since you're royalty. It's terrible in the sense that there's no one to be friends with since the king, my father, forbade me from becoming friends with anyone. There's also the chance of being assassinated or kidnapped at any moment, which was what happened to me."

"You make royalty seem terrible," Yata scoffed.

"In a way, it really is," Aika said with a sigh. "I wanted to get away from it, but I wasn't exactly sure how. Being kidnapped wasn't the way I wanted to leave the citadel, but I'm actually quite happy that I get to have this experience. Though, in the end, I would prefer to eventually go home."

"Yeah, understood, princess," Keimaro said.

"There were many luxuries as well. I got to have anything I wanted and everyone would have to do whatever I told them, I suppose." Aika examined the room around her. "Though, I got sick of it after getting spoiled for so many years. This is actually a nice change of scenery. I don't have to see glistening gold and jewels everywhere."

"Don't expect to be treated like a princess in Bakaara," Yata said simply, folding his arms as he looked at her with a rock-solid stare. "The times are tough, and there isn't a lot to live off of. There are fewer luxuries in comparison to Faar as I've heard. You'll be posing as my sister since no one knows whether or not I have surviving relatives. You can't speak the same way to other people as you would to commoners either, Aika. For example, that accent." Yata paused, waiting for his words to sink in. Aika tilted her head as if to say, *What accent?* Yata ignored the motion and said gruffly, "Go into the other room and get dressed into the clothes that Keimaro brought. We will show you around the town after."

"I'm afraid I won't be able to stay the entire time," Keimaro muttered with a shrug. "I'm beginning my training with my father today. He is finally teaching me swordplay. We should make the tour brief if anything."

"Alright," Yata said. "She's gonna be here for a while, so she'll adapt to it eventually."

The two of them waited in an awkward silence as the princess shuffled around in the other room while changing. She came back into the room in some rather short, torn shorts and a small gray t-shirt. It was a bland look for someone who maintained natural beauty, but Keimaro still found her quite beautiful. She definitely would stand out in their village, he could tell right away.

Keimaro blinked a few times as she toyed shyly with her long brown hair and looked at him with her royal blue eyes. "How do I look?"

"You look great," Yata said before Keimaro could answer and pushed himself off of the bed with a grunt. "All right, you two, let's get this over with! We have a lot that we are going to have to teach her before the day is over if she's going to survive within these walls."

The two of them spent the long morning showing Aika around the village—the farms, the marketing area, the social area, and the living area. Many of the inhabitants of Bakaara actually lived on their own farms, providing their family with enough

Teen Book Box Rating Card

PLEASE RATE THE BOOK YOU RECEIVED IN YOUR BOOK BOX. WE HOPE YOU ENJOYED THE SELECTION. THANK YOU!

YOUR NAME:_____

NAME OF THE BOOK:_____

COMMENTS:_____

_____

_____

_____

★ ★ ★ ★ ★

food to survive the year as well as maybe sell some off at the market for a profit. But those who worked at places like schools or blacksmiths were assigned to a living quarters that were something like apartments. Those who made a good living were sometimes able to afford a house set away from the rest.

The social area was the part of the village that held the schools and areas for teenagers and kids to mingle. There were parks and such for people to walk around and feel free, as if they weren't trapped inside of a ward. The social area was also where a small palace was located, containing all of the elders and every soldier who actually was trained to fight. This meant that there was practically no one else in the village that could fight. If there were an attack, the villagers would probably all be massacred, but the soldiers had been relocated to the palace to protect the elders at all costs. Any other threats to the village would be handled by officials, who enforced the law but weren't trained in combat.

In the market, many people sold different products, none of them very exotic. It was difficult to sell something new because only certain materials were available in the small area of Bakaara. There was a large open area where people would set up their portable tents and shops to sell items. It was probably the loudest area in the entire town because everyone was trying to yell over one another in a rivalry to win customers. Surrounding the entire area was a large amount of buildings such as the general store or blacksmith that were rather essential in meeting people's daily requirements. Keimaro knew that Yata worked at the blacksmith as an apprentice, which was why he was tough and knew how to fight, unlike the other people in the village.

"Wow," Aika said in awe at the large amounts of people that were walking in the marketing section. "There's a lot of stuff to see here!" she exclaimed excitedly, clapping her hands together with a smile. "Oh my, this is all so exciting! Why would you want to leave a place like this? It's so lively, and there are so many people!"

Keimaro scratched the back of his neck with a light sigh, watching as Aika got overexcited at the tiniest of things. "It's not that exciting," he muttered, shoving his hands into his pockets and playing with the jingling copper coins found deep in his pants. "You've never been to a market before?"

Aika shook her head, and Keimaro blinked, surprised. "I always had people who shopped for me. I was never allowed to go and buy anything at the market. I was never allowed out of the castle, as I told you before! I never knew that the markets were so crowded! Why are there so many people here? Do they all want to buy things?"

Keimaro shrugged. "Yeah, I guess. Recently, we've had a shortage in terms of supplies. This area can recycle only so many resources before we eventually run out. But, because of these wards, we aren't allowed to go outside and get the resources out there. People are buying a lot of supplies before winter comes because the crops will be sparse. So, people stock up in surplus so that they can survive during the winter, which is probably the hardest time to survive around here. I suppose you never know who's going to starve each year when we go through the dark season. I'm assuming that there is another secret way to get out of the ward that only certain people know about. Otherwise, when you think about it, we don't have enough extra food to sustain everyone through the winter. The elders are probably getting some resources from the outside."

"You think so?" Yata muttered, bumping Keimaro gently. "Wait, don't talk about that kind of stuff out here in the open. Keep silent about it."

"So, how was this place found? And how does this huge force field stay up all the time?" Aika asked curiously. "I mean, why stay self-sufficient and isolated from everyone else? Doesn't really make sense to me."

Yata winced at the question. "Hey…."

Keimaro touched Yata's shoulder, silencing him and proceeded to answer the question. "Well, I'm not exactly sure why we're self-sufficient. I suppose that it's been this way for so long and that everyone's gotten used to it. No one really wants to change. As for how this force field holds up, I heard that the elders cast it over the village in order to protect the civilians from the monsters that began to terrorize the people," he said. "Other than that, I don't really know much. They don't tell us how the force field was put up because they think someone might try to take it down. The elders of the village, the ones who founded this place, are really secretive about a lot of things."

"Oi, Kei!" a familiar voice called out in the open.

A shiver ran down Keimaro's spine, and he gulped. *No, not now. This guy … he couldn't be here at this moment!* This was a terrible time, especially since he would probably ask questions about Aika.

Keimaro glanced back to see Buu standing there with several of his cronies. Their hair was slicked back, and they were wearing black coats; of course it was only the finest material in the village. A sliver of Buu's curly hair came down over his blue eyes, and he had a wide, wicked smile on his face, a reprehensible sign.

Keimaro should've known what was coming. He sighed as he turned to face the bully before he was quickly kneed in the stomach without warning, a complete reenactment of the previous day. He gasped, doubling over onto the ground. The wind was driven straight from his lungs, and his vision slightly blurred into a flash of white.

"You thought you could just get away with punching me yesterday, huh?" A second foot came downward and drove hard into Keimaro's back, forcing him harder onto the ground. He winced as his face hit the dirt. He grunted, still gasping for air, helpless as a child fighting a tiger. "Die, you filthy piece of—"

"What was that?" Yata asked rhetorically, and the boys were suddenly quiet. The entire market, actually, was now in complete silence. Public displays of violence were rare within the village, but no one seemed to be willing to step forward and help Keimaro. Yata ran his hands through his hair as he began to step forward, each step making a light crunch from his boots. He grasped his hand and cracked his knuckles, letting out a loud pop in the silence. "Back off! Otherwise, I'll smash all of your faces in. None of you will be able to see tomorrow. I'll make sure of that," Yata warned, giving Buu a deadly glare.

Keimaro winced in pain and was kicked backward onto his back, only to find Aika kneeling at his side, pulling him close. "Are you okay?" Her words went through one ear and left the other because Keimaro was too busy watching Yata encounter the bullies before him.

Yata was off being strong and fighting for Keimaro. He didn't have to. The mere sight made Keimaro feel weak and powerless, as if he were nothing but an ant in a quarrel between colossal titans. He felt small and invisible.

"Was that a threat?" Buu snapped, his friends immediately advancing on their new opponent. But Yata didn't seem to care. His fists shot out in a single motion and slammed hard into the noses of both of the boys as he stepped forward. His arms rocketed forward with incredible speed and cracked into their faces with solid blows. Blood burst from their faces as they yelped, flying backward. The two boys landed hard on their backs at the same time. Dust drifted around their writhing bodies, and they grabbed their faces in pure agony as they released screams of anguish into the air.

Yata moved forward and brought his foot downward on each of their faces mercilessly, snapping their noses and knocking them unconscious. People gasped as they watched, shocked that Yata was performing such a violent and beastly act. Yet, Keimaro could see the anger in Yata's eyes, the hatred, the darkness. The boy seemed calm, but he was fighting with emotion.

Yata brushed the hair out of his eyes and glanced at Buu with an apathetic look on his face. "Some bodyguards you got there," he said sarcastically as he poked at one of the bodies with his foot. "I suggest you man up and face me yourself. Or you can turn away and run. If you ever mess with Kei again, I will personally break all of your limbs."

Buu stared at Yata in shock and then glanced at his unconscious friends who lay at the beast's feet. "Y-You're insane!" he yelped and turned, running away in the opposite direction. He broke through a line in the crowd before he vanished from sight.

Only moments after the boy had fled, the crowd began to separate as two guards made their way forward, armed with iron swords. Metal helmets were clamped upon their heads, making them look like tin-men. Beneath their daily clothes, they wore weak chainmail armor. Such an outfit wasn't particularly professional when representing the government, but Bakaara couldn't afford to spend more on equipment, especially since law enforcement wasn't typically an issue in the village. It was rare that people would actually decide to break the law. The only people who broke the laws were the bullies who picked on Keimaro, but the guards always looked the other way in that case.

Yata raised an eyebrow at the men and rolled his eyes. "Come to arrest me, have you?" He scoffed and held out his hands as if he were already accepting his fate.

Keimaro had caught his breath and nodded thanks to Aika when he slowly pushed himself to his feet. He threw himself between the guards and Yata with his arms outstretched in an attempt to form a wall between them. "Wait, don't arrest him! He was just helping me! Those boys were bullying me and—"

The guards pushed past Keimaro as if he were nobody and shoved him to the ground unintentionally. They didn't even bother to glance at him, splayed out on the floor. They kicked Yata to the ground and began to barrage the young boy with a wave of heavy blows, which thumped loudly against his flesh. "One night in prison."

Keimaro stared in disbelief at the guards. They had completely disregarded him as if he were invisible. He slowly pushed himself to his feet, his eyes glaring at the backs of the guards. Why did they knock him aside as if he were just … dirt? He watched as one of the guards picked up the unconscious Yata and slung the boy over his shoulder. The guards took one glance in Keimaro's direction and then began to walk away.

Was he going to let them take Yata away? His first friend? Why should Yata be punished for saving him? "Oi!" Keimaro yelled, grabbing a rock off of the ground. He hurled it at one of the guards, hitting the man in the back of the head.

The metal helmet that the man wore protected him, and he glanced at Keimaro over his shoulder, his eyes wide as if he were looking at some type of foreign monster. "Don't do that again. Otherwise, I will gut you, kid."

Overwhelming fear shivered through Keimaro's body, leaving him standing there in utter silence. The words of the soldier seemed confident and filled with unreasonable distaste. The guard clearly wanted an excuse to kill him, yet they had never even met. Keimaro bit his bottom lip, wanting to let his frustration out on something. He felt Aika tug lightly on his sleeve.

He glanced over his shoulder at her, relaxing his body and giving her a reassuring smile. "Don't worry. Yata's going to be all right." Keimaro knew that he couldn't confront the guards with Aika here. She was still too suspicious.

Keimaro took her hand, his heart pounding as he led the young princess away from the marketplace and back to Yata's house, making sure that they didn't run into anyone along the way. He closed the door of Yata's home behind both of them and walked forward, slamming his fist into the wall. His knuckles blistered from the punch, but he ignored the pain. Winding up for another punch, he drove his fist into the wall once more.

"Why?" he snarled, his chest heaving with his breath. "Why do they always treat me like I'm dirt? Like I'm nothing. I don't understand…." He sighed, exasperated, and pressed his forehead against the wall. "I don't understand why they treat me different from the other children. They threaten to kill me. They let the bullies beat me up every day. In their eyes, I'm just nothing. I'm nothing. And I'm so sick of it!" He smashed the wall once more, blood dripping down his knuckles.

Aika stood there in the doorway, quite appalled by such barbaric behavior, driven by blind rage. But she could also understand his pain. She had seen the way that the boy in the marketplace had beaten him. She had seen the look in Buu's eyes. It was unlike anything that she had seen before, filled with murderous intent and madness all alike.

"That's not true. I might not have known you for that long, but I know that you're not nothing and that you don't deserve this cruel treatment. You have been so kind to me to supply me with a place to stay and food and a home…. Maybe Yata knows why the others treat you badly! We can ask him," she offered.

Keimaro pressed his back against the wall, locking the both of them in silence. Everyone treated him badly. Maybe Aika was right. If everyone treated him badly, then everyone must know why … right? So, maybe Yata *would* be able to tell him. It just seemed so wrong, considering he had done nothing to any of these people.

He sucked in a deep breath and pushed himself from the wall, smiling slightly at the princess as he nodded. Leaving the house again sure would be a drag, since he had to keep covering Aika up from everyone else. But he knew more than anything that he wanted to find out why it was that everyone hated him. To him, this journey trumped everything else. "Yeah, let's go talk to him."

3. TRUTH

In the distance stood two men wearing dark black cloaks that covered their bodies entirely. Their hoods were pulled over their heads. They stood upon a lush green hill, staring through the wards around Bakaara with wicked grins on their faces. "The civilians of Bakaara have been living underneath such weak barriers this entire time? I'm surprised that even the behemoths of the forest cannot break through. We should have no problem, though. Are you sure that the princess is located here, Tobimaru?"

The second cloaked figure sighed with a sound of annoyance in his voice. "Of course she is. There's no other place she could be. Though, I don't understand how she would be able to enter the barrier. But you can feel it, can't you? Her aura. It's easy to sense the aura of someone of royal blood."

The first cloaked figure chuckled with a nod. "Yes. This is quite convenient since the next meteor should be falling nearby into the forest. And what else do I sense in this village? A surviving member of the Hayashi clan? Oh, the aura is so sinister and filled with so much hatred that it is far too obvious. One of your brethren, Tobimaru?"

Tobimaru rolled his eyes underneath the cowl of his cloak

and decided to say nothing about the matter. "Our first objective should be to obtain the power cores from the meteor and then decide to move in on the princess after that. We shall figure out what to do about the survivor later. He is not yet mature, meaning that he shouldn't prove to be a threat to us … yet." He looked up into the afternoon sky, sighing as he turned away from the village before him. "Let's go. There's no point in dawdling here. We should try and pinpoint where the meteor should land so we can harness its power."

"Yeah," the first cloaked man muttered, "but if we decide to fight the Hayashi clan kid, can I take him?"

"By all means."

***

Keimaro could see the prison from a distance, a small hut that probably contained only three or four cells. There weren't many criminals in Bakaara, so there wasn't a particular need for the prison at all. The guards used any sort of reason to jail someone, whether it be from stealing to getting into a minor fight, like Yata's case. There was no restriction on visiting, so it was easy for Aika and Keimaro to walk through the open hut, past the guard, and stand before Yata's cell.

The cell was rather small with simple iron bars. The bed itself looked like it was beaten up with ripped and used blankets that looked as if they hadn't been washed in months. Yata sat on the floor on a ripped red carpet, glancing up as Keimaro and Aika walked in. He was leaning back against one of the cold stone walls. He had a bruise underneath his eye from the guard, but Keimaro knew that Yata had taken multiple beatings to the body as well.

Keimaro tossed an apple through the bars to his friend, who caught it and munched into it eagerly. "I'm sorry," he said softly. "I didn't mean to get you in trouble. You didn't have to stand up for me either. I'm used to it."

Yata twirled the apple in his hand and then raised an

eyebrow at Keimaro with a light smile as he took a swift bite into the fruit. "Man, stop being such a little girl, Kei," he said with a chuckle and sighed. "You don't deserve to be treated that way. No one does."

There was a moment of lasting silence that stretched out as Keimaro and Yata stared at each other. Keimaro finally blurted out, "So, why do they hate me?"

Yata remained silent, chewing the apple and swallowing slowly. When it became obvious he wouldn't answer, Keimaro muttered, "You know, don't you? There's a reason why they treat me differently from others. They take advantage of me. Parents and teachers look the other way when I'm beaten up. If I was killed, people wouldn't even care." He reached out and gripped the iron bars of the cell, staring into Yata's blue eyes. "I know you know. Please, tell me."

Yata's eyes widened at Keimaro's words, and he broke eye contact. Before he could look away, Keimaro caught the despair in his eyes. He knew that look, though Yata was trying to hide it. He was trying to put a mask over his emotions to conceal them, just as Keimaro had done for most of his life.

"It's not for me to tell," Yata muttered simply. "The only thing that I can tell you is that it has something to do with your heritage. Haven't you ever wondered why your last name is different from your parents'? You're adopted. Have you never looked up your last name? Never been curious?"

"All documents regarding my last name have been burned and destroyed."

"It's against the law in Bakaara to even speak of your heritage," Yata said. "Let alone tell you who you are. That would condone my death. I don't intend on being executed or committing a crime while I'm already in jail."

Keimaro squeezed the bars of the cell even tighter, his knuckles beginning to whiten from how hard he was gripping it. He had always known that he was adopted, but parents had avoided his questions. He'd found it odd that there were no records with the surname Hayashi, and he'd had no other way to find information—how could he, when he had no friends? Yata's words filled him with dread and excitement. Why hadn't he seen that his name could've been a reason behind why people treated him badly? What was the story behind the Hayashi name?

"What's your last name?" Aika asked suddenly.

Yata and Keimaro were both silent as the two of them looked at her. "Wait, you can't tell—!" Yata began, but Keimaro interrupted him.

"I'm Keimaro Hayashi."

Aika gasped and brought her hands to her lips, covering her mouth. "Y-You're—"

"Aika, you can't—"

"Shut the hell up!" Keimaro yelled, and Yata jumped backward. Keimaro's eyes were no longer the dark color that they had been. Now they were glowing red as if they belonged to a demon rather than a human. He stood there with his black hair coming down over his eyes and snarled, "Don't interfere."

Keimaro's eyes returned to their normal dark color as he finally turned back to face Aika. "What is it? What's wrong with my name? Who was my family?"

Aika paused, biting her bottom lip. She looked at Yata, who shook his head in disapproval, but the princess spoke anyway. "The Hayashi clan was an entire clan that was massacred during the Hayashi clan genocide. Every single member was brutally murdered by the command of the gods. The High Priests delivered the message that the Hayashi clan were supposedly descendants of demons. The people believed them. Who wouldn't? When a member of the Hayashi clan matures to their full age, they obtain a power known as the Shokugan. I've never seen it for myself, but I studied about it in the libraries. It's an eye that looks exactly like that of a demon and glows bright red when the Hayashi clan member becomes angry, emotional, or filled with hate. Stronger members of the Hayashi clan are able to control whenever their eyes turn that way because it allows them to see something practically before it happens, giving them an edge in combat."

Yata averted his eyes and shuffled his feet as Aika paused.

"Faar went in and massacred every single member of the Hayashi clan. It was said that the Hayashi clan was extinct. I don't understand how it's possible that you're even alive...," Aika said with a gulp, putting her hands behind her back as she looked down at the ground, feeling guilty.

Keimaro's lips quivered as he heard the words of his family's tragedy. His hands tightened on the rusty bars. They had lied to him this whole time. Everyone! Everything was false! Everyone hated him because he was labeled a demon. Everyone wanted him dead, so he would be just like the rest of his real family. He exhaled a deep breath and blinked a few tears that streaked down his cheeks but didn't say anything.

"Kei...," Yata said with a sigh, "look, not everyone knows the full story to that extent, but—"

"Everyone thinks I'm trash, that I'm some monster," Keimaro scoffed and walked past Aika. He looked to see a guard standing outside of the hut with a wooden club gripped in his hand. It was obvious that the man had been listening to their conversation the entire time. The young boy eyed the club, and then his eyes flickered back to the guard's eyes, which were just like everyone else's. They were just like Buu's, just like the bullies', just like his father's. No one in this village cared about his existence.

"It seems you know everything now, huh? Demon child."

Keimaro's eyes flashed bright red, and he leapt into the air in a single flash of movement, all fear drained from his bones. He smashed his fist solidly into the man's face, ignoring his scream of agony. He stomped his foot downward on the guard's wrist, forcing him to loosen his grip on the club. Keimaro grabbed the club from the man and watched as the guard tried to lash out and grab him. But he could already tell what the man was thinking, what he was about to do. Everything that this insignificant human did was processed and examined by Keimaro. The contracting of his tendons and flexing of certain muscles—Keimaro saw it all, and he still had enough time to think of how he would counter it. He swung the club and smashed it into the man's hand that lashed out at him, breaking the man's wrist in a clean snap. Then he whipped the club downward and smacked the man upon the top of his head with a loud crack, leaving the man unconscious.

This was it. He wasn't about to wait years to learn to fight. He would leave this horrible village of Bakaara now. He couldn't stand one more minute in this place. What was the point in living in such a terrible place where the inhabitants mistreated him for something that was out of his control? Had all those fourteen years of his life been wasted in solitude because of his heritage? Because he was believed to be a descendant of a demon? How foolish. He was breathing heavily as he looked down at the unconscious man before him. He clenched his hands into tight fists. A demon, such a thing was absurd. There was no such thing! *Right?*

Leaving Aika and Yata behind, Keimaro stormed to his house. His heart pounded as he approached his settlement. His family had hid his true heritage from him. His father was even one of the people who thought that he was a demon. He spotted his father at the side of the house, whirling a sword about.

He slowly straightened his back as he saw Keimaro approaching him. "Son, I've been waiting for your arrival!" he called out with a light smile but frowned when Keimaro stopped in front of him. "What's with the look?"

"Heh...," Keimaro muttered, looking down at the ground, "it's really funny that you called me that."

"Called you what?"

"Son," Keimaro growled, glancing up to meet his father's eyes. "You called me son, but you aren't even my dad. You may have raised me, but where are my real parents, the members of the Hayashi clan? Where are the descendants of demons, huh, father? Did you kill them? And you couldn't bring yourself to kill an innocent child, so you took me in. Is that what happened?"

His father stood there completely frozen with shock and blinked a few times. "Kei ... I...."

"How dare you ever call me your son?" Keimaro roared, slamming his fist against the side of the building. Blood formed on his scraped knuckles, but he bit his lip to ignore the pain. His heart was racing. "Every word you've ever told me my entire life has been a lie. You never told me a single thing about my real family. You hid the massacre from me the entire time. When did you plan on telling me? You probably were the one who killed my true parents!"

"Who told you about the massacre, Kei?" his father demanded, reaching to touch his shoulder.

"Don't touch me!" Keimaro snarled with hostility, slapping his father's hand away. He heard the door close and glanced over his shoulder to find his mother standing there with Mai. He didn't care. Normally, Mai's presence would have kept him from yelling. He cared for her more than anyone else. But right now, nothing mattered. "Stop acting like you're my parent. You never were from the start!"

"Kei, you don't even know what you're talking about."

"Oh, I don't? This at least explains why you always look the other way when something happens to me," Keimaro snapped. "This explains why you have been such a terrible father my entire life. You've never been there for me." Tears began to form in the corner of his eyes. "My suffering has been your fault all along."

"The Hayashi clan was ordered by international law to be completely purged. Every single member of the Hayashi clan was therefore killed. You are lucky to even be alive!" his father exclaimed and sighed. "Please, Kei ... just calm down. Let's talk about this."

"Calm down?" Keimaro said with a chuckle, a shadow

covering his hatred-filled eyes. "Why the hell should I calm down? All of you, every single last person in this damn village, is scum!" His eyes were glowing bright red with the power of the Shokugan, filling his father with fear and rooting him to the earth. "I am going to leave this village and go and see the world. I finally understand why I've always been undermined and looked down upon my entire life." He turned and began to sprint away, tears forming in his eyes as he ran past his mother, who called out his name. "Never think of me as your son ever again!" Keimaro yelled, dashing off into the distance, across the lush green plains of Bakaara and outside of the shield. He never wanted to stop.

But he did. Tired, exhausted, and depressed, Keimaro pressed his back against the bark of the apple tree outside of the village, grieving in silence. Night was beginning to reign over the world, blanketing it in darkness. He ran a hand through his hair, wondering if he had been a little too harsh to his family. No, they weren't his family. They never had been. They had taken care of him just because they couldn't bring themselves to kill him at a young age. It was all so pathetic! Everyone in Bakaara was pathetic. Who would believe that a human could be half demon?

"Huh," he scoffed in the silence of the night. "What a legend."

After hours of sitting in isolation, the sound of shuffling grass caught Keimaro's attention. He glanced up and saw Yata and Aika walking toward him from the flat plains outside of Bakaara. They ascended the hill to sit down beside him. He made no effort to stop them, but he didn't speak to them either. His emotions had drained with his tears in the hours he'd spent weeping.

"Are you okay, Kei?" Yata asked, plopping down on the grass beside Keimaro.

"How did you escape?" Keimaro muttered, ignoring Yata's question. He stared forward, unable to meet Yata's eyes. Instead, he watched as Aika sat down on the other side of him and placed her hand on his shoulder as a form of reassurance. He didn't bother moving the hand but didn't feel any better either.

"You knocked the guard unconscious in anger, and Aika just took the keys and got me unlocked. Then we came out here to find you. We went to your house and saw your mom crying, so we figured you'd be here. We brought some weapons, in case you went into the forest," Yata muttered, holding two meager iron clubs. "They aren't really much, but we figured that since we were going after you, we might as well come armed."

"You thought it was a smart idea to bring the princess out of the barrier of Bakaara?" Keimaro said with a weak chuckle, rubbing his left eye with the back of his hand. "Why would you come after me into the forest? We've known each other for such a short time. Why would you risk your life to come after me?"

"Because we made a promise that we would go together,"

Keimaro was silent as he glanced up at the sky. Yata was right. A promise was a promise. It was at that moment he saw a glowing star streaking across the sky and frowned, realizing that the star was moving much faster than normal. "Is that a shooting star?"

"Yeah," Aika said with a bright smile, "quick, make a wish!"

What would Keimaro wish for? Freedom. Freedom from these terrible lies that haunted his life. Freedom from these restricting chains that prevented him from seeing the world. He wished that he could leave Bakaara and find this freedom and that he would obtain power in order to claim vengeance on those who undermined him.

"Wait, why is that star moving so fast?" Yata said with a blink, and the three of them noticed that the projectile was coming in their direction. Their eyes widened when they saw a massive glowing blue light streak through the night sky and down toward the forest, smashing into the earth. The ground quaked and rumbled from the force of the meteor. Trees were ripped out of the ground from their very roots and toppled over from the enormous force of the alien object, sending dust everywhere. A moment later, a beam of glowing white light burst from the area and shot off into the dark night sky, piercing the heavens.

Keimaro pushed himself to his feet and glanced off into the forest, his heart pounding furiously. There was no way.... Something had fallen right out of the sky! He took a few steps forward and saw that the beam from the area somehow hit the sky as if it were solid. Radiating waves of vibrant colors filled the dark night, like ripples in the sky. "It landed over there. Quick, Yata! Hand me one of those clubs. We're going to check it out."

"What?" Yata exclaimed. "That's the forest! And it's nighttime! Why would you ever go in there? Are you mental?"

"We wanted a bit of adventure, didn't we?" Keimaro said, beaming. He grabbed a club from Yata and twirled the weapon in his hand, testing its balance. Then he glanced at his two friends. "An adventure just fell straight out of the sky. This is an opportunity that we will never get again! Are you just going to toss it away like it's nothing? Fine, you don't have to come! I'll go alone."

4. A WISH

The forest was at its darkest, surrounding Keimaro and his friends in an overwhelming shadow that cast out all light and happiness. The aura of the forest spread an overwhelming sense of fear. They could see the beam of light in the distance, and Keimaro felt sweat beginning to form on his brow as they slowly made their way to the fallen meteor. He could sense the shadows of creatures that were watching and did his best to ignore them, hoping that they wouldn't lunge out. He gripped the handle of the club tighter and felt Aika's gentle breath on his neck, realizing that she was probably even more scared than he was.

About ten minutes into their walk, he saw a blue light glowing behind a bush. Keimaro gulped, holding his breath as he brushed the bush apart and looked over the rustling leaves to see that the ominous glowing was coming from the dark mouth of a cave. As the light beamed, he saw its reflection coming off of the cave walls. The beam that entered the sky burst from the top of the cave as well.

"Did the meteor fall inside of a cave?" Yata asked with a raised eyebrow, standing beside Keimaro. "Aren't meteors supposed to, like, create big craters in the earth or something?"

"How would I know? I've never seen one fall from the sky

before," Keimaro muttered. There was something odd about the cave. The glow had an ominous feeling that drew Keimaro toward it. He didn't like it, feeling oddly attracted to the alien material. That was when his eyes locked onto Yata beginning to walk through the bushes and out toward the cave opening.

"What are you doing? You have no idea what's out there!" the young boy exclaimed.

"Who the hell cares?" Yata said, glancing over his shoulder, holding his club out in front of him. "Come and explore with me then! This is a huge chance! When we are old and are sitting and looking back at our lives, don't you think you'd wish you went into the alien cave when you had the chance? I'm willing to take the chance."

That sounded exactly like what Keimaro had said earlier. He sighed and grasped Aika's hand. He pulled her with him through the bushes and out toward the opening of the cave. Feeling multiple eyes locking onto him, he gulped and looked around at the darkness. He knew that someone or *something* was watching him, but he had no idea what it was. He glanced at Yata and already saw that the boy was beginning to walk into the cave.

"Let's go, Aika," Keimaro said and pulled her after him.

"Whoa, this place looks pretty creepy, doesn't it?" Yata said with a chuckle, the sound of his footsteps echoing off of the cave walls.

"Yeah, I guess," Keimaro said, finding it rather hard to see through the thick darkness. "I can barely see, though."

"Yeah, neither can I," Yata said. Then suddenly the cave glowed evanescently with turquoise energy, illuminating the entire area for a brief second. "Whoa!"

Keimaro blinked as he looked around and walked deeper into the cave, examining the stalagmites that held up the natural structure. He finally locked his eyes onto an enormous glowing rock that somehow rested in the center of the skinny cave. The rock had deeply embedded cracks but was otherwise normal. The cracks were glowing bright turquoise and shined as bright as a miniature sun every few seconds. "Are you guys seeing what I'm seeing?"

Yata whistled as he leaned against the cave wall with a nervous laugh. "It seems we have made quite the discovery, huh? What exactly is this thing? Does the educated princess happen to know anything?" he joked, glancing over his shoulder at her.

Aika pouted lightly and shrugged, folding her arms and sighing. "I've never seen anything like this before or read anything about it in my books. I mean, I don't think there have been many meteors in this entire world's history that have landed right in the earth! It's simply unheard of!"

Keimaro felt himself being drawn closer, taking a few steps at a time toward the large meteor. Its glow, its jagged edges—all he wanted was a single touch. He wanted to know what it felt like, an alien rock that came from somewhere beyond the planet. Even adventurers on their planet had yet to see such a thing. Keimaro had always wanted to journey around and see the wonders of the world. But now, he was witnessing one of the wonders of the universe. This was beyond the simplicity of their world. This was something else.

An invisible hand wrapped around his body with its fingers curling around his waist and guiding him toward the meteor. He reached out. As his fingers brushed the rock, the entire cave pulsed. What happened next was unexplainable.

A massive explosion sent Keimaro, Yata, and Aika all rocketing back through the air. The world began to spin wildly. Before he knew it, Keimaro found himself on the ground outside with no idea how he got there. His head was pounding furiously, and an annoying ringing battered his ear. He winced and coughed a bit of dust, turning to find Aika lying on the ground beside him. His heart was pounding, and he glanced back at the cave to see that there literally had been an explosion that had detonated inside of the cavern. An odd blue smoke rose from it.

Keimaro glanced down at his body, feeling his chest

growing extremely hot. He winced as he saw blue energy pulsing from his chest and gasped, knowing that the meteor had done something to him. He panted for a moment, staring blankly into the sky. He pushed himself into a sitting position, and rubbed his eyes. He didn't know what had just happened, but touching that meteor probably wasn't his best idea. He glanced at Aika and Yata and saw that a blue current of electricity was surging through both of them, causing them convulse uncontrollably. He stared at them in absolute shock, unsure of what to do. All of this was his fault....

Yata stirred, and his eyes opened as he rolled over onto his side, gripping his stomach with a slight twinge of pain shivering through him. "Gah ... what the hell...?" he muttered, coughing before he pushed himself onto his knees. He groaned. "W-What just happened?"

Keimaro grunted as he pushed himself to his feet, finding that he wasn't harmed at all. Not even the slightest part of him ached despite the enigmatic explosion. He shook his head at Yata, not particularly sure what to say, and reached down to turn Aika on her back. He stared at the young princess's unmoving body, and a sensation of fear burst through him. What if she was dead? It would be his fault. He reached down and pressed his index and middle fingers against her neck to feel for her pulse. She was still alive, thankfully. A wave of relief flowed over Keimaro, and he sighed lightly, lifting the princess up over his shoulder and picking up his club as well. "It's dangerous here. We need to get back to the village. Let's go, Yata."

"Look, it was my fault that we went in there...," Yata said, still on the ground. "I didn't mean for.... I'm not sure what just happened, but if anything did, I take full responsibility for—"

"It's fine," Keimaro said with a reassuring smile at his friend, placing his club down on the ground and offering his hand to Yata. "Let's get going."

Yata looked at Keimaro's hand for a moment, his lip quivering. It was the first time that Keimaro had seen even a sliver of fear on his face. His hand shook lightly as it grasped

Keimaro's. He struggled to his feet and took Aika from Keimaro, holding her in his arms instead. "Take both of the clubs and wield them just in case something comes along."

"Why would you give me the clubs? You have more fighting experience than I!" Keimaro exclaimed.

"I don't have fighting experience," Yata said with a chuckle. "I just have confidence. All it takes to fight is to swing those things around. Your mental strength is what really matters."

Keimaro sighed and picked up both of the clubs, holding the metal weapons in his hands. At Keimaro's nod, the two young boys began to race through the forest at incredible speed. Surprisingly enough, no creatures of the night came at them. The faster they ran, the more confidence seemed to rise in Keimaro's heart. The heat in his chest radiated throughout the rest of his body and pushed him onward to increase his speed, letting off some energy. A gust of wind blew through his hair, and for some reason, he felt good. No, not just good. He felt amazing.

***

Two cloaked men stood outside of the mouth of a cave with the remnants of the meteor. Mere pieces of the alien rock were scattered across the area, and one of the cloaked figures kicked at the rubble in annoyance. "What in the gods is this? How is it possible that someone got here before us?" He pulled down his hood, revealing a man in his forties with white hair and a red tattoo running across his right eye. He scoffed in disbelief, running a hand through his naturally snow-white, slicked-back hair as he clicked his tongue. "Did someone know about the operation?"

Tobimaru didn't say anything, though he glanced to the side with an interested smile. "It seems like the kids that we were examining before came out for a little exploring. They know how to breach the ward, meaning I can find the weak spot. Catch up with the children and buy me some time. The Faar army was waiting for us to bring down the ward anyway so that they could go and take this beloved village of theirs. The kids stole the energy from the meteor, so I suppose it's only fair if we steal everything from them."

***

Keimaro and Yata rested against the apple tree outside of Bakaara, panting. Keimaro was completely exhausted from the long run. His eyes felt heavy, but he knew better than to fall asleep outside of the ward. They weren't one-hundred-percent safe yet. He sighed, knowing that he would have to go home and apologize to his mother and father for his behavior. He had been so angry about being lied to. But, now that he had cooled down a bit, he knew that his parents still loved him despite everything; otherwise, they wouldn't have even taken him in or cared for him all of these years.

Aika lay in her sleep right next to Keimaro, snoring soundlessly on the soft grass. Keimaro was reluctant to wake her but was about to reach for her when suddenly he heard a shift of movement and a grunt. Keimaro turned and saw Yata being lifted off of the ground. His feet dangled inches above the ground as he choked, gasping for air and grabbing at the arm of the man who was holding his neck. Keimaro's eyes widened and glared at a white-haired man wearing a black cloak. The man stared into Yata's eyes with a crazed look, licking his lips slowly. An odd tattoo crossed his right eye, making it look as if he had been brutally slashed with a blade across the right side of his face.

"Hey, Tobimaru!" the white-haired man said with an evil cackle. "Looks like I found the fresh meat! They were off resting!" He squeezed Yata's throat tighter with a snarl. "You wasted the meteor's power on yourselves, huh? How selfish of you! Don't think you'll get away with it, you little brat!"

Keimaro looked past the man and saw another black-cloaked man. When his eyes met those of the man named Tobimaru, Keimaro's heart thumped, feeling an instantaneous connection to the figure. It was as if he could recognize the man through the cowl of his cloak despite not being able to see his full face. "Who are you guys?"

Tobimaru ignored Keimaro's question and simply turned to face Bakaara, a gentle breeze blowing through his cloak, swaying it ever so slightly. "I've located the weak point in the barrier. I'll bring it down. After I do so, signal for the attack, and we will begin the operation."

Keimaro's eyes widened at Tobimaru's words, and he gripped his club tightly. This guy was planning on bringing down the barrier? That would mean the deaths of all of the citizens. That was the only thing that kept the villagers safe from the dangers of the forest. Hardly any of the guards actually knew how to defend themselves and would probably run in the face of danger. It would mean the death of his family.

A surge of anger shot through his veins, and he rushed forward, leaving Aika's side to sprint at Tobimaru. He leapt into the air, gripping his club with both hands as he brought it crushing downward upon Tobimaru. The white-haired man moved in an attempt to save Tobimaru from the blow, but he wasn't nearly fast enough to match Keimaro's speed. However, what happened next was something that surprised Keimaro entirely.

Tobimaru swung around without any warning and slammed his fist solidly into Keimaro's face as if he were able to know exactly where to hit before the boy had even attacked. The fist sank solidly into Keimaro's face, stopping his swing entirely. He flew backward, hitting the apple tree's trunk with a heavy thump. Tobimaru looked at Keimaro for a moment longer before smiling and turning away, vanishing directly before his eyes.

Keimaro stared at the place where Tobimaru had been only a second before. That guy … he had red eyes. They were demonic and filled with hatred, just like the way Aika had described the Shokugan. Keimaro thought he might have used it during his brief fight against the guard outside Yata's cell, but he had never actually seen what it looked like. Was it possible that this Tobimaru person was actually also a member of the Hayashi clan? And how had he disappeared? Was that another form of magic?

"Gah!" the white-haired man grunted suddenly, staggering backward, and Yata fell to the ground. There was a bruise on the side of the white-haired man's face from a heavy blow. He raised an eyebrow, turning toward Yata with a scowl on his face, snarling. "You annoying bastard...."

Yata's skin had transformed from its flesh into a shining metal that reflected the moon's light. He glanced at his own body and blinked a few times in disbelief. "What is going on?" he muttered, clenching his fists and chuckling lightly. "I don't know what this is, but I like it."

He leapt forward and swung his fist into the white-haired man's face. "Kei! Get Aika and head after that other guy! He's going to go and assassinate the elders. I think the meteor did something to us, but there's no time to waste finding out! You need to head there and stop that guy right now! Otherwise, everyone in Bakaara is dead; you hear me? I'll hold this old man off!"

The white-haired stranger worked his jaw, cracking his neck to the side with a broad grin. He swung his fist, conjuring a burst of concentrated blistering wind that swept forward and slammed into Yata. The wind shook the apple tree to its core, and the leaves began to fall off into the air. Keimaro braced his arms in front of him as the fierce wind struck him like a cannon, blowing his hair back and flapping his shirt everywhere. He grunted, closing his eyes to protect himself from the powerful breeze.

When the wind calmed, Keimaro opened his eyes and stared at the two super-humans fighting like gods, obliterating the earth with their supernatural powers. It seemed that Yata's newly developed powers were rather easy to control, consisting of nothing but punching. However, the white-haired man was using advanced techniques that involved controlling the wind from different angles and concentrating the amount of pressure that he used with each blow. The attacks didn't seem to be doing substantial damage to Yata because of his metal-like body, but Keimaro could tell that this man had gotten his powers the same way Yata had—from some alien source.

But, since Yata had obtained new powers, did that mean that Keimaro and Aika had gained some from the blast as well? It was quite possible. But when would he be able to use them? And would the powers be the same as Yata's or different? This was his wish coming true: a foreign power was now sweeping over him and would grant him his ability to become strong. Was he supposed to be happy at this moment? Happy that he had now achieved power? Or should he be distressed that a rogue was entering the ward with the intention of bringing it down, thus killing everyone Keimaro had ever known?

Keimaro reached down and picked up Aika like he would an innocent child. He glanced toward the two men fighting and saw their battle raging with Yata constantly swinging his fists and the white-haired man throwing his harmless gusts of wind at the metal boy. The battle was stagnant, but Yata had purposely drawn the man away so that Keimaro would have a clear path to escape. He needed to get Aika to safety and then head after Tobimaru. Hopefully the guards in the social district would be able to hold Tobimaru off until he got there.

5. TRUE DESPAIR

Tobimaru walked through the calm village of Bakaara during the silent night. This was the easiest job he'd had in a while; he had entered the village without any resistance. He didn't have anything to gain from destroying the village, but he was eager to see how the young boy from the Hayashi clan would do in combat. In fact, that one attack earlier had shown Tobimaru that the boy was filled with rage. Listening to the tone of his voice and the strength of his battle cry, Tobimaru understood that the young boy was filled with hate, anger, resentment, and sorrow. That boy probably understood solitude more than anyone else in this village. That was the destiny of the Hayashi clan's survivors after the massacre.

Tobimaru trudged through the city, absorbing his surroundings meticulously. He could feel the auras of many different humans in the area, but only five elders were capable of holding up such a ward. He scoffed in disappointment when he located them, finding that they were hiding in plain sight. Such insolence came from the humans who hid behind a barrier, thinking that it would always be there to protect them. It was a foolish to believe one would always be safe behind a shield. Without fail, someone eventually would be strong enough to break through.

By this point, the elders had probably sensed his aura and alerted the guards, but Tobimaru knew that Bakaara had been hiding behind its barrier for many years already. Its warriors hardly had any combat experience—if there were any true warriors at all. Most of the soldiers in Bakaara likely enlisted as a guard or a soldier to reap the benefits rather than actually serve and put their lives on the line. They, too, believed that the ward would always protect them.

As Tobimaru reached the large building that hid the elders, he saw about thirty or so guards outside the doorway with their steel weapons bathed in the moonlight, pointing at Tobimaru. To him, they looked like a bunch of little boys holding pointy sticks that they found in the woods and decided to use as weapons. It was pathetic and almost hysterical to Tobimaru. His sword was sheathed across his back, and he slowly reached up over his shoulder and gripped the hilt. He slid the blade from its sheath with a slithering hiss, the metal scraping silently against the holder. As he whipped the long katana about, his eye color morphed from its original dark color into a glowing demonic red, which instilled terror in all of the guards. They trembled before him, their teeth chattering and their legs quivering.

"Don't tell me ... it's a member of the Hayashi clan!" one of the guards gasped.

Tobimaru sprinted forward. In a flash of steel, Tobimaru cut down the men one by one, relentlessly severing their lives from their bodies, leaving their corpses deformed by the time he was done with them. One by one, they dropped at his feet, forming pools of crimson blood beneath his leather boots. He continued onward, stepping over their lifeless bodies as if nothing had happened, his soul filled with apathy.

Tobimaru threw open the door to the silent building. He saw the five elders huddling together, wielding nothing but their canes made of the wood of an old yew tree. They were covered in their red capes and hoods, their faces hidden and their eyes downcast as they accepted their fate. He twirled his sword with a sigh in the direction of the elders. The entire building was completely empty other than the old men—without even a piece of furniture.

"What do you intend to do once the ward is gone?" one of the elders demanded, raising his head to look Tobimaru in the eye. "Will you give mercy to the civilians or simply massacre the peaceful people that have lived here for decades?"

Tobimaru pulled back his hood, revealing his spiky black hair and young face. He raised his eyebrow as he gazed over all of the elders, who saw his resemblance almost immediately. He looked almost exactly like the Hayashi clansman they had been hiding.

"One thing that you should understand about me," he said with little emotion, his eyes filled with resentment. "I know what you elders have done to the Hayashi clan. I also know that members of this community contributed to the Hayashi clan massacre, which is why there is a young boy still surviving here. His parents were killed, weren't they?" he said, tightening his grip on the hilt of his sword. "As he is one of us, I hereby condemn your entire village to death and complete eradication."

"What? You can't just—"

Tobimaru's mouth spread into a wicked smile that stretched across his face, his eyes glowing red with pure malice. "Oh, but I can. The Faar army has been waiting to take over this piece of land for quite some time. Its natural resources are phenomenal. It's been enough to support this whole village for decades without any need to step outside to trade with others. They will sweep in and murder everyone in this village. There is simply no hope for you anymore." He whipped his blade downward upon the elders, splaying their ancient blood across the walls. "There is no hope at all."

***

Keimaro panted heavily as he stumbled through Yata's house and gently placed Aika down on a bed, his heart pounding rapidly. By now, that Tobimaru guy had probably already located the elders if he had the same magical capability as his white-haired friend. However, on the way to Yata's house, he hadn't seen any destruction. Perhaps Tobimaru hadn't gotten through the barrier after all.

Then a shrill scream shattered the dead silence. Keimaro's eyes widened, and he raced to the window. He could *see* the barrier. It was a purple force field that formed a massive dome around the entire village. But as he watched, he could see that it was slowly melting away. The assassinations had already followed through and been successful. How was it possible to bypass all of the guards in such a small amount of time?

Keimaro squeezed the hilt of his metal bat, hearing the thundering roar of warriors in the distance. He saw what seemed like hundreds—and maybe even thousands—of soldiers, racing toward the village across the lush green plains that surrounded Bakaara. That was the Faar army that Tobimaru had been talking about earlier. His bat rattled in his hand, stirred by his spasm of fear.

We're all going to die. That was his first thought. Then he thought about his father and mother and Mai. He couldn't just let them perish. But, leaving Aika here probably wasn't the smartest idea either. "Damn…," he swore, throwing the door of Yata's house open as he raced outside. He needed to check on his family and bring them to Yata's house. That way he could try to defend everyone in one place.

Fear filled his heart at the very thought of his family's fate. As he ran in the direction of the marketplace, he could see raging fire engulfing the village as people ran about, screaming in absolute terror. A conflagration swallowed entire buildings, transforming the village that he had remembered into a burning inferno. He kept his distance from the actual marketplace but could see people being brutally slaughtered by axes, swords, and arrows from the Faar army. The villagers were being mercilessly killed. What madness was this that the officers would order their soldiers to unleash their fury upon innocent and unarmed people? Flames roared in the air as they engulfed buildings, swallowing them in a cloud of ash. He had seen these buildings every day of his life, and it was shocking to watch them crumble.

Keimaro ran around the marketplace to avoid any soldiers. Hopefully they would spend their time looting before they decided to head over to the farms, where his family lived. He sprinted forward, his heart racing when he finally saw the dirt roads that led to the farms. They were filled with bodies—people who had been running for their lives and were brutally murdered and slashed to the dirt. The earth drank up their blood, leaving only stains in the ground. His heart was still beating rapidly as he slowly walked forward, stepping over the bodies of some that he recognized from school. Young girls and boys had been killed. Their parents were piled upon them, trying to shield them from the sharp weapons of the Faar soldiers. He stumbled forward and felt his stomach roll, his head spinning with dizziness. He vomited onto the ground, gasping. *The Faar invaders have already been here.* This could mean only that the Faar soldiers had actually struck the farms first before the marketplace.

Keimaro blinked and began to dart home, his breath heavy as he dashed. The wind blew through his black hair as he leapt over the corpses in the road. They had to be okay. They just had to be! When he got home, everything would be just like the way he had left it.

But it wasn't. In the distance, he could see his house blazing in bright flames with several men standing outside, watching it raze. They were Faar soldiers, wearing large white tabards emblazoned with a red cross. They wore their tabards over their iron armor and held their brandished swords into the air, calling out victory as if they had just slain a majestic dragon.

Fire. His house was on fire. His next actions turned him into a beast, but he did it nevertheless. His hands squeezed the metal bat with incredible force, turning his knuckles white as his eyes glowed a frightening red. He raced forward and yelled as one of the soldiers turned around at the sound of his presence. He swung the bat with incredible force, connecting it with the jaw of the first soldier. With a sickening crack, the man's entire jaw shattered and blood spurted from every possible opening in his face.

That was not enough to clear Keimaro of his rage. He

brought the bat downward as the man fell to the ground. He smashed the defenseless man's weak skull with relentless force, killing him instantly. It was like squashing a watermelon. Time seemed to slow as he looked into the eyes of the newly deformed man, and his throat tightened, sickened at the atrocity he had committed. The eyes of the man were staring upward and fixed at Keimaro, but they stared straight through him rather than at him. Blood was stained across his mutilated face, leaving him unrecognizable. This man was dead. Keimaro had taken someone's life. He was just as ruthless as these soldiers.

Keimaro could hear a roar around him and watched as the remaining three soldiers raced at him from all directions. They had fighting experience, sword training; they had everything. What chance did he have? He whipped the bat and swung it, releasing the handle. The bat spiraled, spinning openly through the air, and connected solidly with one man's throat, sending him crumpling to the ground with a gasp. Keimaro grabbed the sword of the first man he had killed and slipped the blade from its sheath, watching the gleaming steel enter the air. It was rather heavy, much heavier than the bat, but he knew for a fact that it was much more deadly.

He turned around and saw one of the soldiers swinging his sword at him. What was he supposed to do? He had read stories about warriors who battled with others. The proper thing to do would to be to dodge in order to avoid pain, but one could parry the sword if one had to, in order to survive. He didn't have much time to react, so he raised his sword in a clumsy position and their blades slammed against one another in a vicious clash. Keimaro almost lost his grip on his sword, stumbling backward as the man's blow overpowered him completely. He nearly lost his balance, but the man pressed forward, raising his sword to bring it slashing downward.

Keimaro's eyes locked onto the exact movements of the man, and he sidestepped, allowing the blade to come down and smash into the dirt rather than his unprotected flesh. History said that warriors would slash and aim for the throat, unprotected by armor. Keimaro gripped the hilt with both hands and whipped the blade upward, slicing cleanly across the man's throat. The outcome was gruesome and almost too much for Keimaro to even look at. Blood spurted into the air as mere droplets at first and then poured out like a fountain as the man's face paled as if he were a ghost. The man choked and gasped for a moment. Then he fell to his knees with his head moving slightly as if he were confused and shocked at what had just happened. Finally he collapsed to the ground, his face smacking against the earth, unmoving.

Keimaro stared at the bodies of the two men he had just killed and saw a third man already swinging at him. That was when another figure leapt outward and swiped his sword in an advanced and fluent motion, whipping it upward and slashing it across the soldier's arm. Keimaro's eyes turned and looked to see that it was his father, slashing the man's arm and then spinning his own sword to cut the man down with a flowing downward blow. The advanced sword style was beyond anything that Keimaro had ever seen, not that he was particularly keen when it came to sword fighting. However, his father's sword style seemed to involve releasing the weapon in the middle of combat and then catching it to confuse the enemy about where the next blow would come from. This process also would speed up attacks.

His father twirled the blade and raced at the final soldier, who had been hit in the throat by Keimaro's bat. He spun his entire body and used the momentum to bring the downward slash across the man's chest, leaving the man on the ground bleeding. His father slowly straightened his back and stood tall. In the moment of silence, Keimaro and his father listened to the sound of the burning fire.

Keimaro stood there for a moment longer before growing sick at the fact that he had just killed someone. He coughed, about to retch once more, when his father came over and patted his back gently.

There was no response.

Keimaro turned to his father, who finally turned away from the bodies and looked extremely pale as if all of the life had been sucked straight out of him. He looked almost exactly like the men who had fallen on this day.

"Dad, where are Mom and Mai?" Keimaro asked. When there was no response, Keimaro dropped his sword and grasped his father's shoulders tightly, giving him a shake. "Tell me, where are they?" he demanded, his voice rising to a yell.

"Go around the house and have a look for yourself," his father said quietly, his voice shaky and his lip quivering as he dropped his sword to the ground, staring straight past Keimaro, completely lost in his own thoughts.

Keimaro could tell from the look in his father's eyes that something had happened. He knew the fate of his family members before he went around the house to look, but denial kept him from breaking into tears before he actually saw the sight for himself.

As he walked around the burning home that he had lived in for so many years, he locked his eyes onto his mother, who had been completely skewered with a sharp sword. She was lying there on the ground with her eyes fixed onto the dark night sky. Keimaro's heart pounded. In that single moment, the world stopped. It was just him and her body—the body of the one person who had cared about him throughout the many years that they were together, now lying dead before his eyes. Her innocent, pure blood pooled around her unmoving corpse, and her pale skin looked the color of snow.

Like a soldier stabbed in battle, Keimaro fell to his knees as tears began to form in his eyes. Then he cried like he had never cried before, tears streaking down his cheeks and his wails splitting the dead silence of the night. At the moment, he felt like everything was just over. Everything. He heard footsteps behind him and bit his lip, tasting the saltiness of his own tears. "Who did this?" he snarled to his father.

"The same man who took Mai. An acquaintance of yours," his father said. "You know the truth about your origins now, don't you?"

Keimaro nodded and slowly stood up, wiping his eyes with the back of his sleeve. He was drained completely of tears and emptied of all happiness and hope. Someone took Mai. An acquaintance? Could it have been that cloaked man named Tobimaru? Keimaro didn't recognize the man by name, but he could recognize the eyes. Was it possible that…?

"Ah! Keimaro Hayashi!" a voice exclaimed. A man with a black cloak thrown over his body appeared miraculously at the foot of Keimaro's mother's corpse. His hood was pushed back, revealing a wide smile on his face. The figure was completely bald with a rather interesting purple diamond tattoo located on his forehead just above his brow. His irises also gleamed the abnormal color of violet, his widened eyes reflecting his insanity. He looked to be in his forties, and his expression had absolutely no trace of negativity. He held his hands outward as if giving an imaginary hug to the air. "Oh, what a world it is that we live in!" he said, inhaling a deep breath as he smiled sadistically at Keimaro. "Do you smell that? The burning of your village has a rather unique scent to it. Could it be that it is because you are using natural resources that are different from what I'm used to? Or is that simply the miasma of burning filth? Oh, well! No point in asking. The question is, young boy, do you know why we are here today?"

Keimaro heard a thump and glanced over his shoulder to see that his father had been knocked unconscious. Perspiration formed on his brow as he saw his father collapse to the ground. He spotted a shadow looming over his father's unmoving body and glanced up to find another cloaked figure, whom he recognized immediately—Tobimaru. Meanwhile, the bald man was walking in his direction. Keimaro wanted to go to his father, but he knew that he was trapped between these two cloaked men who seemed to be somewhat associated with each other. But they didn't wear the same tabards as the rest of the Faar soldiers. Who were they?

"You're here for the princess, aren't you?" Keimaro questioned, though he knew that it couldn't be the only reason. It must've been the meteor, if anything. But why were they massacring the villagers and obliterating everything in sight?

None of it made sense. "Who are you?"

"My name is Junko," the man said with a broad smile as he knelt down and brought himself face to face with Keimaro. "I am a member of the Bounts. As a Bount, I am able to use magic. In fact, we are currently some of the strongest humans that are known to walk upon this very earth. You're so very lucky to be in the presence of two of us right now. Though, I wouldn't expect you to know of us. After all, you've been trapped in this bubble for quite some time now, haven't you?"

Keimaro looked past Junko and at the corpse of his mother, his fists shaking at his side with unbelievable rage. "And what is your purpose for being here? To dispatch me?"

"No." Junko grinned. "So that you will become one of us."

"What?"

"Isn't it obvious?" Junko exclaimed, standing up tall and putting his hands on his hips as he examined the chaos in the distance. He rubbed the back of his neck with one hand and sighed. "You are living in a city that confines your potential. You've hidden from the world for long enough. The Faar Empire has come in its own personal conquest to conquer the land, take back their princess, and kill you. It's time to make a choice. Die by their hand or join us."

"Why me?" Keimaro asked.

"You know why," Tobimaru said from behind Keimaro, his sword unsheathed and dragging across the dirt. The sharp steel carved into the earth cleanly, and Keimaro winced as he heard the scrape of the blade against the ground. He sucked in a deep breath and exhaled his fear.

"You're just like me then, huh?" Keimaro said, looking forward, taking his eyes away from Tobimaru. "I recognized your eyes when I first saw you an hour ago back at the apple tree."

He lowered his eyes. It was hard to believe that only an hour ago he'd thought he would return to his parents. It was two hours ago that he and his friends had thought they were going to explore the forest for the first time. Tears began to form in the corners of his eyes, and he shut them tight, trying to keep them from streaming down his cheeks. It was three hours ago that he was sitting alone at the apple tree, thinking about what he had just done. It was even less than four hours ago that he had been with his mother and father and yelled at both of them. Why had he done such a thing? Now his mother was dead. His father was unconscious and probably was about to be killed. Yata was in danger, fighting one of these Bounts, and Aika was left in Yata's house completely unprotected while the soldiers of Faar razed the city to the ground. Why had he been so stupid? He put his head in his hands, looking between his fingers at the ground, his eyes darting in panic. What could he do?

"Yeah," Tobimaru said with a sigh. "Members of the Hayashi clan. Our families were both killed, and it somewhat disgusted me to see you thinking of these imposters as your parents." He kicked Keimaro's father over onto his stomach, raising his sword into the air. "It sickens me to think that you ever had a connection to these filthy people. These murderers who deprived our loved ones of their lives and us of our happiness!"

"Shut the hell up," Keimaro growled suddenly.

"What was that?" Tobimaru narrowed his eyes, lowering his sword and giving Keimaro an irritated look. His grip on the hilt of his sword tightened and his eyebrows knit together in an annoyed scowl.

"I told you to shut the hell up!" Keimaro yelled, his eyes glowing bright red. His body was swaying lightly, sapped of strength. *Happiness?* "Look, I don't know what you're talking about. Whatever my parents did in the past, I don't care!" he snarled, turning around to face Tobimaru. *In the end, these are the people that raised me. And I won't forgive you for this.* "I don't care about any of your crap—or what you think is best for me! That was *my* mother! *And you took her from me!*"

"She isn't your—"

"She is to me!" Keimaro screamed, rage sparking inside him. His chest felt extremely hot, as if he were literally on fire, but he ignored it. His mother was dead now—the woman he had grown up with. The one who had always been there to listen to his problems when he was down. She was gone! Forever! And the ones who took her from him were right before him. Was he going to be helpless and weak like he always was in the face of danger? *Hell no. This is my chance to finally do something. I'm done being powerless!*

A burst of flame suddenly sparked from his chest, and he closed his eyes as he gasped, a growling fire surrounding his body to accentuate his rage and determination. His eyes widened with shock at the astounding amount of flames that had conjured from nothing and beckoned at his very call. They surrounded his body in a massive vortex of bright gleaming fire, howling into the night as the fire stretched toward the sky in a brilliant display.

Junko's eyes grew wide with the excitement of a little child as he clapped his hands with an outburst of laughter. "Oh my, oh my! Tobimaru, it seems that this young lad has gotten his hands on the meteor's power! You never told me that he beat you to it! And to have such an outburst of magic at once! This could only be the power of the Hayashi clan's rage!"

Keimaro locked his eyes onto Tobimaru now, confident with his new power. His wish had come true. Now he would be able to fight and destroy this bastard who took his mother from him. He didn't care if the two of them weren't related. His mother and father were his family and would stay that way, forever. All of the fear in his soul had been completely eradicated, and his mind was set on killing this man before him. He cared for nothing else.

"You're angry," Tobimaru said, pulling back his hood to reveal that he had a similar hairstyle as Keimaro as well as the same colored eyes. They looked extremely similar except for the fact that Tobimaru looked significantly older and more mature than Keimaro. He stepped away from Keimaro's father and began to circle the young boy calmly with his blade scraping across the ground, creating a small path behind him. "I remember when I used to look like you—filled with defiance and anger, wanting to destroy everything in my path. I had not a care for anything else in the world. I'm telling you now, you will fail. And if you don't accept our offer to join the Bounts, then there truly will be no one to pick you up when you fall."

Keimaro leapt up into the air, the flames swirling around his body and soaring downward into the earth, creating a massive explosion that erupted outward. The fire buffered his strength, creating a large crater in the ground while swirling dust and smoke surrounded his body, drifting out of the destroyed area. The young boy slowly exhaled, trying to let out some of his anger. He rose back to a full standing position at a leisurely speed, trying to peer through the screen of dust before him.

"Not bad," Tobimaru said, and Keimaro found that the man had appeared inches from his face in a mere millisecond. There was hardly any time to react, and Keimaro hadn't even sensed the speed of this Bount despite his enhanced reactions. A fist was driven straight into his face, and a crack of pain burst through him as he was rocketed backward, flying off of his feet as he flipped through the air clumsily. He slammed into the ground and rolled a couple dozen meters before he finally stopped, his body feeling practically broken. The energy had been sapped from his body and the breath from his lungs. He closed his eyes as a cloud of dust breezed over his body.

After a few seconds, his eyes cracked open as he fought to stay awake. Had he been so easily defeated already? A single punch had rendered him defenseless. As he watched Tobimaru standing before him, he heard a small cry and saw his younger sister, Mai, standing before him.

He wanted to reach out, grasp her tiny hand, and tell her that it would be okay. He wanted to comfort his younger sister, who was sobbing at the sight of her family lying motionless on the ground. But instead of Keimaro holding her hand, it was Junko. The Bount stood there with a bright smile on his face as he nodded at Keimaro before turning and beginning to walk off with the young girl. Keimaro stretched out his hand in the direction of his younger sister, trying to speak but unable to muster the strength.

No … I can't lose Mai, too. I can't lose everything! Please … give her back!

His eyes began to tear up once more as he tried to stretch outward for her. There was nothing he could do. He was powerless in the end. Always powerless.

6. THE PROMISE

An endless darkness enclosed around Keimaro, trapping and grasping his very soul. Its tightening grip choked the life out of him, and soon he could hardly hear his own breath, only a choking sound that was made as his heart pounded in response to pure panic. Oh, how he dreaded the thought of death. His eyes were looking forward into the dark abyss that surrounded him, and he wondered what was grasping his throat. Then a pale, ghostly face came into view inches from his, and his eyes widened when he saw that it was his mother's, coated in impure blood. Her eyes lacked pupils, and all that he could see was a blank stare, one that brought him dread and miserable pain. *Why didn't you save me?*

The young boy's eyes snapped open, and he found himself lying with his back on the ground staring up at the dark night. The stars themselves gleamed as if there were hope, their lights flashing in the blackness that coated the sky. His breath was heavy, and he no longer felt as if he were choking. He winced at the agony that was inflicted upon his body; his ribs might have been cracked, and his cheek was bruised. He turned to see his father standing there before a burning fire.

Keimaro could see that the fire was made from his mother's deformed corpse, which was being broken down into ashes and drifting off into the wind, scattering amongst the earth. He could see tears brimming in his father's eyes, gleaming salty tears that he had never witnessed before.

But the boy had no more tears to spare. All he could do was whimper at the sight of the woman who had been there all of his life as she was cast off into the world, something that he had ironically wished he could do. His eyes lowered, and he pushed himself to his feet, ignoring the aching pain that dragged out in his body. By now, Tobimaru and Junko had probably escaped. Had that been Mai walking with them, or was that merely a figment of his imagination? No, it had been her. He recognized her cries. Aika had probably been taken away as well. Yata was probably dead. His mother was dead. The rest of the village had been burned to the ground in a roaring conflagration and was probably being devoured by the forest's creatures. Soon he would be next.

He wiped his eyes with a tired swipe of his sleeve. He trudged over and stood by his father. In the end, everything he had known was gone in the blink of an eye. Now he had nothing except for his father. His resentment for his father had diminished and had only redirected itself at the Bounts. The sound of the fire popping and crackling was the only thing to break the dead silence before his father finally spoke.

"I know what you're thinking," his father said, his eyes mesmerized by the soft flame before him as his tears began to dry on his cheeks. "You think that I wish you and your mother would switch spots. That she was the one to survive and that you were the one to die. Is that what you're thinking?"

Keimaro was silent. It was exactly what he was thinking—and he didn't mind the thought either. He now understood what Yata had felt when his mother was hanged. His mother hadn't done anything wrong. In fact, she had been the most pure woman that he had ever known. Why had she been the one to be slaughtered? What gods that watched over them would allow such an atrocity to occur? He turned to the fire and allowed the blazing flame to reflect into his dark eyes.

"I don't. I don't wish the two of you had switched. In fact, I'm glad that you're still alive, son," his father said, bowing his head with a shake as he chuckled weakly. "Everything I've done up to this point has been for your own good, to make you strong. In the end, the Bounts ended up coming and killing everyone. And now Faar will eventually be back to take complete control over this area. I'm glad it is you that survived because you will be the one to restore our honor."

"Honor?"

"You will avenge your mother and save your sister."

Keimaro looked at his father with shaking eyes, and he clenched his clammy hands. Revenge? Was that what he wanted? He felt an empty hole in his heart, as if a blade had skewered him straight through his chest and burst out of his back. Would complete destruction of his enemies fill that void? His hands were tightened into fists at his side and his head lowered, a dark shadow coming over his face. This new power had activated out of pure hatred, and he remembered roaring flames howling around him. His younger sister had been taken. His mother had been slain. The people he had grown up with were massacred and now lay dead on the land that he had once wandered endlessly, searching for freedom. He closed his eyes, locking his mind in absolute darkness. It was ironic that the moment he would gain his own freedom, he was also bound to the past of this village. He had suffered, and now he wanted to destroy Faar. He abhorred all of those in the empire and its king for what they'd done. He hated the Bounts even more so.

"You don't have the strength to do so now," his father breathed and shook his head slowly, "but I'll teach you. One day, you will end the lives of the men who took your mother's. Do you understand?"

Keimaro watched his father for a moment as droplets of rain began to fall from the sky, starting off as one or two and then coming down in showers, making the light of his mother's fire flicker. He watched it die down for a moment and saw nothing but ash where she had lain only moments earlier. He felt just as he had when he'd first seen the body of his mother—incapable of stopping anything. Powerless. Not even able to keep her flames alive for a few minutes while she was being cremated. Training underneath his father, he knew, would improve his chances of growing stronger. He would be able to defend himself and would never feel powerless again. Rather, he would obtain the strength to avenge his mother and all of those who perished on this day. He lowered his eyes and saw his father beginning to rise from his knees to his feet. The man turned to his son and looked him straight in the eyes.

"How many men would you kill to save your little sister?"

The young boy was speechless as he looked into his father's eyes and saw the seriousness of the matter. Today had been the first day he had slain a man and stolen a life. It felt horrible. He knew that, from this very day, he would be haunted by the screams of anguish that came from the men he killed. But he had done so in self-defense. Was that not the right thing to do? What his father was asking was if he was willing to taint his soul in order to save his younger sister. Mai was the one who gave him a reprieve from the horror of abuse that he constantly suffered. She returned innocence to his life, and he felt an unexplainable connection to her. He wouldn't let those men take her.

His eyes began to glow a demonic red as rising abhorrence for the men who had kidnapped Mai grasped his heart. "I would kill them all."

His father nodded casually and pointed to a young boy who was lying in the dirt a few meters away. "Tend to your friend. He tried to recover Mai while you were unconscious, yet he was defeated as well. I will train both of you, and you will both become my legacy when I pass," he said softly and turned away as if he had just seen a ghost. He glided silently away with no particular destination.

Keimaro rushed over to the unconscious boy, knowing immediately that it was Yata. He touched the boy's neck, feeling for his pulse, and sighed with relief when he felt it. He watched as Yata's eyes began to crack open, his body filled with agonizing pain. He winced as he awoke from his slumber.

"Stay still. You're injured," Keimaro whispered

"Where's the little girl?" Yata gasped, leaning his head back into the mud around him.

"She's been taken."

"As has Aika."

"We'll get them both back," Keimaro said with a weary smile. "Just you wait."

Yata didn't feel like complaining or arguing against such a bold statement. The men they had fought were unlike anything that he had read or studied in all of the books and lore of man in this world. They used unnatural human abilities, like the new powers the two of them had obtained. Were they monsters? No, monsters were common—but humans who could control unique powers were not. This new phenomenal gift that had been bestowed upon them was something else. It would help them find their friend one day, though Yata knew that the day he would see the beauty of the princess would not be so soon.

As Keimaro's eyes wandered upward and locked onto the cloudy skies that blanketed the land in its shadow, raining down forceful droplets as the gods wept for the lost souls, Keimaro didn't feel pain. Despite losing everything, for some odd reason, he felt numb, as if nothing had happened.

7. REBORN

Four Years Later...

The eighteen-year-old boy stood upon the hill that he had once lain upon as a child, having looked up at the twinkling stars. The apple tree no longer grew there. It had been burned down when Bakaara was invaded four years earlier. A gravestone stood in its place. The young man stood at the gravestone, his throat tightening. He looked at the stone with dark eyes, a shadow looming over his darkened expression. A gentle gust came, blowing his hair ever so slightly. His hands were relaxed at his side. Rain was pouring from the sky just as it had when his mother had passed, and when his sister had been kidnapped. He remembered that day so vividly. It was more than just a dream and clearer than just a memory. He remembered every detail, every ounce of hatred that he had felt on that day. He hadn't seen his sister since then, and he had just buried his father beside his mother. Together. That's what his father would've wanted. Keimaro remembered burying his mother's bones, a painful experience that was imbedded into his mind.

His hair had grown a bit longer, and he had grown to be just below six feet tall. His muscles were toned and shaped to perfection after years of his father's vigorous training. His bangs spiked down close to his dark eyes, which were calm and barely opened, as if he wanted to close them forever. He looked much older than eighteen; his body had matured dramatically over the years. He wore a black cloak that was tightly wrapped around him, a cape draping behind him. His cloak was buttoned up to conceal his white tunic underneath and draped all the way down to his large black boots. A leather belt was curled around the waist of the cloak and tightened to keep it from flapping whenever he moved or when the wind blew. It had been his father's until recently when it had passed on to him.

He heard a sound behind him and raised his head lightly as Yata walked up. The boy was older with strong, broad shoulders and had grown a significant amount over the years. His dark-brown hair was longer and wavier, nearly coming down to cover his eyes. He wore a black shirt with torn sleeves, exposing his rippling muscles. His signature weapon was a simple metal bat, which he carried in his hand everywhere he went. He had left the bat at the bottom of the hill today and walked to the tombstones of Keimaro's parents unarmed. He had felt as strong of a bond to Keimaro's father as Keimaro had, and was also quite traumatized when he had passed from a heart attack. But now, at least he would rest in peace with his wife in the afterlife.

"It has been a couple of days now," Yata said, knowing that Keimaro wanted to stay in the area. But Yata also knew that staying here when they had been training for four years would be pointless. "It's time to go to Bassada," he urged, naming the capital of the Faar Empire. "There'll be an escort caravan moving from Bakaara through the forest to the city. We can follow close by and make use of their escorts and protection."

It was a good plan. A lot had changed over the years. The Faar weaponry was much more advanced, and Yata was sure the escorts would be able to hold the monsters of the forest at bay while they stayed close behind.

Still, the sound of the rain falling was the only response.

"Kei—"

"Did you know that there was an elite escort team that

77

came by last week?" Keimaro said suddenly, looking over his shoulder at Yata. "That stopped by in Bakaara. What would an elite escort team want in Bakaara?"

"I don't know. Maybe there's something—"

"A chest that was kept in my room all of these years was supposedly destroyed in the fire. I never checked or scavenged the remains of my own house after that day. And when the new settlers came in, I never decided to go down there and check for what had become of my old home and whether or not the chest was still there. I did some research and interrogated some people," Keimaro muttered, slowly standing and leaving lilies at the grave. He turned to face his friend. "The king has found keen interest in the chest from the looks of it and has it in his custody. Some say it's the reason that he destroyed Bakaara. The chest was apparently indestructible and survived the fire when my house burned down. No human has seen anything like it. A master locksmith couldn't even open the chest to see what was inside. They've been trying to open the thing for years."

"They hired a master locksmith to find out what was in a chest in your room?" Yata said with a raised eyebrow. "And how is it possible for something to be indestructible?"

"It isn't," Keimaro said. "That's why I'm thinking that there is some magic involved. If those Bounts that assaulted our city many years ago still work with the Faar government, then we know that they were the ones who called for the elite team of warriors to escort the chest back to the capital city. Which means…."

"We have a lead."

"Correct."

Yata sighed and rubbed his head, looking at his friend with a sign of sadness in his eyes. He was so set on his goal. But in the end, what would come out of this revenge? Yata had pledged to Keimaro's father to travel this path of darkness as well. He wanted to see Tobimaru and the rest of the Bounts brought to justice for what they had done to the people of Bakaara. He had hated the people of the village, but no one deserved a massacre such as this. Keimaro's father had died believing that Yata and Keimaro would fulfill his dream and avenge the deaths of all of those who had perished on that day. But sometimes, when Yata looked at his friend, he saw a person that had sunk even deeper into darkness than he.

Keimaro walked past Yata and began the journey down the hill, a sullen look upon his face as he sauntered across the green grass. He closed his eyes as the rain continued to fall upon him, sending small, cold droplets running down his cheeks, looking almost like tears. He reached back and pulled his hood over his head, covering his face in a dark shadow. He looked much like the Bount organization members that he had seen four years ago. His cold, hard eyes locked onto the new industrialized village of Bakaara, which now had soldiers and an improved infrastructure. The newly formed ten-foot walls had been constructed around the perimeter of the village in order to replace the force field.

"We are going to infiltrate an export caravan and interrogate them. After we get any information out of them, we are going to disguise ourselves as them and sneak into Bassada through the front door."

"Sounds like a plan," Yata said, bowing respectfully before the grave of Keimaro's parents before following his friend down the hill toward Bakaara. "It's somewhat risky," he murmured, "but I'm sure that we'll make it. We were trained for this, after all."

***

A soldier by the name of Gavin was tightening his hold around the hilt of his sheathed blade as the caravan began to move into the dark forest that bordered Bakaara. He listened to the wheel of the cart bump over rocks as he and several other soldiers walked into the abyss. Even in broad daylight, the forest itself looked pitch-black. He could already feel the darkness closing in around him, making his throat tighten and dry. The man wore an iron helmet clamped over his head, covering most of his curly, dark hair. A white tabard was thrown over his chainmail, with a red-cross insignia upon it—the symbol of Faar. He had just joined the army, but the first job he had was to perform a simple escort? It was almost insulting to do so; the job had virtually no pay. But the fact that it was in the Forbidden Forest meant that it was all the more dangerous.

He brushed his curly, dark hair out of his blue eyes, trying to adjust to the darkness that encased him. His heart was pounding harder than usual, and he felt a bit panicked for some odd reason. Nothing was happening, but he could hardly see two feet in front of him. He could hear the clanking of the soldiers' armor around him and the trot of the horses that pulled the cargo. He could hear the spinning of the mechanical wheels from the wagon. But, his inability to see anything around him made him all the more frightened of what was to come. Panicked. What if a monster was watching him at this very moment? He could be killed on the spot. The soldier would never see broad daylight ever again, and he wouldn't even have a chance to defend himself. He would die alone, and no one would care that he went missing—other than his family, of course.

Oh gods, he was a soldier in the army. Why in god's name was he so scared? Gavin closed his eyes, disappointed in himself as he tried to calm down, his hand loosening its grip on the hilt of his weapon. He exhaled through his nose, trying to gather some control over himself. *That's it. I'll be fine.*

That was when he finally heard something that was alien, not from the cargo escort. The entire escort stopped, and soldiers unsheathed their blades, filling the silence with scraping steel. The warriors stared blankly into the darkness around them, completely blind as to what was out there. Even if something were there, they wouldn't be able to engage. They would just be a bunch of blind idiots swinging their weapons at nothing.

"What the hell!" a man screamed suddenly as he began to choke, his voice cut off almost immediately. There was a thump, the sound of his body hitting the ground.

Gavin's heart skipped a beat as he held his sword out in front of him, witnessing as streaking shadows rushed across his line of sight. There were slashes and thumps that echoed from the points of blackness in his vision. Screams echoed from the lips of his comrades, and he could hear their bodies hitting the ground. They weren't alone. Something was here with them. Or someone.

There was a heavy slam, and the entire cargo escort creaked, the wagon rocking back and forth slowly. That was when Gavin saw red eyes appear in the darkness, lighting up the shadows with its demonic presence.

"Gah!" the soldier exclaimed, taking a step backward. His scream was caught in his throat, and nothing came out other than a gasp.

A flicker of flame appeared, bringing out the light in the darkness. Gavin found himself face to face with a dark, cloaked boy who looked about his age. But, how on earth was he holding fire in his hand? Gavin stared at the flame in the boy's palm, dancing calmly on his skin. And why were this boy's eyes red? Could it be that he was a member of the Hayashi clan? Gavin had only read stories about them since they were killed off when he was a young child. Supposedly, they were all dead. The clan was extinct! But, despite the tales he had been told in his youth, this person before him seemed to match the description.

The boy lashed out with a quick jab from his left fist that came at Gavin's face. The soldier grunted, reacting accordingly and tilting his head. The blow flew past him. He whipped his sword upward at the mysterious boy, watching as the flame died out and thrust him into darkness. His blade sliced through open air, and sweat began to form on his brow as he sat alone, consumed by an even thicker fog of blackness after being blinded by the flame. Gavin blinked faster, trying to get his eyes to adjust to the darkness. His heart began to race faster and his throat tightened as he was haunted by the ominous silence. He was alone now, wasn't he? The other caravan members weren't making any more noise. *Damn! What do I do? There's nowhere to run, and I can hardly….*

A spark of flame appeared, and the soldier realized that his face was inches from the boy's. "Boo," the mysterious person said and drove his fist hard into Gavin's diaphragm.

The blow sank deep into Gavin's stomach, doubling him over in agony. His mouth was open, ready to gasp in pain, but no sound came out. He choked on any words that he had to say and fell forward, slamming hard into the ground, gasping for air. Drool began to run down his chin as he looked up weakly and saw that there were actually two boys standing over him. One of them was wielding a metal bat and had flowing brown hair. The other was the mysteriously cloaked boy. His eyesight kept blurring as he watched the boy, trying to stay conscious for as long as he could. Focusing his vision, Gavin's eyes widened when he saw the lifeless corpses of his comrades that were lying on the ground. Fear struck him and surged through his body, causing him to begin breathing even heavier.

"We have a few questions for you," the boy with the bat said simply, squatting down and poking at Gavin's face with the end of his bat. "You're the last survivor of this caravan. Unless you want to die like the rest of them, I suggest you cooperate. You got that? You don't owe these Faar bastards anything, so you better answer truthfully. Otherwise…."

"Enough, Yata."

"But…," Yata muttered, glancing at Keimaro.

"You'll scare him, and we won't get anything." The boy sat down, leaning against a tree. He grabbed a rather large stick off the ground and lit the entire thing on fire with a touch of his hand. The light was blinding to Gavin after having been in complete darkness for several minutes. "Hey, soldier, what's your name?"

"G-Gavin…."

"Gavin? Right. All right, Gavin, we are some impatient

fellows. My name is Keimaro Hayashi. It doesn't matter if you know my name because, if you tell anyone of my existence, I'm cutting off your tongue." The boy raised an eyebrow. "You understand?"

"Y-Yes. I got it."

"All right," Keimaro said and pointed the flaming stick toward his friend. "That's Yata. When he gets impatient, he likes to beat people with his bat until they say something. He starts from the bottom up until everything is broken. I'm sure you don't want that, right?"

These guys are absolutely insane, Gavin thought. He nodded his head, fearing for his life. He didn't want to end up like the rest of his dead comrades. But, at the same time, he realized he was being given too much information—which meant that these guys probably wanted Gavin to stick around.

"Good. You're in the army, right? That means you have access to certain information."

"Yeah, I do."

"Perfect," Keimaro said with a smile, tipping Gavin's chin up so the soldier would look the boy in the eyes. "First things first, there was a chest escorted from Bakaara to Bassada. Do you know anything about this chest?"

"N-No … but I heard about it. They said that it was really important cargo and that it was not to be opened. I heard that it was delivered to the king personally. B-But it had nothing to do with me! I swear it!" Gavin exclaimed, looking Keimaro in the eyes.

Keimaro could tell that the soldier was telling the truth, just from the fear in his eyes, the quiver of his lips, and the sincerity of his look. He smiled and leaned back against the trunk of the tree. "I have yet to understand Faar's government. Is the Bount organization associated with the government in Faar?" An image of Tobimaru flashed in Keimaro's mind, and he gulped a mouthful of anger that arose in him.

"The Bounts? They're a terrorist organization that's actually wanted by the Faar government. It's been that way for a while now," Gavin said with a raised eyebrow. "We even have one of the members in custody."

Keimaro blinked for a moment, staring at Gavin in disbelief. "What?" Gavin was still telling the truth … but how was that possible? He specifically remembered the Faar army coming into Bakaara because of the Bount organization. Could it have been that the Bounts weren't working with the Faar government? He remembered that Tobimaru had said that the Faar army would come and destroy the village.

He exchanged a confused look with Yata and sighed, shaking his head. He slowly stood up and extended his hand toward Gavin. "You're with us now. You're going to help the both of us get into Bassada. That chest belongs to me."

"Why would I help two terrorists?"

"Terrorists?"

"You aren't with the Bounts?"

"Who said we were?" Keimaro muttered.

"You're wearing the cloak of one."

"This was given to me by my father. It is the cloak of a full-fledged Hayashi clan member, not of a Bount," Keimaro snarled. He knew the cloaks looked extremely similar, if not identical. But he knew that he was nothing like the Bounts. "I want to find out what's inside of that chest. It belongs to me. Besides, if you don't help us, I will just kill you now."

The soldier glanced down, and he sighed, closing his lids. "Fine, fine."

"You're with us until I say otherwise. Even the slightest hint of betrayal will end with your decapitation. Honestly, I don't have time for stupid setbacks," Keimaro said, poking the corpse of a soldier with his boot. "As you can see, I have no problem with taking the lives of others."

"Yes, sir."

"Well, both of you, come here, and I'll tell you the plan."

***

The young princess of Faar sat in her golden throne beside her father, her back straight. The throne room was a gigantic circular room surrounded with an entire perimeter of soldiers who were fully armed and trained in years of combat. They were an elite force known as the Royal Guard that stood and protected the royal family every hour of every day.

The princess sighed as she leaned back, her brunette hair falling down past her shoulders and toward her white dress that covered her body down to her diamond slippers. She touched the small gold crown upon her head, which was considered a baby's in comparison to her father's. Nevertheless, wearing it and sitting upon this gold throne gave her a sense of authority, and she liked it. Even though she didn't do anything with her power, she always felt that it was nice to have. She played with the hem of her dress for a moment and then relaxed, folding her hands over her lap and resuming her perfect posture in order to impress her father.

"Aika, you were at the village of Bakaara four years ago, were you not?" the king said with a broad smile in her direction. He leaned against the left arm of the throne. Aika's eyes flitted to the large, gold crown upon his head, which was much larger than hers with every sort of different jewel embedded into it to make it glisten brightly. He had curly, brown hair with a beard that came past his chin a bit, but not too far. His royal blue eyes glowed with excitement like a young child's as he extended his hand to the far side of the throne room toward two massive doors. Each door was the size of a cottage wall and was made of dark metal in order to fortify the throne room in case of an invasion. The doors were strong enough to hold out long enough to evacuate the royal family in case of an emergency.

Aika sighed and nodded in response to her father, her blue eyes looking up at the sky and the bright morning sun, which peered through a small, circular window in the ceiling and shone down into the center of the throne room. Bakaara? She hardly even remembered the place since she had been there for only one day. However, she remembered the two boys that she had spent the whole day with. Her first adventure outside of the castle.

But the last thing she remembered was when she had awoken in Yata's house as she was being carried out by some of Faar's soldiers. In the distance, she could see the burning flames of the village that she had seen fully intact only hours before. She had witnessed the complete destruction of Bakaara. She remembered being carried by soldiers over piles of corpses from the massacre. That specific image was burned into her mind, seared forever. It haunted her in every nightmare. She had never learned what had become of Keimaro and Yata. The chances were that they were probably dead. As much as she hated to admit it, her two friends were probably among the thousands of dead bodies she had seen on that day.

Had she known them along enough to be able to call them friends? Well, they were definitely the first ones to stay true to her. They hadn't liked her because she was a princess. They hadn't tried to protect her just because of her status or how rich or important she was. They had saved her life twice because they truly cared about her as a human being. After the explosion of the meteor in the forest, they could've left her there to be eaten by the dark creatures of the forest. But no, they took her to refuge. In exchange, the soldiers of her own city had obliterated their home and probably taken their lives as well. Why should she want to remember such a painful time? Bakaara was the first time she had experienced the happiness of freedom and the wonders of friendship. However, it was also the first time that she had felt pain and loss. And it was the first time she had spent weeks crying herself to sleep, haunted by the nightmares of her deceased friends.

Two Royal Guards stepped forward from their formation around the perimeter of the room. They didn't wear any helmets for protection. They didn't need to—they were renowned for their combat skills and were never struck upon the head. They wore what looked like simple tabards rather than thick knight armor that would prove as a much stronger protection against attacks. But looks were deceiving—all of the members of the Royal Guard were given a layer of abyssalite armor to wear beneath their plain white tabards. Abyssalite was the lightest ore in the entire world, yet it was also stronger than steel, mined from the darkest abysses by dwarves and other creatures that lived deep within the shadowy mountains to the north.

The pair of Royal Guards wore their blades sheathed at their sides, and they bowed their heads in the direction of the king as they moved toward the door and gripped the two heavy latches. Their sleeveless tabards revealed their bulging muscles and showed the strain on the soldiers as they began to pull the massive doors open.

The large, metallic doors creaked as they were pulled open, revealing two more Royal Guards who began to walk forward, carrying a large chest between them. Holding the chest as if it were as fragile as glass, they slowly carried it to the center of the throne room and set it down gently.

The king smiled as he nodded toward one of the guards, who allowed for another man to enter from a side door in the throne room. His clothes look tattered, as if he had just gotten into a fight with a bear. His face was caked in dirt, and heavy bags hung underneath his tired eyes. "This is June," the king introduced the man. "He is the most skilled human in the entire world for creating keys and lock picking. This chest holds the reason we went into Bakaara many years ago."

"It wasn't to save me or take the land?" Aika asked with a raised eyebrow. She had thought that the entire operation had been in response to her kidnapping.

"No," a cloaked man said with a light chuckle, suddenly appearing in the center of the room. Darkness curled around his

87

body in a black mist that hissed with life.

Blades were brandished and, within seconds, all of the Royal Guards around the perimeter of the throne room had unsheathed their swords and pointed them at the single man in the center of their formation.

"And why are you threatening the man who has merely come to make a proposition?" the man said with a smile, pulling back his hood to reveal his bald head. His purple eyes lifted and met with the king's.

"Proposition? I don't believe that we negotiate with terrorists," the king muttered. "You told us that you would deliver the chest many years ago. However, you failed to do so. It took us years of scavenging in order to finally find it."

The Bount reached up and scratched his neck, shrugging as he smirked at the king. "So, what you mean is that you don't negotiate with terrorists anymore? Since when did you change your mind, milord? So, you hired the world's best picklock in order to unlock a chest that is sealed with the strongest and darkest magic in existence."

"If there's a magic seal, then I'll get a mage or wizard to dispel it…."

"There are some things that are out of even your reach, milord."

The king raised his eyebrow and glared at the man before him, tapping his index finger impatiently on the arm of his throne. "What is your name?" the king demanded.

The Bount smiled wickedly, his lips stretching from ear to ear. "My name is Junko of the Bount organization. You see, I've traveled quite far today to reach you. At any moment possible, everyone in this entire room could be dead at my feet, so it is clear that I haven't come to harm you. I have a particular proposition, however, that could possibly interest you."

"And what is that?"

Junko nodded his head over at the chest, not taking his eyes off of the king for a single moment. "The boy whom I seek is also the one who has the key to this chest that you have before you. I can tell you his name and what he looks like. I can also tell you the name of his clan, which will immediately identify him to any of your men." He tilted his head back as the dark mist began to rise upward and wrap around his body once more. "I suggest you tell your men to stand down. I do not come to harm any of you."

The king gave a slight nod, and the Royal Guards lowered their swords and retreated to surround the king, standing between the throne and the foreigner Bount. Their blades were still held up but were no longer directly pointing at Junko.

The king sighed, calling out to the Bount, "Who is the boy that you are looking for, and why is it that you want him?"

"I want his body, his eyes, and his DNA," Junko said, licking his lips lightly with a chuckle. "His name is Keimaro Hayashi, and he is one of the last of the Hayashi clan. He is age eighteen and perfectly capable of fighting. At the age of fourteen, he obtained power from a meteor that granted him the ability to control flames. The destruction of Bakaara led him to great grief, which thus filled the Shokugan with immense power. The boy was given the key to the chest by his new father but has now been separated from the chest. He is on his way to reclaim what belongs to him."

"And you believe that we are incapable of handling a simple boy?" A general by the name of Mundo stood tall and began to walk forward through the large door to the room, after watching the series of events unfold before him. He was wearing golden armor that gleamed upon his chest, his armored leggings clanking against his heavy boots. He looked like a shining angel sent from the heavens. His skin was a dark tan, and his eyes were a glistening blue. His hair was black and curled, and he had a shaved goatee that was trimmed at his chin. "If he's a member of the Hayashi clan, then the gods have already condemned his soul to hell. He is already going to be killed."

"You see, sir," Junko said, holding up two fingers as he addressed General Mundo. "This young boy is beyond your human capacities. However, I understand that you want to handle this situation by yourself, correct? That is fine! You are free to call me whenever you would like." Junko turned away toward the closed doors of the throne room. "However," he said, stopping and glancing back at the king over his shoulder, "the Bount organization will obtain control over Keimaro. And once we do, we will not give the key to you."

"Wait," the king muttered.

"Milord," General Mundo warned, his head whipping around as shock flashed across his face. "You cannot be considering actually cooperating with these terrorists! It was bad enough that we did it once! We don't need an entire terrorist organization's help in order to capture a single boy!"

"Silence," the king said, holding up his hand as he closed his eyes and inhaled deeply. The general gulped, straightening his back as he looked at Junko. "What is it that you want, Junko?"

Junko raised an eyebrow with a light smile and turned back to face the king. "What is that it that I want? Power. Allow me to be your advisor, and I will ensure your capture of Keimaro Hayashi."

"That is out of the question!"

"Then we don't have a deal," Junko said with a loud laughter that echoed off the walls of the throne room. "Just call if you need me, milord! It won't be long before you understand the danger that you're in!" He stepped through the door, his body exploding into a burst of black mist that vanished in a mere instant, leaving the throne room completely silent.

The king put his head in his hands and groaned, leaning back against the golden throne. "Master Locksmith, continue your work on the chest and attempt to open it. General Mundo,

I want you to find this boy. He will most likely be coming for the chest. There is no doubt about that. We will intercept him. I don't care if he's alive or dead. You need to—"

"Father!" Aika exclaimed, her heart pounding rapidly. All of this talk … Keimaro Hayashi! That was the boy that she had met many years ago, the boy who had saved her life twice. It was because of him that she was still alive. Her hands were tightly wrapped around the ends of the throne arms, gripping them so hard that her knuckles had turned a ghostly white. "There's no need for more bloodshed! You can—"

"He's a member of the Hayashi clan. Therefore, he is a demon, a monster, nothing to society at all," the king said with a shake of his head at his daughter. "He will be either executed or killed on sight. It is preferred that he is brought in for a proper execution. However, in the end it doesn't matter which way he is killed. The gods have made it quite clear that the Hayashi clan is never to be trusted and that they are to be eliminated. Huh, I thought we killed off the last of them years ago. To think that there were some of them walking amongst us … those sneaky bastards."

Aika leaned back against her throne and gulped, shaking her head in disbelief. She remembered when she had first told Keimaro about the Hayashi clan. The memory was a bit blurry after four years, but she still remembered seeing the pain in his eyes. He had thought that he was the same as everyone else. What was the difference between him and another human? They looked the same. Only the eyes made him look like a demon, but that wasn't his fault. What gods would declare the complete eradication of their own creation?

Her eyes lowered, and she sighed, knowing that arguing with her father wouldn't result in anything but him angry. Aika's father always wanted things his way and for him to always be right even when he was blatantly wrong. She just wished that she could at least see Keimaro again, just once more.

***

Tobimaru stood on the peak of a mountain, the freezing air biting at his cheeks. His skin was pale, and he felt the heat being sucked from his body, turning him as cold as a corpse. But he stood nevertheless, watching outward over the land with his demonic, glowing red eyes locked onto the massive Faar Empire that stretched across the land. His black hood was pulled tightly over his head, and he scoffed, his hands pressed heavily into his pockets. With every breath a cool mist gently left his lips. His boots were deep within the several feet of snow that covered the ground, making his toes feel numb from the cold. A strong wind gusted behind him, and he glanced over his shoulder at Junko, who had just appeared. "So? How did it go?" he asked, turning to face his superior.

"They didn't accept the offer, as was expected."

"So, we allow Keimaro to wreak havoc on Bassada? The soldiers could kill him," Tobimaru muttered. "How do we know that Keimaro has the heart to destroy? For all we know, he could be a weak, peaceful man. He might be captured easily by Faar."

"Peaceful?" Junko almost burst out laughing on the spot. He walked forward to the edge of the peak, looking outward over the land as Tobimaru had been doing. "Why would a man who lost everything he loved be peaceful? Once someone's soul is tainted to such an extent, he has entered an abyss so dark that he will never find his way out. Keimaro has experienced a taste of pain and intends to cleanse himself through revenge. He is a lot like you, craving vengeance, but he will come to our side with time."

Tobimaru scoffed, glancing away from Junko and instead looking at the blanketed snow that covered the peak of the mountain. "If he gets attention, then he will be found by *him*."

"In the end, none of that matters. We'll kill everyone who gets in our way and obliterate anything that isn't of any worth to us," Junko said with a sigh. "It's a shame they didn't take the opportunity right away. That would've saved a lot of time. Oh well, let Keimaro mess around in Bassada like the little child he is. They'll come to us begging for help sooner or later."

"And what if they don't?"

Junko turned and smiled at Tobimaru with a small, childish giggle. "The Bount organization contains the world's strongest individuals who have mastered power beyond belief. Nothing is out of our grasp except numbers. Kuro will be awakened, and our goals will be complete. If the king doesn't come to us, we will go to him once more—and we will take the crown by force."

8. NO PLAN

The hot sun beat down on the young men as they continued forward across a green field, their boots crushing blades of grass in their wake. Keimaro felt extremely uncomfortable while wearing the restricting armor of the escort soldiers. The armor felt heavy in comparison to his cloak, which had been made out of abyssalite and was given to him by his father. It was supposedly the symbol of a Hayashi clan member, though he didn't understand why his second father would have such a possession, seeing as he wasn't a member of the clan. Perhaps it had been passed down, but Keimaro never got to hear the story about what had happened to his real family. In the end, his second father had died with whatever secrets had been locked up within him. No key would be able to unlock those secrets. Still, Keimaro had been given a particular key, which had dangled upon his neck for several years. He wore it in remembrance of that night when he'd lost everything.

His head ached from the heavy helmet clamping down upon his face, and he groaned, walking beside Yata, who wore the same armor. They couldn't even recognize each other without looking up close to examine each other's faces. "How the hell do soldiers wear this all of the time?" he muttered, tugging at his collar as he sighed, the heat increasing dramatically within the helmet.

He looked forward at the massive towering walls that looked down on him like an insect, leaving him in their shadow. He whistled as he studied the dirt path before him, which began to wind toward a large opened gate made of some type of stout wood. Perhaps it was from a yew tree; Keimaro had read that those were some of the strongest trees with incredible trunks that would withstand days of lumbermen axes. Or maybe it could be the great oak, which was decently strong as well. His curiosity as a child led him to read about so many different types of trees that existed in the world. It was wonder how there were so many varieties. He wondered where they all came from.

After a long two hours of walking, they finally reached the gate. The caravan's horses slowed to a stop, and Keimaro raised an eyebrow when Gavin began to engage in some type of silent conversation with the guards at the gate. He couldn't tell if Gavin was trying to help them get through, or if he was ratting them out. His hand was wrapped tightly around the hilt of his sword in the event that he would need to act. However, only moments later, the guards stepped to the side and let the escort continue through the entrance and into the city.

Keimaro blinked a few times as he walked through the gate. The bright sunlight began to shine down on him once he walked through the gateway. His eyes widened and glistened as he looked at the wonderful sight before him. It was the city— Bassada, the capital of Faar, and therefore one of the busiest, liveliest places on the planet. Everywhere he looked, he saw people busily minding their own business. The crowds surged as if they all had somewhere to be, pushing past each other and talking. Their words melted into a giant rambling sound that Keimaro couldn't quite make out.

He swiftly took off his helmet, flipping his hair to the side before looking outward and taking in a deep breath of fresh air. "Wow, this is something," he said in awe.

"Twenty times busier than Bakaara," Yata whistled. "No, make that a hundred."

"So, I got you in," Gavin muttered, folding his arms as he leaned back against the wagon. "I'm assuming you don't actually intend on delivering this cargo, do you?"

"Nope," Keimaro said with a sly smile. "We are going to find a place to stay. Meanwhile, we will discuss our plan. But, Gavin, don't think that you can get away from us," he muttered, tossing his helmet into the back of the caravan with the rest of the boxed cargo. "A single move that indicates that you'd betray us, and I'll kill you."

"Got it," Gavin said with a sigh as he began to walk forward, holding the reins of both of the horses that pulled the cargo wagon. As he guided them through the streets, the people began to separate around them, letting the animals trot forward on the tiled streets.

The buildings around them were much more complex than the houses in Bakaara. They were built with stronger wood, and some were even made entirely of stone. The rooftops were tiled and looked much more beautiful from their bright red coloring. The street constantly branched off into more walkways that looked nearly the same as the one that they were walking down, making Keimaro believe that perhaps the city was much larger than he'd believed. He imagined that it was like a giant tree and that they were traveling along the trunk. Many branches of streets came off of the main trunk and split off into even more alleys and roads. *Is every part of Bassada packed like this?*

He noticed the houses began to get more and more advanced as they continued along the main road. Some of the buildings were taller and much larger than others, and others were painted in different ways. Keimaro's eyes locked onto a rather large curved stone archway with a stone path that led down straight through a lush, beautiful lawn to a massive mansion that towered high above the other buildings. White pillars supported the orange tiled rooftop, and a long cobblestone pathway led to an auburn wood door with a golden knob on it. No doubt that this belonged to someone of royalty or wealth.

Keimaro stopped suddenly when he saw a man with slicked-back red hair, standing there in front of the door of his mansion. He couldn't help but see that the man was also wearing a black cloak that looked considerably similar to his own. Perhaps he was a Bount? He closed his eyes, tearing his gaze from the man and his house. He shouldn't have been making assumptions. Right now, he just had to concentrate on the task at hand. Yata touched his shoulder.

"What's wrong, Kei?"

"Nothing," Keimaro murmured as they continued forward. The buildings went by quickly, and soon he found that they were walking in a marketing area. The city's main square was similar to that of Bakaara's, except on a much larger scale. It was probably thirty times bigger with stalls, tents, and buildings installed everywhere in order for merchants to maximize the amount of products that they sold and to advertise what they were selling. Men and women yelled and called, bartering with merchants as Gavin led them away from the crowded square. People were everywhere, making it near impossible to walk without bumping into someone.

Keimaro turned and saw a large stone statue of a man in the center of the square on top of a fountain. Glistening water rained down around the majestic, strong man that held a mighty scepter up into the air. The cascading water made his image glimmer, making him look superior to everyone around him from his height and look. As the boy noticed a crown resting upon the statue's head, his hand slowly tightened into a fist, his knuckles cracking. So, that was the man who was responsible for the massacre of everyone in Bakaara ... and the death of his mother. He memorized the face in an instant, and turned away to find that he was walking out of the square and down a street lined with taverns, bars, and inns.

Keimaro's eyes wandered to the swinging sign that hung from the rooftop of a large building. The sign bore a symbol of a large mug, overflowing with ale beneath a simple name: *The Hearth*. What a name for a tavern. Surely enough, Gavin decided to lead the horses to the front. By now, people were complaining that they were moving horses through crowds of people.

Keimaro glanced over his shoulder and saw two guards who began to walk in their direction, making him suspicious that leading a wagon and horses through the city was illegal. He glared in Gavin's direction, knowing the boy had something to do with this. The soldier hadn't warned them, and their movement surely did attract a lot of attention. Could he have purposely led them through the city in an illegal manner to attract guards? "I'll deal with you afterward. Yata, stay with Gavin and make sure he doesn't make any sudden movements."

He turned and began walking toward the guards.

"Hey, escort," one of the guards said. Keimaro recognized his tabard and insignia almost instantly. It was the same one that he had seen many years ago on the day of Bakaara's destruction. The man was in his mid-forties and had a rather short, brown beard. He sighed, tapping his helmet as he stopped a few feet from the young boy. "You're the ones delivering the *special* cargo, right?"

Keimaro blinked for a moment, glancing over his shoulder at the wagon and the cargo inside, covered by a white blanket. Special cargo? Suddenly he felt as if whatever they were carrying around in that wagon was of actual value. He turned back to the guard and nodded his head, going along with the conversation. "Yeah, that's us."

"Really? I thought there would be more of you, considering the importance of the package."

"Well, most of us were assaulted in the Forbidden Forest," Keimaro said with a sigh of exhaustion, shaking his head as if saddened. "Many monsters of the night came at us, and we barely made it out alive. But, we managed to hold on to the cargo, and we made it in one piece."

"That's disappointing that you lost so many lives," the guard said with a shrug, clearly not actually caring. "Well, what are you doing all the way over here anyway?" He put a hand on his hip. "You were supposed to deliver the cargo straight to the king, were you not?"

"Yeah, but we just figured we would stop quickly—"

"Do you even understand how important this cargo is?"

"Not particularly, we weren't told what was inside."

The guard sighed and shook his head in disbelief. "Privates. Oh well, the king has sent us to escort you to him to personally deliver the cargo. I expect that he has something he wants to talk to you men about. Perhaps a report on the mission, nothing big. So, whoever is in charge of you guys should come with us."

Keimaro blinked a few times and finally cracked a smile as he nodded, walking forward with the two guards. "Take care of Gavin," he called to Yata over his shoulder as the two men from the Royal Guard led him away.

A shadow fell over his face as darkness welled up in his heart. This was his chance, practically handed to him on a platter! They were allowing him to waltz up to the king himself. He would be able to kill the man who was responsible for the destruction of his family—well, one of them, at least. The others were the Bounts. He would have to plan this assassination carefully; otherwise, he could jeopardize his own life. But in the end, he wasn't thinking about careful procedure. Rather, his mind was consumed by the very thought of the king's absolute annihilation, nothing more.

***

Yata watched as the Royal Guards escorted his friend away, not really sure what to do now. This wasn't part of the plan. They were supposed to find somewhere to stay, not go off to see the goddamn king. He sighed when he saw two more random guards come by about a minute later, moving to the cargo and lifting up several massive boxes. It took two men to carry each box, indicating that whatever was inside was extremely heavy.

The guards stumbled off with the boxes in the same direction that Keimaro had traveled only moments earlier.

Not according to the plan—that was how Keimaro always tended to do things. If he tried to assassinate the king at this point, he would only get himself killed. Yata hoped that Keimaro wasn't actually stupid enough to follow through with such a foolish plan.

Yata went to the back of the wagon and picked up his bat along with Keimaro's cloak. He slung the cloak over his shoulder and shrugged at Gavin. "We're going to need a room, so I suppose that we'll start with that. Buy us a room, and we'll get started with our plan. It seems that you'll be going along with it, seeing as you have no choice anymore."

"What?" Gavin exclaimed in disbelief. "I thought that you guys were going to let me go once I got you inside! Are you honestly going to make me do whatever you terrorists—?"

"We aren't goddamn terrorists," Yata snarled, lashing forward and grabbing Gavin by the shirt. He yanked the soldier close to him, their faces inches apart. He glared into the warrior's eyes, which were filled with fear. His hands squeezed the shirt, and Gavin gulped, beads of sweat beginning to stream down his forehead. "Remember this: what we are doing is not for ourselves. It's so that no one else will have to suffer like Kei and I have. You freaking understand that? Don't forget: one false move, and I'll bash your skull in. I don't mind killing you in front of people, either. I'm not like Kei. I'm much more heartless," he muttered, shoving Gavin toward the door of the inn.

The soldier stumbled a few feet and sighed, understanding that there was no way out of this situation. But, how could he live with helping terrorists? These guys were obviously up to no good, and the fact that one of them just went to see the king was even more of a problem. Hardly anyone ever met the king in person; why was this boy who had just entered the city getting a chance to do so?

Gavin opened the door and walked inside with Yata behind

him. He scanned the inn and whistled when he saw that it was filled with lively people. Fast fiddle tunes were playing as people danced on tables and on the floor. Mugs filled with beer were being passed around as if people were celebrating. Every corner of the packed room was filled with cheers and laughter, and Gavin couldn't help but smile. These were soldiers of Faar, definitely. Why were they not at the barracks or the mess hall doing their celebrating?

He walked forward and pushed his way through the crowds of people to the bar. There, he smiled at the owner of the inn, who wore a brown vest and had a beard of aged gray hair. "May I have a room for…?" He glanced over his shoulder at Yata, who was looking at the men around him as if they were all monsters, astonishment printed upon his face. "Well, I'll take a room for three days and pay when we leave. A room for three. Sound good?"

"Yeah," the innkeeper said with a nod of his head. He reached to his belt and unhooked a key, handing it to Gavin. He nodded once more in the direction of the staircase. "Second door on the left once you reach the hallway."

"Thanks," Gavin said and took the key. He looked at Yata and led him up the wooden stairway to a long hallway. Small candles were placed everywhere to illuminate the dark area. Night had fallen during the short exchange with the innkeeper, leaving the rooms darkened. He inserted the key in the door and felt dismay swarm over him. He was helping this scum in the pursuit of his goal.

He opened the door to their room and walked in with a sigh as he saw three beds perfectly aligned on one side with a table and chairs on the other. A window was open against the darkening sky as the sun set and vanished over the side of Bassada's outer wall. The soldier walked over to the window and gripped the windowsill, watching the sun's rays streak red across the sky and disappear. The sound of music and voices had died down once the door was closed and were muffled behind the thick wooden walls.

"What is your purpose here in Bassada?" Gavin muttered, glancing over his shoulder at Yata.

"To obtain a chest that was stolen from Keimaro," Yata said, closing the door behind him. He tossed his bat onto the ground and threw Keimaro's cloak onto one of the beds. The boy leapt upward and landed heavily on one of the beds, bouncing from its spring. He leaned backward on the mattress, feeling as if he were on a cloud; it had been so long since he had slept on a bed this comfortable.

"Is that so ... and what else?"

"To assassinate the king."

Gavin's eyes widened and his body went stiff upon hearing such a sentence. That was the highest form of treason. Simply saying such a thing could result in an execution. His hands balled into fists; he knew that he couldn't let these men get away with this. Keimaro had been the dangerous one in the forest, and the reason he had been successful in his assault was only because he had the Shokugan and could see through the darkness. Gavin had the upper hand in this situation, the element of surprise, and Keimaro wasn't even here—not to mention the fact that Yata was actually unarmed and defenseless. This was his chance to stop these assassins!

He grabbed the curtain and threw it at Yata, the white blanket falling down upon the boy. The soldier bolted across the room, snatching the bat off of the ground. He lifted it upward into the air, holding the handle with both hands. "Long live the king!" he yelled, slamming the bat down onto the surprised Yata, who was covered in the sheets.

Gavin's eyes widened as the bat jarred his arms and he heard the clang of metal against metal. Whatever he had hit felt solid, as if he had just whacked an iron wall. He blinked a few times; had Yata been wearing armor? Why was there metal there? Even the guard armor wouldn't make such a solid sound if hit at full power by a bat.

"Man, you sure are a handful, aren't you?" Yata muttered, slowly rising as the blanket slipped off of him.

Gavin stared in disbelief at the abomination before him. There was no flesh to hit. Yata was completely metal, his skin gleaming as if he were some type of statue. How was it even possible for Yata to be moving while in this form? So, he was like Keimaro and had some type of special power as well.

Gavin grunted as he was kicked backward, smashing into the tables and chairs. He gasped as the table splintered and he landed on the ground, his head spinning from the tremendous force of the kick.

The soldier looked at Yata, the outlines of his vision blurred and turning white as he gasped for air. He was lifted high above the floor and thrown across the room once more like a ragdoll. He yelped as he smashed into the wall and fell, his head hitting the mattress as his body fell into the gap between the beds. He lay in an uncomfortable position and groaned, trying to recollect what was happening. Then he saw Yata standing there, tapping his bat against his shoulder.

"So," Yata said simply, kneeling down so that his face was close to Gavin's, who was slumped in between the two beds, "I can either kill you right now and tell Keimaro about what happened ... or we can cooperate and perhaps you'll understand why we have to do what we have to do, got it? I still need you alive, so stop being an idiot and trying to overpower me," he muttered, flicking Gavin in the forehead with a sigh. "Stop trying to fight someone who is above your level."

He rose and tossed the bat aside once more. "I don't like the fact that I have to trust you, but Keimaro decided to let you tag along with us instead of killing you on the spot. I'm sure he has a particular reasoning for his choices. Make sure not to make him regret his choice; otherwise, you'll end up like every other soldier in that forest, understand?"

Gavin nodded with a groan as he rolled over. He climbed up into his bed and placed the pillow over his head. He had been so easily defeated by Yata; it was almost as if he hadn't stood a chance against him. He knew that he still had a lot to see and understand in the open world, but this was insane! A human that could change his body into metal? If every soldier in Faar could obtain this power, they would be invincible as an empire! They would be able to dominate to the edges of the continent with ease. But he had never heard of anyone obtaining such an exotic ability before.

He glanced at Yata from the corner of his eye, hidden beneath the pillow. It looked like Yata would want to do the complete opposite of helping the Faar Empire. What was their goal, revenge? The soldier let out a sigh of exasperation and closed his eyes in exhaustion. Either way, if he just stuck with them, he would find out eventually. Depending on their real goals, he would act accordingly. He only had to wait for the opportune moment.

***

The city of Bassada was at least a hundred times bigger than the village Keimaro had grown up in. The people were much livelier as well. Through many parts of the town that Keimaro saw, happiness was printed on most of the faces of people who strolled through the streets. But, he also saw many parts that hinted at a lasting poverty existing in Bassada. They walked past a particular section of the city scattered with destitute people. They were wanderers in civilization and seemed to own little or nothing at all.

Keimaro walked through the streets silently as if going through a ghost town. This was supposedly a shortcut in order to get to the citadel where the king was currently held, a cut straight through the slums. The buildings were rundown, and the wood was rotted with mold growing in the cracks. Some of the buildings looked similar to the small cottages that Keimaro had seen back in Bakaara, like the one that Yata had lived in. But even those structures were considered a luxury in this part of the city.

The people themselves were wearing ragged clothes that left them looking as if they had just gotten into a fight with a bear. A single man caught Keimaro's attention, for his skin was extremely tan from what looked like long, grueling hours in the sun. Keimaro figured he probably worked somewhere outside of the city, but what snatched Keimaro's eye was the overall emaciated look of this man's figure. He looked like an undead zombie that had risen from the dead and was moping around slowly, dragging one leg behind him. His sunken cheekbones showed how deprived he was of nutrients. His shirt was ripped as if slashed by a sword, exposing his chest. His ribs were prominent, evidence of his starvation, and his stomach actually seemed distended as he breathed heavily, his throat letting out a raspy choke. He was alive, but in Keimaro's eyes he was basically dead. In fact, he probably had only a couple of hours to live without any sort of food.

The Shokugan in his eyes allowed him to see that there was actually an infection in the man's throat as well as his bladder. It seemed that his ankle was twisted, which was why he was dragging it behind. His stomach was swollen because he was filled with gas, and his body looked fatigued from prolonged malnutrition because he hadn't eaten for an estimated four to five days. The fact that the man kept smacking his lips together showed a lack of water and possible dehydration as well.

Keimaro stopped suddenly, causing the two Royal Guards that accompanied him to stop as well. They glanced at him with confusion printed on their faces, about to ask why he had stopped. The young boy reached into his pocket, remembering the money that he had looted from the dead corpses in the forest. He had never really cared much for money. It was just useless junk, though people placed value on it for some reason. He walked over to the old starving man, who slowed down, looking at the young boy with widened eyes. Keimaro pressed a few coins into the man's rough, bony hand and nodded lightly in his direction. The boy saw tears beginning to glisten in the man's eyes. Keimaro gave the poor man a reassuring smile before turning back to his escorts without exchanging a single word. They had spoken with their eyes, and that was enough.

One of the Royal Guards raised an eyebrow in amusement and chuckled with satisfaction. "You don't see such chivalry in the guard anymore, especially from a private. Anyway, what's your name? The king will probably want it presented."

Keimaro blinked a few times as he walked with the soldiers, listening to the clanking of the cargo behind him as the men carried the boxes around. His name? There was no way that he could use his real name—that was, unless he wanted to be captured and executed. "Riku Hikari," he said simply, making up a name out of the blue.

"Riku Hikari, huh? Sounds like a foreign name," one of the Royal Guards said with a shrug as they took a final turn to an enormous citadel that towered high into the air. If anything, it looked more like a church than a fortified building. The only strong part about the building was probably the door, which was as tall as one of those cottages in the slums. At least eighty normal guards were positioned outside of the building, surrounding the entire perimeter of the citadel.

Not bad on security, Keimaro thought as he was led straight through the front door, walking inside. He truly wasn't surprised that this "citadel" was actually just a church. The king could meet wherever he wanted. With this amount of security and protection he wouldn't have to worry about any assassins. Any ordinary assassins, at least. But he was concerned with why the king would decide to meet with a random nobody private who had escorted the cargo. It all seemed far too fishy. Was this a trap? No, it was impossible that anyone could know his true identity. He was dead to the world. He no longer existed.

The inside of the church was huge, the ceiling rising at least fifty feet. Many wooden benches lined both sides of an aisle, and the church was lit by thousands of candles that were positioned on the walls. The colorful stained glass windows on both sides of the church allowed for only a slight amount of light to pass through, and Keimaro realized the sun was setting. It was night already? Time was fleeting faster than he thought.

On the far side of the church, Keimaro saw that the king

was sitting upon a massive chair atop a royal red cushion. His face matched that of the statue in the marketing square. Behind his throne was a large mosaic of some type of giant beast that looked like a drake. A dragon.

The king had a grizzly brown beard that went down to his chest, a symbol of courageousness, apparently, in the Faar tradition of kings. He held a small golden scepter in his hand with a gleaming ruby at its tip. Royal blue robes were pulled over his body along with the finest white linens underneath. The robes drooped down all the way to his boots, which were made of the best leather and were probably as comfortable as walking on clouds. His sapphire blue eyes locked onto Keimaro as the large doors of the church creaked closed behind him, locking them in an eerie silence.

Keimaro was escorted to the front of the church to an altar, where it seemed recent offerings had been made. He looked down at the table that was before him. There was a half-eaten chicken leg, some corn, and some green slime that was splattered onto a plate. These were offerings to their gods? They were more like insults than offerings. He looked past the king's throne at the gigantic golden statue of a dragon, which apparently represented the "gods" that they were worshipping. He blinked, realizing that he had zoned out for a brief second. Regaining focus, he noticed that he was in front of the king, the most important person in all of Bassada—and the man that he despised deeply. He looked on both sides of him and saw that his escorts had knelt down with their heads bowed and were whispering for Keimaro to do the same.

The boy hated to bow down before someone else, but he knew that he would have to do so; otherwise, his cover would be blown immediately. He couldn't allow for honor to get in the way of his goals that he had trained so many years for. He closed his eyes and got down on one knee, pressing his right fist to his chest, over his heart. He bowed his head low so that he was looking at his own feet, mirroring the exact posture of the Royal Guard. "Your majesty, you called for my presence?"

"I called not for anyone's specific presence. I merely called for a personal report on your recent escort mission through the Forbidden Forest on the outskirts of Bassada's borders," the king spoke loudly in a deep voice, showing much authority. He leaned back in his throne with a sigh, twirling his scepter in his hand as a bored child would with a stick. "However, I am quite interested in knowing how the escort mission went. Were you attacked?"

"Yes, my liege."

"By whom?"

"By creatures that lived within the Forbidden Forest, my liege," Keimaro said, not daring to lift up his head to face the king himself. That would be incredibly disrespectful. "We left Bakaara with eighteen men and arrived with only three."

"There were no humans that assaulted the cargo or attempted to hide in the wagon at all during your journey?" the king said with a raised eyebrow.

"No, milord."

"Interesting, do you know why I am asking these particular questions?"

"No, milord."

"It is because there is a survivor of the Hayashi clan actually out there in Bakaara," the king said with a heavy sigh, tapping the arm of his chair impatiently. "His name is Keimaro Hayashi, and he is one of the last surviving members of the Hayashi clan. Intelligence has told us that he is coming to Bassada for a particular chest that was delivered to us earlier this week. Do you know what you delivered in the cargo today?"

"No, milord," Keimaro answered by rote, his mind distracted. *He's telling me far too much. Does he already know who I am? Is this a trap? And how the hell does he know that I'm still alive? I've been in hiding for four years. Who gave him this information?*

"You delivered the blueprints to a new technological discovery," the king said, standing up from his throne as he began to pace back and forth, holding his scepter up high. "You see, there are many different creatures and intelligent humanoid forms that exist in our great world. This globe has yet to be explored. One of the most well-known masters of technology would be the gnome…. Are you familiar with this type of creature?"

"Yes, milord."

"Tell me what you know."

"Gnomes are small humanoids that live in peace with another race known as the dwarves. These two races live in perfect harmony in the mountains of the northern continent. It is said that they live in an underground city powered by technology invented by the gnomes. What they lack in physical strength, they make up for with brainpower. They are said to be eighteen times smarter than the average human. That is all I know, milord," Keimaro muttered, a bead of sweat forming on his brow.

"Ah, good. Well, recently, Faar got its hands on our first ever gnome. We captured it and created blueprints for a new type of weapon that will forever change the nature of war! There will be no more bows and arrows, no ranged weaponry that requires a physical nature. Now there will be only precision with the technology that we have created. A rifle, a weapon that fires a small, circular projectile at such a high speed that it is capable of killing or wounding the enemy. All it takes is the pull of a trigger. That is the rumored weapon that you have delivered to us today. Because of your incredible contribution to our military and for helping Faar become a stronger empire, I will give you a chance at prosperity."

Keimaro blinked a few times, wanting to raise his head, though he wasn't exactly sure if he was allowed to yet. Prosperity? What the hell was this old fart talking about? He didn't want prosperity. All he wanted to do was kill the king. And what was this new weaponry that he was rambling on about? It sounded extremely dangerous. A weapon that could fire

109

projectiles that fast without any physical action but pulling a trigger seemed almost too good to be true—and too terrifying for Keimaro to even imagine. "A chance, milord?"

"Now that I've told you all of this, I am giving you a chance to either live and become a member of the Royal Guard, or die trying," the king said with a chuckle, sitting back down in his chair comfortably. He leaned back, and his lips curved into a wicked smile. "Are you prepared for what's in store?"

Keimaro slowly raised his head and looked up at the king with a sly smile as he pushed himself to his feet, standing tall. He lowered his head slightly, a dark shadow coming over his face as he saw and heard the movement of soldiers from the perimeter of the room converging in on him. "So, milord, is this some type of a test?"

This is exactly what I wanted.

"Yes," the king said with a chortle of amusement. "Whether or not you leave this citadel will depend on your skill. I have been looking for a loyal personal bodyguard for quite some time now. It's time to prove yourself."

Keimaro sensed movement around him as the soldiers suddenly drew their blades, brandishing swords in the moonlight, their steel cutting at him from multiple directions. The boy had yet to react when the weapons were already about to cut through his body. The look on the king's face belonged to that of a bored child, yawning drolly. The boy stomped his foot into the ground, and his sword shot out of its sheath as if the weapon had sprung to life. The soldiers were still in mid-flow of their attack and watched in surprise as the boy caught the hilt of the weapon in the air, holding the blade backward. It was unlike anything they had ever seen before.

Keimaro reacted to the slashes at the last moment, ducking his head with incredible speed and flexibility. The soldiers' blades hacked into open air. His hair came over his face and then lifted as he spun around in a perfect, fluent motion, his sword slashing across the face of one of the soldiers as if he had been wielding a dagger. Crimson blood misted into the air and splattered onto the ground at Keimaro's feet. The man crumpled to the floor.

The boy was ready for the second soldier's attack from behind, though the man probably thought that Keimaro would be caught off guard. Their attacks were far too predictable. In fact, the Shokugan was unnecessary to fight these weaklings. He smiled to himself as he glanced at the man over his shoulder, seeing the jab coming straight at him from behind, a backstab. His body rotated, and the tip of the broadsword flew past him.

Far too predictable.

Keimaro's sword drove straight through the man's chest and burst out of his back as the life drained from his fear-stained face. The smell of urine filled Keimaro's nostrils, and he scoffed in disgust as he twisted the blade, feeling the man's spine. These men were responsible for the murder of his village; he felt no remorse when he killed them. He ripped the blade from the man's body, dragging a stream of blood across the ground before the man collapsed silently. He turned and glanced at the king, looking for approval. He smiled when the superior motioned for more soldiers to come at him.

Keep them coming. I'll teach them all a lesson.

This time, five soldiers rushed forward, two of them with long spears. They gripped the wooden shafts and jabbed outward, the sharpened stone slicing cleanly through the air at his legs in the attempt to wound him. He saw the movements clearly and sidestepped so that the first spear went between his legs and the other jabbed past his right leg. He kept moving, stepping around, making sure that he wouldn't get tangled in any of the spears. His eyes flickered from soldier to soldier, realizing that they had surrounded him. Though, there was no hint of fear in his heart, which kept a steady and calm beat throughout the fight.

A soldier jabbed with his spear, and the boy grabbed the wooden shaft, yanking hard. He smiled as the man flew forward, losing his grip on his own weapon. How boring. The weakest point of a spearman was when he jabbed; he loosened up because he thought that he would hit a target. His grip weakened in the split-second before he pulled his spear back. That was precisely the moment when Keimaro yanked, sending the man stumbling toward him. Completely defenseless, the man's entire upper half was slashed open with a brief whip of Keimaro's blade. He fell to the ground as Keimaro whirled the spear over his head, using a single hand, and slammed it downward into the shoulder of the second spearman, who bellowed in agony. He fell to his knees, the spear bulging from his body as his screams split the air.

The boy turned to the swordsmen now, kicking backward without even looking. He drove his foot into the face of the wounded spearman, knocking him into unconsciousness. He spun his sword in his hand experimentally, his eyes locked in the direction of the remaining soldiers, who were sweating and shifting uneasily. The Hayashi clan boy could practically smell the fear coming off of them—or was that just the fact that they had all pissed their pants in fear? Perhaps it was both.

Keimaro leapt forward, engaging all three swordsmen. Their blades slashed and hacked at him in a flurry of blinding movements. His eyes darted back and forth, swatting their blades away from him, parrying hard in the attempt to open up some of their weaknesses. He alternated exchanging blows with each of them, smiling when he saw them beginning to spread out in an attempt to surround him. That was their downfall.

The boy slashed at one of them, who parried and stumbled back from the force of the blow. The man behind him seemed less tense since Keimaro was now attacking one of his comrades rather than himself. Unfortunately, he was the next target. Keimaro whirled around in an instant, slashing the man's leg as he spun, while ducking two slashes from the other swordsmen. The injured man yelped in agony, but Keimaro had already turned away from him, casting him away as no longer a threat.

He faced the two swordsmen who were still standing tall. He smirked, swinging his fist in a fast blow across the face of one of the swordsmen. The impact was an instant knockout, sending bloody teeth flying into the air as the man's cheek jiggled from the force of the blow, his face already turning red from the punch. Keimaro whipped his sword upward, ripping the man's chest open in a hissing cut from his blade. His hand released the hilt of his weapon, letting the sword spin in the air above him. He spun around and lifted his leg, driving his heel in a heavy kick across the second swordsman's cheek, stunning him momentarily. Lashing out, he grabbed the hilt of his sword, taking advantage of the fact that both of the soldiers were stunned from direct blows to the face. His hands curled around the sword's hilt, and he swung it with full power. The blade tore through flesh and bone, flaying their bodies as fountains of blood gushed into the air. Both men were cut open with a single slash of Keimaro's sword that practically tore them apart.

The boy relaxed and stood tall as they collapsed at his feet. He turned to the man who had been cut across the leg. The soldier was crawling toward his comrades, who were hesitant to step forward and help their friend, which was against the king's orders. He caught sight of the struggling, wounded man and smiled to himself. He walked after the man, spinning the weapon in his hands, and positioned himself over the soldier.

Feel my pain. Feel my hatred.

Keimaro brought the blade slamming downward into flesh, panting as the familiar sight of blood began to pool around the man's unmoving body. His look hardened as he wrenched his weapon from the cold corpse, swinging it once more. The blood on the blade splattered onto the ground, and his heart thudded at the silence that surrounded him. He'd done what the king had asked, hadn't he? It was an awfully odd test for the king to give, for his own subjects to kill one another. He glanced up at the king and saw his bright smile, now resembling that of an excited child on his birthday. Perhaps the king was simply insane.

The king was clapping his hands together rapidly, the sounds echoing through the silent church. The soldiers shifted uneasily as they watched the man who had slaughtered seven of their comrades. Several guards staggered forward, grabbing the corpses of their friends and pulling them away. Keimaro watched as bloody drag marks began to stain the floor, but two servants rushed forward and began to scrub the blood with sponges in order to hide the evidence.

So, the entire test was actually planned before Keimaro had even gotten here, meaning that the king was simply insane. Keimaro had originally thought that the king was wary of his true identity and was trying to kill him with this test. However, it occurred to him that it was impossible for the king to know what he looked like. He watched for a moment as the servants rubbed the bloody stains, their faces clearly disgusted at the stench of corpses and blood.

"Very well done, Riku! My, my, I haven't seen talent like that in ages! It is no wonder you were one of the very few men who returned to the city alive! I thank you for your cooperation with this dangerous activity. You are hereby a member of the Royal Guard. You displayed incredible skills before me today and are probably even capable of assassinating me, were you not so loyal. Might I ask, are the other survivors as skilled as you are? Or did you merely protect them throughout the escort?"

Keimaro didn't want Yata or Gavin to get involved in the Royal Guard like he had, so he simply shook his head with a sigh. "They are simply lucky that I was around is all. They were both nearly killed on the way here," he lied without any sense of emotion, and the king nodded with a sigh.

"Oh well, couldn't have expected that much talent in a simple escort mission," the king said with a wave of his hand. "Anyway, I'll have Judal bring you to your chambers tonight. The Royal Guard always sleeps in the same castle as the king. This is a bright step forward for you, Riku Hikari. Make sure to grasp this opportunity the best you can. You are honoring your empire with your service. I will give you two days to pack and bring anything you want to your room."

"Thank you, milord."

Keimaro watched as one of the original Royal Guards that had escorted him here stepped forward. So, this was Judal. His skin was a dark color from what looked like either ancestry or long hours of work in the sun. His eyes were a light brown, and his full lips were pursed together as he stood there with his tabard thrown over himself, his toned muscles exposed from the sleeveless uniform of the Royal Guard. The soldier held out a tabard and a suit of armor to Keimaro, the uniform of the Guard.

"Go and get changed in the back room. Leave your clothes here, and I'll be showing you to your chambers. You don't need to spend the night there tonight. Your job starts in two days. Two days from now, your life will be dedicated to protecting the king, understood?"

"Yes, sir."

"Good."

Keimaro accepted the abyssalite chain-vest and the tabard. He quickly scampered off to the back room of the church. He took his armor off, letting it clank to the marble floor. He slid the abyssalite vest over himself, accustomed to the lightweight material. Impressed, he also put on the tabard and shrugged. What was he even doing, taking this job? Why hadn't he just killed the king on the spot? Even if he wanted the chest, he didn't have to join the Royal Guard in order to obtain it. He probably could just kill everyone in the citadel and take it straight away. That was, unless the Bounts interfered. But after Gavin said that the Bounts and the king weren't in association, he felt that there really was nothing to fear. Killing the king and obtaining his vengeance came first. Getting the chest was second; then he would save Mai. Perhaps his priorities were a bit scrambled up, but he was closer to the first two goals than anything else.

So, why didn't he just open the door right now and kill everyone? This was the opportunity of a lifetime. He could just kill every single soldier and the king and be done with it. The king was outside his castle; he was defenseless. No one would've known that he was the one to do it. His heart was throbbing, though. It was longing for something more. Keimaro already knew what it was, but hated to admit it.

He wanted to see Aika.

He wanted to see if she was still alive, if she was okay, what the meteor's foreign powers had done to mutate her. He wanted to see her progression, her changes, what she looked like. He especially wanted to hear her voice once more. He had thought about her all the first week after the Bakaara massacre. Afterward, she had slipped his mind when he began to focus on his revenge. But when Keimaro looked at the king and into his eyes, he saw the resemblance of royalty, and he remembered Aika's gleaming royal blue eyes that had mesmerized him the day he had seen her underneath the apple tree.

Keimaro slammed his fist into the wall of the dark, empty back room. Huh, how stupid of him. He was letting a girl that he had met for only a single day, many years ago, get in between him and his goal. Sure, she was the only girl that he had talked to at the time, but was she more important than his vengeance? His hands were balled into tight fists, and he gritted his teeth as he heard a knock on the door and glanced in the direction.

"Oi, Riku, is everything all right?"

"Yeah," Keimaro said softly and pushed the door open, walking out to Judal with a nod. "I'm ready. Sorry for the hold up."

"Faster than lightning when he cuts down warriors, yet he's slow as a snail when it comes to changing," Judal said, and the soldiers in the room burst into laughter. He shrugged and waved for Keimaro to follow him. Keimaro saw that all of the Royal Guards had already left the area, and now normal guards and soldiers were filing out of the church.

Keimaro saw that the king had also left, and he sighed with disbelief. His chance had slipped away. Aika was the princess, and he would be able to see her in two days' time. But, there was also the possibility that she would recognize him. That could prove a problem—and killing her father in front of her would probably also arouse some hatred.

Ugh! Why the hell did he care about what she thought or how she felt? All that mattered was killing the king. Why was he even considering her feelings? The old man deserved every spike of pain that he would get from a blade driving through his chest. He deserved it all!

The boy closed his eyes, feeling heat rising to his face as he exhaled a deep breath. He was frustrated with himself. What did he want—to see Aika or to complete his mission? In truth, he wanted both. And there was no way he could keep Aika satisfied with him. He would have to kill the king before her. Hopefully she would understand why he wanted to do this. No, he didn't want to do this. He *had* to do this.

Keimaro lowered his head as his teeth ground together. He'd promised. He would kill every last man that got in his way, and he would make the entire empire of Faar suffer for what they'd done to him. Nothing else mattered.

9.   THE FIERCE WOLF

Yata's eyes were closed, and he was locked in a deep darkness. His body felt like a feather floating through the air. He was just about to drift into sleep when he felt a nudge. The single touch was enough to make his eyes snap open, and he grabbed Gavin by the ear, making the boy yelp in pain. "What the hell do you think you're doing, huh?" he snapped, pulling the boy's earlobe as he snarled into the soldier's ear. "What do you think is so freaking important that you have to wake me up in the middle of my nap?"

"Well … there's a guy," Gavin grunted, wincing as he balanced on one foot, "and he's been standing outside of our window for the past hour and a half. He's got a black cloak and looks really ominous, so I figured I'd tell you…."

Black cloak? Yata released Gavin's ear and stood, pushing the boy onto the bed. He snatched his bat off of the wooden table and spun it in his hand as he walked toward the window. Sure enough, there was a black-cloaked man standing across the road from him. His head was lowered so it was impossible to see his face, which was cast in shadows by his cowl. Was it possible that this guy was a Bount? No, the style of the cloak was a bit different than what Yata remembered—and if it was, the Bount probably would've attacked by now. So, what was this guy doing here?

A carriage rode by, making Yata blink in confusion. A carriage? He had thought that carriages weren't allowed in this part of town. Just as he had suspected, the cloaked figure was gone the very moment the horses left. His heart skipped a beat as he caught a flicker of movement, just before the window shattered. Glittering glass flew through the air and rained down on Yata, whose body had already solidified into a strong metal. The boy stumbled backward, raising his bat as he saw the cloaked figure standing in front of him.

Gavin had unsheathed his sword and was holding it out in front of him as well, his heart racing. "I told you that he was ominous!"

"Who are you?" Yata demanded, ignoring Gavin.

The cloaked figure reached upward and pulled his cowl back, revealing an incredible, unnatural sight. His hair was spiky and snow-white, something that both Yata and Gavin had never seen before. His eyes were a bright turquoise, making his face stand out even more than it had otherwise. The boy himself looked to be only around nineteen, yet he smiled confidently in the face of the two armed opponents before him. He threw his hands into the air and laughed. He called sarcastically, "Oh man, you got my weakness! Bats and small knives. I suppose I might as well surrender myself and tell you everything." He lowered his hand and struck out with lightning speed.

Yata was thrown backward, not understanding what had happened. The world spun at ridiculous speed as he found himself tumbling, breaking through solid walls and flying out into the open air. He grunted, smashing into the wall of the building across the street from the inn. The blow hadn't dealt much damage; Yata felt as if he had been punched by a three-year-old. But the fact that he had literally been thrown straight through a building from a single blow meant that his opponent was strong. Getting all of this attention from spectators wasn't good either. He shook his head, trying to clear the dust from his eyes, and pushed himself to his feet. He rubbed his head, enduring a brutal headache that had struck him after slamming into that final wall. There was no way that Gavin could've survived an attack like that.

Yata looked up and saw the white-haired boy standing in the hole of the wall with a smile on the face, thrilled as if he were playing a game. He whistled and scratched the back of his neck innocently. "Wow, you went pretty far on that last hit! So, I heard that you had a friend! Where's he? Heard he was pretty strong, too! Hayashi clan, right?" He smirked.

Yata's expression hardened at the mention of Keimaro. How did this guy get information on where Keimaro was? How did he even know Keimaro existed? "Oi, princess! Tell you what—you beat me, and I guess I won't have to go to your mother's house to tell her that her son has no manners," he snarled, tapping the metal bat to his shoulder. "I bet she didn't tell you a lot of things! Like how you're a bastard child."

"Keep the insults coming, tin-man," the white-haired boy scoffed. "I don't have time for your idiocy. The more time I spend talking to you, the more attention I'm attracting. My name is Yuri. I am not your ordinary opponent, as you can tell," he said, tilting his head back to reveal an array of sharp teeth that gleamed like shining daggers. "The old man told me that I was supposed to fetch Keimaro. However, he didn't mention anything about a Faar soldier and a freaking tin-man! Why the hell do you have Hayashi stench all over you?"

"Hayashi ... stench?" Yata snarled, his fist tightening in rage. *Using that word, stench, as if he's a type of dog or monster. As if Keimaro's different from him or me!*

"Yeah, they smell differently from—"

Yata stomped his foot, and the ground erupted, a giant fissure separating the earth for a moment. There was a single millisecond of silence before a giant steel cone burst from the earth, slicing straight through the entire inn. The building was obliterated and began to fall apart, wood flying into the air.

The white-haired boy had thrown himself off of the building before it was destroyed and landed heavily on the ground, rolling to break the impact. "You idiot! What do you think you're doing? There are innocent people in—"

Yata tilted his head back with a gleam in his eyes. He smirked, unbothered by his heinous crime. He walked toward the boy, his bat dragging across the dirt as people began to gather around them, watching the spectacle. "You think I give a crap about the people in this city? I'll do whatever I want! Are you going to stop me?" He lowered his head and released a low growl. "Then do it."

***

Gavin coughed a few times, not exactly sure what had happened. He felt something heavy on him. He tried to open his eyes, but honestly he wanted to simply keep them shut and just lie there and sleep. But, he knew he needed to get moving; this place was dangerous … wherever he was. His eyes fluttered open, and he blinked some dust away to find that he was actually underneath debris of the inn, not exactly sure how the entire structure had come apart. His chest burned with an agonizing pain, and he groaned, leaning forward. His back was pressed up against a wall that was still upright. One of the pillars that held the upper floors had fallen over and had almost landed on him. It was hovering inches over his legs. Feeling uncomfortable, Gavin quickly drew his legs back and began to push himself to his feet. Dust was everywhere, and he couldn't help but hear the grunting and clanging of combat nearby.

There's no doubt that's Yata. What happened?

Oh, yes. That mysterious white-haired boy had somehow teleported to their window and knocked them through several walls. Apparently now the entire inn was destroyed, too. Perfect. Simply wonderful! He knew he was gaining an affinity for Yata. Not really.

Why hadn't that stubborn piece-of-work listened to him earlier? No, why hadn't he gathered his own guts and warned

Yata earlier? Perhaps then they wouldn't be in this mess. Now the people in the inn were most likely killed, dozens of veterans from the war. Yata probably didn't care, but Gavin knew that those men didn't deserve to die in such an unexpected way. Now that he thought about it, how had that boy gotten to their window so fast? And how did he have super strength that excelled beyond even Yata? *Don't tell me he's another one of those freaks with super powers.*

Gavin stepped over the destroyed pillar and looked at the desolated area around him, his eyes wandering over dozens of corpses that had been buried underneath debris. Blood was splattered across the ground, forming multiple pools around bodies. He staggered a few steps, finding it rather hard to walk. Each step was as if he were drunk, incapable of walking in a straight line. His legs were shaking as he tried to go in the direction of the fighting. He didn't know why he was even going to Yata. He could run away right now, but there was something about this boy that seemed to draw him back in. He had been spared for a reason, Yata had said. What was that reason? They trusted him? He was a random stranger; why in the gods would they choose to trust a random *enemy* soldier? There was no logic behind their decision. *So, why am I trying to help these terrorists again?*

Gavin lost his balance and fell over, grasping another pillar. He leaned his chin on it, groaning. The unyielding stone gave him a bruise as he slumped over the debris and looked outward to see Yata and the boy exchanging heavy blows. Surprisingly enough, the enemy was much faster and even stronger than Yata.

Yata was swinging his bat furiously, but the opponent was able to dodge easily, as if he knew what was going to happen next. His image would flicker, and he would reappear somewhere else in the next second. It was near impossible for Yata to read the opponent's moves because the boy's speed was unreal. The boy had reappeared beside Yata and rotated his body, driving a full fist into the solid metal of Yata's face. Normally, punching that solid body would've at least hurt since the opponent was punching metal, but that didn't seem to stop him one bit. With an explosion of power, Yata was rocketed backward through the air, flipping out of control as he smashed solidly through a building, sending more dust everywhere. Debris rained down as the wall of the building began to crumble.

Gavin stared at the white-haired boy, incredulous. He was unbelievably strong; it was simply unnatural. A single punch, capable of sending a full-metal young man through a building. This boy had undoubtedly obtained his power from a similar place to where Keimaro and Yata had gotten theirs. But from where? A twisting feeling grasped at his gut, and he suddenly felt the need to go out there and help Yata.

But what could I do? Gavin thought, looking down at the dirt. *All I would do is give Yata a distraction for maybe a second or two before this guy sent me through more walls. I'm not superhuman like Yata is. I'll be killed. I'll die. Isn't the point of helping these guys just to survive? And if Yata is a terrorist who wants to assassinate our savior, our king, why should I help him?*

Yata's body had shifted from its metallic form, morphing back into human flesh. The white-haired boy grabbed him by the hair and dragged him from the wreckage of the destroyed building. He threw Yata to the ground, where he gasped for air, blood smeared across his chin.

Yata placed his palm onto the ground, trying to push himself upward, but he was swiftly kicked and driven back into the earth. The boy had never felt so powerless against such a strong opponent before. Defeated so easily, being humiliated without a single chance from the very beginning. He saw his bat a couple of feet away and reached outward in a final attempt to fight back. To his despair, Yuri kicked it away. A bolt of fear shot through Yata as his eyes widened. He realized he was now unarmed and unable to defend himself. Was he going to die? Was this the—

The mysterious boy interrupted Yata's thought process with a heavy kick to the cheek. Yata's face snapped to the side before he went limp and hit the ground, his eyes closed, unmoving. The white-haired boy bent over and scooped Yata off of the ground, slinging the unconscious body over his shoulder. He turned and saw Gavin, giving the soldier a slight smile and a nod. "The soldiers will be here soon. I suggest you get out of here," he said, not specifying who he was acknowledging. Gavin heard, and he watched as the boy began to walk off into an alleyway between buildings.

Gavin's throat felt dry, and he felt extremely hot. *What do I do? Follow him and possibly get killed? It would be the right thing to do so that Keimaro at least would be able to save his friend. Ugh, why the hell am I so reluctant to go after them? This other guy is not exactly a hero either. Both Yata and this other guy are bad. Damn, what do I do?* Yata at least had smidges of humanity in him, despite the fact that he was extremely aggressive. After all, he had been the one to spare Gavin's life twice. Damn it.

Gavin leapt to his feet and stumbled over the debris in the direction of the alleyway where the boy had vanished. He couldn't just leave Yata to go off and be kidnapped. That would haunt his nightmares. He had to try to save him at least. Staggering forward, still feeling extremely dizzy, he leaned against the wall of one side of the alleyway as he began to move forward more cautiously, wary of the fact that dwelling within some of these shadows was the dangerous white-haired boy that they had encountered. He could hear the sounds of soldiers yelling behind him, questioning people. If they caught him, it would only slow things down and he would probably lose track of Yata. It was better if he just stayed quiet and kept moving.

The soldier's eyes squinted as he peered through the pitch-black darkness before him, feeling as if he were simply looking at a black blanket. He couldn't see a thing. Why in hell was it so dark? He supposed that it was nighttime, but this was beyond any type of darkness that he had encountered in the city. It reminded him of the Forbidden Forest. He shivered at the very thought of that darkness that entranced adventurers, then locked them into an abyss from which they would never escape. Even as a young boy, he had been one of those children to boast that he would be one of the explorers to go and camp out in the Forbidden Forest and survive. He would be a legend. But as a child, he had known nothing of this darkness or this silence—the silence that drove even the strongest of men mad. He blinked a few times, thinking that his eyes would've adjusted to the darkness by now. Yet, they didn't, and he continued walking, deeper and deeper into the void.

"*This is your friend, then?*" a voice suddenly spoke softly in Gavin's ear. It was so subtle, a simple whisper, but in this dead silence, it was like a horn blowing right into his ear. Gavin nearly leapt at the sound and glanced around, his heart thudding harder against his chest. He couldn't see anything. He didn't know why he bothered to turn around. Even if there were someone there, he wouldn't have spotted them.

"Who's there?" Gavin demanded and finally realized that the sound of soldiers had been gone for a while now. There was no sound at all, and he was locked in this shadow that grasped him. His throat tightened as visceral fear filled him. This was no alley. This was something else beyond his comprehension. A void. He gripped the hilt of his sword, ready to unsheathe it. But even he knew that there was simply no point. Why was this happening? He didn't want to die. Not in a place like this. Not in this darkness.

"Gavin, the soldier. A trained warrior from the simple barrack of Faar. What is someone like you doing with two strong, independent killers such as these? Keimaro and Yata are both very dangerous men. I heard they were traveling alone. So, who are you?" the voice whispered once more, coming from all directions. "You seem bothered, warrior. Are you afraid? Yes. Yes, you are afraid! I can smell it. Your fear."

Sweat began to form on the warrior's brow as he stumbled backward and found that the wall he had seen only a second ago was no longer there. What wizardry was this? Something from mythology, no doubt, locking him in a void of absolute darkness and silence; he was being tormented. Yes, he felt fear. So much of it. He feared death more than anything in the universe. He cared for his life infinitely more than others. He regretted going after Yata already. Now he was going to perish in this dark world. "L-Let me go...."

"Let you go? Why, I haven't trapped you. You came after me. I have merely come for a single reason. Keimaro Hayashi. We want to speak to him. Come to the old warehouse of the lower city. Come with Keimaro Hayashi, and perhaps your friend here will live. All will be explained. Come unarmed."

A sudden gust of wind blew, and Gavin found that his eyes were closed. They snapped open, and he found himself on the floor of the alleyway, his face coated in a layer of hot sweat. He was relieved that he had escaped that darkness—so relieved that he curled into a ball and began to sob silently. Perhaps it was out of the fear that he would be trapped in that darkness forever. Scared of the dark? Why was he a soldier if that was all it took to scare him? Why, indeed?

***

Keimaro followed Judal up a long set of stairs that led from the lower city to the noble district, where all of the land belonged to the royal family or the nobles of society. Upon reaching the top, he raised an eyebrow at the sight before him: outstretching plains of lush grass that gleamed healthily even under the moonlight. A fountain spewed glistening water that gushed down from a statue of the king into the well, mimicking the exact same fountain that he had seen in the city square. Stone pathways were carved into the fields, leading to gigantic mansions that looked at least eighty times larger than the ordinary cottage. They filled the land with their magnificence.

The boy was led down the stone pathways behind Judal, looking around him in awe. *Wow*, he thought, *look at these buildings! The luxury is beyond comprehension. These guys must be loaded.* Of course they were. They were nobles, the highest rank in society besides the king. One building that Keimaro saw had massive pillars in the front to support the stretching tiled roof. The windows themselves were tinted different colors for some odd reason so that the moonlight shone through them, displaying an array of dissimilar light. Even the doors themselves seemed to have golden doorknobs or knockers, worth enough to probably buy Keimaro's entire home village. A boy with golden hair peeked from a window on the upper floors, watching Judal and Keimaro pass by. But, without so much as a nod, he fled.

While all of this was wonderful and luxurious, Keimaro couldn't help but wonder. If all of these nobles were living large and could afford extra things like golden doorknobs, clearly the money wasn't being distributed evenly. He remembered that starving old man that had looked like practically undead in the lower city. Judging from these buildings, there clearly was enough money to go around to everyone. Clearly enough food as well. Yet, it wasn't being distributed, and the economic system was definitely flawed. It bothered him that there were people here living like this while the others in the lower city were suffering. He supposed that, by assassinating the king, perhaps things would change for the better. At least, he hoped they would.

But Keimaro had yet to see the final building at the end of the pathway. He wasn't even sure if it could be called a building, for it was the size of ten of these mansions put together. A hulking citadel stood before him, towering high into the sky. It consisted of buildings that stacked upon one another, creating layers to make the castle look massive. Gargantuan towers were placed on top of lower buildings and stretched even higher up until Keimaro saw that at the very top was a single tower. All of the other buildings that were combined to create this single castle led up to this final tower that seemed to pierce even the heavens, so high that one could stand on top of it and perhaps even touch the clouds.

It was clear that Judal could see the disbelief painted on the boy's face. He chuckled lightly to himself as he nodded to two guards at the door, and they continued walking forward.

Passing a courtyard, which seemed to have many different plants and trees, Keimaro drew his attention away from the size of the castle to see a single tree that he recognized immediately. An apple tree. Right there, on the courtyard in front of the castle. Glistening apples that reminded him of that single day. He remembered the first time that he had met Aika underneath that tree. *Haha, she was practically unconscious. Yet, she reached for that apple anyway. And the next day, she ate another.* Keimaro was about to see her once more. He couldn't help but wonder how she had changed.

Massive doors that were the height of ten men slowly swung open, allowing for Keimaro and Judal to walk in. They stepped into a long hallway that was filled with soldiers on both sides, positioned perfectly. Their posture was flawless, their backs completely straight with their swords held out two inches before their face, unmoving and emotionless. They stood and made no noise as Keimaro and Judal moved forward through the hallway along a blue carpet.

Keimaro noticed many side doors through the hallway that probably led to a variety of different rooms. He wondered how many rooms were in a place as large as this. Surely over one hundred. Maybe even a thousand. Ah, that number seemed so high, but he knew it was true! Hundreds of candles illuminated the dark hallways, and Keimaro watched as the door to the throne room was slowly opened.

Gleaming gold shined in his eyes, and he found that he was looking at three great thrones, two of which were filled while the last stood empty. The perimeter of the room was lined with Royal Guards that wore the same attire as Keimaro and Judal. Through a convenient window in the ceiling, glowing moonlight shined and bathed the king, who was mounted upon the centered throne. Then Keimaro's eyes flickered to the figure sitting on the second throne.

A beautiful girl—no, a woman—sat upon the golden throne. The light in her royal blue eyes was enough to shine through the room, brighter than any fire or any amount of gold in the entire world. Her long, flowing hair came down past her shoulders in a straight, perfect descent, cascading down to her lower back. Her full lips were pursed together as if she were pouting, having just spoken to the king. Her soft skin was untouched, pure, and delicate, as if a single rough tap would be enough to shatter it like glass. She wore a long, tight blue dress that matched her eyes, wavering past her ankles to reveal her glass slippers that shined with fragile heels that touched down softly upon the marble floor. She batted her long eyelashes a few times and opened her mouth when she saw Keimaro as if she had seen a ghost, but she said nothing.

Keimaro did his best to hide his surprise, but he could already feel the heat rising to his cheeks. His heart was skipping beats, pounding excitedly at the sight of the girl he had long forgotten. She truly was beautiful. In fact, for a moment, Keimaro forgot where he was entirely. Everything else in the world had been completely locked out except for her and her elegancy. Their eyes met, and he gave her a slight smile. Then, he realized where he was and hoped to god that she wouldn't give away his name if she happened to recognize him.

"Ah, Aika!" the king exclaimed with newfound excitement, clapping his hands together as he indicated Keimaro with an extension of his hand. "We have found our newest member of the Royal Guard, and without doubt one of the strongest at our disposal as well! His talent must've been hidden all of this time, for I never heard of such a prodigy until I saw him in action today!" Aika gazed over the Royal Guards wearily, tired after the long day. But when she looked at Keimaro, she seemed to prop up straight.

Keimaro smiled. He bowed his head lightly as he and Judal walked to the center of the room and knelt before the thrones. "Milord, you are too kind. The adrenaline and threat of death were what drove me. That is all."

"Ah, but in combat, your life is always at stake. Therefore, you will always be a triumphant warrior, Riku!" The king clapped his hands a few times with a chuckle, nodding his head toward Aika. "This is my daughter. Your job, when you begin in two days, is to be her escort. Judal will accompany you. Understood?"

"Yes, milord."

"Judal, show Riku to his quarters. I think I'll be heading to bed soon."

Judal stood back up and nodded for Keimaro to follow him. They walked out through a side doorway in the throne room toward a long hallway. Keimaro couldn't help but glance back over his shoulder to look at Aika, and for a single moment, their eyes met. A spark ignited between the two of them, but Keimaro immediately broke eye-contact, his face growing hot. He continued to follow Judal through the hallways of the castle, candlelight lighting their path. He couldn't believe Aika was really there.

The shadows crept along the corridors, and Keimaro raised an eyebrow as he saw squads of guards patrolling through random hallways. There was a long blue carpet running straight through each corridor. Every hallway had candles, thousands of them, lit for illumination. Sometimes there were torches, but they ruined the elegancy of the castle, according to Judal. Every hallway had about three doors on each side and maybe a few interesting paintings and some sculptures to differentiate each corridor from the next. Other than that, they were all the same.

Keimaro would undoubtedly get lost in a place this big. They had taken random twists and turns in the castle, and he hardly could recall how he had even gotten to where he was. But before he knew it, he was standing in a room with Judal, who was apparently going to be his roommate. Interestingly enough, the room was humungous. Two individual beds flanked a table set up on the far side of the room with a basket of fruit in it. Each bed was well made and completely lacked wrinkles with the smoothest white sheets that Keimaro had ever seen. This truly was the definition of luxury. The window had a view from the upper part of the castle, which indicated that they were well above the first floor.

Keimaro walked across the room to the window and brushed aside the red curtains. The translucent window refracted the moonlight onto the table, making the fruit gleam brighter. He looked out the window at the glowing moon and whistled as he saw the gardens outstretched below them. But, what fascinated him was the beautiful view of the city beyond. He could see it all. The thousands of buildings each gave off its own tiny glow in the night from small candles or torches. Millions of small lights in the city crawled all the way up to the walls that surrounded Bassada. Simply amazing.

"Nice place," Keimaro said with a small nod to Judal. "So, I'll be reporting to you in two days' time, correct?"

"Yes," Judal said casually, lying down on his bed. He had his arms crossed behind his head and yawned, clearly exhausted from the long day. He closed his eyes. "Meet me at the front of the stairway at first dawn two days from now. I'll help you learn the princess's schedule."

Keimaro nodded and turned, opening the door from whence he came. He stepped through and closed it behind him, looking at the hallway before him. He gave a heavy sigh. How was he going to escape this maze?

The young boy wandered, taking random turns in hallways, clearly without any idea where he was going. He eventually turned into a massive room that seemed to stretch three stories high. The room was divided into layers, all of which were overrun with huge books. Shelves were stacked upon one another and stretched up to the ceiling, filled with thick books of all varieties. As if the entire castle hadn't been a maze enough, the royal library seemed to be even more so. *Hopefully there's someone here who can help me find my way out of this place.*

Keimaro walked forward, weaving in between bookshelves, not sure where to go. There were ladders with wheels at the bottom that leaned against the tall bookshelves, which towered over Keimaro. He walked about, realizing how late it was, and noticed that many of the candles were actually going out. Soon the entire library would be filled with darkness, making it all the more difficult to navigate—that is, without using the Shokugan. But if he used the Shokugan here and someone saw him, he could blow his cover almost immediately.

After a few minutes, the entire library was dark, and Keimaro found himself stumbling over stray books that had been left on the floor and tripping over the bottoms of ladders.

How much worse could this get? His eye caught sight of a small light coming from ahead of him, and he blinked a few times, walking slowly in that direction and making sure not to make any sound. He saw that the light was coming from behind the shelf. He reached for the shelf and grabbed a single thick book. He slid it out, revealing a small hole that he could peer through. He looked through the opening and, to his surprise, found Aika sitting there at a table with a lantern and a book in her hand, unguarded. She was alone.

Keimaro couldn't believe that someone so important would be alone. A part of him wanted to go forward and confront her, to speak to her, but his heart was fluttering and almost a thousand excuses popped into his mind. *I'll blow my cover! I'm sweaty after that fight earlier today; I probably smell bad. She's a princess; I'm just a simple undercover guard.*

Damn. Where were his guts? He felt completely powerless over his own actions and sucked in a deep breath. He wasn't afraid when the tip of a blade was pointed against his throat, yet he was like a little child in the face of a beautiful woman. How ridiculous. He ran his hand through his hair, toying with the pages of a book. *All right, I'll go and talk to her.* Keimaro made a quick nod to himself and went back to looking through the hole, only to find her on the other side, looking straight back at him.

"Looking for something?"

"Gah!" Keimaro exclaimed, completely surprised. He stumbled, tripping over a book. His head hit the shelf behind him, and dozens of books rained from the sky, burying him. *Kill me now.* He heard shuffling and sighed as he lay there, a pile of books on top of him. He was so embarrassed that he just didn't want to move at all.

"You're Riku, right? My new bodyguard?" Aika asked curiously, getting down on her knees as she began to help take books off of Keimaro.

Keimaro blinked a few times, leaning forward so that some of the books fell off of him. She didn't recognize him. Well, it was for the best. He nodded. "Yeah, that's me." He scratched the back of his neck and began to scoop books up. "S-Sorry about that! I was just getting used to the job. One day you're off escorting cargo through a forest, and the next you're the princess's bodyguard."

Aika giggled lightly and picked up some books as well. She began to set them on the shelves neatly in perfect order. "Well, you moved up the ranks quite quickly, didn't you?"

"Yeah," Keimaro said, raising an eyebrow as she continued to organize the books on the shelves, knowing where each one went. "It seems that you spend a lot of time in this library, princess. You know where everything goes?"

"Ah, yes," Aika said, slightly embarrassed. "I spend a lot of time in the library. There isn't much to do since I'm the princess and my father won't really let me do anything. Weird, right? I just managed to escape my other guards and come here to have a good read. It's much better when I read without my guards staring at me for hours."

Keimaro began to put some books on the shelves as well and chuckled at the image of guards staring at her as she read. "It sounds quite irritating, your highness. But it seems you have yet to escape me." He flashed her a warm smile and could see her blushing.

"I suppose so. And what are you doing here? Spying on me?"

Now it was Keimaro's turn for his cheeks to beat bright red. "N-No! It's not like that, your highness. It's … uh, well, I got lost on my way from my chambers to leave the citadel. I don't actually live here until two days' time, you see." He scratched the back of his neck nervously, averting his eyes from hers. But he could tell that she was smiling.

"Call me Aika."

"Er … yes, Aika."

"Now, would you like for me to show you the way out?"

"That would be the reverse of what should be happening. The princess escorting a common guard," Keimaro grinned. "What an interesting twist of events. Sure, but your father would be unhappy to see you unguarded."

"Ah, I'll show you a special way out. As long as you promise to keep it a secret, okay?"

Keimaro blinked a few times, knowing that Aika hated to be confined to the castle grounds. But, did this mean that she knew a secret passage and was able to sneak away? Surely not, the guards must've had an eye on her. But then again, here she was in the library, completely vulnerable and alone.

He nodded to her, and she swiftly took his hand and began to lead him away. He blinked, not sure when the last time a girl had held his hand, and stumbled after her. "Whoa!"

She led him out of the library maze with ease, walking out into the hallway. She looked both ways, making sure that one of the patrols was not walking by, and quickly began to move down the corridor, dragging Keimaro behind her. She took another turn into a hallway before grabbing the doorknob of one of the many doors and turning it, walking through the entrance into a new room.

Silence reigned as Keimaro blinked a few times, looking forward at something he had never expected to see: a greenhouse containing an incredible amount of exotic plants from around the world. He recognized a few of them. One was the Phoenix Heart, a small edible flower with red petals that were completely engulfed in flame. When the flame went out, the flower would die. It usually didn't coexist with other plants because it typically created a forest fire, so Keimaro thought it was smart that this plant was isolated from the rest.

Some plants had frosty mists circulating the stems. Others gave off different aurora colors that reflected off of the glass ceiling above. The moonlight shined down and gave all of the plants a glow, making them all the more magnificent to look at. It must've taken years or even decades to collect so many exotic plants of this rarity. Keimaro couldn't help but stare at some of the flowers in awe but soon realized that the princess had walked past the rows of plants to the very back of the room. He walked quickly after her and frowned when she moved a rather large pot that contained a fake plant, revealing a secret hole underneath. Who would've guessed?

Keimaro blinked a few times as he peered into the pitch-blackness of the hole and whistled. "Uh, Aika, as your future bodyguard, I really don't advise you to go down there. You don't know what's in there and—"

"Oh, don't be a poor sport, Riku." Aika sighed, gripped a ladder that had been concealed in the shadows of the hole, and began to climb down. "I showed you this because I trust that you would keep it a secret. After all, you are my age. You know that a girl has to have a night out every once in a while, right?"

"Y-Yeah, but if you are found out of the castle…."

"It'll be my fault, not yours. I won't let any punishment come to you," Aika said, disappearing into the darkness. "Besides, I've been through this tunnel already. It's safe. Coming?"

Keimaro rolled his eyes, not particularly sure what he had gotten himself into. He felt something ominous from the hole, but he ignored his intuition and leapt down, landing in soft dirt beside the princess. It was extremely dark around them, and it took a few moments for him to adjust to the blackness that engulfed them. Aika, however, seemed perfectly able to navigate her way through such thick shadow, her hands guiding along jagged stone walls as she began to progress through the tunnel.

Keimaro slowly unsheathed his sword and shook his head in disbelief that the princess was leading the way through a potentially dangerous area. Why wasn't he stopping her? He watched her closely and smiled to himself, knowing exactly why he wasn't stopping her. She reminded him of himself back in the day when he had wanted to search for adventure. The castle grounds were the same as the barrier that had confined him to Bakaara. And now she was out searching for adventure, just as he and Yata had done.

The tunnel led out, and soon he could make out the shape of a ladder. His eyes were squinted from the minimal amount of light that cracked from the ceiling above. They were definitely underneath the castle. Why was this tunnel even here? Perhaps it was a secret tunnel for the king to escape in case of an invasion? Maybe. Who knew?

Aika was climbing up the ladder and began to move something above, keeping one hand on the ladder as she did so. Keimaro made sure to position himself below her in case she were to slip so that he could catch her. He blinked a few times when the moonlight shined through the ceiling as she moved whatever was blocking the hole. He glanced away, making sure not to look up Aika's dress, a crime worthy of capital punishment. When he looked back, the princess had already climbed out of the hole and was motioning for Keimaro to follow.

When he pulled himself from the hole, he found that they were on a rather large, flat green field, somewhere in the noble section that overlooked the city. He admired the beautiful view of the city below and smiled at its magnificence. He was about to say something when he heard a rumble. Then an explosion. A burst of dust and a shockwave knocked over multiple buildings in the distance, and Keimaro's eyes widened. A giant spike made completely of metal bulged from the earth—a technique learned by Yata. Without a doubt, it was him. The fact that he was resulting to using such strong techniques would mean that he really was in trouble. Was it the Bounts? It definitely wasn't Gavin; that soldier was far too weak to drive Yata that far.

"Aika." Keimaro glanced over his shoulder at the princess, who was staring with wide eyes at the explosion. "Your highness! We need to get you to safety. Go back into the tunnel, got it?" He gripped his sword tightly, knowing that he should stay with her to ensure her safety. But right now, his prime priority was seeing if Yata was all right. "I'm going to go see what happened. Go back to your room and make sure you're safe."

***

Aika stood there for a moment, staring at the explosion with disbelief as Riku ran off, his sword raised high in the air. Her hands were shaking at her side, and she couldn't believe what she was seeing. Four years ago, she had awoken with an abnormal ability that wasn't known to man—an ability of healing that could instantly mend any wound, no matter how bad it was. The only thing that she could link her foreign powers to was to that meteor that had fallen out of the sky. It, without a doubt, gave her this odd power. She'd always wondered whether or not it had given Keimaro or Yata powers, but that Bount by the name of Junko had clarified that for her. He had said that Keimaro Hayashi had the ability to control fire. Magic. So, everyone who had been within range of that meteor was given a power. That disturbance in the distance—was that the doing of Yata and Keimaro? The destruction of her city?

Then again, she supposed that she could understand their hatred for Faar. Their armies had destroyed everything that they had. Bakaara had been completely massacred without warning. In fact, they were wanted dead as well. Why must things be so complicated? Why was there even war in the first place? All that remained after a war was a desolate wasteland of destruction littered with corpses. The winners never cheered nor celebrated, for the loss of their comrades haunted them so. In the end, there was always sorrow and nothing more.

And then there was this boy, Riku. There was something about him, something that Aika couldn't quite point out. She felt as if she recognized him, which was why she had led him into the secret tunnel. She'd immediately felt as if she could trust him with everything. She had no idea why. The way his eyes looked at her made her melt with warmth. The way he smiled was the one thing that had made her giggle in a long while. Yet, he was a commoner. A simple guard. Any relationship, whether friends or more, was completely forbidden. Her father would just have him executed if they got too close. Thinking about friendship or beyond was simply nonsense, especially for an important person such as her. But she didn't want to be alone forever.

The princess had climbed down into the tunnel and walked into the darkness alone. The dead silence truly was disconcerting. She made her way back to the royal garden and pushed the plant back into place with a heavy sigh. She really did hope that Riku didn't reveal the tunnel to anyone. *Why did I trust my only secret way out from these walls to a complete stranger?*

She heard another rumble and felt the ground shaking ever so slightly. To be able to feel such an explosion from this distance was incredible. She turned around and looked off into the direction of the city through the glass panes of the greenhouse. What was going on?

***

Keimaro couldn't believe what he was seeing. The entire inn was obliterated, pieces everywhere. Corpses of men and women lay inside, scattered about in the debris, and soldiers were trying to pick up the pieces or at least identify the bodies rather than finding out what had happened. A huge crowd had surrounded the area but was being blocked off by mobs of soldiers who had recently arrived.

The young boy began to push his way through the crowds, looking for Yata or Gavin. He hoped to the gods that they weren't amongst these unidentifiable corpses that lay on the floor. The mere image of all these bodies under the debris reminded him of the massacre of Bakaara four years ago. He shook away the thought and trudged on through the debris until he saw small pieces of metal on the floor, tiny shards in a concentrated area. He walked up to the spot, knowing that this was where Yata had been defeated. He had been beaten in his metallic form, as indicated by the metal, which meant that whoever was here was truly a strong opponent. Then he looked down and saw blood. His eyes followed a trail of small droplets that led into an alleyway. There, he saw Gavin leaning back against a wall, breathing heavily with his head tilted back.

Keimaro walked up to the soldier and stood beside him, expecting him to say something, but he never did. He slowly knelt down beside Gavin and touched his shoulder. "Hey, are you okay? What happened here?" he said calmly, trying not to lose his cool.

Gavin's eyes were barely open, and he sucked in a deep breath. "A guy came. He had white hair and was so fast and strong. Yata and I didn't stand a chance. They took him to the mansion that we passed by on the way to the inn; you remember it? It's disguised as a warehouse to the ordinary eye. But certain people can see it as a mansion. I'm assuming that you were able to see it. It's called Z's mansion, a rumored place where only magical beings are welcome."

"Z?"

"The richest man in the city. No one ever sees him, and he's supposedly the one who kidnapped Yata," Gavin murmured. "That's where we'll find him."

Keimaro nodded and stood up once more. *Why would those guys want Yata?* "Can you walk?"

"Yeah."

"Then let's go."

10. TWO HEROES

When they arrived at the gates to Z's mansion, they opened automatically as if they'd been expecting Keimaro. The boy walked forward with Gavin closely behind him, both of their weapons sheathed at their sides. They walked along a tiled pathway made of some type of expensive marble that led out into a garden and eventually to the mansion itself. The mansion towered high and looked exactly like one of the nobles' houses. Compared to the other houses that surrounded it, this building was massive. The grandiose pillars supported the red-tiled rooftops. Stone statues of naked angels had water pouring out of their mouths and into fountains on the lush green lawn.

Once again, it made Keimaro wonder where all of the money was going to in this *civil* society. Someone living so high and mighty seemed to have far too much in comparison to someone who was barely scraping by in order to survive. At the door, he saw a boy, a few years older than he, walking in his direction. He had snowy white hair with a pale skin tone. His eyes were an abnormal turquoise that narrowed onto Keimaro with seriousness. He wore a tight red scarf that was curled around his neck as well as a white sleeveless shirt, revealing his toned muscles. This was the guy who had defeated Yata supposedly.

Beside him was a girl around the age of nineteen from the looks of it and a man who was probably in his early twenties. The girl had light brown hair that was tied into two ponytails. Her hazel eyes gave off a stare that would probably make most run at the very sight of her. In her hands was a type of weapon that Keimaro didn't recognize, a rather long weapon with a barrel. It looked like some type of ranged advanced technology. If anything, it was the single shot rifle that Keimaro had heard about. He had also heard it took forever to reload that weapon— but, for someone like her, perhaps it took only one shot in order to take down her targets.

The man had glasses and was completely unarmed. He had dark brown hair that came down to his forehead, and he wore an expensive black suit with a red tie as if he were going out to dinner for a special occasion. He smiled calmly at Keimaro and stopped along with his comrades a couple of meters from the boy.

Keimaro had noticed that the gates had closed behind him, and he smiled to himself. *Then no one will be able to see me massacre all of these bastards. Fine with me.*

"My name is Yuri," the white-haired boy called out. "I have no intention of hurting you or your friend. All that we ask is that you come in and have a talk with us so that we may—"

"Show me Yata."

"Look, lay down your arms and—"

"You know who I am, don't you?" Keimaro said, annoyed, his eyes turning from their original dark color into a glowing red. He smiled when the girl lifted up the rifle and aimed it straight at him. He saw Gavin tensing up and instinctively taking a step back, but he stood his ground and glanced at the girl. "Give me back my friend, or I can't be held responsible for what happens next."

"Is that so?" Yuri said, his eyes turning red as well, albeit a different kind of red. This red wasn't demonic at all. Instead, it

141

was monstrous and beastly, as if he were losing control. "Well, then we will force you to listen to what we have to say."

A crack entered the air, and Keimaro's eyes sensed a small lead ball leave the rifle in the girl's hands. The ball spiraled, gaining incredible speed as it soared toward him, but Keimaro's sword had already left its sheath. It slashed upward, cutting the bullet directly in half without much effort. The bullet split and flew around Keimaro, digging into the dirt behind him. Splintering pieces of lead glittered before his eyes as he glanced at the girl, his blade hissing through the air. The girl was staring at him with disbelief that he had just cut the bullet in half. That amount of strength and reaction timing was unreal, let alone the fact that the sword was strong enough to withstand the force of the projectile.

Keimaro sprinted forward at the girl, who was desperately fumbling with her rifle, trying to reload her weapon. The man with the glasses had taken a step forward to form a barrier between him and the girl, raising his hands. Instantly, a solid yellow wall was conjured in between them, transparent as if it were glass. Keimaro raised his eyebrow at the man's ability. More foreign magic. *So many freaks in one place. Perfect.*

He slammed his foot into the ground, igniting a small jet of flame that sent him flying into the air above the wall. He performed a flip while in the air, generating fire along the metal of his sword, and smiled wickedly as he came down, smashing into the earth as the two opponents leapt away. A wave of flame radiated outward from his blow.

Smoke rose from the area where Keimaro had landed, and the grass around him was seared and singed from the flame, small amounts of smoke drifting from the lawn. He stood once more and twirled his sword in his hand as the man engaged him, conjuring a blue hammer in his hand made from the same foreign substance. Hammers were perfect against swordsmen, for they shattered their steel and usually overpowered them. However, they were extremely slow. Unfortunately for this man, Keimaro always had speed on his side.

The man brought the hammer crashing downward upon Keimaro, but the boy took an easy step to the side, reading his opponent's moves perfectly. He rotated his body and grinned, driving his fist solidly into the man's face, cracking his glasses with a single punch. He released a jet of flame straight through his knuckles and into the man, sending him flipping through the air and landing several meters away. The man slammed heavily into the earth, landing on his back, his body going limp upon impact.

Yuri was still standing there watching, rather impressed with the progress that Keimaro was making against his friends. He had his arms crossed and chuckled. "Not bad, demon scum," he called out with a smirk.

Keimaro ignored the comment and stomped his foot into the ground, a wall of flame appearing in front of him. He punched the wall of flame, sending fireballs outward like little missiles at the girl, who leapt about, trying to dodge the barrage of concentrated flames. But one could dodge only so much. Eventually a ball of fire caught her in the shoulder and exploded upon impact, sending her flying backward into the ground, gasping for air. The boy then turned to Yuri, his hands tightening around the hilt of his sword. "There's something abnormal about your hair, too, snow-white."

Yuri raised his eyebrows and sighed. "You know, your friend called me the same thing." His image vanished, and Keimaro's heart leapt when the white-haired boy reappeared inches in front of him, his fist soaring forward at Keimaro's face.

With barely enough time to react, he tilted his head to the side, dodging the blow. Wind from the force of the blow blew his hair back, and his heart thudded with self-doubt. He had never seen someone as fast as this person in all of his years—not since Tobimaru. He staggered backward after narrowly avoiding the blow but found that Yuri was already striking once more with a barrage of fast blows, some of which were impossible to dodge.

The first blow that Keimaro took was excruciating. A sinking punch to the stomach drove the wind from his lungs and damaged his diaphragm. He felt saliva gathering in his mouth as he stumbled away once more, trying to disengage and rethink his strategy. But Yuri wasn't giving him the opportunity, for he leapt forward once more.

Keimaro swept his hand outward, and a wave of flame shot out, forcing Yuri to take a few steps backward in order to dodge. He was breathing heavily, but Yuri was simply smiling at him, still filled with energy.

"Oi, what's wrong? I thought you were going to beat me up," Yuri called with a lively chuckle.

"Shut the hell up, you stupid mutt," Keimaro spat, grasping his stomach.

"What did you call me?" Yuri yelled, reappearing in front of Keimaro. He whipped his fist to the side and slammed it into Keimaro's cheek, a sinking blow that cracked the boy solidly, sending him rolling across the grass. "You're in no position to talk, nor are you in any position to fight me, Hayashi scum. Maybe we should just kill you so that we can end your pathetic species! I know everything about your story. Powerless and weak … that's what you are. Incapable of protecting the ones that you love. You think you can treat others as if they're lower than you just because you've got those eyes and a few sparks of fire, huh?" He appeared in front of Keimaro's body and kicked him across the ground once more, sending him rolling a few meters away. "Stop acting so big, like you can do anything you want. Four years in hiding, training, and this is all that you can muster up to fight me? How are you going to defeat the Bounts with such a lowly power?"

This guy knows everything…. Who the hell is he? Keimaro's ribs felt cracked, and he gasped for air, spitting blood onto the grass. His eyes were unfocused, and everything was a blur. He placed his palms on the ground in an attempt to push himself up once more. But it was hard. His body felt ten times heavier than usual, and his muscles were straining to pick him up. He felt powerless. *Just like that one time.* An image of his burning city flashed into his mind. Mai. His mother. All taken from him because he was too weak to defend them. He had trained four years to grow stronger. Was that not enough?

Yuri walked over to Keimaro, watching him as he tried to get up. He lifted his foot upward and brought it crashing down onto his back, sending him to the ground. "Stay down! Don't even think of getting up! You deserve nothing." Nevertheless, Yuri watched as Keimaro tried to get up before driving his foot back down into the young boy, sending him back to the floor. He sniffed the air and sensed a familiar presence. He smiled when he saw the soldier finally rushing toward him from behind with his sword raised. Yuri spun around, driving a kick solidly into Gavin's ribs. With a crack, an explosion of force sent Gavin soaring across the lawn to slam into the gate. His body went limp as soon as he hit the solid gate, and he collapsed to the ground, unmoving.

Keimaro stared at the body of the soldier who had attempted to save him. A boy who had been a stranger only yesterday was now trying to save him. At this rate, they were both probably going to be killed. Then he remembered an image of his father. He recalled his father's words: *How many men would you kill to save your sister?*

Yes … I remember. Another kick. *What was my answer?* A third kick.

Yuri rose his foot upward to squash Keimaro's skull.

I would kill them all.

As Yuri's foot came down, Keimaro swung around, grabbing the white-haired boy's ankle and redirecting the kick into the earth. He swung upward and slammed his fist solidly into Yuri's stomach. He pulled back, seeing the pain in the boy's face, and began to concentrate flames into his palm, gathering fire into a ball. He curled his arm around Yuri, grabbing him by his back and pulling the boy toward him. "I already promised myself I wouldn't die until my goal is complete." The ball of flame smashed into Yuri's stomach. "I don't break promises." *Not to Mai. Not to anyone. Especially not to myself!*

145

The ball of fire grew smaller upon impact into the size of a tiny marble, and there was a millisecond of complete silence before a massive explosion. The sphere erupted, creating a huge roar of flame that extended up into the sky and sent Yuri flying backward. A vortex cloud of dust surrounded Keimaro, parting around him as he walked forward. His eyes were filled with apathy, and he stopped, watching as Yuri slowly began to push himself to his feet, smoke drifting off his clothes.

"Not bad," Yuri snarled, his voice growing deeper as his body grew bigger. "About time I took you seriously." His spine began to twist and lengthen, stretching upward. White fur burst from his skin and covered his body. His teeth sharpened to daggers, his eyes still glowing bright red. His fingernails lengthened into sharp claws that dug into the ground, his ears growing bigger as well. By the time the transformation was complete, Yuri was an eight-foot-tall white werewolf, a creature that Keimaro had only read about in books. They were only rumored to exist.

Keimaro took a few steps backward at the sight of Yuri's transformation, his heart thudding rapidly against his chest. It reminded him of the beast that he had saved Aika from four years earlier, except Yuri seemed to have full control over himself. He was intelligent despite his enhanced strength and speed in this new form. Keimaro sucked in a deep breath of air, exhaling through his nose in an attempt to calm his nerves. Being afraid was only going to mess with his head. He could not allow himself to succumb to fear. "Huh, looks like I was right about you being a mutt, then."

"Enough."

The voice came from behind Keimaro, who glanced over his shoulder to see a middle-aged man standing there with spiky, red hair. His hair was extremely long and slicked backward, as sharp as daggers. He wore a black cloak that was wrapped tightly around himself, and he sighed as he began to walk forward past Yuri's friends, who had gotten up and were recovering from their wounds. It was that same man that Keimaro had seen earlier in the day standing at the mansion's doorstep.

Keimaro lowered his sword at the sight of the man and turned to face him, sensing that Yuri was drawing back. "Who are you?"

"My name is Z," the man said with a small smile before he looked at the singed grass and destroyed lawn and slapped his forehead with frustration. "My, my, Yuri! He is our guest! Why did you have to confront him in such a way?"

"The punk asked for it." Yuri snarled, not taking his eyes off of Keimaro.

"You want round two, dog-breath?" Keimaro snapped.

"Round one isn't over until you're done breathing, Hayashi scum," Yuri retorted.

Z watched the two of them bicker for a moment. He tried to speak up, but their words overlapped his. Z raised his eyebrow at their rudeness. Then he snapped his fingers and conjured a giant red hammer into his hands. He gripped the handle tightly and began to swing it, red light streaming behind the head of the hammer. The hammer slammed into both boys with a single swing and sent them flying backward, skidding along the ground.

Keimaro rolled across the lawn and landed on his back. The blow hadn't really hurt as much as it had confused him. He was dazed, not sure what had just happened. His vision was blurred white, but nothing really hurt except for his head. He leaned forward, rubbing his forehead, and something smacked onto his chest. He glanced down, and his heart thudded when he saw it was an odd, slimy, green substance that was moving abnormally around his body.

"Eh?" he exclaimed, beginning to struggle, but the odd substance curled around him, expanding until it had covered his entire body. The boy watched as the red-haired man snapped his fingers once more and the green substance solidified, trapping Keimaro completely so that he was incapable of moving. "Tch, stop your tricks, old man!" he snarled, attempting to break the foreign solid, but it was just like the substance that the man with the glasses had used.

"Old man? I hardly look old."

"But you are old," Yuri muttered, stuck in the same situation as Keimaro, though he seemed much more calm. He leaned back so that he was lying on the soft grass, apparently getting settled in since he seemed to know they would be there for a while.

"Shut up, Yuri," Z said with a scoff and put his hands in his pockets, giving Keimaro a look of reassurance. "Don't worry; we aren't here to hurt you. Actually, we just wanted to get your attention and to see if you were the real thing. The walls of my mansion are fortified with a gigantic ward so that no one can get through. In fact, most people can't even see my house."

"Huh?" Keimaro muttered. *Looks like Gavin's rumor was true.*

"You see," Z explained, "when one looks at the gateway of my mansion, one sees only the gates to an abandoned, eerie, old warehouse. In fact, the rumor around here is that it's haunted. No one dares to come near it. You must've seen people with shifty eyes when you were walking close to it, right? It isn't exactly the liveliest place from a distance. You can't see anyone who is walking inside of the ward either. The gate itself is impenetrable by most humans. But I remember you from earlier today. You walked by, and we locked eyes. You saw me. That's when I knew that you had arrived in Bassada. So, I sent Yuri to go and fetch you. Instead, he brought back your friend as bait so you would come to us. We want to offer you a proposition."

"I don't want to make a damn deal with any of you people. I have my own goals and—"

"We have the same goals," Z said with a chuckle, "the destruction of this corrupt government, the assassination of the king, and the eradication of the Bount organization. You hate them as much as we do, correct?" He looked Keimaro in the eyes now with his smile wiped clean off his face. His eyes were deprived of their former cheer, which had been replaced with apathy and seriousness.

Keimaro stared at Z for a moment, gulping. Who were these guys? They hated the Bount organization? They all had weird magical powers, too, just like him. Were they former Bount members? No, maybe they were Bount organization members who were trying to bait him! He couldn't be sure if these guys were for real. But, when he looked around, he found his answer. He saw Yuri's head lower at the very mention of the Bounts. The girl with the rifle had looked away and was tightening her grip on her weapon. The man with the glasses was touching her shoulder.

"No." A look of surprise came across Z's face, but Keimaro spoke once more. "I hate them much more than any of you ever could."

The smile returned to Z's face, and he nodded. "We are a resistance group that has formed against the Bount organization. Yuri here is the first person to ever kill a member of the Bount organization, the strongest terrorist group in the entire world. They contain men and women with capabilities beyond human comprehension, and they have mastered their abilities to the point where they are able to shift continents, change nature, destroy armies, and obliterate nations. Three Bounts have been assigned to this city, which is why we are here to hunt them down. We come to you today because we are sure that you recognize their names: Tobimaru Hayashi, Hidan, and Junko."

Keimaro's ears pricked up at the very sound of their names. He despised all of them so much. No one would understand. They had taken everything from him. He had sworn that he would destroy them all. Mai was probably dead after all of these years; he hadn't seen her or even heard a single mention of her existence since that day. His eyes were glowing a bright red, and flames were beginning to flicker around his shoulders. "Yeah, I know them. And I'm going to be the one to kill them. I'll crush them with my own two hands. I don't need your help with anything, old man."

"Stop calling me old. And how is your disguise as a member of the Royal Guard? Soon the Bounts will be forming a plan with the king of Bassada, and they will be working to end all freedom on the continent. Humans will be ruled underneath the Bounts. They'll gain power politically, and soon an army will be at their disposal. Is that what you want?"

"I'll stop them before—"

"You were hardly able to fend off Yuri in his human form!" Z snapped. "And you believe that you can handle three full-fledged Bount members and a whole empire by yourself? Don't be such a loner, Keimaro. You have your goals, correct? I recall them being to get your revenge on Faar, kill the Bounts, and save a particular someone. Your little sister, right?"

Keimaro's eyes widened at the mention of Mai, and the flames intensified, beginning to spread outward. "How the hell do you know about Mai? You know where she is, don't you? You sick—" A glob of green substance smacked across his mouth and solidified instantly. He tried to speak, but it came out muffled.

Z smiled at Keimaro and winked. "That's much better. You believed that your sister was dead this whole time without even proof? My, my, sounds as if you're giving up on a member of your own family. How pessimistic. She's alive. The Bounts intend to use her for something that is unknown. My group will be the ones to confront the Bounts and the king. You can either be a part of our operations or sit back and watch us fight the battles that you want to be involved in. Fight with us. In return, we will ensure your sister's safe return."

Keimaro's breathing slowed, and he began to calm down. Her safe return? She was alive. All of this time, she had been okay. He wondered what she looked like after all of these years. She was eight now, wasn't she? These people seemed strong. He wasn't in a particularly good situation to go against them either. Gavin was unconscious, Yata was captured, and he was stuck surrounded by people who could quite easily defeat him. *Looks like it's not just me and Yata anymore.*

The flames began to die down around him, and he closed his eyes. The green material vanished as if it had disintegrated into thin air. He looked up at Z and worked his jaw. "I'll work with you on the condition that I am the one who gets to kill Junko."

Z smiled. "Of course."

"Where is Yata?"

"Unconscious inside the mansion. We will provide you with training—"

"I don't need training,"

"Straight to it then? We will go over the plan soon. Can you walk?"

"I'm not hurt," Keimaro said, pushing himself to his feet. He swayed, wincing at the sharp pain in his ribs. *I'll be fine. I just need to rest a bit.*

Z extended his hand to the girl and boy at his side. "This here young lady is Lena. She is an expert with the rifle, explosives, and technological advances. She studied amongst gnome engineers for most of her life. She's quite good with hand-to-hand combat as well and doesn't have any magical capabilities. But, she makes up for it with her talent and hard work."

Keimaro nodded his head and blinked a few times, his face turning red. "Uh, sorry for … hitting you with fire earlier, Lena," he said, holding out his hand in the attempt at a handshake. He didn't expect her to shake it—and, of course, she didn't.

"I'll make you pay for it later," Lena snapped, one hand on her hip as the other brushed some ashes from her shoulder.

"This is my son, Noah. He is quite the smart kid, if I do say so myself. He is mastering the same type of magic that I do. Some call it bending; some call it conjuring. We create anything that we want out of thin air using the colors that we can see before us. If we see green, the conjured magic is green. It really depends on what we concentrate on. It's quite a strong attack but focuses more on defense and utilization than offense, which was why you were able to easily defeat him. He needs to work on a few things in order to maximize his proficiency with this style of magic, but overall, I suppose, he's all right."

"Sorry for punching you in the face."

"No, it's completely understandable. We were enemies at the time, after all," Noah said with a warm smile, adjusting his cracked glasses with a single poke at the lenses. "I look forward to working with you."

"Likewise," Keimaro lied.

"And this is Yuri. He is the king of a faraway city known as Horux and is, as you witnessed earlier, a werewolf. He is capable of transforming at will, and he has a few tricks up his sleeve in addition. He was the first person to kill a member of the Bount organization when they invaded Horux, just as they are doing to Bassada. You two will be working together."

Keimaro and Yuri locked gazes for a moment, looking into the red glow of each other's eyes, never having seen someone else like them. Immediately, they understood each other from a single glance: the pain, the hatred and anger mixed with agony that derived from memories of the past. They glanced away, and Keimaro watched as Noah began to walk toward Gavin's unconscious body to pick him up.

Z nodded at Keimaro. "We will walk you to Yata. Meanwhile, I want to debrief you on how you will contribute to our revolution. A revolution doesn't happen in one day. As lucky as you were to get your position as a member of the Royal Guard so easily, not everything will happen so smoothly." He began to walk across the singed grass toward his mansion. "We have many assassins and willing warriors who all share a piece of our circle of hatred for the Bounts. But, in order to eliminate the threat of an entire army, we must first eliminate Faar. Do you understand?"

"Yeah," Keimaro said as they arrived at the door and began to walk in. The boy's eyes widened when he saw the largest room possible in history, bigger than even the king's throne room. The ceiling stretched higher than he had thought possible with floating candles that magically bounced about in the air, levitating. A winding stairway led to many different floors in the giant tower-like structure. The inside of the house was shaped more like a tower than the mansion it had looked like on the outside. Rooms were located on a platform that circled around the room, creating entire floors. This winding stairway consisted of only floating steps with two railings that spun around the structure, leading to the very top. *Magic.*

"I understand that you will be living in the castle for the time being, but you will surely have plenty of time at night to come and be here, correct? So, please, treat this place as you would your home," Z said with a nod, walking forward through what seemed like crowds of people.

Keimaro saw literally hundreds of boys and girls, young and older, walking around everywhere, fitting inside of this mansion. *Each of them is an assassin?* he wondered. They all hated the Bount organization. How could this be? There were so many of them. Could the Bounts have affected this many people? He bumped into a few of them as he walked past and glanced at Z. "Where's Yata?"

"He's fine," Z said and walked to the far side of the massive room, past many of the boys and girls. He stood on a large blue platform that seemed to be made of some type of glittering, soft, padded material and looked more like some kind of elevator than anything else. He waved his hand, indicating for Keimaro, Lena, and Yuri to follow. "Noah will take your friend to the infirmary. I'm assuming that your friend will be staying with us?"

"I suppose so," Keimaro muttered, pushing past the crowds of people. He sighed, stepping onto the massive blue platform, which was large enough to fit dozens of people. He blinked a few times, not really sure what was going to happen on this platform. The only thing he was sure of was that he was going to be surprised. And, sure enough, he was.

As soon as Yuri and Lena were secured on the platform, there was a flash and Keimaro felt his body being ripped apart. Well, not exactly ripped, because that sounded too painful. It was more like being taken apart meticulously. After a single second of blackness, he found himself standing in a completely different room, which was much smaller. He looked down to see that he was still on the platform still, and then he blinked, looking around.

The room looked somewhat like an office with multiple red leather chairs and a long wooden desk covered with a map of Bassada. Colorful darts had been slammed down into the piece of parchment. He watched as Yuri and Lena calmly walked forward and sat down in the leather seats.

Lena glanced back over the chair at him and snapped, "Hey, stop standing there gawking. Get over here! We have business to attend!"

"Uh," Keimaro said, still confused, scratching his neck. "How did I get here?"

Z had sat down in a large black leather chair on the other side of the desk. He had spun around to look out the window, which took up the entire wall on the far side of the room. It offered a beautiful view of a lush green plain with a few hills, surrounded by yet another wall. "You were standing on a teleporter. With the right coordinates, the platform can disassemble the particles in your body and reassemble them in a place where another teleporter marker is located." He spun around in his chair and leaned his elbow on his desk with his chin against his palm. "You don't understand how many trials it took to get that thing to work—and how many people died in order to test it. Gnome technology, cool, huh?"

Keimaro gulped. He didn't like the thought of his body

being taken apart and pieced back together. Though, the idea of a teleporter was rather interesting. He had never read anything about its existence and had always thought that such a contraption would be much more futuristic. He assumed that its invention hadn't been publicized yet.

He walked forward, sat in a leather chair beside Lena, and sighed, leaning back into the seat. *These guys have a lot of resources, it seems. Didn't Gavin say that Z was one of the richest men in Bassada?*

"Now," Z said, tapping his hand on the map. "We are eager to get started with your cooperation, Keimaro. If you are willing, that is. You will be meeting up with Yata later on tonight. He is currently resting. But, I shall tell you our plan as well as what we know of the Bounts' plan."

Keimaro nodded. "I'll cooperate."

"Good," Z said, leaning back into his chair and placing his hands on the arms. "Now, you are rather valuable to us. You are a member of the Hayashi clan and have one of the very rare magical abilities—the kind that are only given by a meteor, a foreign rock that falls from the sky. This rock originated from an outside source that isn't from our planet. Only two have ever been recorded to hit the earth, and the creator of the Bount organization harnessed one of them."

Keimaro frowned. Two had hit the planet in recorded history? Was Junko the one who harnessed the power, or was someone else the creator of the Bount organization? And what the hell was causing these meteors to hit the earth? Where did they get their own power?

"Other magic is known as artificial magic, which is given through potions that can be created only from components of certain animals, herbs, or even sometimes humanoids from different continents around the world. That is why few have obtained magic—it is either extremely expensive or very dangerous to obtain since one would have to journey around the world in order to get it. Mastering artificial magic is even harder since it isn't natural, but your magic is by far the strongest.

Unfortunately, it can also be the wildest and hardest to control, for it becomes a part of you."

Keimaro slid his hands into his pockets. *Artificial magic. So that would be what Noah and Z both have. Users of artificial magic have limits. But I don't.* Keimaro smiled. *Perfect.*

"However, that isn't the only reason you're valuable, Keimaro. You are also valuable because of that necklace you wear—the one with the key."

Keimaro blinked, looking down at the key that dangled from his neck. "What does this have to do with anything?"

"It is the key to the chest that will decide the fate of this continent," Z said with a slight smile. "I'm not sure you understand the full story of the Hayashi clan yet, Keimaro. Do you even know why the Hayashi clan is doomed with these demonic eyes that make others judge you?"

"I always figured that we were born with it in our—"

"Members of the Hayashi clan share the same ancestors as ordinary humans. At a certain point in time, their genes changed, making the Hayashi clan different from all other humans," Z said as he pulled out a cigar and handed it to Keimaro with a smile. "This will be a long story. Will you light this for me?"

Keimaro snapped his fingers, lighting the end of Z's cigar with a flicker of flame. He leaned back into his seat, waiting for the elder to begin speaking.

"I am an extremely old man; that is a given. Whether or not my looks may deceive you, I am one of the three immortals that dwell on this world. My name isn't really just Z. It is Zylon. I am four-hundred years old due to a journey long ago when I sipped from the Fountain of Youth. Now I am blessed and cursed with eternal life until killed by unnatural forces. This means that I was around when the Hayashi clan was first created and separated from the rest of humanity.

"It may be hard to believe, but long ago dragons were common. They would fly in the sky and lay eggs on the highest peaks of mountains. They would swallow humans whole—and for an age, humanity despised the beasts and sought to obliterate their existence from this world. Humanity had gathered so much hate for the majestic creatures because of their ability to take everything away from a human in a single instant. Humanity's pain drove the creation of the Hayashi clan.

"Skytera was a flourishing, massive island that was embedded with ancient runes that allowed the chunk of land to float in the air. These runes were created by the dragons themselves, and thus the majestic beasts found a place that they could finally call home. Soon they created a huge chain of islands that floated in the sky and hosted most of the dragon population. There, they would mate and bear their children out of the reach of any human. Dragons, the superior race, continued to grow in strength, safe in their haven above the clouds.

"Humanity searched for decades to find a way to the clouds so they could destroy the dragons for good. But they never could. So, the dragons slept safely above the clouds and rained jets of flame down on human cities during the day, pillaging and obliterating all in their path. They drowned themselves in their favorite ore in the world, gold, and continued to destroy kingdoms in search for more.

"That was when the first human conquered a dragon.

"The first human who ever mastered magic was Kuro, the creator of the Hayashi clan. Kuro had obtained his power from a meteor that fell from the sky. Using his newfound abilities, he conquered one of the strongest dragons at the peak of the highest mountain in the world, battling him with the most advanced magic known to exist even to this day. Mountains were crushed; the continent quaked with fear as the two forces battled for dominance. A single human against a dragon, it was unheard of. And Kuro won. He defeated the dragon and chained it up.

"The king of dragons demanded that Kuro release their brethren, but the man insisted that there be an exchange. In

157

exchange for the dragon's release, he was to obtain the all-seeing eyes of a demon to become dominant over humanity. Kuro was granted his wish and betrayed the deal. With his newfound power, he looked into the eyes of the dragon that he had captured and began to control it. Using his power and the strength of this dragon, he was able to fight the entire race of dragons and defeat them. Thousands of dragons were massacred, and the rest transformed into impenetrable statues to avoid being killed off by Kuro. The statues were left at Skytera to rot for eternity.

"I met Kuro myself. Together, we were the first ones to arrive at the Fountain of Youth and take a sip, obtaining eternal life. Over time, Kuro's demonic genes began to spread to other humans through his offspring. Generations passed, and eventually people noticed the difference in the eyes of humans with Kuro's genes. They began to be categorized as a clan known as the Hayashi.

"The gods supposedly didn't favor Kuro, for he had obtained his power from luck that was out of their control. Finally, seventeen years ago, the time for the purge had come. The High Priests, the only humans who can communicate with the gods, ordered that every human empire in existence must purge their population of members from the Hayashi clan. And, thus, the Hayashi clan massacre began.

"Kuro himself watched as the gods destroyed members of his family. They were killed off one by one before his eyes, executed by the humans that he had always found to be his brethren through his centuries of survival. It was then that he developed a hatred for humanity. In fact, he developed a hatred for the gods as well. He declared war upon the world two years into the Hayashi clan massacre. He promised the world that he would be the one to destroy everything that the gods had ever created and that he would then rule the world in place of the gods. That would be their punishment for destroying his family without any true purpose. And so, he created an organization known as the Bounts. He formed the organization in order to destroy humanity."

"Destroy humanity?" Keimaro exclaimed with disbelief, slamming his hands on the table. "What? The creator of the Bounts is a member of the Hayashi clan? I'm related to him?" A bead of sweat began to form on his brow.

That would explain why Tobimaru is in the organization. But what's all this talk about dragons? How could dragons give someone the eyes of a devil? Were they really that powerful that they could grant wishes like that?

Z nodded. "Kuro Hayashi is currently the most dangerous person on the planet. The only reason that he hasn't destroyed humanity is that he is currently in a slumber due to an event that happened six years ago. He is strong enough to obliterate humanity already, but with every day that he sleeps, he becomes stronger. No one is quite ready to wake him in order to finally put an end to him. Humanity would rather just wait in hopes that he will never wake up."

"What does this all have to do with the chest?"

"Within that chest is a single whistle. That whistle will awaken the strongest dragon in existence that was controlled by Kuro. Did you ever wonder why the Forbidden Forest has its name? Did you ever wonder why there are so many monsters in that forest or why it's pitch-black in there? The ominous aura of the most evil beast in history slumbers underneath that forest. The dragon will awaken along with Kuro, and that will signal not only the end of the continent or humanity, but the world," Z said, leaning back into his chair. "So, that's quite an important key you've got there. The king of Bassada has gotten his hands on your chest. But, as long as you have the key, it won't be possible for the dragon to awaken. The Bounts know this, which is why they are beginning to take matters into their own hands."

"What do you mean by that?"

With his arms crossed over his chest and his eyes closed, Yuri began to speak. "It means the Bounts are going to try to take over the Faar Empire so that they have access to the largest army on the entire continent. Then they will use their army to find you, kill you, and take the key to awaken Kuro," he said simply. "That's their current plan, from the looks of it. Once Kuro is awakened, it's over, so you need to keep that thing safe. But, at the same time, you are the only one with foreign magic. So, we can't let someone as strong as you just sit around and lounge, doing nothing. We still need your help to stop them, so that's why we ask to take your key—"

"No."

"What?"

Keimaro touched the key with his hand, feeling the bronze against his skin. "This is a memento from my father. It reminds me of his death. It reminds me of my mother's death, and the destruction of Bakaara and my clan. It reminds me of my pain. I won't let you have it."

Yuri stood up from his chair, towering over Keimaro with an annoyed look on his face. "Look, you stubborn bastard! This is more than just you! Stop being selfish for two freaking seconds and think about the world! Your goals aren't the only things that matter here!"

Keimaro's eyes glowed red with the Shokugan, and he glared at Yuri. "Yeah? Why would I trust some random strangers that I just met with a key that I treasure more than anything else?" He stood up with his face inches from Yuri's. "My existence is formed from my goals. The only reason I haven't killed myself to end my pain is that I want revenge. I want the Bounts to suffer as I have. And I want the king of Faar dead at my feet."

"Not exactly the *hero* type, wouldn't you say?" Lena said with a roll of her eyes, leaning back in her chair and looking away with a scoff, tapping the leather arm impatiently with her index finger.

"I'm not here to become a hero," Keimaro muttered, "nor am I here to satisfy anyone else but myself. I am here to obliterate all of *my* enemies. So? If the Bounts get their hands on me, it's the end of the world. Interesting. What are you going to do with me then? Lock me up? Attempt to take this key from me?"

"Neither," Z said simply. "We are merely going to cut down the government slowly. There are many political leaders as well as military leaders that need to be brushed off. You seem to have no problem with killing others. In that case, we will have you cut down all of the king's supporters. If we kill the king straight away, the power will only go to someone else with the same intentions as the previous king. We need to cut down anyone who supports the king."

"In other words," Keimaro said, leaning forward in his seat, "you want me to become an assassin to fulfill your little deeds and do whatever you want? Huh, I came here to kill the Bounts and the king, not kill his henchmen." He was tired of arguing. He just wanted to rest. His eyes were heavy, and he could feel his head going completely blank. At this point, he didn't even know what words were coming out of his mouth. He could hear Z speaking, but the words passed straight through him as he felt exhaustion finally hitting him. Before he knew it, he was asleep, leaning back in his chair with his eyes shut.

Z was about to continue talking and smiled when he saw that Keimaro was asleep. "He must be exhausted. Yuri, Lena, make sure that Keimaro is escorted to his room safely. Be sure to be careful; we wouldn't want to disturb his sleep."

***

Yuri rolled his eyes as he heaved Keimaro's arm around his shoulder, the other arm around Lena's. Together, the two of them walked down the hallway toward the nearest open room. Yuri gripped the doorknob and heaved Keimaro onto his large bed. He didn't bother turning on the lights since it might wake him up. Still, the kid must've been pretty tired if he was able to sleep through Yuri and Lena dragging him across the hallway. Yuri had never seen someone fall asleep faster than this boy had. "He's had a long day," Yuri said, turning to leave the room. "Let's give him some rest."

Lena stood in the doorway, looking at Yuri with worried eyes. "Yuri ... do you actually think we can trust him? He's dangerous, and ... I mean, how do we know that he's the *one*? Can't you just defeat the Bounts like you did at Horux? Wouldn't that be easier than trusting a complete stranger?"

Yuri stopped walking forward with one hand in his pocket and smiled at Lena. "No, I don't think we can trust him. Quite frankly, this boy is out of control. He is consumed by hatred to the point where he would probably kill anyone, even a child, in order to obtain the revenge he thirsts for. His aura is evil; I can smell it. His eyes represent the devil, which he seems to resemble with such heinous intentions. In fact, I wouldn't be surprised if he turned on all of us and killed us all. However," his look became serious in a mere instant, "I can also see good in him. He cares for his friends and allies. If he didn't, he wouldn't have come all this way for his friend, Yata. He wouldn't have fought us with such fierceness. I feel that there's more behind him than just a hateful boy. After all, he's had the chance to assassinate the king, being his guard and all. Yet, the king still lives."

Lena lowered her head, looking away. "You really think that he can kill them? That he can accomplish what you can't? You're stronger! So much stronger...."

"Yes," Yuri said with a chuckle. "For now. The thing about natural magic is that it reacts with your emotions. I, too, have natural magic, though it isn't from a foreign source. Keimaro's magic is different. It fuses with his hatred and becomes stronger. It can evolve into a much stronger form, where mine stays the same. Keimaro has the potential to become something stronger than even me." He scratched the back of his neck with a sigh. "Though, we don't know if he will live long enough to get there. Tobimaru Hayashi will be after him; that's for sure." He stepped past Lena, glancing at her over his shoulder. "All we can do is trust that he will become strong—strong enough to destroy the enemies that we can't."

Lena's eyes watered as memories began to flow back into her. She sniffed and shut her eyes as she reached for Keimaro's doorknob. She was betting everything on a complete stranger. She wasn't sure whether to be worried or not. Could she put her trust in Keimaro? Would he destroy the Bounts in a representation of their revolution? No one could know, not even Yuri. She opened her eyes and watched the sleeping Keimaro as she slowly closed the door, the shadows eventually swallowing the young boy in darkness. All that she could do was hope.

11. A NEW REASON TO FIGHT

Keimaro's eyes opened, finding that the ceiling was rather blurred. *Hmm? Where am I?* Everything came back into focus at once. The room was dark and silent, and he was lying on something extremely comfortable. That was all he knew. He sat up, slowly leaning forward and rubbing his forehead with a groan. He was on a bed. Where? He didn't remember going to an inn.

Memories of the previous night began to flash back, and he sighed, looking down at the white blanket that covered him. Everything was much more complicated now that he knew what the Bounts were up to. World domination using a dragon, a mythical creature. It sounded absurd, but it was possible. After all, Keimaro hadn't even seen much of the world yet. He had to assume that any legends or stories that he had ever heard about were real after seeing werewolves, magic, and falling stars. He had to assume that dragons really did exist. But the mere thought of such a majestic, yet frightening beast, sent shivers through his body.

He reached up and touched the key that dangled from his neck, feeling the cool metal on his fingertips. Yuri or Z could've stolen this from him and simply left him. But they hadn't. Instead, they had just given him a place to stay. *Can I really trust these guys?*

The door suddenly flew open, and a burst of light filled the room, blinding Keimaro. He covered his eyes with his hands and groaned, leaning back into his pile of soft pillows. The ephemeral light blinded him for a few seconds, and he saw the outline of a shadow that reminded him a bit of Aika. But, as his eyes adjusted to the light, he saw that it was only Lena.

She harshly threw a loaf of bread at Keimaro and crossed her arms over her chest. "Get up and get ready. Z wants to introduce you and your friends to our plan for today. Hurry up," she snapped and turned around, walking out of the room, leaving as abruptly as she had entered.

Keimaro caught the bread barely, still a bit drowsy from his sleep. He rubbed his eye with the back of his hand and sighed. "What's her deal?" he muttered to himself as he took a swift bite from the bread and pushed himself out of bed. He didn't know girls were so harsh. *Whatever.*

Stuffing the rest of the bread in his mouth, he threw his cloak over his body and walked out of the room, giving Lena a slight nod. He noticed that they were in one of the winding hallways that went in a circle around the tower, apparently on the very top floor. He glanced over the railing of the left side of the platform and whistled, looking all the way down. It looked like a very long fall and a very long climb to get up here. He blinked and realized that Lena was already ahead of him, opening the door to a room. He stumbled after her and followed her into the room.

Keimaro smiled when he found himself walking into a room made completely of wood. It was a rather large room that contained an impressive array of weapons all along the walls. Some were weapons Keimaro didn't even recognize, and each seemed to come in many sizes and versions. *There's enough weaponry in here to supply an army,* he thought. He looked across the room and saw Gavin and Yata standing to the left of Z. To the right were Yuri, Noah, and Lena.

A wave of relief filled Keimaro when he saw that his friends were unhurt. "So," he said simply, "what exactly is your plan then?"

"Well, we test your abilities today. You are quite the angry person, I noticed," Z said with a sly smile, "so why don't we allow you to break loose a bit? You go under the name of Riku Hikari, correct? Well, now I will allow you to reveal yourself as Keimaro Hayashi, the rebel against the king."

"You want me to be myself?"

"While wearing a mask."

"What am I, some kind of masked vigilante?" Keimaro murmured, crossing his arms.

"Pretty much," Z said with a smirk. "You will be yourself underneath a mask while you are an assassin, but you will be living the day as Riku Hikari, a member of the Royal Guard. They won't suspect you. Only when you're wearing your mask can you let out your wild side."

"The king or someone from the Royal Guard would recognize my voice if they ever heard me speak underneath the mask. They could also recognize my fighting style," Keimaro said.

"I doubt they will match your fighting style since they don't witness your combat often. Anyway, I looked into the voice problem. I have a mask prepared for you." Z turned around and revealed several complete outfits and masks already set up. He reached up, took one of the masks from the wall, and held it out to Keimaro. "Try it on."

Keimaro took the mask, feeling that it was rather hard, like clay. He placed it on his face and blinked as it began to bind itself to his flesh. *What the hell?* He grunted, suddenly panicking as the mask became one with his skin. He touched around his neck, only to find that he could not take it off. *"What is going...?"* The way he spoke had changed completely. It was filtered somehow so that, when he spoke, it sounded extremely deep, as if he had put a hollow can over his head and was speaking into it. How interesting.

"The mask is enchanted with magic that allows it to bind to you, adjusting to your size. When you speak, it filters your voice so that you are unrecognizable. Effective, right?" Z said with a clap of his hands. "The Bounts are currently in hiding, but when they see that you exist, they'll come out. That's when we will strike, do you understand?"

"So, you're using me as bait." Keimaro said after he yanked the mask off of his face, forcing it to detach from him.

"Essentially, yes, while also taking care of another issue at hand. Somewhat like multitasking, you could say. You teens are quite good at that, aren't you?" Z said. "Now, in order to get the Bounts' attention, we are going to need quite the entrance, aren't we? Imagine it, the world finally realizing that the Hayashi clan has yet to be exterminated, excluding Tobimaru, of course. You'll make a grand entrance tonight at the public political speech. The king will be there; everyone will. The Bounts will see it right away, and we will bring them out of hiding. Understood?"

Keimaro nodded. "So, what's the plan for tonight then?"

"I'll explain…."

***

Tobimaru leaned back into the stony walls of the cave in which he slept. Reduced to sleeping in caves, pathetic. He toyed with the small fire lit at his feet with a sigh as the shadows began to recede to the back of the cave. The sun once again began to take its place in the morning sky. The clouds seemed rather scattered today; perhaps it wouldn't snow like it always did. *Screw that Junko, leaving me here to suffer in the frozen cold. We could finish the job in a day.*

A single gust of wind announced the arrival of the man's partner. "Hidan, so? What's going on outside?" He poked once more at the blazing fire with his stick before he leaned back to look at the white-haired Bount beside him.

167

Hidan shrugged, scratching his head. "Not particularly sure. Doesn't seem that Junko wants us to strike quite yet. He seems quite eager to wait until the opportune moment to strike rather than us just blowing up half of the city in a fight against Z and his little apprentices." He sat down on the ground across the cave from Tobimaru with a sigh. "I don't particularly like his orders for us to stay here. There's nothing to do."

Tobimaru leaned his head back against the cave wall. "I don't see what's wrong with killing everyone in the process anyway. After all, if the goal is to obliterate mankind...."

"In order to destroy humanity, we still need its help. When Kuro is awakened, I don't believe that he will be able to face Sparta and Athens alone, even with that dragon of his," Hidan muttered. "Either way, I heard that your little cousin is in town. What do you intend on doing with him?"

"I intend to kill him."

"Really now, isn't he of Hayashi blood? There isn't much left. Perhaps it isn't wise to spill it."

"He's lost his way," Tobimaru muttered. "His sight is too narrowed, and his idea of revenge is nothing in comparison to what I want. Keimaro wants the kingdom and the Bounts to suffer. That is all. However, I want the entire race of humanity to suffer. I want the gods to plead for forgiveness for what they've done to me. I want humanity on the brink of extinction. The gods' greatest creation, obliterated because of their single mistake. I will make them regret their decision of genocide forever," he snarled, his head lowered as a dark shadow came over his face.

Hidan chuckled, standing up and stomping on the fire with a single step. A gust of wind blew the ashes all around in a slow, swirling vortex until they settled gently on the cave floor. He walked to the mouth of the cave with a sigh. He looked out across the snow-covered peaks of mountains and saw Bassada in the far-off distance on a stretching plain, hundreds of miles away. "You sound just like Kuro. That's good. Maybe you'd make a good leader as well. At any rate, killing Keimaro might be beneficial. Since he is of natural magic, the magic can be transferred to someone else. If you kill him and touch his chest once he is dead, his powers will transfer to you. Just as the powers from the meteor transferred to him, they will leap from host to host. At least, that's what Junko told me."

Tobimaru raised an eyebrow as he stood up from his seat on the ground. *Junko had said that?* "He didn't tell me that. Why, does he intend to kill Keimaro himself and take the natural magic for his own?" His eyes began to glow bright red with annoyance at Junko. He had hated that man from the very beginning. "Tell me!"

"I…" Hidan was about to speak but saw a young girl emerging from the shadows behind Tobimaru and immediately stopped talking. "Ah, good-morning, Mai," he said with a smile. "Did you have a good sleep?"

Tobimaru glanced at Mai over his shoulder and scoffed. "Whatever."

Hidan sighed when Tobimaru walked past him and out of the cave. The white-haired man walked up to Mai, who was rubbing her eyes with the back of her hands and yawning. He knelt down on one knee and patted her head softly. "Ah, don't mind him. He's just a little grumpy. Did you sleep well?"

Mai, now about eight years old, had her black hair tied into a single ponytail. She yawned once more and nodded her head. "Yeah. Why is Tobi always so grumpy? Did I make him mad?"

"No, no, no!" Hidan exclaimed with a reassuring laugh. "He's just having some time coping with some memories. All of us have bad memories. That's why we need to keep moving forward, right?" He poked her nose gently and turned around, offering her a piggyback ride. "At any rate, we are moving again. Do you have everything you need?"

Mai blinked a few times before running off into the shadows of the cave once more. She returned with a small pack that she put on. A small teddy bear poked its head out of her bag. The young girl leapt onto Hidan's back with a gentle giggle. "Go! Go!" she exclaimed, pointing off into the distance.

Hidan smiled and began to walk to the entrance of the cave. He inhaled a deep breath as he stepped outside onto the edge of the mountain. Mai reminded him so much of his own daughter. He shook his head with a smile, and with a single gust of wind, they were gone.

***

"So," Z said with a raised eyebrow, "it seems that Yata and Keimaro both have magic of natural properties, but Gavin doesn't. Perhaps I can interest you in a particular type of artificial magic then? We have many types."

"No, thank you," Gavin said with a slight shake of his head. "I don't have much interest in getting magic myself. I'm a simple soldier of the Faar Empire. I shouldn't be involved with whatever plans you have going on—"

"You are a spy then?"

"No!"

"You're an ally then."

"Not that either!"

Keimaro sighed as he scratched the back of his neck, listening to Gavin plead his case. "He's a soldier that I forced to work with us in order to get us into the city. I threatened to kill him if he turned against us. But, he's not an enemy. He proved himself when he risked his life to try to help me while I battled Yuri, Lena, and Noah."

Z raised his eyebrow at Keimaro and smiled at Gavin, clicking his fingers. In an instant, Lena had twirled a giant blunderbuss from nowhere and was pointing it straight at Gavin's face. She cocked the gun, and the pistol clicked. With her finger on the trigger, her eyes lacked any emotion.

Z tilted his head at Gavin and slid his hands into his pockets, inhaling a deep breath of air. "You know, I'm not one who likes to put people on the spot," he looked Gavin straight in the eyes, sending a shiver through the soldier's body, "but tell me: are you with us, or are you against us? Don't lie; I can tell if you're lying. Give me the honest truth."

Gavin stared at the pistol that was pointed at him, his heart skipping a beat. Beads of sweat began to form on his brow, and he rubbed his fingers together at his side. What should he do? Did he trust these guys? He remembered that Yata had spared his life despite his refusal to cooperate. He knew that Keimaro wasn't a heartless terrorist because he put his friends above all. Despite the fact that Keimaro had just met the king, he hadn't performed the assassination, which meant that there was more to him than met the eye. But Gavin didn't agree with their decision to kill the king! He lowered his head, his throat tightening. He didn't want to die. He had gone along with all of this so that he could survive, but he didn't want to participate in an assassination.

"Oi, old man!" Yata snapped, taking a step forward. "What the hell do you think you're doing? You can't just threaten him! Whether or not he's with us is completely irrelevant!" His right hand curled into a fist, and he continued forward when Noah swiped his hand and created a magic blue wall between Yata and Gavin that separated them. "Put the gun down, or I swear to god, I'll kill you all!" he snarled, his arm transformed into a chrome metal that gleamed.

Gavin sighed, looking at Yata. These guys that he had just met were willing to put their lives on the line for him. Why was that? Killing other strangers seemed so easy for them, though killing wasn't something that he believed was ever justified. But, if that were the case, why was he even in the army? Why was he afraid of death? He liked these new companions of his, but he didn't support what they were doing. If he died, at least he would die with his beliefs. He tilted his head back and closed his eyes.

"I am not with you. I am with Keimaro and Yata. However, I don't support their decision to go against the government. The king has done nothing wrong, and the empire is flourishing. Its people are happy. You would be using supernatural powers to destroy a peace that took generations to establish and maintain!" He slammed his fist against his chest in the soldier salute that he had practiced. "I am still loyal to the government and its order! Kill me if you wish! I swore my life to protect what I believe is right." He lowered his head and fought back tears. He was going to die. At least it would be quick.

Z looked at Gavin incredulously and smiled. "Very well," he said, nodding toward Lena.

She pulled the trigger, and the pistol clicked, firing a single bullet that soared forward, cutting through the air as it made its way toward Gavin. The soldier stood in his salute, unmoving, accepting his fate as the projectile flew toward him. A blade came down and slashed the bullet, cutting the projectile in half and sending the pieces flying around Gavin.

Silence stretched, and Gavin's eyes opened. *I'm alive?* He saw Keimaro's black cloak flapping from the fast movement. The boy had darted across the room to cut down the bullet and save his life. His heart was racing, and he watched as Yuri and Noah both stepped forward in response to Keimaro's unsheathing his sword. *Is causing trouble for people all that I'm good for?*

Keimaro raised his head and looked at the assassins before him. He twirled the blade in his hand and lowered it, pointing it at the ground to show that he meant no harm. "He's our comrade. Whether or not you accept that is up to you. But I won't have you killing him off."

"And why is that? How long have you known him?"

"A little over a day."

"The bond clearly is strong, isn't it?" Yuri said with a sarcastic scoff.

"No," Keimaro said, "but he had many chances to run away. We gave him the freedom to leave us whenever he wanted, but his curiosity drove him to stay with us. And his good-natured conscience was what brought him to tell me that Yata had been kidnapped. He could've left and allowed Yata to be captured without informing me. He also could've left after telling me where Yata was. He could've left while I was fighting Yuri, but instead he risked his life to save mine. You all know that there's more to me than meets the eye—and my eyes tell me that there's more to him than you know."

"I don't want you going on an instinct," Yuri snarled. "If he messes up a single operation, it could be the end of all of us. Don't you see that? And he knows our plans! We can't just let him go either."

"Then we continue the original plan," Keimaro said. "He does what I say. If he disobeys, I will kill him."

Gavin gulped, not particularly favoring that plan either, but he supposed that it was better than being shot on the spot without being given a chance at life at all. He closed his eyes and sighed. At least Keimaro was trying to negotiate to save his life.

"We will let him stay," Z said. "I understand why he doesn't support us. He doesn't hate Faar. In fact, he respects the empire as well as its leader. None of us have even given a single legitimate reason for hating the empire. All that we have stated is that we hate them for our own reasons. While Keimaro and Yata have a personal drive to destroy the Faar empire, we have our own reasons for wanting their downfall."

"Are they true reasons," Gavin said, "or are they just personal conflicts that you had?"

"Both, actually … and I'm sure you'll be intrigued by both," Z said, tapping Lena's arm so that she lowered the pistol. "At any rate, perhaps I'll have Noah show Yata and Gavin around the city so that they know how cruel the Faar government is. As for Keimaro," he turned to the boy, "Yuri and Lena will show you how you will execute your entrance tonight so that we can make it the most effective. We want to draw attention."

Keimaro nodded and looked at Yata, who nodded back. "Keep out of trouble," he said to his friend as Yuri and Lena walked past him. He turned and began to follow them, glancing back at Gavin and Yata over his shoulder for a brief moment. This whole plan was to make him like some type of celebrity. It was well-thought-out if the masks had already been created and enchanted specifically for the mission. It was as if they had known that he would be coming to the city. The thought of Z knowing all of his plans was unsettling—but, then again, perhaps it was just coincidence. He shook his head, trying not to think of it.

Upon leaving the house and walking down the pathway that cut through the front lawn of the mansion, he saw that the grass, which had been singed with fire earlier, was already repaired. It looked good as new. He raised his eyebrow with amusement at how fast they had fixed the lawn despite the large-scale fight that had occurred. They began to walk through the streets, and Yuri pulled a black hood over his head, just as Lena did. Keimaro blinked, supposing that he should do the same. He wore his black cloak over his Royal Guard abyssalite armor. He had left the rest of the uniform in his room. Feeling his sheathed sword clanking at his side, he looked around and saw that the other people in the streets were not as heavily armed as they were. Though it made sense, it also made them stand out a lot more— a few sketchy, cloaked people walking through the streets with enough weapons to supply a squad. Where were the guards? They didn't even care that a small group of armed people were waltzing through the streets without identification?

That was when Keimaro saw a small group of guards huddled in the corner of an alley, sitting on top of boxes and barrels, playing cards. They were laughing while smoking pipes and cheap cigars. Empty glass bottles of beer were scattered on the ground around them. He winced at the very sight of the men that were supposed to be the protectors of this city. These guards reminded him of the soldiers in Bakaara before it had been invaded—they were all talk and took advantage of their job position. All they did was lounge around all day and drink rather than actually protect the average citizen from danger.

Keimaro sighed as they pushed onward through the crowds of people. From the looks of it, it didn't matter if a couple of people died. The population in this city was huge. There was no room to even walk. And every street or two, Keimaro would spot a dead body on the side of the road somewhere. Usually the people seemed to have died from either starvation or beatings, perhaps from the guards. He looked forward and saw that Yuri and Lena had disappeared into an alleyway, the shadows swallowing up their image in a mere instant. The boy stumbled after them, unable to see them. He blinked a few times, trying to adjust to the thick darkness, but found it hard to see.

Keimaro looked up and saw that Yuri and Lena were climbing up the side of a building to get to the rooftops. He frowned, quite astonished at how they climbed the building with such ease. They simply grabbed onto windowsills and cracks in order to haul themselves upward. That definitely took some practice and a huge amount of upper-body strength. Still, it couldn't be that hard. After all, during his four-year training while in the forest with his father and Yata after the Bakaara massacre, he had climbed many trees in order to stay away from the beasts of the night. Climbing a building couldn't be much harder; he just needed grip.

Yuri and Lena sat on the tiled rooftop, looking down at Keimaro and waiting patiently for him. Yuri was emotionless, whereas Lena had cracked a smile, knowing that Keimaro was hesitant in following them. "What's wrong? You coming?" she teased.

Keimaro glared at her and took a few steps back from the building. *It can't be that hard.* He ran at the wall, planting a single foot on it. He pushed upward and ran two steps up the wall before slamming both of his feet against it. *Except, I'll do things my way.* He released a small jet of flame from his feet that shot him backward, flipping through the air. He landed on the other wall with his feet and released another jet of fire that sent him flying upward into the air over Lena and Yuri. His arms flailed, and his legs were mush in the air, but he was smiling nevertheless as he reached the peak of his flight. He had a clear view over the entire city's rooftops. He landed heavily on the tiled roof and turned to look at Yuri, who stood up, unimpressed.

"Let's go," he said. He walked past Keimaro and broke into a hard dash across the rooftop. He lowered his body and put all of his weight down into his feet, kicking off of the edge of the rooftop and using his momentum to send him flying through the air. He landed on another rooftop, leaping across the gap between the buildings with graceful ease.

Keimaro raised an eyebrow when he saw Lena mirror the action. He stood there with his mouth gaping and sighed, taking off after them. His breath was heavy, and he was nervous, which was rather rare. He kicked off of the roof and was sent flying into the air over the gap. A moment of fear shot through him as he looked down at the ground below. He could fall right now, and he would never see Mai ever again. He raised his head and looked outward at Yuri and Lena, who were still racing along the rooftops like a bunch of monkeys.

Will I ever see Mai again? Is Z telling the truth about her still being alive? I mean, I always wished that she would be alive, but the reality of it all…. Why would they keep her alive? A mere child? He landed on the roof with a solid thump and continued running forward. *The Bounts keep only what they have to gain from. Why would they keep her?*

The boy began to slow down when he caught sight of a massive tower before them that stretched up into the sky and was topped with a gleaming, gigantic bell. He scratched his neck when he saw Yuri pointing to the very top and whistled. "That's a long climb. I'm assuming that we aren't climbing this the manual way, are we?"

Yuri shook his head and pointed down toward the bottom of the tower, where a wooden door was guarded by two armed guards. "We are going to break in and place a chip at the very top. Then we will escape using a zip line." He reached into the pocket of his black cloak and pulled out a tiny blue chip that matched the color of the teleporting pad. "This," he said, "is the key to our grand entrance tonight. It enables us to particle transport to the exact location where it is planted. After that, I'll explain how we are going to execute tonight's plan."

Keimaro nodded and sat on the edge of the roof, his legs dangling off the end. He pointed to the guards. "So, we are just going to bust inside? Are we allowed to kill or…?"

"No, we can't," Yuri said. "If we kill anyone, they will be investigating the area for at least a day or two. That's too much time. We need to just bust in and run away. We are going to plant the chip without them even knowing. Follow my lead, and we will get this done quickly. Cover my back, Keimaro. Lena, make sure to prepare the zip line gear."

He leapt off of the rooftop and landed hard on the street, startling civilians around him. He paused to take in the shock from the height of the fall before he broke into a sprint forward. He barreled through the guards and the door before they were even able to unsheathe their weapons. The door screeched as it was ripped off its hinges from the tackle, and the soldiers slammed hard into the ground. Yuri was already on them with his fists raining down upon them with heavy punches.

Keimaro was still sitting there, watching the scene with his mouth gaping. Yuri had just gone in there so easily and so fast without even a care for his surroundings. The civilians around him were already screaming and running around, signaling for more guards to come. He supposed this was when he came in to support Yuri. He leapt down from the rooftop as well and landed, wincing at the shock from the fall that burst through his legs and traveled up through his body. He could see the crowds of people scattering with armed guards pushing their way through. The boy heard Lena jump down behind him and glanced over his shoulder to give her a swift smile as they began to race forward. Keimaro had to make sure that his hood was always up during the encounter so that no one recognized him. He still had to conceal his identity as a member of the Royal Guard. After only a day of getting the job, he shouldn't be caught fighting guards in the street.

Upon reaching the door, one of the guards turned to him, and he responded with a crack of his fist across the man's jaw. There was no warning. Just his fist, slamming against flesh and bone. A dribble of blood spurted from the man's lips as he crumpled to the ground. Ignoring the throb of his knuckles, Keimaro had no intention of fighting the other soldiers that surrounded him. He quickly made his way through the open doorway, stepping over the unconscious bodies that lay still on the cold marble floor.

The inside of the tower seemed extremely simple. A table had been knocked over, and poker cards were scattered everywhere among three more unconscious guards that reeked of alcohol. No doubt they had been slacking off while the two guards at the front were clearly doing their job, though not effectively. From the looks of the destruction and smashed beer bottles, Yuri had been through here. The walls were made up of simple cobblestone with a winding stairway that climbed all the way to the very top.

Keimaro gave Lena a guiding push toward the stairs as he turned around and kicked at a few of the guards, trying to drive them back. They had already unsheathed their blades and were fully ready to kill. He winced, remembering that he wasn't to kill any of them; otherwise, it could ruin the entire operation for tonight. Without a way to defend himself, he grabbed a beer bottle off of the ground and hurled it at the mob of guards. The projectile exploded into a million glittering pieces of translucent glass that became stained with blood upon contact. Spurred on by the shrill screams of agony, Keimaro raced up the stairs, avoiding eye contact with the wounds of the men behind him. He could hear them racing up the stairway, attempting to catch up to him.

They kept climbing. The stairs seemed to go on and on, eventually making Keimaro feel exasperated from the strenuous exercise. He pushed onward, hearing the slowed clanks of armor behind him, getting closer. When he reached the top, he saw that

Yuri was standing there with Lena, giving Keimaro a nod of satisfaction that the job was complete. *So, this chip is planted, mission complete?* The only question was: how were they going to get down? Keimaro had never once heard of a zip line before. Was it a new type of technology?

"Lena?"

Lena nodded upon hearing her name and pulled out a massive pistol that was apparently loaded with a harpoon. *A harpoon gun?* She aimed it high into the air and fired, a long rope following the harpoon through the air. The projectile lodged itself onto the rooftop of a lower building, across the street. Lena gave the rope a good tug to test it before she sliced off the end that was attached to the gun. She tied the rope against a pillar that supported the roof over the enormous bronze bell that stood in the center of the room. A cool breeze blew through the tower, causing the bell to make a whistling noise.

Yuri took a small bar from his cloak and positioned himself in front of the rope. He put the bar over the rope and gripped both ends tightly, bravely kicking off of the tower as he flew out into the open air, zip lining down toward the building below.

"You've got to be kidding me," Keimaro muttered, knowing that he was next. *I didn't sign up for this.* He could already hear the clanking of the soldiers behind him. Lena handed him a bar, which he took reluctantly. He positioned himself just as Yuri had, the bar over the rope. However, his hands were shaking as he looked down at the hundreds of meters below to the ground. If he fell now, he would be squashed like a bug. His breath was heavy as he felt sweat forming on his palms, increasing his chances of slipping and falling. *Damn, Kei! Why are you being so freaking negative? Just get it over with! You've done worse!*

"Hurry up, Hayashi!" Lena snapped as the men began to stumble up the stairway, panting and coated in sweat. "They're here!"

"But!"

"Go!" Lena kicked him in the back swiftly, and he grunted, his feet leaving the safety of the tower.

Keimaro's mind went blank with fear as he looked down and saw his legs dangling through the air, rooftops zooming past him. He would've yelled, but his throat was clogged with panic as he thrashed and kicked. He heard the bell suddenly ring, and he glanced to see Lena coming down behind him. The soldiers were plugging their ears in an attempt to block out the sound. He turned back to look at where he was going and slammed face-first into the roof. He fell, smashing into a cart of some sort. Dust flew off in all directions, and he blinked a few times, looking up at the sky, rather dazed. *Not the best landing I could've had. Ugh, at least I'm alive.*

Yuri poked his head over the roof to look down at Keimaro while Lena landed graciously on the ground beside him. She grinned as she squatted down, patting his head gently as if he were an injured pup. "Not bad for your first zip line, Kei." She giggled teasingly and stood up. "Thanks to you, we have everyone's attention. Better get up and start running. Otherwise, your cover is blown."

***

Yata sighed as he walked through the streets of Bassada behind Gavin and Noah, feeling uncomfortable with the large amount of people in the area. He felt as if they were all being aggressive whenever they bumped or pushed him unintentionally. He had a strong urge to efface every single human being in this entire city. The way they looked at him, touched him, spoke around him—they all disgusted him. Nevertheless, he kept his eyes forward and attempted to repress his fury. He tried to think about something else, but every time he did, he could only think of his failure when he had fought Yuri. That white-haired bastard had absolutely obliterated him in combat. He didn't even seem to be trying when Yata had been giving it his all. Yata's hands were clenched tightly at his side, and he shook his head in disbelief. Was all that training for nothing? So he could lose in combat to some random boy from the streets working for a rich old man?

His eyes narrowed as he glared at the back of Noah's head. He didn't dare say such rude and dishonorable things in front of Z's son, but he was curious as to how much power this boy contained as well. All of this seemed so bizarre. The group seemed almost too good to be true, fighting for the exact same things that Yata and Keimaro had been training for over the past four years. But, Yata had never really had a reason to want to kill the king or smash the sovereignty of the crown. He just wanted the man dead for destroying his village. Revenge. As puerile as it sounded, it was all he wanted. Selfish or not, Yata had no legitimate reason for wanting Faar to be eradicated other than his own personal hatred.

Giving him a real reason would just make him even more determined to destroy Faar. Yata glanced over at Gavin. In order to convince such a dedicated soldier, Noah would have to show something that probably wasn't in the public view—something that would be enough to convince even the most loyal of soldiers to turn against the government. But, from the looks of it, they were simply walking in the public streets, not anywhere where any secret government things would take place.

Noah suddenly took a turn into a street that looked like a ghost town. The houses were tattered and old with rust and mold growing all over the wooden structures. Bodies were sprawled across the sides of the street from starved homeless individuals that had passed but hadn't been cleaned up from the streets. Some of their flesh was decayed, with flies and bugs buzzing around. The very sight almost made Yata want to vomit. Gavin actually did.

"I know that poverty is a problem in our society, but that isn't a good enough reason to convince me to execute the king," Gavin muttered, wiping his mouth of sick. "There's poverty in every prosperous nation. There is no society where everyone is living high and mighty—"

"That's not what I came to show you today," Noah said simply, walking toward one of the buildings. At the building's side was a latch in the ground, camouflaged by a patch of grass. "My father has a large amount of prototype samples of artificial magic. These bodies that you see out here are not just from starvation. Would you like to see the truth? It is a rather sickening sight." He reached down, grabbed the hidden latch, and pulled. A wooden doorway came up, some dust entering the air, and absolute darkness was all that could be seen beyond.

Yata truly didn't want to go down there. Perhaps it was a personal fear about entering catacombs. Well, not just catacombs. It was any type of underground activity, for that matter. He gave a smug look, but Gavin and Noah didn't seem to quite catch it because Gavin followed Noah forward, rather curious as to what the darkness held. Yata gave a small shiver as he inched his way over, dragging his legs until he fell stagnant at the entrance of whatever this opening led to. "Well, it's your call, Gavin. I'm going to hate the government, no matter what, but this is to convince you to join our side, right?"

Gavin shrugged. "I'll see what he has to show me."

Damn it.

Noah nodded and flicked his wrist, summoning a glowing red stick that appeared in his hand. Such conjuring magic truly seemed like a very useful trick, fit for many different types of situations. He gripped the stick and pointed to the darkness, revealing a descending staircase that led into the abyss. He began to walk downward and conjured a glowing stick for Yata and Gavin to use as well.

Gavin went second, and Yata followed after. Being in the back of the group was something that he didn't favor at all. He definitely wasn't afraid of the dark since he had embarked on his short trek through the Forbidden Forest. But the moment that they stepped down into the dark corridors of this underground facility, he was overwhelmed with a disconcerting feeling. Perhaps it was the clamminess or even the scant light that radiated from the small sticks they held. Other than that, it was pitch-black, and Yata followed the shadowed image of Gavin, who walked before him. The corridor was extremely narrow and scarred with some type of markings, carved delicately with deep incisions into the stone walls, as if they were in an ancient burial ground. Seldom was he this uncomfortable, yet here he was. His heart pounded as it had when he was a child whenever he felt fear. Nothing had happened, yet he already felt this foreign feeling—how cowardly of him. He blinked when he found the narrow hallway opening up into a massive room filled with blackness, their tiny glow sticks lighting up only a small percentage of the abyss that engulfed them.

"How does your magic work?" Yata asked Noah curiously.

"Anything that I imagine in my mind becomes a reality. I can create any type of shape or form using creative magic," Noah said, clicking his fingers. A large glowing set of green tracks began to set its place in the air, spiraling around the room, illuminating the darkness a bit. But what fascinated Yata was that Noah conjured a train next, supposedly a dwarven model of underground transportation. The magical train followed the tracks, lighting up the entire room as it spiraled until it reached the very top of the ceiling and exploded in a burst of green light that attached itself to the wall, fighting back the darkness.

"If anything," Gavin said, looking at the magic in awe, "wouldn't your type of magic be the strongest type? Since it is essentially fitting for any situation and also allows for the creator's imagination to form as a weapon to defeat his opponents? It seems that it would be even more powerful than Keimaro's flames."

"Ah, it is very strong. My magic is tactical and can be helpful when I can't utilize my surroundings. It is also quite a defensive power. But in terms of strength, it is not optimal. The magic can be shattered by someone as strong as Keimaro—and with such rowdy and angry flames, he could easily overpower my defenses and defeat me," Noah said and then pointed forward to an enormous curved archway that led into yet another large room. "This is where you will find the truth of what the Faar government has been doing behind the backs of the people."

Yata watched as Gavin began to walk forward into the next

room and gasped. The boy followed the soldier and found many large tubes filled with human beings in odd, glowing, colorful liquids. Tables were filled with different types of bubbling fluids of a variety of colors in vials and flasks. A giant lab.

Yata moved closer to one of the tubes and gulped, realizing how skinny this human being was. It was a girl—an ordinary girl with long jet-black hair and slender arms, probably from being left here to starve. Small tubes were attached to her skin and seemed to be pumping odd fluids into her body. Immediately, Yata regretted coming down here. He turned away, ready to empty his stomach.

"What is the meaning of this?" Gavin snarled, looking at the hundreds of massive glass tubes that contained humans inside of them. His eyes were wide with disbelief at what he was seeing. His hands were shaking as he looked all around, taking in his surroundings. "What the hell is going on?"

"The Faar government has been trying to develop a way to give artificial magical power that is on a whole new level of strength using merely chemicals rather than natural substances from the world. They intend to create an army of magicians in order to give them the upper hand in war against the Spartans or Athenians so that they would be able to conquer the land," Noah explained. "These test subjects are humans that were taken off of the streets of the lower district. Poverty. No one would miss them, so the government kidnapped them and performed sick tests on their bodies to see if they could create the ultimate weapon."

"Did they succeed?"

"I'm not sure," Noah said. "These humans seem to be mostly dead, and the place is pretty much abandoned."

Yata was watching the girl in the tube once more. She had been taken from the streets and used as a lab rat by Faar's alchemists and chemists. His hands balled into tight fists at his side. *I won't forgive them for this atrocity.*

The girl's eyes snapped open and flashed a brilliant red. The two of them stared at each other for a brief moment before Yata yelped with surprise and staggered backward, bumping into a table. Glass vials and flasks exploded into glittering shards as chemicals spilled off of the table. She was alive! How was that possible?

Gavin dashed over to Yata and grabbed the hilt of his sword. He quickly drew his blade, whirling his weapon before him as he looked at the girl in the glass tube. "She's ... alive?" he said with surprise and grunted as he swung at the tube. A single slash was enough to shatter the glass completely, raining shards down onto the ground. Odd fluids that stank of waste poured out onto the ground from the shattered tube.

Yata rushed forward and grabbed the girl as she fell before she made contact with the sharp glass. He blinked as he held the naked stranger in his arms and quickly pulled the cloak off his body and wrapped it around her. "She's alive," he said, reaching out and touching the girl's throat, feeling her pulse. It was subtle but there. Her eyes were now closed, her breathing normal, but she was definitely unconscious. They had to get her out of here. He lifted her into his arms and looked at Gavin and Noah. "We'll bring her back to the mansion and help her. Are all of these people alive?"

Noah shook his head. "No, most of them are dead. In fact, they should all be dead since they were left here for such a long time without any food or anything. It's a miracle that she's alive."

"Well, let's get her out of here as soon as possible." Yata turned to Gavin. "That enough to convince you?"

There was a sudden bang, and everyone went down, ducking behind the same desk in unison. The sound of footsteps echoed loudly in the hollow laboratory room. The metallic clanking sound that accompanied the footsteps of at least a dozen men indicated that these were armed guards.

Gavin gripped his sword tightly, now knowing that this was definitely a government project—a government that he no longer respected if this was how they treated their own people.

Yata was still holding the girl in his arms and examined her before he looked away. Her flesh had caved in after the small tubes had been detached from her body, making her look like a deflated skeleton. Nevertheless, she was still alive, though not for long at this rate; she looked as if she hadn't eaten in weeks.

"General Mundo," a man said, clearly venerating the higher position as he saluted the general. "It seems that Project X has escaped. No, rather, someone was down here and broke her out."

"How recent?"

"Only minutes ago, sir. The preserving fluids are still warm. Someone must have bumped into the desk nearby as well, for there are shattered vials and flasks," the soldier said. "Shall we perform a search, sir?"

"As soon as possible," General Mundo said. "I want whoever was down here caught and executed immediately. I also want Project X to be captured alive as soon as possible. No doubt whoever these people are, they were humane enough to try to free her. They'll probably keep Project X alive until we get our hands on her. Get the tracking dogs on the job."

Noah, Gavin, and Yata all looked at each other in despair. Tracking dogs? There was no doubt that they would be caught with this odd smell. Preservative fluids, was it? It smelled more like urine. They had to get out of here.

"When I use my magic," Noah whispered, "we make a run for it, got it? We destroy as much stuff as we can and close the tunnel so that they can't follow us. Yata, I'm leaving that part up to you. Gavin, take hold of the girl and take point." He flicked his wrist, and a burst of green light shot up into the air, exploding, sending streaks of energy outward and attaching to soldiers. The attack smashed bottles and glass tubes everywhere, causing chaos as Yata and Gavin began to make a mad dash for the exit, Noah following closely behind.

Yata's heart was pounding heavily. *All I have to do is destroy the tunnel. Easy enough.* When they reached the corridor, Yata's fleshy arm morphed into pure metal. He began to rapidly smash it into the wall, causing dust to crumble down from the ceiling and the wall itself. Cracks began to split around the archway as Yata grunted, putting more and more effort into his punches, digging deeper into the structure as he slammed it with more force. *Harder! More power!*

He looked and saw Noah holding off the soldiers with his magic, blocking rifle bullets and sword blows with his glowing blue shield as he cast different shapes outward to counterattack. Yata gasped as he pulled his hand back, pieces of debris crinkling from his fingers. His hand curled into a solid fist, clenched tightly. He planted his feet firmly into the ground, and his eyes widened, his body rotating, gathering speed as his fist rocketed toward the wall. He yelled when it made contact, the cracks in the wall suddenly giving way as the entire structure began to collapse. Rocks crumbled from the archway entrance, smashing into the earth.

Yata turned, pride rising in his chest, until he saw Noah. The man was pinned, and rocks were already raining down around him. "Noah!" Yata exclaimed, stretching his arm out to the man while debris fell relentlessly. He could get Noah out of here. All Noah had to do was grab his hand, and he could yank him clear of the doorway before any debris buried him. He watched as Noah shook his head, without even trying to reach out, as if already accepting the inevitable. The debris began to fill up the gap, and Yata could've sworn that he saw Noah smiling before the soldiers forced him down onto his knees. Then he was gone.

Yata stood there in the dead silence, staring at the place where Noah had been only a moment earlier. *No....* He placed his forehead against one of the rocks that filled the doorway, his heart thudding. Then a blood-curdling scream of agony erupted from the other side of the debris. Yata's hands were shaking at his side, salty tears beginning to form in his eyes, his stomach giving way. He listened to Noah's screams until eventually they stopped, and he was gone once more.

I could've saved him. I could've reached a little further and grabbed him! He fell to his knees, his arms limp at his side as tears streaked down his cheeks. He lowered his head, beginning to sob. He was powerless to do anything, just like before. The last time he had cried like this was when he saw the dead from the massacre, four years earlier. He hadn't cried when Keimaro's father had died, but he hated the fact that Noah had just sacrificed himself to save them. The son of the man that was leading this mysterious rebellion. *Gavin wanted to come down here. He wanted to see why he should hate the government. Noah wouldn't have died if it weren't for Gavin. This is all his fault.*

Silence. Yata didn't want to blame Gavin. The soldier seemed dedicated enough to want to stay by their side rather than run back to his barracks. But now Noah was dead. A young man they had only met hours ago had sacrificed his own life for them. What would he tell Z? He pushed himself to his feet and looked at the pile of debris once more. He exhaled as he wiped his eyes in the crook of his arm, turning away and beginning to walk after Gavin. What, indeed?

12. THE PROTOTYPE

Keimaro had been running from the guards for quite some time now. They had somehow climbed onto the rooftops and were following him closely, yet they hadn't gotten a clear glimpse of his face. His ebony cloak was pulled tightly around him, flapping in the wind. His hood came over his face, creating a dark shadow that obscured his facial features. His boots thudded loudly against the rough tiled rooftops of the city as he continued onward, leaping across gaps as Yuri and Lena had done. No doubt they had escaped already because it seemed that the guard was focusing everything on capturing him. At least a dozen soldiers followed him on the rooftops and maybe two dozen on foot, yelling at him to stop running. It didn't seem that any of them were willing to shoot him with their rifles, though, for some odd reason. He would've thought that one of them would've at least fired a shot, or perhaps an arrow. It made sense, though. The prototype and blueprints had been delivered only yesterday. It was a miracle they had already produced so many guns. The soldiers probably didn't even know how to use them yet. Sometimes Keimaro would see soldiers slipping between the gaps of the buildings and fall, which caused him to snicker a little. Though death was never a laughing matter, something intrigued him when they slipped and fell. How inept could get they get? They were imbeciles for following him this far.

He looked around for a better way to escape, but couldn't

really see anything. Then he spotted a canal filled with stagnant water that stretched throughout the city. Swimming in there would give away his position. He rushed forward on the rooftop, but something else caught his eye. His Shokugan eyes activated, causing a glowing demonic red in his iris. There was a small crack in a weakened part of the roof. Interesting.

Keimaro reached the weak part of the rooftop, eager to see what would happen. He saw that the guards were so close behind him anyway. He had nothing to lose. He leapt up into the air and smashed his feet into the crack. He lost his footing as the entire roof collapsed, dropping half a dozen soldiers into the open air. Time seemed to slow as Keimaro's glowing eyes flickered from left to right, scanning the area as he fell. It looked as if they were in some type of warehouse. Wooden bars crossed the top half of the structure, their purpose supposedly to support the roof. But they were also good footholds—not to mention, it was much better than falling twenty feet only to hit the inevitable solid ground. There was nothing else in the empty warehouse to grab on to besides the bars. Conveniently, the bars led up to a small circular window across the warehouse, which exited above the canal. He lashed out with his hand and grasped one of the bars, his body weight dragging him down. Soldiers' bodies crunched loudly as they hit the ground. Keimaro winced as he heard the sickening thuds and began to haul himself upward.

Keimaro saw several soldiers peering down through the massive hole in the roof as he balanced on the wooden bar. His legs were shaking as he moved forward, but he figured that the slower he moved, the harder it would be to balance. He turned away and began to sprint forward, stumbling a bit as he felt his balance being disrupted. As he neared the circular window, he realized it was extremely small, perhaps large enough to fit a baby. He looked over his shoulder and saw soldiers on the bar already beginning to follow him, having dropped down from the rooftop cautiously. The boy grunted as he sucked in a deep breath and dove through the window, making his body slender and straight as an arrow as he flew through the small opening and out into the free, fresh air towards the canal.

He closed his eyes as he hit the water with a clean dive, his body slicing through several feet of liquid before he slowed into a float. His eyes snapped open, and he blinked when he saw that he could see clearly despite the slight fog in the water. He gave a swift kick and began to make his way through the water, trying to hold his breath as long as possible. He knew that the canal was still and that the soldiers would look through the window searching for his whereabouts. By staying underwater, he hoped they wouldn't spot him.

Keimaro broke the surface while underneath a curved bridge, brushing his black hair out of his eyes. His iris's color changed back into its normal dark brown, and he pressed himself against the bridge, looking up at the giant structure above him. "Well, that wasn't that bad of an escape," he muttered and quickly began to strip himself of his cloak. He sighed, throwing it over his shoulder as he began to climb out of the water. In order to avoid being recognized, he would probably have to sneak around town to get back to the mansion. The authorities were probably looking for him. Perfect.

It took quite some time and navigating for him to finally find his way back to the mansion without getting caught or recognized. Nevertheless, he did it, and he was still dripping wet when he walked through the door. Only a few boys and girls were walking about on the ground floor, but Lena was sitting on a red leather couch on the far side of the room, her legs folded, beside Yuri. She waved at him with a little giggle when she saw him completely soaked. "Wow, how did you decide to escape?"

"I fell through a roof and dove into a canal," Keimaro murmured, walking over.

"Sounds like you had a fun time."

"Oh yeah, *wonderful*," Keimaro muttered with a roll of his eyes as he raised the cloak over Lena and squeezed some water onto her, causing her to squeal. "How did you guys escape?"

"We let all of the guards chase after you and slipped away into an alleyway," Yuri said and raised his eyebrow at Keimaro, leaning back into the couch. "You're too loud and too noticeable. Sure, that'll be perfect for tonight, but in a real assassination and a real getaway, you're going to need more than just luck in order to escape. You'll need to memorize every part of your surroundings in an instant and analyze how you'll be able to use it to your advantage for your getaway. You understand that?"

"Yes, sir," Keimaro muttered.

The door flew open, and Gavin staggered into the building with Yata. Absolute silence fell as all of them looked at the bony naked woman in Gavin's arms. Everyone began to walk toward them, but Gavin held up a hand, completely out of breath.

"Someone help her! She needs medical attention!" Gavin exclaimed, placing her down on the ground gently. He put his hands on his knees and panted, out of breath. He watched as Lena lifted the girl and began to race away with other students toward the teleporter so that they could get her to the infirmary.

Yuri pushed his way through the crowd along with Keimaro until they stood over Gavin. "Where's Noah?"

Gavin's eyes were lowered. Yata took a step forward, his eyes solid and unwavering. "He was separated from us. Either the guards got him, or he's dead. He chose to sacrifice himself in order to save us." His tone was harsh and straight to the point.

Keimaro blinked a few times, barely able to take this in. "What? Are you serious? What in the hell were you guys doing? Being chased by guards? I thought that Noah was just taking you guys to show you why the government should be hated, not a secret mission! And who was that naked girl that you brought in? She looks as if she hasn't eaten for weeks!"

"Kei, calm down."

"I won't calm down! One of our comrades just died!" Keimaro snarled, pointing at the door. "We should head out there and go—"

Yuri slammed his fist solidly into Keimaro's face, his body rotating and sending the boy flying backward. Keimaro hit the ground hard on his back. Yuri pulled back his fist as the crowd of assassins around them gaped. They watched Keimaro, who was grabbing at his face and gasping.

"Hey," the werewolf snarled simply, raising his fist. "When you said you would work with us, I told you I would help make everything work out. But you listen to what I say, got it? This isn't your lone wolf thing anymore! You're with a group. And you listen to me."

Keimaro pushed himself upward, his eyes flashing red. "I don't work for anyone, and no one is my superior. I choose to be here because you benefit me. I don't support your freaking cause or—"

"Do you want to see your sister again?" Yuri snapped.

Keimaro's heart thumped, and he lowered his head, glaring at Yuri with even more hatred. His hands were tightened into fists that trembled at his side, burning rage flaring up in his chest. He exhaled through his nose and released his hatred for a moment, his fists relaxing into limp hands. He didn't bother answering, knowing that Yuri knew the answer for him.

"You're dismissed until tonight," Yuri said simply, one hand in his pocket. "Go explore the tower and its many public rooms. It has many services to offer that could possibly interest you. However, you will leave the issues regarding your two friends to me. Is that understood? In exchange for your cooperation, we will return your sister. We promise."

"Promises aren't always kept."

"Ours are."

Keimaro pushed himself to his feet, rubbing the bruise on his cheek from the punch. He turned away from Yuri and began to walk off into the crowds of boys and girls from the rebellion who dispersed as soon as he walked past.

Every door on the first floor of the tower was supposedly public, and there were dozens of them. Trying to get his mind off of that humiliating event, he opened a random door that led into what looked like a feasting hall. Without doubt, some type of enchantment had been placed on this mansion. The feasting hall alone looked larger than what the mansion would be able to hold. The ceiling stretched up infinitely; magic again enabled actual clouds to hover in place of a ceiling. The boy didn't even bother questioning the limits of magic.

At the moment, the angered boy was in no mood to marvel incredulously at the magnificence of the wonders around him. Rather, he went and got a keg of beer from a table of what seemed like unlimited refreshments and sat down at one of the longer stretching tables in solitude, separating himself from the rest of the boys and girls that were eating together.

Keimaro took a heavy gulp of his beer, wincing as he felt an odd burn from the strength of the alcohol. What kind of a beer was this? He set down the keg angrily, shaking the table with a bang. *Who the hell does Yuri think he is, bossing me around? We have just met. He is not my superior, and thinking that he will save my sister is foolish. I don't even know whether or not she is alive. And now Noah is dead. Perfect. More and more lives are lost, and that old man Z probably won't take the news too lightly, especially since it was his son.* He took a couple more swigs and closed his eyes, exhaling through his nose. *All I have to do is do what they say until Mai is safe. Then I can do whatever I want. I can even kill everyone here.*

There was a second bang, and Keimaro watched a boy plop down on the seat beside him. The boy had a long scar across his right eye but nevertheless wore a smile across his face. His hair was light blond and rather short, slicked back with some type of fancy oils that probably came from nobility. His clothes also indicated that he was from a rich class. His garment consisted of multicolored silks of blue, red, and white.

He flashed a warm smile in Keimaro's direction. "You must be new around here. I haven't seen you before! What's your name?"

Keimaro tried to ignore the noble, but the boy rambled on. "My name is Aladdin. I am a noble from the upper district, but I came here when Z offered me this incredible opportunity to become something more than just a lazy, fat old man sitting on my bum all day. I don't want to be like my father. I want to be much more, someone big and powerful!"

Keimaro scoffed, glancing at Aladdin from the corner of his eye. "So? That's why you joined the rebellion? So that you can become something more than just a fat lard?"

Aladdin smirked. "Not just that. There's more to me than just that. But overall, I want power—power to destroy my enemies. Not just magical power. I want political power as well. I want to obliterate my opponents, but I also want to inscribe my name in history," he said with a bright smile, flashing perfect white teeth. "I want to become king."

Keimaro almost choked on his beer and coughed a few times before he set down the mug, looking at Aladdin only to find that the noble was completely serious. He smiled. How interesting. "Well, I'm sorry to spoil your dream then. The only person to assassinate the king will be me. I have a personal accord to settle with that old man. It's good that you aren't like him, a fat old man sitting on a throne wasting his days signing useless laws and filling his belly with the finest foods, ripping his rich silks from how big he gets. How is it to be a noble?" He remembered the poor man on the side of the road who had been practically starved to death, his ribs caving in to his own body. Keimaro's eyes flashed a fiery red. "You guys just have everything, don't you? What, your rich father doesn't keep tabs on your whereabouts? Is that how you're here?"

"Quite hostile, aren't you?" Aladdin said with a shrug, understanding. "I wouldn't blame you. Not many like the nobles since they take so much of the wealth in this city and leave so little for the rest of the people. When I become king, I intend to change that. I want to alter this social structure that we have. Why should one family be more revered than another? Why should someone be king who doesn't even deserve the throne?

My reign will change everything," he beamed, "and what is your goal?"

Keimaro was rankled by this noble's attempt to get him to speak. Still, he opened up his true intentions. There was no reason to hide them, not here. "I intend to kill every member of the Bount organization. Then I shall destroy the entire empire of Faar. Every soldier who opposes me will be turned into ash in the face of my hate-filled flames. I'll eradicate every bit of opposition against the Hayashi clan and take my revenge for the deaths of my family and village."

"Ah," Aladdin said with a laugh, "so you're Keimaro Hayashi."

"You've heard of me?"

"We all have." Aladdin grinned. "You're a celebrity around here. Your name, at least. The boy who killed his first man at the age of fourteen and obtained natural fire magic from some meteor from space. Lucky chap, aren't you? Not to mention you've already earned a spot on the Royal Guard after being inside of the city walls for less than twenty-four hours. Now that's either impressive or just damn lucky."

Keimaro shrugged. "That happened not a day ago. I'm surprised that word spread so fast."

"Not much to hear about except for the successes or failures of our members," Aladdin said, leaning back into his chair with a sigh. "You've got a nasty bruise on your face; what's that from?"

"You've got a nasty scar on yours. Why don't you intrigue me with your story, and I'll amuse you with mine?"

Aladdin's face paled a bit at the mention of his scar, but he gathered back his smile within a few moments and guffawed loudly, his voice echoing through the halls but dying quickly in the noise of the rebels around them. His face grew serious, and he shrugged, taking a long gulp of beer before speaking. "Fine,

I'll tell you. As a noble, I was usually untouched and treated well because of my position. As a young boy, my skin was perfect, and I was undoubtedly the most handsome boy amongst all of the nobles—even more handsome than the prince himself."

"There's a prince?"

"Yeah, you didn't know? He's been gone for a while now, off fighting some barbarians with his army, but I'm sure he will be back before you decide to destroy the entire empire single-handedly," Aladdin joked, and Keimaro rolled his eyes with annoyance. "At any rate, the king didn't seem to like me very much. When Aika began to favor me at a rather young age, the king said something about me and called me filth. Interestingly enough, Aika still took a liking to me."

The mention of Aika made Keimaro awaken even more to his story. Aika had taken a liking to this boy? Keimaro looked at Aladdin and could see that indeed his face and hair were matched close to perfection when he took away the scar. "And what happened?"

"Ah, we were so young that it didn't particularly mean anything," Aladdin said, "but the king had a man cut me when I was only twelve so that my face would be ruined. He wanted to separate Aika and me. In fact, it was to set the example that Aika wasn't allowed to be attracted to any males for a while. It was quite painful and scarred quite a bit across my eye. Luckily enough, I still have vision in both eyes," he said with a smile. "At any rate, I have hated that man ever since. A man as disgusting as him shouldn't be upon the throne. I want him off, and I want myself as king. I want him punished for what he did to me and everyone else that he's hurt."

Keimaro lowered his eyes at Aladdin's story. His face had been cut by a blade for his natural beauty? That was a terrible reason. No doubt the noble's family shared a hatred for the king as well. "My story is just that Yuri decided to punch me in the face for being disobedient."

"You don't seem like the obeying type."

"I'm not."

Aladdin smiled at him and leaned back in his chair, inhaling deeply. "So, you're taking place in tonight's show, huh?"

"You know about it already?"

"I heard a few birds chirp here and there."

Keimaro shrugged.

"Are you nervous?"

"Should I be?

Aladdin leaned his elbow against the table and sighed, spinning his empty mug on the table, bored with Keimaro's responses. "Well, you've got to assassinate a few politicians in front of the king, who is the most heavily guarded person in the entire empire. No doubt there'll be dozens, maybe hundreds, of guards against such a small number of you. A large number of the Royal Guard will be there as well. I heard they have a strong reputation for being able to cut down enemies quickly. They eliminate our assassins before we are even able to reach the throne room. I heard a couple of us died last week; they've been strengthening their security, no doubt."

"I'm not afraid of anything," Keimaro said boldly and sighed, standing up. "I need another drink."

"As do I," Aladdin said with a smirk, "but before we do get a drink, might I ask something quickly?"

"Yeah?"

"Do you know someone by the name of Buu?"

Keimaro's eye twitched at the mere mention of his name, and he turned to face Aladdin fully. The bully from Bakaara? How did this guy know his name? *Don't tell me....* His face grew serious. "Yeah. Why, is he alive?"

"He's very much alive and incredibly strong, one of the finest warriors out of all of our assassins. Well, maybe not the finest, but definitely the most aggressive and daring. Ironically, you're from the same village, are you not?" Aladdin said with a sly smirk. "The two of you come from the same place and take your spots at the top of the assassins. What's your secret?"

"We both lost everything," Keimaro muttered. "Not just a cut to the face. Our families were killed before our eyes, and every human we had ever known was left burned to ash or slaughtered on the roads of our own homes. Babes were dashed against walls, and children were left to hang. Everyone else met the brandished steel of Faar," he paused, coughing awkwardly. "So, Buu is eager to see me?" *Do I really want to see that bastard?*

"Quite," Aladdin said. "In fact, overly excited, really. He's been fighting triple the amount that he usually does in the sparring ring. The original amount was already a lot, but now he just fights and fights and fights. Undefeated, he is. I think someone ought to bring him down, you know? I figure he's trying to get your attention."

Keimaro scoffed, sitting back down at the table with Aladdin with a disbelieving shake of his head. "So, that's why you came to me, to find someone to defeat this incredible, undefeated champion of yours?" He looked forward, fire blazing in his eyes. He wanted to fight Buu badly. He wanted to show that bully that he no longer needed Yata as his bodyguard. He wanted to show Buu that he was stronger than he was before. *Much* stronger. Wroth heat shot through his veins, and a smile spread across his face. "I could use a fight. A good one, at least. I have to blow off some steam after Yuri gave me a good whack to the face."

Aladdin's expression brightened as he stood up, patting Keimaro on the back with a grin. "That's it! Show him. I've already bet money on you!"

"What?"

"Oh, well…," Aladdin said with a nervous smile, scratching

the back of his neck. "It's a bit of a rumor that you're a hot-head, so we kind of knew that you would go after Buu. So, there's a bit of a pool of betting going on...."

"How much?"

"Enough to make you rich."

"I get half of your profit if I win."

"Rather greedy, aren't you?" Aladdin murmured with a pout.

Keimaro thought about Aika—and buying her some flowers, but he blinked the thought out of his head. She was royalty; this wasn't his place. Nevertheless, he figured that sooner or later he would need some money. He might as well scrape some of it off of this noble while obtaining some pay from the king for being his Royal Guard. "Quite so. Otherwise, there won't be a fight to see."

Aladdin rolled his eyes and scoffed. "Whatever, fine, fine. Just make sure that you put your maximum effort into this fight. I won't be losing my weekly allowance because you decide to mess around."

Keimaro stood up, cracking his neck. He exhaled air. "I don't mess around. I don't make jokes. I always do my best. And I always win."

***

Darkness. Noah's glasses were cracked on his face and dirtied to the point where he could hardly see anything except shards of images. His hands were stretched into the air and bound by heavy metal clamps like those on his ankles. He was in an empty cell with nothing but rats and disease-infested blankets. Not a single bit of light could be found. Some liquid dripped down from the ceiling; whether it was clean or not couldn't be known, but Noah found himself catching the liquid on his tongue regardless, so parched that he thought he would die from dehydration without any nourishment. He had been beaten relentlessly by the soldiers of Faar and tossed into this cell with no food or water. It had been only a few hours, but his uncomfortable position combined with his broken ribs and injuries to make it feel like an eternity. He wondered when someone would come and just kill him already.

Footsteps sounded nearby, echoing through the underground jail. Perhaps the guards were taking him away for questioning or an execution. Noah closed his eyes and sighed with regret. Why hadn't he taken Yata's hand in that split-second when he could've been saved? Why had he just given up and accepted his fate? The look in Yata's eyes had been so filled with hope.

He yanked on his chains, trying to move forward. They were heavy and ponderous, allowing him to make no progress in moving across his cell to at least touch the iron bars that confined him. Seldom had he ever felt this defeated.

The footsteps grew louder and echoed through the dark recesses of Bassada's underground cells. A light flickered in the distance, a blazing torch that blinded Noah. He turned his head away and winced, writhing against the light. He looked past the torch and saw a large, burly man with heavy, gold-plated armor clamped over a layer of chainmail. At his side, his hand gripped a caged knight's helmet with a red feather hanging loosely from the top. His other steel, gold-rimmed gauntlet was wrapped around a large, thick torch with blazing flames. The man's face was shadowed by the darkness around him, and he was unfamiliar to Noah's eyes.

He walked over to a brazier that had been so encased in the darkness that Noah hadn't noticed it. He lit the brazier, and the area brightened. The shadows retreated back to their corners, and soon Noah felt relieved to be around any sort of human company at all.

Noah saw that the man had a black beard that had recently been trimmed to smooth stubble. His dark eyes wandered over Noah near the fire, and he smiled, showing a golden tooth. His sword was sheathed at his side, the blazing steel hidden. He stood there for a moment in complete silence and sighed when he spoke, "What did you see?"

The question was utterly idiotic. The man knew everything that Noah had seen, yet he still asked the question. Noah knew that this would lead to more beatings, and he closed his eyes, shaking his head. "We didn't see anything," he lied straight to the man's face.

"My name is General Mundo," the man said simply, reaching out and grabbing one of the rusty iron bars with his large gauntlets, squeezing the metal. "I command three of the king's largest armies alone. I am a legend among legends, and you break into a laboratory that is under my supervision and think that you can simply lie to my face?"

"You shouldn't leave entrances to your secret laboratories in a public area then," Noah snapped.

General Mundo raised an eyebrow in amusement at Noah's tenacity and clicked his tongue, pacing back and forth. "Well, well, how do you think we get our experiments? Since there's no reason to hide anything anymore, I figured that I might as well tell you. I capture curious cats that go down there and perform tests on them so that perhaps, one day, Faar can become the ultimate superpower of this planet. A god amongst humans. And the rest of the humans in the world will bow down before our almighty king—or, rather, the genius that created such an invincible army." He smiled at Noah. "The only reason you aren't in a tube like the rest of those poor slum children is that you know specific information regarding Keimaro Hayashi's whereabouts, don't you?"

Noah blinked a few times in disbelief. How the hell did this guy know about Keimaro? Had they already performed the assassination? No, it couldn't be night already. Could it? Then again, who knew the time in a place as dark as this? He lowered his head, a shadow looming over his face. Keimaro hadn't even been with them, and no one else had been caught. How could they even know that he was associated with Z's group? "I don't know who that is," he said simply.

"You're lying again," General Mundo growled. "My intelligence tells me that he has been spending time with your band of blubbering buffoons and that he was spotted last infiltrating the clock tower near the central square this morning while you were off exploring my laboratory." The general was pacing back and forth as if in deep thought with a sly crack of a smile across his face. "And each time I hear his name, the people seem to say it in fear—as if, by some chance, he might actually be a threat to our empire. The guards themselves couldn't confirm him. They could only recognize his voice since they heard him speak, but with that black cloak that he wore, no one can be sure if it was him. Though, some spectators seem to believe that the boy had red eyes. A black cloak … that could be only one of two things, the Bount organization or your group of assassins. Shall I question everyone in this city until I find him? My guards will recognize his voice. Tell me, do you know him?"

Noah shook his head, unknowing. "I don't know! I wasn't informed about any mission involving a clock tower. I don't even understand why they would go up there!" he exclaimed, raising his head to shout, his voice bouncing off of the walls of the dark jail.

General Mundo turned to face him, lacking emotion, his arms robotically at his side. "Well, then, I suppose we will have to extract what you know."

Noah watched as a second figure stepped from the shadows. *What?* he thought. *There was no way that this person could've come here undetected by me. He was standing there the whole time, and I never noticed him?*

A black cowl came over the man's face, and silver skull chains dangled from his neck, posing as a replacement for an amulet. His face was obscured by shadows, and his sleeves ran down much too long for him. The border of his entire cloak itself was red as blood, and all that Noah could see underneath his cowl was a wicked smirk filled with evil. There was no doubt about it; this was a Bount. But even Noah knew that the Bounts were no longer associating themselves with the government. In fact, they hardly had any history together other than hatred. As far as Noah knew, the government and the Bounts were trying to destroy each other. So, why was this Bount member here working with General Mundo?

"Who are you?" Noah demanded, his heart thudding against his chest as he thought of the horrible, torturous things that a Bount could do to him. He wanted to die, to be spared from future pain.

"My name is Danzo," the Bount said with a flashy smile, his face still unknown. His voice was raspy and old, as if stolen by age. He held out his sleeve, an eternal darkness gaping at Noah. Two silver chains burst from the darkness of his sleeves and lashed outward at Noah, wrapping around his arms and legs and finally his throat.

Noah gasped, feeling the air choked from him—or perhaps it was his life. The silver chains began to glow, and the young man felt his memories flash before him. He could see it all. His father, his mother, sitting alone at the side of a beautiful lake, outside of the confines of human society. They were in solitude, a wonderful solitude where they could enjoy the peace of silence. He remembered his mother's long, auburn hair and her flashy white smile that was so bright it could blind even the strongest of men—that, or mesmerize them, like it had Noah's father. Her beauty was incomprehensible, and her blue eyes smiled just as her lips did. He remembered her laughter as they sat beside the lake on that wonderful summer day. The sun beat down on them as they enjoyed a picnic on the softest sand that could make a man fall asleep just from lying in it. It felt like clouds. His memory was vivid as the scene flashed in his mind.

Noah's mother graciously handed him a piece of bread just as men in black cloaks waltzed from the forest behind them, walking on the sand and kicking it up into the air. Dark, ominous clouds filled the sky and blocked out the light of the sun, casting a gloomy shadow across the earth that sapped all happiness. Noah was just a child, still biting on the piece of bread when he glanced to see the man who began it all, the entire Bount organization, Kuro.

The man stormed forward as if he had no time at all, but his smile also showed that he had not a care in the world for anyone as he kicked sand onto their picnic blanket. He stopped before them with two of his men positioned behind him. His black hair had come over his eyes and spiked upward into the air, and he looked only in his thirties with his teeth showing a sly smile.

The features of his face did not age a bit over the years. He put one hand on his hip. He wore different attire from the rest of his men. He had a black shirt that exposed his muscles, squeezing his arms to make them bulge all the more, looking as if he were suffocating his own flesh. A black belt was wrapped tightly around his waist, inscribed with some type of golden text that Noah had not been able to make out. His pants drooped to the ground, ripped and tattered, as if he had borrowed a slave's clothing. But what caught young Noah's attention were his eyes—those glowing red eyes that could make anyone stare at them in absolute wonder. The two rubies that gleamed brighter than any gems in all of the kingdoms and all of the continents, filled with the glow of life. He smiled and spoke to Zylon, Noah's father.

Zylon looked the same as he did now and retaliated with some words that were muffled in Noah's memory, incapable of remembering any specifics. Then Noah watched as horror after horror took place.

Kuro moved forward to strike Zylon, knocking Noah's father to the earth with a single flick of his hand. He raised his fist to smash Zylon into the ground once more, but Noah's mother leapt between them, latching onto the Hayashi man's arm. Kuro glared at her with annoyance and swatted her with the back of his hand, sending her back into the ground. He burst out with laughter at the woman's insolence. This was the first and last time that Noah had ever seen his mother humiliated and downgraded in such a horrible way that he could hardly watch. Yet, watch he did, with his lips quivering and tears filling his eyes. He could do nothing but sit there and watch as Kuro drew his blade in annoyance.

Zylon had gotten up and was ready to lash forward at Kuro but was grabbed by the other Bounts who slammed him down into the ground, as Noah watched helplessly, apparently forgotten. Zylon screamed, kicking and thrashing as if he were a little boy trying to break free. The word that left his lips was clear and painful to hear: "NO!"

Noah turned to Kuro and saw that the man was now looking straight at him with a vile smile spread from ear to ear. He thrust his gleaming steel downward into Noah's mother, the most beautiful woman in the world. As blood sprayed into the air, young Noah grew numb, oblivious to what was happening. He heard her blood-curdling scream but just stood there, the bread still in his mouth, though he wasn't chewing. A pool of blood began to form underneath her body, soaking into her rich silks as her voice died and Zylon's cries replaced it. The young boy stood there with shock in his eyes, turning to see Zylon watching with a look of despair.

Noah's day had transformed entirely as he lowered his head and tears began to stream down his cheeks, realization taking its place. He sobbed and sobbed, but the men wouldn't stop beating his father. And they wouldn't bring back his mother. All that he could do was cry.

***

General Mundo watched as the boy's eyes went blank, the color erased from his irises. His skin began to pale as he shook furiously as if there were an earthquake. The general glanced at Danzo, who was performing some type of magic through these mystical chains that came from his sleeve. He smiled as the chains went limp and retracted back into his cloak as quickly as they had come, leaving Noah completely limp.

The boy's face smashed into the dirt as he fell unconscious, lying there.

General Mundo looked at Danzo with a questionable stare. "Is everything all right, Lord Danzo?"

"Yeah," Danzo said, "when you enter someone's head, you witness their memories and their pains. You share their mind and feel everything that they have felt. Their frustration, their agony, their pain, their sorrow. All of it. I suppose it's this particular magic that has left me withered and rickety like an old, used toy for Kuro. Nevertheless, I've found a location for Keimaro Hayashi, and I have everything I need. However," he said, raising his head, "the information will be disclosed at the opportune moment. The Bount organization doesn't strike until the time is right. And now is not the time. We will let their band of assassins do as they wish until we are ready. For now, release the boy. He is not a threat. Not anymore."

***

Zylon sat at his desk with a sullen look on his face as he received the news of his son's capture. No doubt Noah was dead. That fool. How could he possibly have let himself be captured like that? He lowered his eyes with a sigh.

At a faint rustle, he looked up and saw Yuri, Yata, and Gavin standing in the room. He turned to Yata and Gavin. "The two of you witnessed his falling, correct?"

"Yes, sir," Gavin said respectfully.

"I reached out to him," Yata said, "but he didn't take my hand. Instead, he let the rocks come down. There was a chance, but...."

"He didn't take it."

"Yes."

Zylon shook his head, closing his eyes as he finally felt age bearing down upon him. For once, he felt like an old man. He spun around on his chair to face his large window, looking out at the green gardens behind him so that his assassins could no longer see his face. "Not particularly the best first expedition out into the city, I suppose," he said, his voice weak. He had learned to control himself for the most part after having lived for several centuries. He had lost many of his good friends in that amount of time. He was used to this numbness that he currently felt. "Was the mission a success?"

"Yes, sir," Gavin said. "The demonstrating and testing of chemicals on live humans is inhumane and should be stopped immediately. The government is being selfish. To make an ultimate empire based on magic would be effective, but the costs are beyond imagining, treating humans as if they are lab rats. Treating the homeless, maids, and slaves as if they are nothing more than animals to be tested on is wrong. They are still human. I will fight beside you. You have my sword," he announced, though his voice showed insecurity, as if he weren't sure if his own life meant much anymore. "I believe that it is my fault for his death, sir. I will take full responsibility. If I had not wanted to go down there into that lab…."

"You brought something back with you, didn't you?" Zylon interrupted, trying to change the conversation from his son. "A human that has been tested on, but survived, correct?"

"Yes, sir."

"You're awfully polite," Zylon said, spinning back in his chair, his hands on his desk as he leaned forward toward the assassins. "So? What exactly do you have for me?"

Yuri took a step forward and began to speak. "It seems that *it* is a human with supernatural capabilities, Z. I don't know what to say about it, but somehow it managed to survive. Its body enables it to actually use two different types of magic at the same time, something that usually isn't capable unless it steals its magic from a foreign power that isn't from this world, like Keimaro or Kuro," he said, and Zylon's body stiffened.

"How is that possible?"

"We don't know," Yuri said. "Lena is examining it now."

208

Zylon nodded and turned around once more to face the window. "Get some rest. Tonight is the public announcement of Keimaro. We need to be prepared for it. Noah's capture will not delay us, for this is a very rare opportunity for everyone to be grouped up like this. Make sure you're ready."

"All right," Yuri said, "but there's one more thing. The lab experiment's eyes. They have the Shokugan. It seems that she could be from the Hayashi clan."

13. OLD RIVALRIES

Keimaro gulped down a piece of meat as he walked through one of the public doors with Aladdin. The door beside it had been completely surrounded with people, assassins lining up simply to access it. He hadn't seen why it was so popular, but the door that he and Aladdin had entered was completely empty. On the other side of the magic door was a dark corridor with torches lighting the path before him and shadows creeping along the walls. The door closed behind him, and he could see a light at the end of the hallway, bright white. His shadow traveled along the dirty stone walls as he followed Aladdin, his boots crunching on the sandy floors, which seemed to be made of some type of clay. His heart was pounding at the roaring cheers of what sounded like thousands of people. "Where are we going?"

"To the arena," Aladdin answered.

Keimaro blinked and stopped at a door to the right of the hallway that Aladdin pushed open to reveal a massive array of weapons similar to the weapons room that Z had kept on the upper floor next to his office. He shook his head, pushing his cloak to reveal his sheathed sword at his side. Aladdin nodded in understanding, closed the door to the weapons room, and continued down the hallway.

"It sounds like there's so many people," Keimaro muttered.

"There's a lot," Aladdin said with a chuckle. "It's the main entertainment around here. We fight each other to become stronger, yes? We spar and use our magic to create even more devastating fights. Watching them is breathtaking and makes us wonder what we can do. Taking place in them helps you find out how strong you are, and also how weak. Buu has been challenging and fighting in this arena for a while now, and he has defeated everyone he's come across. He's bloodthirsty for some real competition. I hope you're ready to give it your all."

"How in god's name can an arena fit inside of a mansion?" Keimaro wondered aloud. But that wasn't really what was on his mind. *Buu is the champion around here? He must've gotten a lot stronger from when we were kids. Does he have magic?* If Buu had obtained the title of champion amongst a population of magical assassins, he truly must've had something to offer.

"How can you conjure flames from your body? Why don't you ask the gods? Magic." Aladdin guffawed at his comment as they reached the end of the hallway, where an iron gate stood before them.

Keimaro was blinded for several moments as an artificial sun seemed to shine down from the sky. The more he wondered about how they fit this arena in here or how the sky was so blue or how the sun shined so like to the real one, the more he confused himself. Magic didn't have to be explained, he supposed; it was just a wonder. His eyes looked outward in awe and saw a stretching sandy plain that was scorched with flames. Stands surrounded the entire battlefield with seats, and people filled every inch of the area as they cheered, thrusting their hands into the air at the battle before them. Keimaro scoffed. This wasn't much of a place to train. This was a gladiator arena.

Keimaro saw a girl in the arena with long blonde hair and sapphire blue eyes. She danced through the air, leaping gracefully with elegant flips that even Keimaro was sure he couldn't perform. She landed on her feet, whipping a skinny rapier with fast jabs at the air. As he watched, the jabs became physical light, transforming into golden energy as they fired small, needle-like projectiles at her target across the battlefield. The boy's eyes scanned the arena and finally locked onto the person he sought: Buu.

Buu was easily recognizable, not losing a single bit of his ladies' charm. His curly brown hair had gotten a bit longer, and his glowing blue eyes matched Aladdin's, making him look as if he were of some noble descent. His lips were thick, and his skin lacked a single scar or mark upon it, as smooth as a baby's. He wore no top, exposing his large, toned muscles in the sun. His skin itself was a crispy tan from clearly spending much time in the sun—and perhaps too much time fighting in the arena. He smiled with the thrill of battle, and Keimaro could see the fire in his eyes.

The former bully had leapt through the air with elegance and flipped, landing on the ground as the daggers of light flew underneath him, burying themselves into the stone wall behind him. They flickered for a moment and then died out, shattering into gleaming pieces of light before disintegrating entirely. It was as if they had never been there. The former bully's feet planted heavily into the dirt as he grinned. His entire body vanished.

Keimaro's eyes widened, unable to spot where Buu had gone. Was that his magical ability? Teleportation? As he watched, Buu appeared behind the girl, driving his fist solidly into the girl's back. She gasped and staggered forward, swinging her rapier, but Buu was already gone. Keimaro stared, incredulous. *This is insane.*

Buu teleported all around the girl, barraging her with unpredictable patterns of rapid punches and kicks, his knuckles smashing relentlessly into this poor blonde girl as her rapier continuously met open air, incapable of predicting where he would be next. Finally, Buu appeared across the arena. He was winding up his fist, spinning his arm to gain momentum while his opponent was swaying, barely conscious. She raised her rapier in some attempt at defense, but Buu's teleportation was too fast. He had already begun to swing his fist while across the battlefield, but he teleported with perfect time. He reappeared in front of the blonde girl with his fist already in motion, cracking across the poor girl's face and sending her spinning wildly through the air to land on her back, gasping for air. The crowd roared with amusement as boys and girls of multiple ages leapt to their feet and cheered for the champion, clearly thirsty for more bloodshed.

"So?" Aladdin asked. "Are you ready?"

Keimaro didn't answer the noble as he stomped forward. His hands touched the metal with such burning heat that the gate melted, turning into a glowing, red, molten liquid and creating an opening. The metal glowed like bright lava and receded. He stepped through the opening and heard the crowd of entertained assassins go silent as he moved forward onto the sand before anyone was even able to retrieve the girl from the danger zone. The dirt crunched underneath his feet, sounding loud in the dead silence. He felt all eyes on him, but he didn't care. He stopped before Buu, a wind ruffling his black hair so that it blew past his eyes. He could see the wild grin on the boy's face.

"Ah, the gallant Keimaro Hayashi has blessed up with his presence!" Buu exclaimed, his arms in the air. The crowd went wild in response, cheering and stomping their feet, rumbling the earth around them. Buu's eyes were wide, and he licked his lips. "I don't know if you remember me, but I used to beat on your wimpy ass every day since grade school."

"Yeah," Keimaro said, unbuttoning his cloak and brushing back his cape. He took it off as Aladdin sauntered onto the battleground behind him. He tossed his cloak to the noble, who caught it with a questionable look, but didn't complain. Then Keimaro pulled off his shirt to reveal his body just as Buu had so that they were on even terms. The girls in the crowd squealed with amusement as he tossed it to Aladdin as well. The noble rolled his eyes in disgust as he grabbed the unconscious blonde girl and dragged her away. "No armor, just like you."

"You're still picking fights with, aren't you?" Buu scoffed. "I've heard a lot about you, you know. Quite famous, you are. Taking the spotlight with your name, the last of the Hayashi clan. What a joke. You're nothing but a bastard, an adopted child with no real parents. You're of dirtied blood. You're a Hayashi, a demon. Nothing but a monster and an abomination to us all. Why didn't you just die off in the Bakaara massacre? I would've preferred anyone to survive but you and that blabbering idiot, Yata. Why did all of my friends and family have to die, but you had to survive? Huh?" he snarled.

Keimaro's eyes morphed into a glowing red, filled with hatred. "I'm growing annoyed with you and your meaningless words. I came here to humiliate you, not make small talk about the past."

"About the past?" Buu burst out in uncontrollable laughter, his head tilted back as he bellowed. "How can I forget the past? Have you forgotten it? Clearly not, otherwise you wouldn't be here, would you? You and I are here for the same reason. We both want Faar to be destroyed for what they've done to our village and our families and friends. Every single one of my friends was killed! How ironic that you, the demon, survived along with your only friend! How funny is that? You see, I know why Faar came on that day. They wanted you, Keimaro. The Hayashi clan massacre, I learned all about it. You survived, somehow. You survived! And they went to our village to finish the goddamn job! So, what are you doing here, huh? You should've killed yourself and been done with it already! None of us want you here. All you'll do is attract the Faar soldiers to us and get us all killed just like what happened four years ago."

Flames sparked around Keimaro and howled, gathering on his skin, but they didn't burn him. Instead, they wrapped around him like tight armor as he felt hatred surge through him. "Rankle me no more with your pointless prattling. It's about time that someone quelled your small title of *champion*. Your words are like pebbles being thrown at a wall," he said, slowly unsheathing his sword. The blade scraped against his sheath as it entered the cool air, brandishing into the glowing sun. He whirled the weapon and held it out before him. *I'll destroy him. This is payback.*

Buu's face turned red with frustration, but he held his tongue. He reached behind him and pulled out two iron gloves that he slid onto his hands. He clenched the gloves, and the iron seemed to bend into movement with his hands, crunching as they curled. He slammed fist against fist, the metal gloves giving off a spark as they collided. "I'll show you the difference between us in power. And this is perfect! You won't have your little bodyguard, Yata, interfering with your battles any longer. He won't be here to protect you this time!" He roared, rushing forward at Keimaro with incredible speed. His bare feet thumped against the sandy ground as he sprinted, his image becoming a blur.

Keimaro knew that Buu wouldn't rush him directly. He would teleport and come from another direction. But from where, the sides, or behind? He turned around in a random guess but blinked when he saw that Buu had actually come from the right with his fist already in motion. Swinging his fist before the teleportation meant that Keimaro would have less time to dodge. Keimaro grunted as he swung around, the iron gauntlet missing his face by only several centimeters. He felt the force of the punch on his skin. Contact with that iron to the face was a frightening thought. He staggered away, disengaging from his opponent, his heart beating quickly. There was no way to actually escape Buu because he could just teleport across the entire distance in an instant, closing in on him. He had to be on his toes throughout the fight. There was not going to be a single moment when he would be safe.

Buu's fists barraged him, each blow coming from a different direction. There was no particular pattern to his attacks; Keimaro had made sense of that already. After so many times in the arena, Buu probably knew that having a pattern was what opponents could use to dodge his attacks. But without a pattern, it was literally impossible to avoid.

Keimaro grunted, his body furiously being thrashed about as he tried to maneuver and dodge the attacks in time. Yes, his Shokugan eyes allowed for him to see the attacks long before they even reached him, but it was physically strenuous for him to dodge such fast and sudden attacks. His head tilted to the side as a fist flew past his cheek once more, but the second blow coming at his stomach was unavoidable. The iron sank into his abdomen, and he lurched forward, feeling as if all the beer he had just drunk was going to come up. He spat saliva out onto the ground as his breath was emptied from his lungs. His hands grasped onto Buu's forearm and began to release intense heat onto his flesh, burning into his skin.

Buu yelped in pain and vanished from Keimaro's grip before the burn got too serious. He appeared behind Keimaro with a downward kick that cracked down on Keimaro's back, forcing the boy onto his knees. The sly teleporter flipped through the air and gripped both of his gauntlets, coming down with a crashing blow toward Keimaro's skull with an evil grin across his face. His expression changed as a wall of flames expanded outward from Keimaro's body. He teleported away as fast as he could, gasping as he saw the bottoms of his pants singed from the flame. He beat at any small fires that clung to his clothes and glared at Keimaro. "Hey, you've got some neat tricks. Where'd you get that power, huh? Something that the old man handed down to you? You were always such a secretive fellow."

Keimaro grasped his stomach; his diaphragm felt as if it were pulsing, and his ribs burned with pain. He winced as he pushed himself onto his feet once more with a shake of his head. He stood tall, the crowd cheering in response. He cracked his neck a few times.

"I remember vividly now. I saw them kill your mother," Buu said with a chuckle. "You know, I just happened to pass by. They might've had some fun with her, too, those soldiers. I don't know, but I turned away and kept walking so that I could warn my own family. But that's unfortunate for your mother. Why weren't you there for her, huh, Keimaro?" he called out, and the crowd fell silent as they waited for Keimaro's response. *Why weren't you there?*

Keimaro could take any hateful words, but lies like that made him want to murder Buu. He moved forward, his eyes glowing like two coals dipped in molten lava. Smoke rose off of his body as flames generated along his fist. No words could leave his mouth for fear that he might accidentally release a jet of flame outward instead. *Make him pay for everything that he's done to you*, a voice boomed in his head.

"Oh, the demon comes to his senses, huh?" Buu yelled, sprinting forward as he leapt into the air. "You deserve to die. It is all your fault that Bakaara is gone, you stupid, insolent bastard of a child! Your mother deserved every bit of pain she got from those soldiers for raising a child straight from the depths of hell!" His image vanished.

Keimaro's eyes could see everything that happened. He saw the magic somehow. A glowing, swirling void in the air sucked Buu's body into the hole, making him vanish in an instant. His knuckles cracked from how hard he clenched his fist, and he spun around, seeing the portal reappear behind him. With unnatural clarity, he rocketed his fist outward, rotating it before Buu had even appeared. When the boy did, he met a fist solidly to the face. There was a crack as the fire-filled fist collided with Buu's face, Keimaro's body rotating as he drove his opponent straight into the ground with full force. The boy felt drained of energy, but his body was singing with wrath he wanted to unleash on Buu, eager to barrage the former bully with fire-filled punches and tear him apart after what he had said.

But Keimaro did nothing more. Instead, his demonic eyes glared straight into the blue pools of Buu, the boy shaking as blood streamed down from his broken nose. Small burns marked his cheeks, and he stared, trembling, awaiting more blows to rain down on him. None came.

Keimaro knew that Buu could no longer move after a blow like that. In fact, he was impressed that the boy was still conscious. The silence dragged out for a moment longer before the crowd roared in approval, the earth thundering from their bellows of amusement. The boy stared down at Buu with a sullen look before Aladdin rushed to his side and thrust his limp hand into the air to claim the victory.

In his heart, he felt no such victory. All he felt was pain at

217

the reminder of his mother's fate. He didn't believe that she had been abused, but her death was enough to bring tears to his eyes. *Why weren't you there for your own mother when she needed you most?* Keimaro lowered his head, looking away from his opponent. Buu stared at him weakly. He felt that perhaps he had gone too far.

"Keimaro Hayashi," Yuri boomed, his roar silencing every single assassin that had taken the time to watch the battle. They all shrank away as the werewolf stomped forward down the steps of the stands and locked gazes with Keimaro, glaring at him with his beastly eyes. "And what on earth do you think you're doing? You know we have plans for tonight. Why do you insist on risking injury?"

"I was having a reunion," Keimaro muttered, pulling his arm from Aladdin's and grabbing his clothing from the noble. He slid on his shirt and threw on his cloak, his cape flapping behind him as he walked forward to the stands, looking up at Yuri. The ten-foot walls were all that separated them. "So? How might I help you?"

Yuri simply stared at him and rolled his eyes. "We have something that we need to show you. It's confidential. Meet me on the top floor immediately."

***

As he walked up the long spiral stairs, Keimaro was lectured on how he should've been resting and eating rather than fighting in the arena. All he could do was block out Yuri's words and think about how annoying it was to walk up all these stairs. He wished they had just used the teleporting platform like when he'd first arrived at the mansion. He wiped some sweat off of his brow, and Yuri stopped at the top floor, looking at a servant passing by. Keimaro hadn't even been aware that the mansion had servants. Then again, he supposed that it made sense, since Z had to be rich to afford all of these magic rooms.

"Your servant will lead you to the private bathing house. It's indoors, so I warn you to bring a torch—and more than one, at that. Otherwise, it could get quite dark if the water accidently puts out the first one," Yuri said with a shrug. "Not the best experience and not the most pleasant bath either. Anyway, make sure to come to me at the infirmary once you've cleaned yourself up. We have something to show you."

The servant wore a black dress that stopped mid-thigh, while white stockings stretched up several inches past her knees. Her long, brown hair hung down perfectly combed like a princess's without a single knot in it. Her hazel eyes averted from Keimaro as her cheeks flushed red. She held her hands behind her back shyly, inadvertently drawing attention to the red bow at the top of her breasts that kept her dress together. She definitely didn't seem like the type who would normally be a maid. In fact, she already looked quite shaken just from wearing the dress. *Perhaps it's her first day?*

"Around here," Yuri said, "being a servant for a day or a week is typically a punishment for the assassins. Mika here tried to steal food from the kitchens at midnight." He patted her head gently as if she were some type of a dog, causing her to pale and knit her eyebrows. "Make sure not to embarrass her. She hates that. Though she can't do anything about it today, she will make you pay for humiliation afterward. Isn't that right, Mika?"

"I'll destroy you," Mika muttered, crossing her arms with an angry pout.

Yuri chuckled and gave Keimaro a small wave before he walked off.

Keimaro blinked a few times as he found himself left alone with Mika. He scratched his neck gently. "Uh ... so...."

"Just come with me," Mika muttered assertively and walked off down the hallway with a towel in her hands.

Keimaro blinked a few times, watching the sway of her hips as she scampered down the hallway. He sighed, sliding his hands into his pockets as he walked after her. He followed her into a room, unsurprised to find himself in some type of hot spring, despite the fact that they were inside of the mansion. Rocks surrounded a rather large pool of water with steam rising into the air. A white artificial light floated in the air, shining down into the bath. It would seem that he wouldn't need a torch after all. The boy beamed as he looked at Mika.

"This place never ceases to amaze me," he said with a radiant smile. She simply left the towel and quickly stumbled past Keimaro, fleeing to the hallway. He watched her for a moment, not sure what he had done to repel her. He closed his eyes and turned away, closing the door behind him. He sighed as half the room was encased in shadows that crept along his feet.

The boy undressed and left his cloak and shirt on the floor before stepping into the hot springs. The water felt natural and clean—and scalding hot. It took several minutes for him to ease himself in, but when he finally did, he was completely relaxed. He exhaled as he leaned back against the side of the springs, feeling the cool air evaporate the hot water off of his skin. The steam drifted upward, obscuring his vision, creating a screen around him. The rocks that surrounded the hot springs were smooth and, oddly enough, felt more like pillows than they did rocks. Leaning back and relaxing, he looked blankly at the clear waters before him and imagined himself in front of an ocean, just like he had read about in books when he had lived in Bakaara. *Ah, if the Bakaara massacre never happened, I could be pursuing my dream of becoming an explorer rather than an assassin. It's hard to say it, but I miss the old days in Bakaara.*

He sighed. Although he knew that being associated with this organization benefitted him, he felt like an outsider already—shunned, as he had been in his youth. From the stares he received from other assassins, he was clearly the hot topic of the hour. Without a doubt, he would get more of a reputation after his showdown with Buu. From Mika's reaction, fear of him was arising in the hearts of other assassins. Perhaps he had come across as a bully? He hadn't wanted that. He'd never wanted anyone to misjudge him this way. He closed his eyes. This felt like Bakaara all over again. Everyone had a dark perception of him, and he'd been here only a day!

"Why do you care so much about other people's opinions?"

Keimaro's head snapped up, his eyes widening. From the dark shadows of the room, a figure emerged. It was another version of him, except with the Shokugan activated. His eyes were red and glowing angrily, and the clone wore an evil smile upon his face. Keimaro's heart pounded with uncertainty—was he was just seeing things, or was this doppelganger an actual physical being? He stayed frozen in the hot springs, unmoving.

"What, cat got your tongue?" the clone said with an amused smirk, putting a hand on his hip. He wore his cloak and all of his clothing, but the resemblance was purely physical. The doppelganger scoffed, his attitude clearly different from the original Keimaro's. "Your objective here is revenge! Not to make friends, is it? Who the hell cares what these other people think of you? What matters is that you use them to get what you want."

"No," Keimaro muttered. "I'm not just here for revenge. I'm also here to change humanity's views on the Hayashi clan! If everyone fears me, then I won't be accomplishing anything! I'll still be a monster in their eyes, and nothing will have changed from four years ago!" he exclaimed. "Who are you?"

"I'm you," the clone said with a chuckle, his eyes flashing bright red. "The real you. The one who is set on his goal. The one who is willing to do anything in order to destroy his enemies and claim Hayashi clan dominance over the human civilization."

"The Hayashi clan isn't dominant!"

"Why is it that we are faster, stronger, and better than other humans, then?" The clone paced back and forth as he spoke, a smile printed on his face. He never stopped watching Keimaro. "Tell me. Why are we able to destroy entire armies of humans alone? Why do the gods want us extinct? Why is it unfair for us to live on this earth? Why do other humans see us as monsters? Haven't you ever asked yourselves these questions? Oh, of course, you have. After all, I would know," he said, stopping in front of Keimaro so that he was looking down on the naked boy. "It's because we aren't human. We are a whole race separate

221

from humanity. We are an improved version, and the gods knew it was unfair for us to share the same land with their prized, inferior creations, the humans. That's why they called for our elimination, Keimaro. That is why our mother and father are dead! Our true parents, not those fake guardians that didn't give a single crap about us."

Keimaro lowered his head, glaring at the clone. "You've said enough."

The clone wasn't done. "Our lives are ruined by humanity, yet you want to be friends with them, don't you? You're soft. You want these humans to accept you as one of them, huh? Why would you want that? It was humans that killed your new mother, too, and obliterated your village. It was humanity that declared that your entire clan be annihilated! All of the pain that you've experienced in your life," he cackled with laughter, tilting his head back as he did so, "has been because of humans! So why in hell's name do you wanna side with a race as disgusting as them?"

"Shut up!" Keimaro growled, swiping his hand. A burst of flame roared outward at the clone. In an instant, the image shimmered and vanished into thin air. The boy's heart was thumping rapidly and he was gasping when Mika threw the door open, her eyes wide with fear. With a glance, she saw that the towel had caught fire and quickly flicked her wrist. Water came to life from the springs and flowed freely through the air to touch upon the flames. The flow doused the fire's rage, leaving nothing but smothering smoke.

Mika exhaled and turned to face Keimaro with a frown. "What happened? I was worried! Why were you yelling? Who were you talking to?"

Keimaro blinked and realized that the entire thing had been an illusion. Was he going mad? Something like that had never happened before. He shook his head and sighed. "No, it's nothing," he muttered. He climbed out of the springs, water dripping off of his body.

Mika squealed and turned away, her hands folded over her lap as a rosy blush bloomed on her cheeks. "Cover yourself up before you get up like that!" she exclaimed, rushing out of the room.

Keimaro watched her for a moment and chuckled to himself, picking up the ashy towel. He dried himself and put his clothes back on, zipping up the front of his cloak. He cracked his neck, walking to the doorway of the room, where he saw Mika waiting outside to lead him to his next destination. He gave her a small nod before he turned back to glance into the darkness of the hot springs. What on earth had that incident been? Was he going insane? *I should tell Yata about this.* But, at the same time, a part of him didn't want to. Illusions would make Yata worry about him and make him cautious. He could see Yata urging him not to take part in tonight's assassination.

He blinked and closed the door behind him, giving Mika a small smile. He scratched the back of his neck as he tried to explain why he'd had the sudden outburst moments before. In the back of his mind, there was a slight worry because, for once, it seemed that Keimaro was powerless.

***

Keimaro stared in disbelief at what Yuri had to show him. His eyes were widened and his teeth gritted together. His hands shook furiously at his side as he saw a skinny young girl who bore a striking similarity to the man he had seen in the poor side of the city. She looked so malnourished that he found it hard to even look at her without feeling empathy. Where had they gotten her, and how was she important to the organization? The closer he looked, the more certain he grew that he recognized this girl. She was the one that Yata and Gavin had brought through the front door of Zylon's mansion. Her long, black hair had grown to her lower back from a lack of cutting. She rested upon a soft white mattress in the infirmary. She was asleep or unconscious; he couldn't tell. He glanced at Yuri, who was looking at the girl with little emotion. "Who is she?"

"We were hoping that you could tell us that."

"Huh?" Keimaro blinked, raising an eyebrow.

Gavin was standing beside the bed, his position rather stiff. He seemed traumatized after the loss of Noah. Yuri nodded to him, and the soldier lifted one of the girl's lids, revealing her iris was a glowing red color.

Keimaro's heart thumped as he stared. The Shokugan. Why did this girl have it? Were they somehow related? He had believed that the Hayashi clan had been massacred. Were there more out there? She was too old to be Keimaro's sister. Who was she? "Where did you find her?" he demanded of Yuri.

"That's confidential."

"You showed Gavin, a person that you almost killed because you didn't trust him!" Keimaro snarled. "Do you want me to help at all? If so, you should probably stop being so secretive around me and tell me where the hell you found this girl!"

Yuri raised an eyebrow at Keimaro's sudden aggressiveness and exhaled. "We found her in a government alchemy lab underground. They have been performing experiments on humans in the poorer districts—people who were already doomed to die. Many of the lab experiments perished in the process. However, when Yata, Gavin, and Noah went down there to investigate, they found this girl. She's alive. And she has the Shokugan. This begs the question of whether the government is transplanting the eyes of other members of the Hayashi clan into fresh hosts. Perhaps they kept the eyes of those who were killed instead of destroying the bodies."

"You're saying they scavenged the dead members of the Hayashi clan in order to perform tests on live humans?" Keimaro said with disbelief, finding more hatred building up in his body. *These bastards have gone too far. That isn't human! How dare they?*

224

"That is our current hypothesis, yes," Yuri said. "Tests show that she's an ordinary human and that these eyes were actually surgically implanted."

"Has she awakened yet?"

"Nope, she's been asleep for hours now."

Keimaro sighed. "Allow me to speak to her when she awakens. What's the plan with Noah? When are we sending a rescue mission?"

"Rescue mission?" Z's voice echoed as Keimaro glanced over his shoulder to find the man sauntering down the infirmary toward them, his hands neatly behind his back. "And why would we do so?"

"It's your son...." Keimaro frowned.

"And that would only risk our lives for one that is already doomed to perish. Not to mention it would kill time and possibly even resources. If one of us is captured in the process of trying to *rescue* someone who is already going to die, they could give away the location of our hideout," Z said. "Noah cannot give us away. He swallowed a magic tag that makes him incapable of giving away our position. Therefore, we have nothing to fear."

Yata, who had been standing beside Gavin, took a step forward. "It's not right to leave one of our comrades to die like that!" he exclaimed. "He's your son! Don't you care? I could've saved him. But I didn't! Allow me to at least—"

"No," Z said simply, his facial expression completely emotionless. "You all must prepare for tonight's mission. Nothing else must be on your mind. I have already accepted my son's fate. Perhaps it's about time that you all grew up and understood that it's not worth it to be wasting your time with a hopeless chore when there are more *important* things at stake! It's better to put your time and energy into something that will make their sacrifice worthwhile. How did my son die?"

"He let himself be captured so that we could get away, sir," Gavin reported, his head lowered.

"Precisely. It was his intention to be captured, so that you may continue his legacy," Z said. "Don't let his sacrifice go to waste. By going in to try to save him, you will be doing exactly what the enemy wants. They'll kill you. Or, even worse, they'll capture you. And if they capture you, it'll be the end of every single person in this mansion. The entire rebellion will be crushed, and everyone will perish. Thousands of families will be devastated when they find the remains of their children underneath the debris of this mansion. And this world will be destroyed when the Bounts gain power. It's not worth the risk; do you understand? Get prepared for the mission." Z walked past them, ignoring the girl on the bed, and exited through a door on the far side of the stretching infirmary.

Keimaro watched him go and saw that Yata was shaking. He could practically see the guilt and weight of Noah's death upon his friend's shoulders. He wanted to go over and comfort him, but Yuri blurted out, "It's time to go over the plan. We're going to the weapons room. You have ten minutes to get there. We will begin debriefing with or without you," he said simply to everyone before he walked away.

Gavin and Yata followed, but Lena stopped in front of Keimaro before he was able to progress with his friends. "There's something bothering you, isn't there?" she said, putting her hands on her hips with a small smile. "I can tell."

Keimaro blinked. "How?"

"I'm a girl. I know everything!" Lena giggled and walked over to a window beside the unconscious girl's bed. She propped herself on the sill, glancing out the window at the gleaming bright sun. She could see the training fields outside where dozens of rebels and assassins were engaging in combat to hone their skills with hopes that one day their aspirations would become a reality. "So? What is it that's bothering you?"

"It's nothing, really."

226

"You don't want to talk about it, huh?" Lena remarked, still watching the training outside. "You know what really amazes me with this entire *magic* thing? To be honest, I find it quite unnatural to use these weird artificial powers in order to overpower another human being. It's unfair since ninety-nine percent of the population doesn't have access to magic. So, the one percent that does ... well, they're usually considered freaks or supernatural geniuses. Either way, I never really liked the unfair idea of changing your humanity in order to become stronger. Why not become stronger as a human being rather than becoming something else? I guess that's why I never took up magic myself. Not to mention my father would *kill* me if he found me shooting fire around like you do!" She chuckled softly.

Keimaro smiled at her. "Your father knows that you're in a giant rebellion against the king, risking your life every day for the betterment of the people? That's not something that he can brag about, you know."

"Yeah," Lena said, kicking her legs slowly, watching her feet sway forward and back, "but I don't think he minds. He likes that I'm fighting for what I believe in. Besides, he thinks that the government is unjust as well. So many people die every single day. So many people that really could just be living normal lives if the government didn't interfere and tax them to death. It was really the whole lab thing that finally broke the straw for me and made me join Zylon's rebellion against the king. I suppose that's probably what convinced your friend Gavin as well."

"I suppose. Do you have your own personal reason for wanting to go against the king?" Keimaro asked.

"Of course," Lena said, her voice becoming small suddenly. "Everyone in this place does. We all have our own stories to tell. Mine is about how my father wasn't able to pay the taxes one day, so the guards took my mother and imprisoned her. They had their way with her, and I guess that's how she had my little sister. Then they killed my mother since my father still wasn't able to pay off the debt. We got to keep my little sister at least. I just...," Lena choked on her words and straightened her back, her lips quivering a bit, "I don't know why anyone would ever do that to another human being. Just for money...."

"Hey," Keimaro said, putting his hand over hers, which was shaking furiously. He looked into her eyes and gave her a reassuring smile. "We can change things. We *will* change things. Don't lose hope, ever. You're extremely strong; I hope you know that. I promised that I would destroy this disgusting government that they have set up. Today is the first step to our overthrowing of the king. It's like Z said, we won't let anyone's deaths be in vain."

Lena's face lit up, and she smiled, revealing a set of perfect white teeth. "Yeah, you're right. I don't know what I'm being all depressed about. You're really nice, you know, despite all the rumors that they have going on about you."

"Rumors?"

"Well," Lena said with a shrug, "you know. There were already rumors about the Hayashi clan still existing. Most of humanity believes that you guys are demons disguised as humans that are trying to destroy the human race or something. Overall, some of these idiots think that you're evil, but you're not! I...." Lena saw the look of despair on Keimaro's face and knew that she had hit a sore spot. "Oh, so that's what's bothering you. It shouldn't bother you. You don't need everyone in the world to love you. After all, their opinion matters nothing to you."

"They don't? It does hurt, you know," Keimaro muttered, looking down at his hands, which dangled now between his legs. "It hurts to be called a monster by everyone and to never have any friends. It hurts to be an outsider that's always watching others be happy. All that I've ever endured is pain for being the abomination that I have been since birth."

Keimaro suddenly felt her arms around him, and he blinked, feeling his face turn bright red with embarrassment as she hugged him. Never once had a girl shown any type of affection toward him like this. He didn't know what to do and tensed up a bit. But, when he found that she still didn't let go, he relaxed and allowed her to hug him. This wasn't affection. It was acceptance.

"I know the other assassins look at you as an outsider, but it shouldn't matter! After all, you have us as your friends. They'll come to know you as one soon," Lena said against his shirt. "It's always nice to have a friend there when you're down, isn't it?"

Keimaro's expression relaxed, and he couldn't help but laugh to himself. He had never felt this way before. A warm feeling inside radiated throughout his entire body. He felt accepted, something that he hadn't felt since four years ago when he'd met Yata. "Yeah, it really is." He pushed himself to his feet as Lena pulled away. "Well, hopefully they didn't start the debriefing without us. We better get going, huh, Lena? Tonight is the start of the rebellion." He slid his hands into his pockets and began to walk toward the exit of the infirmary.

"You know, I don't hate magic," Lena said with a giggle, and Keimaro stopped to look at her over his shoulder. She was still sitting on the windowsill. "It's amazing how, inside of this mansion, there's enough magic to create an entire world. Magic fascinates me to the point where I sometimes wish I embraced it. There's so much out there in the world that is unknown. I wonder if there's different magic out there even more wonderful than this … being able to create a secret utopia of peace within a mansion."

Keimaro smiled at her statement. "I'm sure that there is. After all, the world is vast. When this is over, we should go exploring sometime! That was my dream originally when I was a kid, to go see the whole world."

"Really?" Lena said as she leapt off of the windowsill, landed gracefully on the ground, and began to skip toward Keimaro. "That sounds like fun. I might have to take you up on that offer."

"It's settled then! When this is all over, we can explore as much as we want."

14. THE GRAND ENTRANCE

Aika personally hated speeches. She hated politics as a whole. Stepping into the world of politics was something she abhorred to the point that she sometimes slept during discussions. They were just long arguments that carried on for days with people offering new proposals that could be put into action. But, no matter how much she despised politics, her father always felt obligated to bring her to the public government speeches. So, she went.

She sat on a golden throne with a padded red cushion beside her father. A small golden crown embedded with beautiful sapphires and rubies sat upon her head, her long brown hair braided and left to dangle behind her. Her hands were covered by white gloves that rested upon the hard arms of her golden chair. Her light blue dress went down past her silver slippers to the very ground. It was rather tight around her breasts, and she felt herself being squeezed with scant room to breathe. A necklace with a silver chain left a diamond locket dangling above her chest. She wore a bored and sullen look as she leaned her cheek against her fist, but was quickly scolded by Madame Dyrus, Aika's womanly advisor, the person who was supposed to make her act like the princess she was.

Madame Dyrus was a frail old woman, but she covered any wrinkles or facial features that spoke of age with makeup or natural remedies. She leaned back in a comfortable red leather seat behind the princess, making note of every movement that Aika made that wasn't princess-like. Her brown hair was tied into a bun behind her long, slender face that reminded Aika of a horse. Sometimes Aika would call her horse-face in her mind. Madame Dyrus had a pointy nose with puffy lips that always made it seem as if she were pouting.

The king was wearing a large, royal blue robe that was wrapped around his gold-plated armor, which he wore to show off, even though he was no longer a warrior. His gleaming blue eyes scanned the crowds of people before him, as his fingers explored the fluffy, snow-white lining of his robe. It was made of some cloud-like wool that made the robe all the more comfortable. He wielded a golden scepter in his right hand as a signal of his power. The scepter was slender with a gold coil around the handle to make it easy to grasp. Different gems were embedded in it to give the scepter a beautiful glow in the moonlight; it refracted the silvery light, casting colorful beams from sapphires, rubies, and emeralds. He stroked his long, fuzzy brown beard with his left hand and wore a bright smile as he heard the cheers of his people upon seeing their king. He wore the golden crown of the king upon his head with spikes that pointed toward the night sky. Diamonds were so scattered amongst the crown that it looked as if ice itself had frozen the crown in wealth.

Aika and her father sat on the balcony of a building high above a large wooden stage. Below the stage, many people had gathered to hear the public speeches of politicians who were giving their proposals for the government. There were soldiers everywhere, fully prepared to guard the king from any assassination attempts. Guards lined every rooftop, and the entire Royal Guard was hidden amongst the crowd, on the stage, or on the roofs as well. General Mundo stood beside the king with his hands behind his back, looking outward, wearing his full suit of armor.

The entrance to the building where the king was located was heavily guarded with four dozen soldiers and nine Royal Guard members. Two members stood behind Aika at the doorway with their perfect straight posture and robotic looks.

Aika watched as the politicians began speaking, but her mind wandered from the very moment it started. For some reason, that boy, Riku Hikari, had leapt into her head. He was the newest member of the Royal Guard and was to be one of her personal bodyguards. She didn't know why, but she had felt a thrill when she had been with him. His clumsiness had made her smile, and he seemed quite adventurous to follow her into the underground escape without even stopping her. She had not been afraid while she was with him, safe in the knowledge that he would be able to protect her. Yet, she had never seen his swordplay. Her father had been blabbering about how effective a swordsman he was and how killing seemed to be second nature to him. Her blue eyes lowered at that thought. She couldn't bear to think of how a human could kill another so easily unless they had a reason for such hatred. But, even so, didn't murder come with a price?

She believed that it did. Haunting images or nightmares. Constant guilt. One way or the other, killing another human would come back to haunt them. Why should one kill when they had the ability to heal another? To comfort rather than to slaughter or injure, that was what she would like to see.

Four years ago, after she had left the destroyed Bakaara, Aika had found that she had obtained an odd healing power. The moment that she touched a wound, the wound would heal. It didn't matter how serious the injury was, for she tested it on multiple animals, too afraid to use it in public. She had tried it on herself as well while doing dangerous experiments involving cutting herself. Though it seemed rather sick and twisted at first, she found that it really did help her gather information. And there wasn't even a scar left. She had wanted to use this mystical ability on a particular boy that she had known for quite some time, Aladdin, but her father had forbidden her from seeing him again, afraid that they would fall in love and attempt to marry. It was true; perhaps if they were allowed to be together, they would have wed even at this young age. But, it seemed her father had other plans regarding who would gain her hand.

A flash of movement caught her attention, and Aika's head turned. A rather small, skinny line shot through the air and buried itself in a building beside the stage. The line was barely visible, but Aika was sure that she saw it. She noticed that General Mundo had seen it as well. His hand gripped the sheath of his weapon, and she saw the indecision on his face: was he seeing things, or was the line actually there? Aika knew that there was no such thing as assumptions in the Royal Guard. They had to be safe.

Her eyes followed the line and locked onto the bell tower in the distance. Her heart leapt a beat when she saw multiple small figures on top of the bell tower, milling about. Something was happening here; there was no doubt.

***

Keimaro had his black cloak wrapped tightly around his body as he felt his particles reform at the top of the bell tower. A gust of wind rushed into his face, blowing his spiky black hair back. His eyes squinted as the breeze blew against his face, and he saw the lights of the city focusing on the stage in the distance. He turned to see that Yuri, Yata, and Lena had placed their white masks on their faces, making them look like ghosts and clowns. Each mask was different. Yata's had a simple line running across the entire white mask with black lines that looked like bars coming down the face. Yuri's had a bright grin that seemed almost creepily happy. Lena's mask was the only one that had a color besides black and white; a small red flower upon the forehead made her seem a bit more feminine. However, her mask had no mouth with only a hole at the nose.

Keimaro's mask was gripped tightly in his hand. Instead of being pale white like the rest of their masks, it was silver. The eyes stretched a bit like a ghost's, and the mouth was merely a single black line that went across the entire mask and thickened into a curved smile at the end. He looked at his fellow assassins and saw that the masks seemed to attach to their bodies and morph together with their cloaks, making their skin look black as night. His hands were covered with black gloves, and his dark cape flapped in the wind behind him. Not a single bit of humanity could be seen just from looking at him.

He lifted the mask to his face and felt it attach. He gasped as the mask latched itself to his face like a leech, small lines of black veins sprouting from the mask and inserting themselves into his flesh, traveling along his skin to meet with the cloak and transforming his entire neck into a black color until not a single inch of skin was exposed. He heard his breathing echoing and realized there was no problem with breathing or seeing. It was as if the mask had become one with him. What an interesting contraption.

"*The operation begins now,*" Yuri said, his voice distorted so that he wouldn't sound like himself. Rather, he sounded monotonic with a new, extremely deep voice that resonated. "*Kei, get on the zip line and make sure to hit the target nice and hard. We wouldn't want any survivors. Lena, ring the bell when Kei hits the target. Let's begin.*"

Keimaro grabbed onto the zip line and pushed off of the bell tower, his heart cleansed of fear. Right now, his mind was only focused on the mission at hand. His hair blew backward as he rushed forward through the air. His heavy breathing sounded as if a massive hollow helmet had been clamped over his head, echoing in his ears as he zoomed down toward the stage below. The crowds gasped as they saw him flying through the air on the skinny line. Originally, he would've thought that a line this skinny would've broken, but now he had no doubts that Lena truly had some effective contraptions at her disposal. His iris morphed from its dark brown into a demonic red, and he saw that the politicians had already stopped their speech and were beginning to get off of the stage.

"*You're not getting away,*" Keimaro's robotic, echoing voice snarled as he kicked outward to give himself momentum. He swung back and came forward once more, a burst of flame emitting from his feet as he released his grip on the zip line, falling into open air.

Lena, Yuri, and Yata watched him, incredulous. *"Is he going to survive a fall that big?"* Lena asked in awe.

"Yeah. Remember, he isn't human," Yuri said, beginning to attach his own zip line. *"Let's go."*

***

Aika watched as the cloaked, ghost-like figure leapt down from the line with flames sending him flying through the air like jets to propel him forward. To her amazement, his body came downward at incredible speed before any of the politicians were even able to leap off of the stage. An immense explosion erupted from the stage. Flames roared upward in a pillar that flew off toward the clouds, spreading outward as scorching fire flew off in all directions, catching onto the roofs of several buildings. Dust flew up into the air in an enormous cloud, but she could already see the mysterious intruder's silhouette emerging from the cloud, slowly standing.

"What on earth is this?" General Mundo yelled, his hands gripping the bars of the balcony, his knuckles white with shock. His face was red with frustration, and Aika could see a vein bulging from his forehead. "Riflemen! Load your weapons and prepare to fire!"

Aika watched as three other black figures dressed in similar cloaks flew down the invisible line and landed beside the first figure, bringing their total to four. In her eyes, they all looked like ghosts with white masks wearing those ominous black cloaks. Were they even human? She had heard the first figure yell before he had hit the stage, and his voice definitely wasn't human. Not to mention the fact that an ordinary human would never survive a fall from that high.

Madam Dyrus gripped her shoulder and urged her to follow the escorts to flee the area. "Princess, we must evacuate! It is much too dangerous! Those are assassins—and inhuman ones at that! They'll have our heads before—"

"*I don't suggest you run,*" a voice from the dust spoke. The cloud began to clear, exposing all four of the cloaked figures to the crowd, who had been panicking but had calmed down slightly when they realized that the assassins weren't yet posing a threat to innocents.

Aika's eyes widened when she saw scattered bodies all over the stage—deformed, burned corpses that were red with raw flesh. Blood was splattered across the shattered wood. The stage itself had collapsed and was nothing but destroyed debris scattered across the area with all of the bodies of the politicians lying alongside several civilian and guard casualties. The first figure that had leapt was the one talking. He stood in the middle with the rest of his comrades behind him.

"And who are you?" the king demanded, standing up suddenly with all of the rifles of his guards trained on the four cloaked figures. "One false movement and you will be pumped with enough lead to supply an army. Choose your next moves carefully, terrorists."

The ghostly figure chuckled, his voice mechanical and dark. He cocked his head to the side as he looked at the king with his glowing red eyes. "*My name is Keimaro Hayashi. You have taken something from me, milord—my honor, my family, my home, and my happiness. You have made my life a living hell. That is why, in the last year, I made a final decision. That I would come here and kill you along with every single person in this empire. I'll take everything from you as you have taken everything from me. With the burning flames of my hatred,*" he growled as he lifted a hand. Roaring flames snarled up, catching on his hand and swirling in a vortex around his forearm that blew the black sleeves of his cloak ever so slightly, "*I will destroy you, king. However, worry not. You will have several weeks before I decide to come for you, for I'll leave you alive to watch your empire crumble.*"

Aika watched as her father shifted nervously and nearly dropped his scepter, staring at Keimaro with shock and newfound fear. That was Keimaro Hayashi? She looked back at the figure. He had obtained some type of odd magical power as well … and he wanted revenge for the Bakaara massacre. Her heart thumped rapidly as she watched him. She wondered if Yata was also amongst those ghosts that stood behind him, lingering silently.

"Making such bold threats, do you think so highly of yourself?" the king boomed, his voice echoing as he stood up from his throne. "You are only a single demon boy with a small band of rogues. You hide in the shadows, but even a demon cannot conceal himself in darkness for eternity against the army of Faar. We will find you and annihilate you before you are even able to make a single step toward your goal. Do you not remember? Your entire clan was condemned to die. Are you really willing to bring your friends into this conflict with you? Are you so selfish and set on your revenge that you would drag your allies down with you for your sick goals? I enjoyed killing your family, Keimaro Hayashi, and it's time for you to die as well. There's no place in our world for a monster like you."

***

Keimaro's eyes glowed even brighter as anger swirled within him, causing his fists to shake at his sides. He felt a hand on his shoulder, but he shook it off as smoke began to rise from his body. He stared at the king as his father's image flashed into his mind. He remembered vividly what his father had said to him.

He had been sitting beside his father's bed when he had passed from the heart attack. That was something out of Keimaro's control. He remembered the constant look of exhaustion on his father's face. "Kill them all," he'd said. "Make sure that Faar pays for what they've done to us. Our lives were lost from the moment that they invaded. We are dead men that roam the earth. We are ghosts that haunt the terrible men that have brought pain to our past lives. Avenge me, Keimaro. Be the one to thrust the blade into the man's blackened heart."

A monster, huh? He looked around at the eyes of the soldiers that had locked onto him. His Shokugan eyes could see that their entire bodies were shaking with fear. It was as if they saw a creature before them, a demon, a monster, rather than a human. Keimaro's eyes flickered to the citizens, who were staring at him with widened eyes as well. Some were whispering together, words that couldn't be identified. But he knew that look in their eyes. He recognized it. Fear. Hatred. All of it crammed together to create the look that they wore—and how had it come to this? How had it come to him, becoming the villain?

Keimaro stared at his hands, which shook before his face. Was it because he had killed murderers? Perhaps that took away his humanity. Maybe he should've given up on this entire thought of revenge from the very beginning if it would've at least helped him keep his purity. *No*, he thought, *it's not because of my actions. It's not because of anything that I've ever done. It's because of my family. It's because of these eyes. It's because I am a member of the Hayashi clan. They all judge me to be some type of monster based on the stereotypes that they have heard in legends and stories. They supported the Hayashi clan massacre. Every last one of them.*

He recalled his mother's smiling face, her long, black, flowing hair with her bright grin every time he had arrived home from school. He recalled her smile fading as it turned to worry every time he came home with a bruise, and he pictured the way she had comforted him and always been there for him. She was the person he had loved most in this world. *They took her from me!*

Keimaro yelled as a pillar of flame burst up from his body and into the dark night sky. It smashed through the inky clouds, exploding in a streak of light flying across the sky in all directions. He rushed forward in the direction of the king. He slammed his hand into the bottom of his sheath, his blade popping into the air. He gripped the hilt and whirled it as he sprinted forward. The crowds of people panicked and screamed as they separated, leaving only the soldiers in his way.

Everyone is responsible.

His sword came down, each time taking yet another life. Blood sprayed into the night air as Keimaro spun around, swinging his sword harder and harder against his opponents. The soldiers couldn't withstand his relentless assault and all lay dead at his feet within moments. There was a crack as bullets began to fly at him from all directions, the riflemen finally letting loose. The projectile lead balls spiraled through the air as they soared toward him. *Kill every last one of them.* He raised his hands, and a wave of flames flew into the air, melting the bullets as soon as they reached the wall from the intensity of the fire's heat. *That is your sole purpose for existence.*

***

Aika stared in shock as Keimaro tore through the line of Royal Guards as if they were nothing. The flames that he had shown off were definitely no type of ordinary magic. That pillar of flames alone showed he had incredible amounts of power. She blinked as she felt herself being lifted up by guards, who escorted her away hurriedly. She struggled, pulling away from one of the guards. She wanted to see him, up close. She didn't know why, but after all of these years, something just drew her toward him. "Father!" she exclaimed, but her voice was swallowed by the sound of roaring flames.

A huge wall of flames sprang into existence in front of the balcony, a wave of heat smashing into her. She winced, covering her eyes from the brightness of the fire, and stared when she saw the flames separating into a perfect doorway. Keimaro flew forward and stepped gracefully onto the marble railing of the balcony. *How is that possible?* Her eyes were wide as she stood there, her mouth gaping open, incredulous. *We're at least five stories above the ground!*

Keimaro's cloak blew from a swift breeze as time seemed to slow. He stood there on the balcony with them, seemingly completely relaxed despite his burst of adrenaline only a moment earlier. The boy's eyes flashed as he flipped off of the railing, slamming his heel into the back of General Mundo's head. With a crack, the man's skull slammed hard into the ground, leaving him unconscious. General Mundo had led Faar's armies into battle dozens—maybe hundreds—of times and had been always victorious. Yet, here he was, being defeated so easily. It seemed to take hardly any effort for Keimaro because he stepped over the unconscious body with his sword unsheathed as he whirled it. He advanced on Aika's father, the king sinking back into his throne, his face pale.

The other soldiers had rushed forward, and the sounds of scraping steel echoed loudly. Then silence fell as all of the warriors pointed their blades at Keimaro. The tip of Keimaro's sword pressed against the king's throat, drawing a small line of blood. Guns clicked as they were armed from multiple rooftops, all aimed straight at Keimaro, ready to pump him full of lead the very moment he decided to assassinate the king. But, none of the Royal Guards dared to make a move. A single movement could provoke Keimaro to assassinate the king right there. Tension filled the air as everyone stood frozen in place.

Aika stared at her father in disbelief and then at Keimaro. "Kei, stop this! Don't you recognize me? I'm Aika, the princess from four years ago! Please, put your sword down! I'm sure this is all—"

"*A misunderstanding?*" Keimaro said, his head lowered. "*No, it's not. Your father means every word that has ever left his lips. He is the one responsible for the death of my real family and my new one. He's the killer who took my mother from me. He's the one who destroyed my village and everything in it. He took everything from me!*" Flames shot upward around him, causing some of the Royal Guard to flinch, but they held their ground. "*So, king, give me one reason why I shouldn't lop off this senseless head of yours?*"

The king gulped as he pressed his back to the throne and gave a nervous chuckle. "Well, I've heard that you've been looking for a particular girl. Would be a shame if she were to be killed after you lopped off my head, hmm?"

Aika saw Keimaro's eyes widen through his mask. Who was her father talking about? Clearly, it was someone dear to Keimaro from the way he was reacting. She could see his free hand shaking at his side as well as his handle on his hilt tightening. This wasn't good. It looked as if her father were actually provoking Keimaro. She wanted to step forward but was pulled backward and away from the scene, gripped tightly by guards.

"Stop, wait!" she exclaimed in protest, but they lifted her up and hauled her away. Her eyes followed Keimaro until he vanished from view.

***

Keimaro couldn't believe what he was hearing. Was this some kind of a bluff? The Bounts had taken his sister, not this old man. Could they have handed her over to the king? His heart was pounding, and he could feel himself heating up internally. He couldn't kill the king now; he knew that. Why was he even up here on this balcony? What had gotten into him that he had been such an idiot as to abandon the mission and pursue his own selfish desires? He glanced over his shoulder and saw that Yuri, Yata, and Lena were all surrounded by soldiers. They had their hands up in the air in a sign of surrender, and the soldiers were advancing on them. He had messed everything up. Now everyone was going to be caught and probably killed because of him.

No, I can still get out of this. I just have to focus. I can't let this old man get to my head! This is what he wanted all along.

The entire time, Keimaro noticed that the king was eying the key that was around his neck. No doubt the king had his father's chest in his possession, but this wasn't the time to pester him about it. For now, he just had to focus on fixing his mistakes and saving his friends. But what to do? He blinked and looked straight at the king, who returned a confused glance. *Why not?*

He reached out and grabbed the king with both hands, lifting him into the air. The soldiers stepped forward, about to slash him at the single movement. "*If you so much as take another step, I can turn your beloved king into ashes before your eyes,*" he said simply, freezing every soldier in the entire area.

"Take the shot!" one Royal Guard snapped to a rifleman.

"I can't! What if I hit the king?" the rifleman countered, knowing very well that if he shot the king, it would result in a death penalty for him and his family. The risk was far too high, and the pressure would've probably caused him to mess up the shot. Not to mention, he had only just begun his training with the rifle. He still wasn't confident in his own ability to make such a gamble.

Keimaro grabbed the king and held him over the side of the balcony, gripping the man by both of his arms to hold him up. His sword had already been sheathed, and he was now unarmed. This had to work; otherwise, he would probably be killed.

"*Step away from my accomplices,*" Keimaro ordered, and the soldiers all looked up in unison, their faces pale. Gasps erupted from the groups of people who still had the guts to stay and watch the spectacle. The soldiers began to slowly take steps backward, freeing Keimaro's friends. They sheathed their swords as they turned to face the new threat.

"*Run,*" he said simply to his friends.

Yuri and Lena broke off into a sprint almost immediately, but Yata stood there staring at Keimaro blankly for a moment before Lena yanked on his arm, dragging him away from the scene. The crowds of people separated around them as they sprinted off, but no soldiers ran after them. Instead, all of the weapons and eyes were trained on Keimaro, who had to somehow escape this dire situation.

Keimaro didn't want to kill the king yet. He knew that the king would know the location of his father's chest, but now was definitely not the time to ask him. He saw that the groups of soldiers were hovering below the king, ready to catch him. Their arms were outstretched, as if prompting Keimaro to drop their lord—and that was exactly what Keimaro did.

Trusting that the soldiers would catch him or that the king would only break a limb from the fall, he released the king. In that single instant, the Royal Guards that had been posted on the balcony rushed at him with their brandished swords, slashing

242

wildly. The crack of bullets split the air as riflemen took their opportunity to fire at Keimaro. His eyes saw the spiraling lead balls flying at him from multiple directions, and he knew that it was impossible to dodge. He spun around, grabbing the nearest soldier who came at him and using him as a shield. He heard sudden thuds as bullets buried themselves into the soldier. Stray projectiles slammed into the armor and bodies of other soldiers, smacking into mail and tearing through flesh. Screams of agony split the air as the Royal Guards ducked down in unison, trying to avoid the friendly-fire.

Keimaro saw the chaos and took the opportunity to make a mad dash for it, ejecting a large jet of flame behind him in order to burst himself forward and through the archway that left the balcony. The soldiers had taken Aika this way; he knew there must be some type of exit. Bullets tore through the walls and whirled through the opening, flying past him. He grunted, throwing himself to the ground, his heart pounding. After a couple of seconds, there was silence. The Royal Guards had begun to stand up already. Perhaps the riflemen were reloading or the Guard had signaled for them to stop firing. Either way, Keimaro knew he had to get moving.

His eyes darted around, looking for some type of an exit. A stairway led downward to the lower floor, but that would provide no escape. Without a doubt, soldiers down there were probably coming up already. *When you can't find an opening, make one.* His father's words echoed in his mind, and his eyes snapped open as he lifted himself up. He spun around, roaring flames generating around him as he grunted, punching out at the wall across the room. A massive ball of concentrated flame obliterated the entire wall, sending a wave of dust flying around him. His body melted into the dust cloud, and he sprinted forward through the opening and leapt through the wall into open air. His arms waved as he broke through the cloud of smoke, flying in the direction of another balcony that was lower and seemed right behind the building.

Keimaro winced as he landed, absorbing the full shock of the fall. He sucked in a deep breath as he heard the yelling of soldiers all around him. He pushed forward, his hair blowing into his eyes as he rushed through a glass door. Glittering shards rained down around him, some cutting his skin, but he didn't care. His heart was pounding rapidly, and he just wanted to escape. He knew that he was leaving behind a large trail, but the intention was to move so fast that they wouldn't be able to follow. He sprinted through a room where a couple lay on their bed. He sighed at the woman's scream but didn't bother to look in her direction because he was already throwing himself through their open window across the room.

His breath caught in his lungs as he found open air and watched as the floor flew up to meet him. His boots smashed into the ground, and he gasped, wincing as he fell to one knee. He knew that his body was much stronger than an ordinary human's so that he could endure higher falls. Nevertheless, the shock from so many falls had taken a toll on him. He felt a sharp pain, as if a dagger were being driven into the side of his ankle. He glanced up from the paved ground and saw that people were all around him, staring at him, incredulous and shocked. The guards were probably close by. To make matters worse, the woman who had been in the bed had run to the window and began to scream and point at him like some type of alarm.

Keimaro glanced over his shoulder and glared at her with his demonic eyes, feeling a sudden need to hurl a ball of flame at her home and obliterate the entire structure altogether. When he looked at her, her voice caught on her lips and died almost immediately. Her face paled, and she took several steps back from the window until she completely disappeared from view, surely scared for her life.

The boy tried to examine his surroundings, remembering what Yuri had told him about using his environment to his advantage to escape any situation. There was an alleyway, but he didn't know where the hell that led. He could already hear the yelling of guards and the clanking of chainmail and armor nearby. He didn't have much time, and the alley was the only place that could provide a possible escape. He was in plain sight, standing in the middle of the street. He sprinted forward, ignoring the pain that split through his ankle, and ran into the shadows of the alleyway.

Unfortunately, a squad of guards was there, coming toward him. He slowed to a stop as soon as he saw the guards running down the alley and grunted, turning to flee back the way he'd come. But more guards had already closed off the exit and were slowly advancing on him with their swords held in front of them defensively.

Keimaro gulped, examining the situation. He was completely trapped between two armed forces. He could kill them all, but that would take time and more soldiers would come. He didn't want to have to kill every single soldier that came at him. He just wanted to escape. He sucked in a deep breath and turned back to the alley, running full speed at the soldiers, not bothering to unsheathe his weapon. The guards blinked in surprise as he ran at them, not sure what the boy was up to. They prepared themselves and held their ground.

"*This better work,*" Keimaro muttered under his breath as he took a single step onto the narrow wall of the alleyway. He released a continuous jet of flame behind him, propelling him forward along the wall. His feet were placed accordingly as he grunted, growing accustomed to the speed. Elated, he realized he was running on the wall. It was working! He grinned stupidly as he flew over the confused squad of guards and landed gracefully on the ground behind them, flying at incredible speed, leaving only smoke in his trail.

Keimaro staggered out of the alleyway into another open road, knowing that he had to get out of the common area. But he was in a city—it was practically impossible to escape! He had to find somewhere to hide. People surrounded him in the street; he had to distract them somehow so that he could hide. He slammed his palms together, creating a huge explosion of flames that erupted into the air. Civilians scattered in all directions, screaming in fear as a huge cloud of smoke swallowed the area. When the smoke cleared, Keimaro was gone. The guards poured out of the alleyway into an empty street.

Keimaro had broken into a random house and locked the door behind him, finding a frightened elderly couple. Actually they weren't frightened. As Keimaro looked closely, they looked quite calm actually in comparison to the other civilians. The woman was holding a pan and was staring at him as if she were looking at a ghost. The elderly man was sitting in a rocking chair, looking in his direction through his squinted eyes. But, neither of them made a sound.

"*I…,*" Keimaro began, but wasn't particularly sure what to say at all. Nothing he could say could really excuse his being dressed up like a marauder. He scratched the back of his neck and reached into his pocket, pulling a few coins out and placing them on the table. "*Look, if you just shelter me for a few hours, I promise I'll make it worth your while. I just—*"

"It's okay, Keimaro Hayashi," the old woman said with a reassuring smile.

Keimaro blinked, heat rising to his face. How did they know who he was? They clearly hadn't been at the speech. His name couldn't have circulated so quickly either. He could silence them both right now and seek refuge in this house in solitude. His hand was twitching at his side, his eyes widening.

What are these thoughts that I'm having? I can't kill bystanders. I would never stoop so low. Two innocent elderly in their own home … I can't do that! I would be just as bad as the Faar soldiers who broke into my home and killed my mother. His hand relaxed at his side, and he gulped, reaching up and taking off his mask. The mask detached from his skin at his touch, and he held it in his hand, sucking in fresh air as he looked over the two elderly. "How do you know my name?"

"Because of me," a boy said, descending a set of winding wooden stairs that led down from the upper floors. He seemed to be several years older than Keimaro with a head of curly brown hair that shined as he raised an eyebrow, smiling playfully at the assassin. He was wearing tattered clothing that was torn to

246

the point where it looked like they had been lacerated by a bear. He scratched the back of his neck with a chuckle. "Where are my manners? My name is Edward, and I'm the one who's somewhat overseeing the mission. In fact, it's lucky that you are here because we need to discuss the many flaws that occurred during your...." A whirring sound filled the air as a bright blue glow shined from upstairs. "Ah, it looks like they're coming to scold you themselves."

Gavin and Aladdin descended down the stairs behind Edward, having teleported from Zylon's mansion. Aladdin had a rather nervous look on his face, while Gavin's was smug. "You almost—"

"Yeah," Keimaro said with a sigh as he shook his head. "I got it. I messed up. I lost control." His hands were shaking at his sides, and he closed his eyes. He had wanted to tear the king apart at that moment. What was this feeling that he was having? It was overcoming all of his common sense! He shouldn't have bolted forward so suddenly or allowed himself to be provoked like that. "Who's that?" he said, pointing over his shoulder at Edward.

"He's one of the assassins who will be helping us in our operations. You're only too lucky that you waltzed straight into his house by chance," Gavin muttered. "Aladdin, take him back to the mansion. I'll make sure to try to calm things down outside." Keimaro realized that Gavin was wearing his guard uniform. He intended to pose as a soldier and control the crowd or lead the guards away. "Edward, we can use that teleporting pad upstairs?"

"It's a small one, but yeah."

"Send Keimaro and Aladdin back."

"What?" Keimaro snapped. "We are done with the mission?"

"It was a success, as far as I'm concerned. You scared the crap out of the people and made quite a scene. Far more of a scene than I could've imagined because you almost killed the king," Gavin said, glancing at Keimaro from the corner of his eye as he took a step forward toward the door, adjusting the iron helmet upon his head.

Gavin exhaled. "However, you would have cost your friends their lives if they didn't escape. You put too much faith in them, assuming that they would be able to escape. What if the Bount organization appeared and captured one of them? With everyone on the run and everything all chaotic, no one would even notice that someone had been captured until we all arrived at the mansion to do a head count," Gavin said, pausing. "You have to take these factors into consideration. You created too much risk. I just hope that everyone gets back safely. That's all."

"You're saying ... I could've gotten someone killed?"

"Yes!" Gavin growled, turning to face Keimaro now, clearly annoyed. "You completely lost control out there today! It just shows us how much self-control you actually have. You left the plan and almost got everyone—"

"And you're the one to lecture me? The person who wanted to go down into that stupid laboratory only to have Noah captured?" Keimaro yelled, his eyes dark and filled with anger. "He could be dead as well for all we know!"

Gavin's eyes were wide, and his lips were quivering as if he wanted to cry. His hands were shivering at his side. He broke eye contact and moved to the door, throwing it open and standing in the doorway for a moment. "At least I admit my faults, whereas you believe that you did nothing wrong," he said, closing the door behind him.

Keimaro stared at the door for a moment, his heart pounding against his chest. *Why am I rejecting the fact that I messed up? I know I messed up.* He turned to Aladdin, who shrugged and began to follow Edward up the stairs. He turned to the elderly couple in the house and bowed his head lightly before he followed them back up the stairway. At the top of the stairs was a small room with a bed pushed to the side and a blue platform placed in the very center. It was small, much smaller than the one that was installed at the mansion, but it could still fit two people. Probably.

Aladdin was waiting on it, and Keimaro stepped onto it reluctantly. He feared the moment that he would arrive back at the mansion. By now, no doubt the entire crew of assassins knew his mistakes. It was inevitable. Information flowed so freely in the mansion. He closed his eyes as he felt his skin tingling once more and sighed. *What was going through my mind back then?*

15. OUTSIDER

Keimaro was practically dragged off of the platform the very moment he arrived in the mansion. Crowds of young assassins were watching the spectacle as two strong, burly men threw Keimaro at the feet of Yuri, who stood tall over the boy. He grunted, annoyed at the fact that he was being looked down on. He tried to push himself to his feet, but Yuri put his foot on Keimaro's back, forcing him back down onto his knees. There was silence as Yuri held his hand up into the air. Keimaro could see Yata standing there in the front lines of the crowd, doing nothing. At the sight of the doubt in his friend's eyes, Keimaro looked away.

"You're so obsessed with your revenge that you left us, your comrades, to die," Yuri snarled, lifting his foot from Keimaro's back. "I knew Z should've left you out of this. You are an untamed beast from the wild, consumed by evil, and you have no compassion. I've seen men like you. In fact, I used to be like you. Always craving that revenge. You always want that man dead, the one person who took everything from you. It's all you can think about, right? Even in your dreams, it haunts you—"

"Stop talking like you know what you're saying!" Keimaro yelled, his voice silencing Yuri's in an instant. It boomed through the crowd, causing assassins to shift nervously. His eyes were glowing bright red as he pushed himself to a standing position in front of Yuri. "My entire life has been dedicated to revenge since the very moment my mother perished! My life is void of meaning without my vengeance. I intend to avenge my father, my mother, and my little sister. The fact that you think you understand me is pathetic!"

He turned to the crowd, roaring, "Do you even *understand* what it's like? To lose everyone and everything that you've ever known in a single instant? To see your own mother skewered by a blade as your house burns. To watch your little sister be kidnapped while you lay there with broken bones, powerless to do anything?" He turned back to Yuri and jammed a finger into the werewolf's chest. "I joined this organization to obtain my revenge. Don't think that there's any other reason."

Yuri raised an eyebrow. "Is that so? I thought that you came here because you believed and hoped that perhaps there was a sliver of a chance that your little sister was alive."

"She isn't."

"We don't know that."

"We do!" Keimaro snarled. "Do you truly believe that she survived even a single year with those Bounts? No, the king himself confirmed it. He knew about Mai, meaning that the Bounts turned her over to the empire. Those experiments that they were performing in the underground lab used Hayashi DNA and transplants. My sister was used as a test subject. A lab rat. At this point her fate is quite obvious to me. She's dead." he choked.

"So, you'll do the selfish thing and abandon the mission, leaving us to die," Yuri said. "Unlike you, we cannot create walls of fire that generate enough heat to melt bullets. Once the volley of projectiles comes at us, we are dead. In an instant, all of us could've been lying on the ground in a heap of bodies. And then you would've been next. I don't think you understand that yet. I do believe that every human has self-control," he said. "Even I, at times, feel weak when I am provoked. I feel a tugging sensation that makes me want to lose my humanity and become a beast. I want to succumb to my instinct. But my mind is better. I know when to make the right choices. Today, you didn't make the right choice. Admit your mistake."

"I won't admit anything, you damn werewolf."

The crowd gasped, and Yuri's face darkened. He whipped his fist around and slammed it solidly into Keimaro's face before the boy could even react. With a loud crack, Keimaro flew backward, smacking against the platform painfully. He grabbed his face, screaming in agony as blood streamed from his nose. His eyes glared through the cracks of his fingers, red as his blood.

But in a single moment, Keimaro's hostility drained from him, and he lowered his hands, allowing the blood to freely stream down his face. He stared in shock at Yuri.

Yuri had tears in his eyes, and his fist was shaking, his knuckles covered with a fresh coat of Keimaro's blood. He was panting, his breath heavy, and he wiped his eyes with the back of his hand. He was about to rush in and attack Keimaro again, but Yata and Aladdin leapt forward, restraining him. "Lena is gone because of you! Where the hell do you think she is?" he roared, struggling against the metallic Yata and Aladdin, his eyes red with fury. "And you won't even admit your fault!"

Keimaro hadn't noticed her absence, and he hated himself for that. His heart was pounding as he scanned the crowd, hoping that he would prove Yuri wrong and find Lena there. But she wasn't. This couldn't be. She couldn't be gone. His hands were shaking, and his lips were quivering with shock. *I know the other assassins look at you as an outsider, but it shouldn't matter! After all, you have us as your friends. They'll come to know you as one soon.* Her words echoed through his head, and he slowly pushed himself to his feet.

Yuri limped forward, sobbing silently. Keimaro could've never imagined the strong and independent leader crying. Yet here he was.

"It's my fault," Keimaro said quietly, and Yuri stopped crying almost immediately. "Lena was captured, wasn't she? It's my fault that it happened. And I'll get her back. Whatever condition she comes back in, you can apply to me ten-fold," he said, his eyes filled with confidence. *What am I doing? Why do I care about any of these people? Aren't they just tools to get my revenge? I shouldn't make a promise like that.* But his expression didn't change, and Yuri exhaled deeply.

"If she's dead—"

"She won't be," Keimaro said. "I'll save her and—"

"You won't be doing anything of the sort." Z's words echoed through the mansion as he walked forward, his footsteps echoing loudly in the dead silence. His hands were crossed behind his back as the crowds of assassins separated, clearing a pathway for him. He tilted his head back as his eyes flickered from Yata and Yuri to Keimaro. "And what do you think you're doing? The mission was indeed a success."

"Lena was captured," Keimaro said, turning to Z. "I wouldn't call that a success."

"And you intend to save her?"

"Of course," he growled.

"I forbid you to do so," Z said. "The key around your neck is the most important object in the entire world right now. If you go after her and it falls into the hands of the enemy, the world will be doomed because you decided to go out there. Leave the key here; then you may go and risk your life if you wish."

"I'm not doing that," Keimaro said simply. "I'm going to go and save Lena and Noah. It's peculiar that you're so concentrated on your goals that you don't even care about your own subordinates. You don't even seem to care about the capture of your own son. You give me no reason to trust you with this," he said, reaching up and feeling the cool metal of the key that pressed against his chest. "Not to mention, I don't work for you. I don't have to listen to anything you say. We are only working toward a mutual goal."

"In that case...." Z nodded to the assassins, who unsheathed their weapons, brandishing them at Keimaro. Glistening steel flashed in Keimaro's eyes, and his heart pounded as he stared in shock at the opposition. "We cannot allow you to leave this establishment. Not to mention, you call me heartless, yet I don't recall you ever caring about anyone here either. I can see it in your eyes. Your obsession with revenge is absolute. Even with today's actions, it is confirmed that you cannot control yourself. You might go off and—"

"Old man," Yuri snarled, stepping up beside Keimaro. He cracked his knuckles as he stood against the blades of the rebels. "I intend to go and save Lena as well. Don't think that you're stopping either of us."

"I'm going, too," Yata muttered, taking a step forward. "It's my fault that Noah was captured. I need to make things right."

Z raised an eyebrow at the rebellion before him. He scoffed, his eyes on Yuri. He grunted and slid his hands into his pockets. As if it were a signal, all of the rebels sheathed their weapons and stepped to the side. Z's face was filled with frustration and annoyance that his own subordinates weren't listening to him. "Why do you want to save these people, Keimaro? You have no connection to them. You've been with us only for a few days. There's no way that—"

"I feel that I have made a connection, a rather small one," Keimaro said with a sigh, scratching the back of his neck. "And I'll admit, it definitely is a drag to go out there and risk my life in order to save someone while in enemy territory. However, something Lena said gave me a new insight on everyone here." He closed his eyes, remembering the words that she had spoken to him right before they had performed the assassination. Her words echoed in his head, and a small smile crossed his lips. "She treated me as a friend, a comrade. She accepted me. If I were the one captured, she would go out there and save me. And if I were sitting in the dark solitude of a jail cell," his eyes came up to meet Z's, which widened as the boy spoke, "I would want to grasp at the hope that maybe one day someone would come and rescue me."

Yata smiled at Keimaro's words and nodded as Aladdin came behind the Hayashi boy and patted his shoulder, stepping in line with Yuri, Yata, and Keimaro. Without a doubt, Keimaro was beginning to see friendship in all of these people around him. Maybe communication with people after all of these years had finally changed his insight on humanity. Maybe not everyone was as cruel as he and Yata had thought after the Bakaara massacre.

"I'm going to be the one to save Lena and your son," Keimaro declared, "and if you really want to spend your time fighting me for trying to do you a favor, go on. I'm pretty sure you'd be wasting your efforts when there's an army of millions of soldiers out there that we categorize as the enemy. Our plans for overthrowing this government and assassinating the king aren't over yet. Fight me, kill me, take this damn key from my unmoving corpse then! See where that gets you. Because even if you fight me," his irises morphed from pitch-black to bright red, "I'll take down as many as I can with me."

Z stood there for a moment, at a loss for words. Then a smile spread across his face, a silly grin that grew from ear to ear. He began to clap his hands and chuckle. "Very good. You have changed quite a bit from the first moment I saw you. Though you are still consumed by revenge, you have at least grasped the essence of friendship. Go on. Go save Lena and my son. If you are captured or killed in the process, though, it is the end of the world. I hope that you realize that."

Keimaro smirked at the old man's remarks. "I won't be captured. Don't worry. And here's the best part: I've got an idea for saving them both."

***

"Kei," Yata's voice froze Keimaro in place as everyone began to disperse from the scene. Keimaro watched the back of Yuri's cloak as the werewolf walked away and then turned to face his friend. "You mean what you said, right? That you're becoming attached to this place."

Keimaro nodded. "Yeah. I think I am."

"Then it would make sense to leave the key here, wouldn't it? I am beginning to trust these people as well and—"

"No."

"No?" Yata said with a frown. "Why not? If we can trust them, then—"

"I trust no one more than I trust myself. I'll keep it safe. There's no reason to risk leaving it here and have it possibly fall into the wrong hands," Keimaro said. "I am becoming attached to everyone here, but that doesn't give me a reason to trust anyone. Anyone but myself."

"Not even me, Kei?" Yata asked with a rock-solid stare that caused Keimaro's eyes to widen. "Hand me the key. I'm staying here in Zylon's mansion while you're off in enemy territory. There's no reason that—"

"No, I—" Keimaro interrupted, but Yata's hands curled into tight fists at his side.

"*Listen to me!*" Yata yelled, his arms transforming into their gleaming metal. Keimaro jumped, shocked. "If you can't trust me, then who can you trust? I've been here for you for four years. I've been there since the time your mother died, and I was there when your father, our master, passed. I was there when you had a fever that almost killed you. Don't you remember that I took care of you when you were weak?

"I was the one you complained to every day about how rigorous our training was. I was there when we first journeyed

256

into the darkness of the Forbidden Forest when we both reached sixteen years. We were almost eaten, but we had each other's backs. You put your life in my hands as I put mine in yours. How can you not trust me with that key when you have already entrusted me with your life? Tell me, Keimaro," he snapped, grinding his teeth. "Do you not consider me your friend? Don't you trust me?"

Keimaro's eyes widened. It had been a while since Yata had yelled at him like this. *Just give him the key.* "I trust no one other than myself, Yata. That's all there is to it," he murmured and avoided eye-contact with Yata. *You idiot.*

Yata watched his old friend with widened eyes, but the look that came after was that of pity that made Keimaro's heart sink. "So be it," he said simply and walked past Keimaro without so much as a single glance.

Keimaro remembered the time that he had placed his life in Yata's hands. It was more than just once. The first time the two of them had entered the darkness of the Forbidden Forest as a team was when they were sixteen, two years after the Bakaara massacre. It had been the second time they had walked on such unholy soil. Alone, separated from their master, they were to survive one night in the dark woods. As night approached, the two had felt the blackness of the forest closing in on them. The fire they had created could not fight back the shadows that crept from all sides, ready to close them in an everlasting darkness. At sixteen, Keimaro had believed that he was ready for anything. After two long years of training with his father to master the way of the sword, he believed that he could best anyone. He was wrong.

A beast of the night had leapt from the shadows and smothered their fire in a single instant, locking the two companions in blackness. At the time, Keimaro had been confident that he could conquer the beast, but the darkness of the forest was too dense; even his Shokugan had trouble penetrating the thick, black fog that blinded him. Igniting his flames, Keimaro realized that the beast that leapt from the shadows was the same black tiger that they had seen two years before. With widened eyes, the teenager had begun to step backwards with fear beginning to course through his veins. The beast leapt outward at him, and Keimaro tripped over a thick root of a tree and landed on his back as the black tiger landed upon him. Keimaro raised his sword forcefully and brought it between the tiger's sharp fangs and his throat. His heart pounded and he began to gasp heavily as he applied pressure, trying to stop the tiger from biting open his throat.

A crack resounded through the night, and the tiger suddenly was sent flying off of Keimaro and into the thick trunk of a tree. The beast whimpered for a moment as it slid to the ground and Keimaro turned to find that Yata had swatted the tiger away with a powerful swing of his bat. The boy extended his hand to Keimaro with a smile. "What's wrong, Kei? There's nothing to be scared about. After all, I'm here."

Keimaro had stared at Yata with shaky eyes and then shook his head, snapping his mind back to reality. He reached out and accepted his friend's hand as he was pulled to his feet. "Thanks for the save. I messed up," he murmured, whipping his sword through the silent air as he turned to face the recovering tiger. He held out his hand, allowing a flame to spark in his palm. "It's our turn."

Now, Keimaro watched as Yata walked away from him, guilt already beginning to build up in his chest. His breath was heavy as tears began to form in his eyes. That was the first time the two of them had fought in a long time. There were so many times when Yata had been there for him. *Go after him, you idiot.* But Keimaro didn't move. Instead, he kept his head lowered and watched his friend's back from a distance. There was no reason for Keimaro not to trust Yata, the person who deserved his trust the most. Yata always had his back, no matter what it was. Keimaro ran a hand through his hair and exhaled. On that night they had entered the Forbidden Forest, Yata had saved his life countless times. *I should be grateful—grateful that I have someone who is willing to put his life on the line just for my sake. What's wrong with me?* He put his face in his hands and groaned. *Only an idiot would push away a friend like that.*

***

Aika darted through the hallways of the castle, her heart racing. Keimaro was so different than she had remembered. So dark. His eyes were unlike anything she had ever seen before. They were filled with even more hatred than the day four years ago when he had been told the truth about the Hayashi clan. His eyes lacked any type of compassion, and when they locked onto her, everything seemed to freeze. She could see the flames of the burning village in the pools of his eyes. The entire past was represented by him; the flames of his hatred were his power that he used to express his frustration. And now he wanted revenge.

She had heard that her father was in his bedroom being tended by multiple doctors. That meant that Keimaro had done something to him. She had received no news on whether her father was okay.

The Royal Guards that had been escorting her opened a large wooden door that led into her father's room. Inside were at least ten doctors, all dressed in white coats. They were scrambling around the king's bed. The decorative red and blue silks hanging from the ceiling had been thrust out of the way, allowing them to work. Everyone was in a rush, but Aika just wanted to see her father.

The princess pushed past some of the doctors and finally made her way to her father's side, only to find that he was completely fine. His head was a bit bruised, and maybe he had a broken bone or two, but overall he seemed okay.

"Father, are you all right?" she asked, just to make sure.

The king nodded with a long, exasperated sigh. "I'm growing too old for that sort of thing, being dropped from a balcony into a group of people," he muttered, leaning back against the dozens of pillows that propped him up. "Keimaro Hayashi is much more dangerous than I could've imagined. That was magic that he used today—and it wasn't any ordinary magic. Artificial magic, which is already extremely rare, requires body movements in order to perform, and it exhausts the caster. But

when Keimaro used his magic tonight, he didn't use any
movements. It was as if the fire were a part of him that acted to
protect and fight for him. It truly was something else, and he, as
the Bounts have said, is extremely dangerous. We need to take
the proper precautions."

"Milord," General Mundo said, walking through the open
door with several Royal Guards behind him. "If I may, perhaps
we might see benefits in calling in Junko and the Bount
organization. They forewarned us about tonight's occurrence
and—"

"I refuse to create a partnership and give terrorists as much
power as an advisor!" the king bellowed but was quickly
restrained by the doctors to make sure that he didn't move too
much. "Send a message to my son. He will take care of this
matter swiftly. Take him off of the Spartan front. We have
internal affairs to deal with before we worry about foreign
conflicts. Inform him about today's events, and increase the
amount of security that we have. And you," the king said,
looking at a Royal Guard by the name of Judal, who stood tall
and saluted his lord upon being recognized.

"Yes, milord?"

"Find me Riku Hikari. We are going to need his skill in
order to protect against this new uprising. It seems that there
isn't just one enemy that we have to deal with. There are many of
them," the king said, leaning back into the softness of his pillow.
"Riku will have to protect my daughter in case there are any
assaults by this rebellion. We have to crush them. Mundo, I
heard that you have captured one of the members?"

"Yes, milord," General Mundo said with a proud grin. "We
have yet to make her talk, but we do have our ways to forcing
one to speak."

"Good, use whatever measures necessary to get her to talk.
Then have her executed in public to send a message to these
rebels," the king muttered. "Dismissed. Allow me to rest."

Aika blinked a few times as the doctors and guards began to

file out of the room, most of the soldiers standing right outside of the door. She turned to her father. "Father, are you sure that you want to bring Darius all the way into this conflict? I mean—"

"Darius is the most skilled warrior in the entire world when it comes to swordplay. He can easily defeat opponents with or without magic. It doesn't matter who they are. However, if it is Keimaro Hayashi that we are dealing with, perhaps his honor will allow him to duel Darius fairly. In that case, Keimaro will be slain; there is no doubt in my heart. He is good, but there is no way that he is good enough to face my son, the heir to the throne."

***

The wind howled against Tobimaru's cloak as he sat upon the rooftop of the bell tower from where the assassination had occurred. So, they had utilized a zip line in order to catch the politicians by surprise and create quite the scene today. Why in hell's name was Keimaro giving himself away so quickly? And why hadn't he just assassinated the king when he had the chance?

Don't tell me that he actually stopped midway in the assassination just because his "friends" were in trouble. How pathetic.

He sat down on the edge of the bell tower, his legs dangling into the open air. "To think that I'm related to a coward like him, tch." He scowled, picking up a small blue chip off of the floor and tossing it into the open air. That was a part of the teleportation mechanism that Zylon had. So, they had used teleportation in order to reach the top of the bell tower without any sort of suspicion, and the event began quickly after. It was a pity this chip had been damaged in the scuffle. A means of teleporting into the mansion would've meant a quick end to this little uprising.

"They must have quite the tactician," Hidan said, the wind blowing as he gusted into the area behind Tobimaru with Mai on his back. The young girl was asleep, snoring soundlessly against Hidan's shoulder. "And an engineer to develop a plan like this with all these gnome inventions. Then again, it seems that everyone has gnome inventions. I heard that the Faar government even got their hands on the recipe for creating rifles. They've been mass producing them."

"That's what I heard, too," Tobimaru said with a bored tone. "When is the king going to realize that he's fighting a pointless battle and that he should come to us for help already?"

"When the king loses his pride," Hidan said. "He's probably going to call in his son Darius from the Spartan front in order to eliminate Keimaro. I've heard rumors that the battle-prince is capable of matching a Bount with his blade. An ordinary human without any magic, able to defeat a Bount. Can you imagine that? He's quite the legend."

Tobimaru looked out at the twinkling bright stars that lingered in the blackened skies. "Yeah? Well, we can only hope that Keimaro kills off that legend. I can already tell that the Shokugan is growing stronger in him, but he hasn't obtained full control over it." He sighed. "In tonight's event, it looked like he almost completely lost control to his Shokugan."

"I still don't understand this whole Shokugan thing," Hidan muttered, "to be honest."

"These eyes aren't just a representation of a demon. By being a member of the Hayashi clan, we are half-demon. We are not fully human. That is, unfortunately, something that all of the people are right about. We aren't like them. When a member of the Hayashi clan activates the Shokugan in order to benefit from its all-seeing prowess, the demonic side threatens to take control. In tonight's case, the revenge and hatred that dwell within Keimaro's demon side took control when the king spoke about the Bakaara massacre. This means that he still hasn't come to recognize the demon part of himself and rule it. He's still weaker than I would've predicted at this point, though his training with his newer father did him well in controlling his flames. That fire truly has become like a part of him," Tobimaru admitted.

"Was that a compliment I heard?" Tobimaru's partner

sneered.

"Shut up," the Hayashi clansman muttered. "And what about you? Why are you always carrying Mai around and treating her like she's your own daughter? It's annoying."

"How is it annoying? It shouldn't affect you if I bring her around or not!" Hidan exclaimed. "And for the record, I told you! She reminds me of my own daughter that I had before I joined the Bount organization," he said, gently putting Mai on the ground and walking over to sit beside Tobimaru.

"Yeah? You never told me about your daughter."

"So you want to know about her?"

"Not particularly."

"I'll tell you anyway," Hidan muttered and smiled when Tobimaru rolled his eyes. "It's important for partners to understand each other, anyway. After all, you should know why I decided to join the Bounts.

"My daughter was nine years old, and she was the most beautiful thing that I'd ever seen. The fact that my wife and I created her made her all the more special to me. I can still remember her dark, long, straight hair and her glistening, crystal blue eyes that would smile at me whenever I looked into them. She was always happy, you know, excelling in every subject that she had in school. I never really got to see her all that much since I was in the Faar army at the time. We were at war with Sparta. I didn't really know why I had joined the army. I was fighting Sparta for no real reason; I had nothing really against them. In fact, Faar was just trying to take over Sparta, and the other empire was simply trying to defend itself. I constantly asked myself whether or not we were the good guys. All we did was pillage, kill, rape, and destroy. At the time, I was quite the master of the staff and used a spear in combat. They called me the Flashing Wind because I always took down my opponents with a single flash and was as swift as wind when I fought. But my mind was always set on seeing my daughter again. In fact, she was the reason that I kept fighting. The government didn't treat cowards kindly. They were executed in public in order to establish discipline amongst the ranks in the army. They didn't care if they killed their own men. The Faar army has millions of soldiers at their disposal. Losing a couple hundred cowards in order to scare the rest of the warriors into fighting for their empire was a small price to pay.

"So, I never left the army, and I constantly waited for the war to end so that one day I could go home and see my wife and child. However, while the end of the war was nearing, the Spartans pulled a fast one on us. Their skills in combat are without a doubt the fiercest and most coordinated that I've ever seen. Their units become one, and they can cut down our soldiers swiftly. Their only downfall is their lack in numbers. In their empire, their population has decreased because weak babies are dashed against walls or killed in their youth because they are incapable of contributing to the military. Quite scary, I dare say. At any rate, the Spartans overpowered us easily in the final push into their territory. We lost hundreds of thousands of men as the Spartans slaughtered us, but the Faar generals didn't tell us to retreat. They told us to keep fighting.

"As my eyes wandered around the roaring battlefield, I could hear the clanging of metal against wood and see the flash of blood spurting into the air. Corpses lay scattered across the desolated plain, which was covered with ash from flaming arrows. The Spartan warriors released a loud battle cry that shook the very earth as if the titans had awakened to condemn us all to hell. And in a swift moment, I knew the fate of this battle. I watched each of my comrades and friends fall, and I began evacuating many of the men. My final and closest friend, who had been in the service with me for ten years, was decapitated before my eyes. There truly was nothing that I could do about it. Without magic, without strength, there was no way that even I could face such a dangerous force as the Spartans. I took command and forced the Faar troops to retreat, which the soldiers had no problem doing. But I paid the price soon after.

"I was lashed relentlessly with a spiked whip fifty times for taking control and saving the soldiers' lives by ordering them to retreat. Apparently it showed weakness in the Faar Empire. An ordinary human supposedly could survive only thirty of those lashes. By then, my skin was raw with bloodied wounds, and my breath was heavy. My eyes could see nothing but an abyss of darkness, making me believe that I had somehow gone blind when I lost consciousness. I was locked in a cell for a week before I was released and allowed to go home. I was relieved that the fighting would be over and that I would finally be able to see my family. Though, I never should've expected to see my family, after having pulled the stunt that I did. When I returned home, I found my wife had been raped and killed. My daughter had been stabbed multiple times and was hanging on a cross in front of my burning home. She was only nine.

"From that very moment, I hated everything. My hatred wasn't directed toward Faar alone. It was directed at the universe. I wanted everything that the gods had ever created to be obliterated. They had done so much wrong with the creation of humanity. There were so many flaws if humans would do something as barbaric and terrifying as what they did to my beloved family. I joined the Bount organization in hopes that one day I would be able to destroy the gods that had done these terrible things to me. Kuro promised me that, when he becomes the new god of this world, he will bring back my family when he recreates the world into perfection. That's all I ever wanted, actually, to see my daughter's face again."

Hidan glanced over his shoulder at the calm, sleeping face of Mai and smiled slightly. Tears had begun to form in his eyes, and he exhaled, his voice strained as he tried to hold back from crying. "It's actually quite hard, seeing Mai's face. It truly does remind me of my daughter's. Sometimes that's good, but sometimes it just reminds me of my mistake. If I had never tried to save those soldiers, then my family would still be alive."

"It's not your fault," Tobimaru said, looking at the city before him. "What you did was what any good man would've done in that position. The only reason that you were punished for it is because of the cruelty of humanity. I always wonder what the gods were thinking when they created humans, believing that they were such a beloved creation. In reality, all they do is bicker and destroy each other. They cause pain, the most terrible feeling in existence."

"What's your story then?" Hidan asked his partner.

"I don't like sharing my life story," Tobimaru said, pushing himself to his feet as he began to walk back toward the bell. Changing the subject, he said, "It won't be long before this idiot of a king decides to communicate with Junko. Get Mai out of here before someone sees two Bounts wandering around the city. I just wanted to see what happened at tonight's occurrence."

Hidan wiped the salty tears that had generated in his eyes and nodded, lifting the young girl off of the ground and putting her on his back. He held her tight as he stepped off of the bell tower and gusted off into the wind, vanishing into thin air.

Tobimaru glanced into the distance, his eyes red with the Shokugan as he saw Z's mansion. *So, he's using some type of an illusion in order to cover up that large mansion of his. Huh, anyone with the Shokugan can see how flashy that is. Not to mention, the amount of artificial magic radiating from that place is impossible not to spot.* He sighed as he looked once more into the sky, this time at the full glowing moon that illuminated the night. He remembered a night long ago that had been just like this one. Just as silent. Just as sad. He didn't make a single sound as he simply vanished, his image completely gone from the face of Bassada in a flash.

16. UNDERCOVER

Keimaro walked in the morning light with Aladdin. He had pushed his fight with Yata to the back of his mind. Though, after thinking about it overnight, Keimaro concluded that he would have to formally apologize to his friend. Yata deserved at least that much.

Aladdin and Keimaro were heading toward the castle, strolling through the lush green grounds of the nobles. Fortunately, he could be seen in public with Aladdin since he was a noble. Keimaro couldn't help but stare in awe as he looked up at the massive structure that towered over him and stretched past the clouds, vanishing into the sky above. The birds chirped and sang as if this were the most pure of places in the world. He glanced forward and saw Judal, escorted by several members of the Royal Guard, walking from the large doorway of the front entrance of the castle.

"Yo, Riku!" Judal called, walking over and raising an eyebrow as he saw Aladdin. He bowed with respect. "Milord."

"At ease, Captain," Aladdin joked with a wink. "I was just having a small talk with my friend, Riku," he said, toying with the fine silks that he wore. "At any rate, I'll let him go on to work. When you're done with him, please send him to my house. I'd like a word with him after he's off duty."

"Yes, milord," Judal said and watched as Aladdin turned away and happily skipped off. He exhaled and straightened his back as he turned to Keimaro. "I'm sure that you've heard about what happened last night, right? The attempted assassination of the king by Keimaro Hayashi and his group of bandits?"

"Yeah, I heard about it," Keimaro said, trying to pretend as if he were disappointed in the outcome.

The captain nodded. "Princess Aika has been secured away in her chambers for the time being until Prince Darius arrives. Meanwhile, we are meant to go and interrogate the would-be assassin we captured. So, for today, you won't be guarding the princess since she is under good protection. You will need to guard the associate and ensure that she doesn't escape. We suspect that some of her friends will try to break her out of jail. For now, just get some information out of her. I'll take you to her."

Keimaro's heart leapt as Judal began to lead him away from the castle. They walked on a cobblestone path, avoiding the green grass, which looked completely untouched. He turned and saw three guards standing around a side entrance to the castle, a small wooden door that would've gone unnoticed on a building as big as this. The boy watched as the captain took a turn from the path that circled the perimeter of the entire castle and instead followed a side-path to the camouflaged door.

The undercover assassin raised his eyebrow as he followed closely behind the captain. He watched as the door opened after a swift nod of Judal's head. Through the entrance was pitch-black despite the bright daylight that was apparent outside. Looking through the doorway, Keimaro thought that he was going to be walking down a staircase to the depths of hell. His eyes were wide as he stared at the abyss before him, but he kept his calm and watched as the captain passed through the doorway and down a small stone staircase. His footsteps echoed until they began to fade as he got farther away.

Keimaro hesitated for a moment before he followed Judal into the darkness, watching as the blackness encased him. The door closed behind him and locked him into a world of shadows, as if a blanket of black had been tossed over his eyes. He felt tempted to activate his Shokugan so that he could see, but he restrained himself, wincing a bit uncomfortably. He strained to see Judal's outline and then blinked as light flashed and a torch was lit.

The captain held it in front of him and gave Keimaro a small nod, beginning to walk forward in the darkness. Without a doubt, few soldiers were down here, wherever this hell was. It made sense: who would want to stay in this darkness? It reminded Keimaro of the Forbidden Forest. He shifted awkwardly as he listened to the echo of their boots thumping on the cold stone ground. Using the light from Judal's torch, Keimaro could see cells with iron bars that separated the main hallway from crammed rooms filled with people. In jails, he imagined that the cell-mates would've been fighting, grabbing the bars, or yelling. But when he looked at the jailed people before him, he saw only a lack of hope in their eyes, many of which seemed to be on the brink of insanity. Some didn't even look up to see the two members of the Royal Guard walking through; instead, they stared at the ground blankly. They seemed completely sapped of energy and hope after having been deprived of light for so long. In fact, most of these people seemed like they would be normal. They were probably just political dissidents or perhaps wrongly accused. Then again, images could be deceiving.

Keimaro forced himself to look away from the cells, knowing that in one of them he would find Lena. He just hoped that she hadn't been mistreated already, especially not the way her mother had been. He would never forgive himself if she were forced to experience that. He held his breath, smelling the acrid odor of urine. Then he coughed when he smelled blood mixed in. By now, the hallways had more torches that were located on the stone walls, illuminating the area. Keimaro could see that guards had beaten the jailed to the point where they were almost dead, and it seemed like these people were half-starved as well. Such unfair treatment made Keimaro sick to his stomach.

Guards sat in chairs that leaned against walls, half-asleep from the silence. Keimaro walked past one of the snoring soldiers and sighed. He supposed that the man didn't need to be too cautious, since all of the prisoners were too weak to attempt to escape. Even if they did escape, getting out of the noble district was near impossible without running into a squad of guards or two. Since they were constantly starved and beaten, it didn't look like they were going to be escaping any time soon. Keimaro snatched a loaf of bread off of the lap of one of the soldiers and stuffed it into his pocket.

Finally, they reached Lena's cell. Fortunately, she was alone, but she seemed much more restricted than any of the other prisoners. Chains connected her wrists to the wall. She was incapable of moving five feet from the wall. Without magic, it was impossible for her to even think of escaping. He saw her head drooping languidly before her eyes flickered up to see Keimaro. She almost smiled but saw that Judal was there beside him, and the hope was immediately wiped cleaned off of her face.

"We've tried to get information from her, but she seems quite hard-headed. See if you can get anything from her," Judal said, opening the cell and nodding to Keimaro. He paused and then lowered his voice, whispering so Lena couldn't hear. "You seem like the type that can make people talk. Just don't kill her, all right? The king has ordered that she be executed in public after we extract the information."

Keimaro stared at the captain, shock registering in his chest. He kept poised and nodded, continuing into the cell and watching as the door creaked shut behind him. He advanced toward Lena, who began to sob, tears streaming down her face. He couldn't do this. He couldn't hurt Lena. It didn't matter who it was. He couldn't do this to someone who was defenseless like this.

"Just get it over with...," Lena whispered, sniffling. Her face was covered in bruises, and there were scrapes across her cheek. Dirt caked her skin, and her clothing looked torn from multiple beatings.

Keimaro's lips quivered as he stood in front of her and gulped, his hands shaking. *I can't blow my cover. Judal is watching. I have to do this.* "Why was your band of assassins going to assassinate the king?" he demanded.

"We didn't want to assassinate the king. That wasn't the plan."

"Then what was the plan?"

Lena said the answer, but she was too quiet. Judal couldn't hear.

Keimaro raised his hand and slapped her across the face with a loud crack as her head snapped to the side. "Answer me!" he roared, tears forming in his eyes. "Louder!"

"It was to show Keimaro off. We wanted to give him publicity so that it would instill fear in the government," Lena gasped, stifling back her cries.

"What else do you want to know?" Keimaro asked Judal over his shoulder.

"Where are they hiding now? That's all we need."

A surge of fear shot through Keimaro's body. Lena couldn't give away that information. If she did, then everyone in the mansion would be killed. It wouldn't be only her life at stake. It would be everyone's. He slowly turned toward Lena and closed his eyes. If she told him, then she jeopardized everyone's life at Z's mansion. But if she didn't … he would have to beat her until Judal was satisfied. *Damn it!*

"Where are the rest of your crew hiding?"

"I don't know." Lena said weakly.

Keimaro raised his hand and slapped her across the face once more, a bit harder, leaving a red mark. "Tell me the truth!"

"I don't know!" Lena cried, tears freely streaming down her cheeks.

Keimaro brought his foot back and drove a kick into her diaphragm. She lurched forward, her breath completely driven from her lungs. He grabbed her by the hair and lifted her head, forcing her to look him in the eyes. He was trying to be as gentle as he could with her, but he could see the pain on her face. She was barely conscious. He swung his fist and slammed it into her stomach, causing her to gasp once more. "Where the hell are your damn friends hiding? If you don't tell me, this will continue!"

"I don't know where they are! We switch hiding places frequently so that if one of us is captured, we won't be able to give away the position! Please...," Lena whimpered. "No more...."

Keimaro stared into Lena's eyes and released her hair, allowing her to crumple to the ground. He stood, leaving her in a heap. Then he turned toward Judal, who shrugged with a sigh.

"It looks like she doesn't know. I would cut off a limb or two, but I don't think the king would like that. He was rather vague on how much we could hurt her. At any rate, she looks like she could hardly withstand last night's torture anyway. That's enough. Looks like we'll have to manually search for their damn hideouts, what a drag. Come, Riku, I have to show you around the castle anyway, don't I?" The captain opened the cell door and began to walk off, leaving Keimaro to follow him.

Keimaro reached into his pocket and squatted down on the ground, putting a piece of bread in Lena's weak hands. He tilted her chin up toward him, but she wasn't looking at him. She was looking *through* him. "What the hell did they do to you?" he whispered, staring into her eyes. He bit his lip and closed his eyes, trying to hold back tears. "We're going to get you out of here. I promise, we won't leave you." He closed her fingers around the bread and quickly turned away, leaving the cell. He couldn't break her out now. That would blow his cover. In fact, he might not even get away since Lena was currently in such a weak state. He closed the cell door behind him and began to walk after Judal. His hands were shaking, stained with Lena's blood.

I cannot believe I just did that. I was torturing and beating my own friend while she was in such a weak and vulnerable condition. The first person in this city to accept me … and I hurt her. His hands curled into fists, and his eyes filled with fire. *I'll make these guys pay for this.*

***

Far away, on the borders of Sparta, a young prince brushed aside the curtains of his war-tent, which was decorated in the red and white of Faar. He walked out into the morning sun, which shined down on him and gave his golden crown an even brighter glow than usual. He was wearing his golden battle armor, which glittered in the sun, the flashiest suit that one could wear. The one to slay this prince would inevitably become rich. However, the prince was renowned throughout all of the kingdoms for his feats in combat. Without a doubt, he was one of the most skilled humans with a blade, and his leadership was well-earned, as many had said. He dominated even the burly and organized Spartans in battle. He stretched, finding that their battle against Sparta was going fairly well. They were pushing the enemy closer and closer to their capital and took more land every day. With time, they would dominate this empire.

The prince's looks fit royalty. His curly, brown hair was without doubt perfection, and he won the hearts of fair maidens with his looks alone. His royal blue eyes could seduce the strongest of women, but they could also be filled with such intensity that he made his enemies feel as if they were naked before him. At the age of only twenty-four, he had claimed many achievements as prince of Faar. His skin was tan from the many days that he spent in the sun fighting beside his men and working with them. Unlike his father, he didn't believe in forcing all of the work upon his subjects. He contributed his amount to help his men and therefore was treated as a brother amongst his soldiers as well as their superior.

"Darius," the prince's squire announced, walking forward with two guard escorts at his side as well as a small messenger boy that stumbled behind them, "a letter has been delivered from your father."

The prince raised an eyebrow, not expecting to hear so soon from his father. Was it time for his father to pass, leaving the throne to him? He chuckled at the thought and nodded, grasping the letter in his hands and seeing the royal seal. *Still alive then, old man?*

He ripped off the seal and flipped open the letter, reading it swiftly. He frowned the more that he read. "My father is drawing me back from the frontier of the Spartan-Faar war in order to deal with a group of bandits within our capital? What am I, a law enforcer?" he snarled, tossing the letter onto the ground in annoyance. "A single boy is threatening his throne, and he needs to call *me* back in order to deal with the issue? How frightening is this teenage boy?" he demanded as he looked at the messenger.

"W-Well, milord…," the messenger stammered, "the boy isn't quite ordinary. He has acquired magic, but it isn't like other magic that we've seen, sire. The magic that he has never tires him, and he can keep using it! It also looks as if it's a part of him. I'm not an expert on artificial magic, milord, but this doesn't look like it. I haven't seen much myself, but…."

"You think that his magic is real?" Darius scoffed as he looked the messenger up and down and smiled. "Is that so? A boy comes into the city, shooting flames about and kills a few of my father's men and the king has already wet his pants? How like him. Fine then, I'll destroy my father's opposition within the empire and then finish the job here. Tell General Killen to assume control over our forces until my return. Push toward the capital, but make sure that he doesn't rush toward the victory without me. I'll be back within the month after I eradicate this threat within our walls." He walked past the messenger and his squire, calling over his shoulder, "Fetch me my horse and a squadron of men. We will deal with this quickly."

***

"Ugh," Keimaro muttered as he walked outside of the castle after having spent the majority of the day exploring it with Judal. Well, he supposed he had to be familiar with where everything was if he was going to be living here. He sighed, scratching the back of his neck as he saw the smile on Judal's face. "What are you so happy about?" he muttered, exhausted.

"The new guys always have a hard time at first trying to comprehend how many rooms there are to memorize in this entire place. Don't worry, the hardest part about this job is knowing where everything is," Judal said with a chuckle. "But with all of the new threats appearing all of a sudden, things could change quickly."

Keimaro nodded as he turned and saw the sun setting over the horizon, vanishing over the edge of Bassada's wall. The bright orange and red dispersed into the skies, filling the clouds with light. His eyes twinkled as he stared with amazement at the breathtaking view before turning to his captain. He hit his fist to his chest and bowed his head slightly. "I'll be heading to meet with Lord Aladdin now, if that's all right with you, Captain Judal," he said, using the same title that everyone else used when regarding nobles.

The Captain seemed rather surprised at the respect that came from Keimaro and grinned, giving the recruit a nod. "As you were, soldier. Go on. You wouldn't want to keep him waiting. Make sure to be back here tomorrow morning. I want to see if we can get some more information out of the prisoner. See ya, Riku," he said, giving a small wave.

Keimaro turned and felt a chill shiver down his spine as he walked along the cobblestone path, making his way toward Aladdin's house. If he was correct, it should be the first house in the noble district. Once there, he should feel safe. But, the thought of Lena being tortured once more was disconcerting. The very thought that he would have to beat his friend again made his stomach churn.

He blinked as he saw Aladdin's house, a flashy mansion with spiraling marble pillars that somehow managed to support the red tiled rooftop. The building itself wasn't as big as some of the other mansions but was without a doubt still a reasonable enough size to leave the boy in awe. Interestingly enough, he recognized this house. He had walked past it his first time in the noble district. Keimaro walked up to the door, which was made of some type of quality wood that gave it a hazel color. He grasped the golden knocker and was about to hit the door with it when he heard the door click.

"Hmm?" he murmured as the door opened and an old, bald man with squinted eyes poked his head through the opening.

The man had a face of wrinkles, and small clumps of gray hair were formed just above his ears. Keimaro could hardly even see the color of his irises for his eyes were so small. He was wearing a black suit with a red tie and was clearly a servant of the house. "How may I help you, sir?" the old man said with a raised eyebrow, holding the open door with his white-gloved hand.

"I'm here for Aladdin."

"His sire doesn't see common soldiers just upon request. You need approval from the house as well as some type of an appointment if it's on working terms. You cannot just come—"

"It's all right," Aladdin said with a warm laugh as he walked from behind the butler and opened the door wide. He was wearing a blue robe that was tied with a small white sash. His blonde hair was wet, indicating that he had just gotten out of a bath. "Make yourself at home, Riku. Yuri is in my room. My butler will show you there. Just make sure to take off your shoes when you walk in, okay?" he said, walking away from the door to go get dressed.

Keimaro blinked a few times and nodded, taking off his boots and putting them on a mat beside the door where other shoes were being displayed. He walked inside, and the door was closed behind him. The butler didn't seem surprised that Aladdin had just let someone into the house without identification. He simply sighed and motioned for Keimaro to follow him.

The entrance to the house was topped by a high ceiling that seemed to stretch at least four stories tall. A shining chandelier that emitted an array of various crystalline lights upon the walls hung from the ceiling. A long pair of marble stairs climbed to the next floor. The butler led Keimaro up the stairs and through a large hallway, filled with candles within some type of transparent delicate paper bags that allowed for the light to be distributed more vastly. He was led into a rather large room where Yuri was sitting on the edge of the neatly made king-sized bed.

Yuri turned his head, his eyes lighting up when he saw Keimaro. He waited until the butler had closed the door behind Keimaro before he began to speak. "Did you find her? Is she all right?" he asked quickly, getting up from the bed and walking to Keimaro.

The boy blinked a few times and nodded. "Yeah, I found out her location. They intend on torturing her more than they already have. It looks like she's already at her limit, though," he said with a sigh. "At this rate, she will crack. I know that you think she's tough enough that she wouldn't, but the things that they could do to her in that cell are endless, and there don't seem to be any laws that protect her against being tortured. We're going to need to get her out soon. They're planning a public execution. I think our only chance may be to rescue her on her execution day. Trying to get her out of jail while this area is under such heavy lockdown will be near impossible without getting caught. Even if we fought our way out using force, there would be no way to escape without the guards eventually keeping up with us since carrying Lena would weigh us down. She is in no position to move on her own right now."

Yuri's fists were shaking, and his eyes were red with rage. "So, what do we do? We can't just let her get tortured until the execution day! She could die by accident, and the pain that she's going through…"

"Not to mention the fact that she could spill important information regarding the location of our base, which would lead to the deaths of more than just a dozen. It would be hundreds," Keimaro said, rubbing his chin. "I don't know a good—"

"We can break her out," Yuri said confidently, looking Keimaro in the eyes. "Tonight!"

Keimaro blinked. "Eh? Tonight? That's not a good plan! She just got in there! The security is tight and—"

"Who cares? They can't be much worse than a Bount! I'll wear the mask, and I'll get away. I'll even enter werewolf form if I have to," Yuri said, closing his eyes. "I can't stand the thought of Lena being in a cold, dark cell, suffering. I know what it's like. I don't want her to endure that hell! I'll break her out; you won't have to worry about a single thing. All I'll need is her location."

"I can't give you the location," Keimaro said, and he felt a pang of heat between the two of them as Yuri glared at him. "You'll get both of you captured or, even worse, killed. I won't let you run off to your—"

"Stop underestimating me!" Yuri boomed, grabbing Keimaro by the collar of his shirt. He lifted him off of the ground by an inch and brought their faces close together, glaring into the dark pools of Keimaro's eyes. "I am much more capable than you are. I don't know why I ever decided to put my trust into you on that mission last night. You almost got us all killed. Lena is behind bars and is being tortured because of your mistake!" he growled, shaking Keimaro roughly. "And you're reluctant to giving me her location so that I can save her from that pain? Are you kidding me?"

Keimaro's lips were quivering, and he just wanted to cry. *But if I give you the location ... both of you will be....*

"The true reason that Keimaro is incapable of giving you her location," Aladdin said, stepping through the doorway behind them with a smile. He wore a fresh blue tunic and long, baggy, white pants that looked like pajamas, "is because he isn't sure whether or not he can put his trust into you. I spent today researching the Hayashi clan background and looked over some of the intel that Zylon has on you," he said to Keimaro with a wink. "In fact, he's got quite a bit. Keimaro has trouble trusting people and depending on them to get the job done. It isn't because someone has let him down before. It's because he's let down someone before."

"What?" Yuri muttered.

"Stop talking," Keimaro growled.

"He let down his little sister when he was powerless to save her."

Keimaro was silent and gulped, feeling anger swelling up inside of him. Though, he had no idea what he was mad at. He closed his eyes as he felt Yuri's hand release the hem of his shirt. He stepped away from his two companions. "I don't intend to let down anyone ever again," Keimaro said, "and living my whole life in regret ... I don't want anyone else to go through that. Especially you, Yuri. If you fail in saving Lena, and she is killed, you won't be able to forgive yourself. But that's not all. I won't forgive you either. The risk is not one I am willing to take."

Yuri stared at Keimaro for a moment, his clenched fists dropping limp at his side. He was speechless. Keimaro sighed. He understood the way Yuri was feeling more than anything. Yuri would keep persisting until he found out. It was better off if Keimaro just told Yuri where Lena was rather than forcing Yuri to have to go search for himself. In the end, the werewolf was going to risk his life anyway.

"She's in an underground facility beneath the castle. There's an entrance on the side of the castle; it'll be easy to miss because it doesn't seem like it has high security. But trust me, once you trigger their alarm, you'll be surrounded within minutes," Keimaro let out without thinking. "Don't expect me to come and save your life either. If I blow my cover, the entire plan with overthrowing the kingdom will be finished. By doing this, you'll be doing it on your own accord. Don't act today. Give it a few days."

Yuri raised an eyebrow and put his hands on his hips. "Huh? Why should I wait a few days?" he muttered, trying to keep poised, his eyes on Keimaro. "I don't have any intention of letting Lena suffer more than she already has."

"By going now, you're increasing the risk that you'll get captured," Keimaro exclaimed. "At any rate, you'll only get yourself killed. Besides, don't you want to rest a bit before you sweep in and save the damsel in distress? After all, we just performed a bunch of operations in the past few days. I don't know about you, but I'm really sore from fighting so much," he said, reaching up and stretching his arms. "I don't intend to get involved with your suicidal plan to save Lena."

The werewolf rolled his eyes and walked out of the room, eager to be alone. As he started to close the door behind him, Keimaro saw a resplendent blue band around Yuri's wrist. He vanished through the door without a single word spoken, and Aladdin sighed.

"Yuri isn't exactly the most diplomatic person around. He's near impossible to convince," the noble said. "Once he's got his mind set on something, he's going after it. There's no stopping him. Anyway, we should talk about the task at hand. I did some research today. I went through the paperwork that they did on recent government prisoners, and there was nothing recorded about even obtaining Noah." He rubbed his chin as he walked over to his bed and sat down. "I knew something was off. I even searched through the secret files, which is illegal by the way, and still didn't find anything."

"That's odd."

"What's even more strange is that there isn't any record of the entire existence of the underground lab. It's as if it never existed. Perhaps the king doesn't know about the lab…. At least, that's my theory."

Keimaro frowned. "That means…."

"That there's an outside force within the government that has obtained some power. My thought is that it's the Bount organization, trying to maintain some influence in the city. Undoubtedly, they'll try to push their way to the throne eventually, which is why we should take it first. However, I don't suspect that there's a large Bount force in the government; otherwise, it would've been noticeable before now. Z hasn't sensed any abnormal activity or auras from the Bounts, so it must be a subordinate."

"Didn't Yata and Gavin see the person who attacked them underground? Whoever was underground must've been with the Bounts. Wouldn't they be able to identify who was down there?" Keimaro said.

Aladdin grinned at Keimaro and gave him a nod, patting him on the back. "Looks like we've got a lead! I'll go ask them tonight, and I'll get back to you tomorrow after duty again. Hopefully Yuri will stay out of trouble tonight. Do you need somewhere to stay?"

"I suppose," Keimaro said. "I'm off duty, and I'm supposed to return to my room with the captain. But I don't think he'll have any objection if I was *ordered* to spend the night. After all, you're my superior now, I guess," he said, rubbing the back of his neck. "Why, you have an extra room?"

"I have dozens."

"Makes sense, in a place this big."

"I thought your job was to protect the princess, but it looks like you've got plenty of free time on your hands," Aladdin said, walking to a mirror and examining himself. He rubbed his chin and sighed, turning to glance at Keimaro over his shoulder. "Don't tell me you're—" He blinked when he saw that Keimaro wasn't there anymore and that the window was open. A light, nighttime breeze blew into the room, and he heard nothing but the chirps of crickets. He walked over to the window, leaning on the sill as he looked up at the moon and smiled. "What a sneaky bastard. I just hope he doesn't do something stupid."

***

Keimaro knew that it wasn't right for him to just leave Aladdin with Yuri in the mansion, especially if Yuri tried to save Lena tonight. Aladdin wouldn't be able to stop him alone. In fact, Keimaro wasn't even sure if the noble was capable of combat. He had never gotten to see Aladdin in action before. Still, something drew him from the noble's house and toward the

281

castle. He wanted to see the princess again. Why? He had no idea. He could name no specific reason, other than wanting to see her face and maybe even talk to her. Before he knew it, he was walking up a narrow stairway toward the princess's tower. When he found the door, it was heavily guarded with five strong, burly men who stood tall with thick metallic armor covering every possible inch of their body. That must've been extremely uncomfortable.

"What is your business here, guard?" one of the soldiers said.

"I'm the princess's bodyguard, so I'm here to—"

"The king's orders are not to let anyone in. *Anyone.* That includes you, rookie," the soldier stated. "These orders will be followed until further notice. If you want authorization, you'll have to get some from the higher-ups. Until then, we can't let you pass. Please turn around."

"But this is my post! Shouldn't I—"

"Turn around. Otherwise…." The soldiers all unsheathed their blades in unison and pointed the gleaming tips at Keimaro, their hands shaking ever so slightly. The timorous soldiers definitely didn't seem ready to combat the rumored member of the Royal Guard who had been assigned to protect the princess. They all thought of him as simply a random braggart from the slums that managed to score a lucky position in the princess's guard. Now that they faced Keimaro in person, for some reason, the boy was giving them an ominous aura—one that relieved them of all their previous bravery and left them sapped and shaking in their rattling knight armor, which creaked with every movement.

"Ah, how ponderous. A group of brawny knights ganging up on a member of the Royal Guard? Show proper deference. The adversity of such a high position is esoteric in comparison to you, those who lounge around all day simply gambling amongst yourselves and drinking to the point where you hardly even know your own place. You torpid fools ought to lower your swords and bow," a voice said from behind Keimaro, and the boy turned to find General Mundo standing behind him with his slicked-back hair and gleaming armor. "Lower your blades and resume your positions. As for you, Riku Hikari, was it? Follow me."

Keimaro looked at the superior for a moment and supposed that it was more of an order than a suggestion. He couldn't deny this man; he was a general. So, the Royal Guard followed the general as they descended the steps. He couldn't help but think that it was unlikely that the general was just randomly wandering and saw the event occurring. Without a doubt, he had been following Keimaro or at least intended to see the princess himself. Though, the first idea seemed more likely since the general had asked him for a walk. What on earth could this man possibly want to talk about?

"I heard about your trial with the king," General Mundo said, breaking the silent barrier between the two of them. "That is quite the feat, if I do say so myself. You've managed to impress even the king with your talents with the sword. I have heard a great many things. I wish that the king had asked for you to come into the ranks of the guard sooner, actually. With the recent assassination last night, if you had been there, perhaps we could've saved some lives."

"Perhaps," Keimaro said.

"So many men were lost just from a simple swipe of Keimaro Hayashi's hand. Can you believe it? Dozens of men were killed. Men with families. I can't imagine what the families must feel like today after finding out that one of their loved ones was incinerated by Keimaro's flames. Last night's events will only arouse rage within the civilian population." General Mundo sighed. "But then again, what can they do? And what can we do? We are simple humans. We don't have powers like that monstrosity of a boy. Born a demon and now he's got abnormal fire powers to match. How much deeper into darkness will he fall, I wonder?"

"I was asking myself the same thing, sir," Keimaro said,

wincing at the mention of how he was a monster. *I don't need some old man telling me what I am.* He kept his calm and watched as the general tittered like a child. It looked as if he were up to something, but Keimaro simply waited until the general collected himself.

"At any rate, the king has told me to send a letter to Darius, the prince of Faar, telling him to come home. He is one of the most skilled humans in existence with a blade. I'm sure that he would be intrigued to have a sparring match with you before the king," General Mundo said. "I was just wondering if you'd be up to the challenge, is all. After all, I wouldn't want to force you into fighting an opponent that you'd be uncomfortable in combat with."

Keimaro raised an eyebrow as they reached the end of the staircase and stopped descending. The general noticed and turned to look at the guard. The boy's eyes were wide and filled with heat and glee. However, not a single crack of a smile formed on his lips. "My only issue is … if I hurt the prince, will there be any penalty?"

"Not at all."

"Then this'll be fun," Keimaro said with a small chuckle, his eyes glimmering though they remained black as the shadows of an abyss. "You can count me in."

"He will be here in a few days," General Mundo said with a wave over his shoulder as he began to walk away. "I congratulate you on your new position, by the way, Riku. I'm sure you'll do great." The general gave a wicked smile that spread across his lips, though Keimaro couldn't quite see it.

Keimaro watched the man walk away, frowning to himself. There was something off about General Mundo. There wasn't any specific reason but Keimaro's intuition told him to be careful about Mundo. A part of him wanted to go and follow the general to find out what was so fishy about him, but he had other things on his mind. Keimaro turned to leave the castle instead. If those guards wouldn't let him go in through the front door to get to

Aika, there would always be alternate ways to get in.

After finding an open window, Keimaro began to climb up the side of the castle. It wasn't exactly difficult, but was more psychologically strenuous than it was physically. Many tiles were loose, but he found plenty of windowsills to grab on to, and his upper-body strength was honed to the point where it didn't even strain him to climb. However, the thought of getting caught or even falling haunted him throughout his ascension. He was paranoid. Even the slightest of sounds would make him glance downward to see if soldiers were wandering around below. Fortunately for him, there weren't. With his white tabard, he blended in partially with the color of the castle. He hadn't thought of how long the climb to get to the princess's tower really was. It didn't seem too far, but it felt like he had been climbing for ages. His fingertips were beginning to ache, and he wondered how he was going to get back down. Each breeze made him want to fall or just release the castle and flow with the wind—though he knew realistically he would fall and probably die, or at least break every bone possible.

Why on earth was he risking everything just to see the princess? Something as suspicious as this could be seen as an attempted assassination or kidnapping. He couldn't possibly be risking his capture for a simple girl! Just to see her, how ridiculous was he being? Nevertheless, he continued onward, pulling himself further up, until he finally grasped the stone railings of the balcony. He hauled himself upward, panting, slightly exasperated from the climb. He landed swiftly and silently as a feather on the balcony floor. The boy glanced back over the railing and almost whistled at how far the drop was. He now towered high over the entire city and could see all the brilliant lights as he had from his own room except to a much greater extent. Now he could see over the walls and out toward the vast fields that surrounded the city. He could even see the edge of the Forbidden Forest.

Keimaro smiled to himself and then turned to see the silk curtains of the balcony blowing to the side. His eyes widened as the curtains gusted, and he saw Aika without her shirt, putting on her nightgown. His eyes gazed upon her smooth, young skin, and a light blush came across his face. He coughed and immediately regretted it because Aika's face snapped to his. She screamed.

Within a single second, the guards barged through the door, brandishing their swords. "What happened? Princess! Are you okay?"

"Yes! Yes! I'm fine!" Aika stammered. "I just saw a bug was all! There's nothing to worry about!" She squealed, her face red as she pulled her blanket around her body. "Now get out of here! I'm not dressed!"

***

The soldiers all flushed red and quickly piled out of the doorway without taking a single glance at the balcony. As soon as the door to her room was closed and locked, Aika turned to face the balcony, but she didn't see him anymore. She could've sworn that she saw Riku. Her face was red as she slowly began to walk toward the balcony, her white nightgown wrapped around her. She stepped onto the soft marble floor with her bare feet, feeling the slight shiver of cold run through her toes. The soles of her feet padded against the floor gently, and she looked around.

The boy stepped out from the side of the balcony, his foot touching gracefully on the railing. A hood was pulled over his head, but he wore his white Royal Guard tabard. He gave her a small smile as he touched down on the ground in front of her. He had been hiding on a ledge next to the balcony. He was fast; she gave him that. But how did he get up here?

Aika glanced past Riku at the railing and shook her head in disbelief. "How did you…?"

"I climbed."

Well, that answers that, Aika thought. But she couldn't believe it. No ordinary human could climb that high. She brushed the hair out of her eyes and tucked it behind her ear. "Why are you here, Riku? You realize this is against the rules, don't you?"

"Yeah, I got it," Riku said, rubbing his neck with a sigh. "I just wanted to check up on you. After all, that's my job, I guess. I wanted to make sure that you were all right after that explosion in the city and then the assassination last night…."

I feel like I know him, Aika thought, biting her lower lip. There was something about him. She felt as if she had met him before and that they knew each other. But, this was only the second time they had even talked. And what kind of soldier cared so much about a princess? Who would climb dozens of stories just to see if the person was okay—particularly if that person were a complete stranger? When Aika looked into the dark pools of his eyes, she saw something familiar, but what was it? Her heart fluttered when their eyes met. Heat rose up in her. "Do I know you?"

***

Why had Keimaro come up all this way? To see her? No, he wanted to tell her something. He wanted to tell her everything. He lowered his eyes when she said those words: *Do I know you?*

Yes. Yes, you do!

Then he bit his lower lip, trying to hold back the words that wanted to leave his mouth. For now, he was just Riku Hikari, right? *Not around her, I'm not.* His heart throbbed, and when he looked at her, an image appeared in his mind.

The beautiful blue skies that stretched for miles and miles that urged him on to explore the world. Keimaro could see himself at the age of fourteen, sitting underneath the beautiful apple tree that had once topped the hill overlooking their village. A light breeze sent every single blade of grass swaying as if they were dancing with the wind. And in a moment's glance, Yata appeared, sitting on the grass beside him. The two of them were laughing and joking with each other, but Keimaro couldn't hear anything. They simply smiled, enjoying the view and the wonderful weather. And then Aika appeared in the image, standing over them with her dirty dress, scolding them for something. But the two boys were simply laughing, inviting Aika to relax with them.

If the Bakaara massacre hadn't happened, then maybe that dream could've become a reality. Maybe they could've been the best of friends. The three of them.

A tear formed in Keimaro's eye and streaked down his right cheek, gathering at his chin. It fell gently and hit the marble floor, dispersing into multiple droplets as it hit. He lowered his head as his heart ached, wishing that he could return to that happiness—sitting underneath the apple tree, free from everything with his friends. He wiped his eyes with his sleeve and raised his head. He had to show her.

Aika's eyes widened when she saw the glow in Keimaro's irises, a flashing red that was unmistakable. She didn't move, and her mouth dropped open as the two of them stood in silence, looking at each other. "You're…."

Keimaro's eyes returned to their dark color, and he gave her a small smile. "Yeah."

"K-Keimaro? It's you? It's really you! All of this time, I'd thought you were dead from the massacre. I mean, until I heard that you were in the city and—"

Aika was interrupted when Keimaro leaned forward suddenly and locked lips with her. The wind gusted as they kissed, sending waves of heat between the two of them, sparks igniting almost instantly. Aika's face blushed bright red as Keimaro pulled back, and she was silenced by the action. She reached out and slapped him, practically shaking. But Keimaro didn't even react; the smile was still printed on his face.

After a few moments of being stunned, she gathered her bravery to speak again. "W-Why did you do that!" she exclaimed, flustered. "I'm a princess! You can't just—"

"I just did," Keimaro laughed warmly and took a step back to lean against the railing of the balcony. "You didn't have to enjoy it, Aika. You really are beautiful, and I've always wanted to do that. I remembered that you were pretty before, but now when I see you, I really can't help myself." He exhaled, looking over his shoulder at the view of the city. "I suppose you're wondering what I'm doing here then. You know, it's weird. I don't know why I climbed this high to see you either."

"Why are you posing as Riku Hikari?" Aika asked, touching the railing and turning toward him. She tried to push the kiss to the back of her mind. "What's the point in that? Are you out to kill my father?"

"If it was something as simple as that, I could've just done it when I had my hands around his throat last night," Keimaro murmured with a shake of his head. "No, it's not him that I want. For the most part, my concentration is on the Bount organization. Although your father's men are the ones that destroyed my village, the only reason they were able to invade was because of the Bounts. Not to mention, they took my sister from me and killed my mother." He growled, squeezing the railing tightly. "The reason that I am here is that I want to make sure that you're all right, that's all." *At least it's part of the truth.* "Members of the Bounts have infiltrated the government, and they will try to target you. I am here to ensure your safety. Though, I just blew my cover a couple of seconds ago, I suppose."

"You really must trust me," Aika laughed lightly. "You know, I might not be the same girl that you remember from four years ago."

"I figured that you owe me one anyway." Keimaro winked at her. "After all, we saved your life in the forest twice."

Aika pushed him playfully, and Keimaro laughed.

"Did you end up getting a power from the meteor that we discovered in the forest?" Keimaro asked abruptly. "Yata and I got one."

"Yes, I did," Aika said, looking out at the city, her eyes wandering amongst the glowing lights. "I gained an odd ability to heal. Whenever I get a cut, it automatically heals, which is why you won't find a single scar on my entire body. I can use the ability to heal other people as well, but that's all that I've learned so far."

Keimaro now knew the purpose of the three powers. The meteor was supposed to give god-like powers to a single person who absorbed its energy through physical contact. At least, that was what Z had said. If the powers were evenly distributed, then each of them got a fraction of the total power that the meteor could've provided. Aika got the power to heal. Yata got the power to protect. And Keimaro got the power to destroy. If those powers were all put together, then they would cause devastation on a massive scale if used improperly. So, that was the power of Kuro. The mere thought of his awakening was enough to bring a shiver down his spine.

The young boy's stay on the princess's balcony was prolonged as he began to engage in conversation about their past and attempted to catch up on what had happened over the years. He couldn't help but realize that Aika didn't treat him like he was a terrorist. She didn't seem to have even the slightest bit of hate directed toward him despite the fact that he had injured her father. And he felt guilty for doing what he had done.

He didn't know why. Perhaps it was because he was beginning to strengthen his friendship with Aika once more, and he felt bad for hurting someone she held close. But, in the end, he knew that what he should've done was murder the king right then and there. In the deepest and darkest parts of his blackened heart, he also wished that he had simply squeezed the life out of the king's throat and ended this whole charade in a single instant.

But as the boy talked to the princess more and more, his thoughts of revenge began to be pushed to the very back of his mind, and his heart thumped every time she giggled at a joke or remark that he made. He felt heat rising in his body, and for once it wasn't anger, annoyance, or hatred. Unfamiliar with this foreign emotion, he ignored it and ended up falling asleep at her bedside after hours of talking. And for the first time in years, there was a smile on his face as he slept.

17. THE PRINCE

It had been several days since Yuri had spoken to Keimaro in Aladdin's mansion. How long did that idiot expect him to wait before he could save Lena? His friend was sitting in a dungeon being tortured every day, and he was expected to just sit there and wait until her execution was announced? What kind of logic was that?

The werewolf sat isolated in the room that Aladdin had provided for him. The noble had left the house early that morning in hopes of asking Gavin and Yata a question regarding their previous mission underground. He still had not returned. The snow-haired boy lay on his king-sized bed and stared at the ceiling with his arms outstretched on the purple and yellow blankets. He hadn't seen Keimaro since that day either. It looked as if he were actually taking his job seriously in the Royal Guard. *How the hell can he take the job seriously when he's the one who will be assassinating the king?* He gritted his teeth and clenched his fists tightly. *That bastard is probably off enjoying himself and forgetting about Lena, isn't he?*

Yuri had almost forgotten what her laugh sounded like after so many days of being separated from her. Noah was gone and now Lena? How could he call himself their squad leader if he couldn't even protect them from getting captured? He closed his eyes and exhaled deeply. It was settled. He had to go and get her himself. He didn't care if Keimaro or Aladdin weren't ready. He remembered the instructions that Keimaro had given him. He didn't care if Aladdin had ordered him to stay inside of this damn mansion. He had to go out there and save Lena. He couldn't allow her to suffer anymore—not more than she already had through her life. She deserved better. Much better.

***

After spending almost an entire week with Aika and Judal, Keimaro found himself "protecting" the princess when in reality they were just spending time together. The Royal Guard leaned back against his wooden chair as he watched Aika studying her books in the royal library. He yawned, patting his lips with the palm of his hand. It was so quiet, like always. Royal librarians were as sneaky as assassins and crept about, careful not to make any noise so that they didn't disturb anyone. The boy leaned against his palm as he watched the princess, who seemed deep into her reading. *What could be so interesting about that book, anyway?*

Aika closed the book abruptly, and Keimaro almost jumped as she smacked him gently on the top of the head with the novel. "Stop staring at me! It's making me uncomfortable."

"Isn't that my job?" Keimaro muttered, putting his chin on the desk. Over the past few days, he had been laying low to ensure that anyone in the government wouldn't suspect him of being Keimaro. He had also been trying to deduce who in the castle was a member of the Bounts, but he didn't have any particular suspicions other than one of the king's royal advisors, General Mundo, and a random servant that had been following him around for about an hour before he broke off the trail. But he didn't have much time to inspect anyone, since he had to keep following Aika around every day. And out of the princess's lengthy schedule, this was probably the most boring period of her entire day.

"Hey, Riku," Judal said, walking over from the door of the library toward the table. He was also assigned to watch the princess during this time. "I heard that you're having a spar with

Darius today; is that true?"

"Word gets around, huh?" Keimaro said. "The prince has arrived already? I wasn't informed."

"Oh, he's arriving this afternoon. That's what I heard, at least," Judal said as he stepped aside to allow one of the librarians to set down a book in front of Aika to read. "Milady, you sure do read a lot, don't you?"

"Yes, I do enjoy a good read," Aika said with a smile, opening the book and beginning to flip through the pages.

Keimaro turned his attention back to Judal. "Really, now?"

"Yep. The princess will be escorted to her father's side at the throne. That means that we will have to go and meet Prince Darius at the main gate and escort him through the city to the throne room. General Mundo is making the battle quite the form of entertainment for tonight. The word is all over the place. I suspect most of the guard might come and watch, not to mention a large population of the nobles."

Keimaro rolled his eyes. "I'm not nervous."

"You should be."

"Your faith in me, Captain, is awfully discouraging."

Judal laughed warmly. "Oh, I've seen you in action all right. I know that you're a phenomenon and a prodigy amongst swordsmen. The reason that you're so unpredictable is because these men are incapable of adjusting their sword style to meet yours. Your style of combat is so unique on its own that one cannot predict the path of your blade. Your speed makes it so that, even if they guess, your sword cuts through them before they are even ready to make a single movement. However, Darius is very similar to you. In fact, I'd say you two are one and the same."

"Really, now? I find the challenge worthy of my interest then," Keimaro grinned.

"Stop talking about hacking each other with blades around me," Aika said with a sigh. "The library is no place for barbaric talk."

"Yes, milady," the two Royal Guards said apologetically in unison, bowing their heads.

"I was joking."

"Of course, milady."

Aika rolled her eyes and closed her book, slowly standing up. "It's time to get going anyway, isn't it?"

Keimaro nodded and slowly pushed back his chair as Judal began to walk in front of Aika while he stood behind. That was the typical two-man formation that they formed when they were escorting her. But, just as Aika had begun to walk toward the door of the library, Keimaro heard a sound just over his shoulder. He glanced, just barely, using his peripheral vision to see if there was anything. Nothing. There was no way that someone wasn't there. He *had* heard something. There was no mistake. Someone had moved, thus showing that they didn't want to be seen. He had to be on his toes.

"So, Riku," Aika said, playing with the hem of her blue dress as she walked out of the library, "I was wondering. Since there's going to be a ball in my brother's name, during his arrival, would you mind accompanying me there? I mean, I have no one else to go with and…."

"So, you're picking me as a last resort plan, princess?" Keimaro said with a teasing smile.

Aika flushed red and shook her head quickly. "No, it's not that!"

"I'd like to go with you, princess," Judal announced proudly.

"Umm…."

"She didn't ask you," Keimaro laughed. "And don't you have a wife, Judal? What on earth are you saying?"

"I have no idea," Judal chuckled.

They continued to chat and laugh as they walked through the hallways of the castle, greeting soldiers as they went by. However, Keimaro's mind was already on meeting the prince. He knew that he would have to assassinate him. Aika had never mentioned her brother and seemed to avoid the topic whenever he came up. Could it be that they were on bad terms? If this Darius was as strong as rumors said, an assassination might be difficult even if the prince were alone. And if he killed the prince, the king might tighten security around Aika and himself. That would surely make things more complicated. They might even increase security around Lena, which would only piss Yuri off even more. It was already bad enough that they had left Lena in that cell for several days now. He closed his eyes. Sometimes he had sleepless nights just thinking about her. He tried to make sure that she received decent treatment and didn't get beaten too often, but she looked skinnier and weaker with every day. An image appeared in his mind—the starved man from the slums he'd seen when he had first arrived in the city.

Keimaro stopped in place, his body shaking. If she turned out like that ... he would never forgive his decision to wait before saving her. Never.

"Yo, Riku." Judal's words snapped him back to reality, and he glanced up to see his captain looking at him with a raised eyebrow. "What's wrong? We are almost there," he said, pointing to the door to the throne room at the end of the hallway. The two guards that were standing beside the door, waiting for the princess to walk through, had already opened it.

Keimaro blinked a few times and shook his head. "It's nothing," he lied and walked through the doorway.

***

Darius wiped a bit of sweat from his brow as he rode his

stallion across the lush green plains at a casual pace. He saw the draped banners of Faar over the Bassada walls and couldn't help but flash a glowing white smile. The trot of horses echoed in his ears, but when he looked at the clear blue skies, he felt as if he were locked in the deepest of silence. The clouds floated and drifted slowly, mesmerizing him with their shapes.

"Milord," his squire said, riding up beside him, "we are almost at the gate."

"I can see that," Darius said with a roll of his eyes. "I want to see this Keimaro Hayashi for myself. A couple days of constant riding have left me impatient. But, knowing my father, he won't let me skip straight to the task at hand. The buffoon will probably be wasting tax money on another ball or party. At any rate, keep on your toes at all times, even when we are in the city," he said to his men and drove his heels into the side of his horse, galloping forward with increased speed.

The gates opened as Darius and his squad of men dismounted swiftly. Their blades were sheathed at their sides, and the prince's red cape hung behind him and touched the ground. He pulled off his golden battle helm, which had a red feather hanging from the top. He held it at his side and looked forward with his gleaming royal blue eyes at the townsfolk who had come to greet their arrival.

This was a large occasion for the city. Their war hero had finally returned, even if it was only for a short while. The appearance was rare and to be celebrated. Soldiers lined both sides of the street, brandishing black clubs and pressing back the crowds of common folk who had come to simply gaze upon the infamous prince. Yet, Darius couldn't help but see two specific soldiers walking through the center of the city along the tiled pathway toward them. None of the other guards were even bothering to stop them.

Darius raised an eyebrow. *Don't tell me. My father asked for two men to escort me to the castle? What a joke.* He sighed when he saw that the two were a simple eighteen-year-old boy and a middle-aged man. He put his hand on his hip as the two guards dropped to their knees, putting a fist to the ground in a bow.

"You may rise," Darius said. "Knowing my father, he would've sent his best men to escort me, though he need not expend the effort. He should've put you men to guarding my sister instead."

"Princess Aika is in the throne room underneath the protection of the Royal Guard. There is no need to worry, milord," the middle-aged man said.

"Your names?"

"Captain Judal of the Royal Guard," the middle-aged man responded.

Darius frowned when the younger boy didn't respond. "I asked your name," he repeated, annoyed.

"Riku Hikari," the boy said, looking up at Darius.

Darius's heart skipped a beat at the look in the boy's eyes. They bore a hint of innocence but also gave off a fierce, intimidating aura for some reason. The darkness of the guard's pupils seemed to stare straight through his flesh and into his soul. The eyes were two voids filled with emptiness, silence, and nothingness. Typically, from someone's eyes, Darius was able to read what a person was thinking simply from the emotions that they expressed. But this boy … there was nothing. It was as if he had no emotion at all. Darius's eyebrow twitched with frustration and annoyance.

"Milord," the squire whispered into Darius's ear, "this boy is a new recruit of the Royal Guard. He killed over ten of the king's men during the tryout. His ability to manipulate the sword and martial arts is supposedly comparable to your style. General Mundo has arranged for you two to spar in the courtyard today."

"Is that so?" Darius said with a small grin spreading across his lips. A young prodigy, huh? Ah, this boy reminded him of himself at the time. But, the young guard didn't know the storm that was coming. "Rise, let's go off to the castle. Riku Hikari, correct? I am Prince Darius, the war hero of Faar, destroyer of the Athenian empire, conqueror of the Spartans, and dominator of Bakaara. Pleased to make your acquaintance."

***

Gavin staggered backward after having been barraged with a flurry of fast blows by Yata. Already, the soldier could see a considerable amount of progress in Yata's combat. His ability to manipulate metal allowed for parts of his body to morph into a variety of shapes that he could use in a fight. It was similar to Noah's magic, except the objects were attached to his body. Yata wasn't capable of creating new matter out of thin air; instead, he simply changed his physical form, so he was quite limited with what kind of metallic transformations he could use.

On the other hand, Gavin was still having trouble keeping his balance while fighting such strong opponents. Sure, he had improved in comparison to the weakling that he had been in the Forbidden Forest. But against Yata, he felt practically powerless. His blows did no damage, and it was near impossible to break through Yata's guard.

Gavin sighed, tossing his one-handed sword to the side with a shake of his head. "This isn't working! I'm not hitting you with enough power." Glancing to his left, his eyes locked onto a brilliant gleaming blade that rested on the wall. It had a golden hilt with a sapphire embedded in the center that radiated a bright glow. The blade itself was forged by what looked to be some type of elven blacksmith and ended with a slight curve at its tip. That meant that the blade would be light but still be extremely powerful. The only heavy part of the weapon would be the gold hilt. The soldier found himself walking toward the weapon, his hand outstretched, hypnotized by its beauty.

"The blade of Kuro," a voice said from behind Gavin.

"Buu," Yata growled, leaving his metallic form. He gripped his bat tightly and began to walk forward with an annoyed look on his face. "I'd remember that stupid face of yours anywhere. You survived Bakaara after all of these years?"

"What, Keimaro didn't tell you?" Buu said, brushing his curly, brown hair out of his smiling blue eyes. A bright red bruise bloomed on his cheek, hinting that he had been punched recently. He touched the wound and winced a bit. "Well, he gave me quite the punch a couple days ago. At any rate, I'm not here to cause conflict anymore. I'm done with arguing with you guys over the past. The only past that I care about is the destruction of Bakaara and how much I'm going to make Faar pay for what they've done."

"Is that so?" Yata raised an eyebrow. "Looks like something we can agree on. And Keimaro and I are not really on the best of terms right now."

"That so? That hot-head finally blow his cap?" Buu smirked, not surprised.

"You two know each other?" Gavin whistled awkwardly.

"Yeah," Buu said with a chuckle, "we are from the same village. We weren't exactly on the best of terms at the time." The boy's body vanished, and he immediately appeared beside Yata with his arm wrapped around the annoyed metal shifter. "But we're fine now; isn't that right?"

"Get your hand off me before I break it."

Buu's image blinked and reappeared beside Gavin as he turned his attention to the sword that the soldier had been marveling. "Oh, well. Past ties are hard to sever. I couldn't help but learn that Yata was up here training, so I figured I'd stop by. Anyway, that blade that you're about to pick up is actually quite the antique. It hasn't been touched for a hundred years. It was the original blade that Kuro used before he decided to toss it for a new one made of dragon bone instead. You see," he said, pointing to the shining blue glow of the blade, "this weapon was made by forest elves, a race of creatures that live on a far-off continent. Their weaponry is without a doubt the most magical of all the races' creations. As humans, we are capable of mass-producing weapons, but the elves take time to create each individual weapon. In a way, you could say, they treat the weapon as they would an actual living being. They give it a name, they spend the time to enchant the weapon, pray for it, and always keep it in the best of shape.

"Now, the history of this blade is rather interesting. Kuro used this sword to slaughter thousands of men after he went into the Enchanted Forest and forced the elves to forge him this weapon. They call it Bloodthirster because it's always thirsty for blood, suitable name. When it tastes blood, it absorbs the fluid and becomes larger. Even though the blade grows, the weapon itself doesn't become any heavier. It simply becomes ten-times deadlier, harder, sharper, and scarier with every man that it kills. However, when deprived of blood, it shrinks back to its original size, until it's like this," he said, nodding toward the weapon.

Gavin stared at the sword in awe. "And it hasn't been touched all of this time?"

"After Kuro killed the world's first dragon, he forged a weapon made from its bones. His armor was forged from that same bone and covered in the dragon's scales. It was the strongest material in the entire world to create a weapon. With no further need of his old weapon, he cast it from Skytera, where it embedded in the earth below. Back in the day, there were competitions for men to pull the blade out of the ground. Supposedly, only the one man who was as worthy as Kuro—and as dangerous—would be able to pull the blade out of the ground. Interestingly enough, the only one who pulled it out was Zylon himself. The old man was Kuro's partner back when they used to go adventuring and such. He brought it back but never used it in combat. Neither has anyone else here. Sure, it's an insanely strong blade, but many of the people think that it's cursed and that it is capable of corrupting the soul. Not to mention, I figure that the blade would get so thirsty that it could even decide to start sucking up the wielder's blood," Buu said with a slight shiver. "Scary thought, right?"

Gavin's eyes stayed on the weapon, and his hands shook furiously. To become stronger, like everyone else, he had to do something! He didn't want to accept magic as the only way to gain strength. He also didn't want to rely on a weapon in order to make himself stronger. But, he did believe that he was strong enough to wield the Bloodthirster. "Is it against the rules to wield the sword?"

"No, it's just…."

"Just that everyone is afraid," Gavin said. *Everyone else is working hard to fight against this corrupt government and to prepare for the battle against the Bounts. I can't be dead weight forever. Will wielding this blade make me stronger?* His mind flashed to the moment when Keimaro had been fighting against Yuri. He had been too powerless to fight against magic this whole time. He had to show everyone that just because he didn't have magic, he wasn't weak. He wasn't powerless!

"But I'm not afraid of this power," he said, grasping the hilt of the golden weapon. The very instant his hand curled around the handle, he felt drained, as if everything was being sucked out of his body—all of his happiness, hope, and joy. He grunted as he hauled the blade into the air. Buu stepped backward as if Gavin were cursed. "I'll show everyone that I can be strong even without magic!" Gavin growled, holding the blade overhead though his arms shook with the effort.

Yata stared at the soldier with newfound respect. He couldn't help but smile, lowering his bat to his side. "Hey, that's cool and all … but you look a bit pale." He chuckled, putting a hand on his hip.

Gavin blinked a few times, realizing he did indeed feel sapped of energy. He groaned and dropped the blade onto the ground. Then he doubled over, falling onto the floor in a heap. "Ugh, I feel terrible. What's happening…?"

Buu sighed, standing over the soldier with his arms folded. "Idiot. I told you! The weapon saps your energy unless you're in real combat. Don't use it to train because you won't be feeding it any blood while you're fighting. If you use it while it's hungry, it'll just start sapping your energy and blood."

"It's like a vampire," Gavin gasped, staring at the ceiling. He chuckled. "So, it sure does take stamina to wield this thing, doesn't it? Good! I'll learn to wield it."

Buu groaned and looked to Yata. "Have you been teaching this guy to be an idiot? Because he reminds me of you."

"All three of you," Z said, walking into the training room. He raised an eyebrow when he saw that Gavin was on the floor with Bloodthirster at his side. A small smile appeared upon his lips, but he said nothing about the spectacle. "We have a particular situation. The girl that Yata, Gavin, and Noah saved has awoken. Come with me immediately."

18. OPERATION DESTRUCTION

As Keimaro followed Darius into the throne room, he could still feel the heat rising in his chest. *This guy … led the destruction of my village? He is the one who physically was present during the massacre. He should be the first one to die!* His hands were shaking at his sides, and his eyes were wide with disgust as he glared at Darius's back. It took his maximum willpower not to kill the bastard right then and there. He could hear the clanking of armor behind him, and he knew that any loose actions would result in his downfall. Nevertheless, that didn't change the fact that he wanted to rip this prince apart and burn his remains.

The boy found himself walking on the hard marble floor once more. A hush fell as the prince moved to stand before his father. Judal and Keimaro separated and stood on either side of the prince. Darius's men stood in a formation behind them as the doors to the throne room closed. Keimaro folded his arms in front of him as the king left his throne to embrace his son. Watching them hug, Keimaro's eye began to twitch. He wanted to cut them both down at that moment. All of his suppressed anger was now coursing through his veins at high speed, making his hand tap against his bicep impatiently. The man who had ordered the destruction of his village and the man who had carried it out were hugging each other right in front of him. Why didn't he just skewer them with his blade right then?

"We should have a celebration in your honor, Darius! Not only have you come to exterminate the rebels, but you have also brought great honor to Faar through your military victories! I'm very proud," the king said with a wide grin as he gripped Darius's shoulders.

"Ah," Darius said with a fake smile, "that would be lovely, father. However, there is something that I would like to test first. Your secret weapon, isn't it? Riku Hikari," he said, turning to face Keimaro with a broad grin. His eyes were filled with determination and eagerness for battle. He cracked his neck as he took a few steps away from his father, grasping the hilt of his sword, which was sheathed at his side. "I've been riding for a couple of days now, and I've been very hungry for some decent swordplay. My squire told me that you're considered a prodigy amongst these guards, hmm?" He slowly slid his blade from its sheath. He twirled the weapon as it went free into the air and held it out in front of him with a nod. "Entertain me a bit then."

Keimaro looked at the king for permission but was ready to draw his own sword. The king simply sighed and nodded, walking back to his throne and slumping into the seat, knowing his son wouldn't stop the fight. He waved his hand, indicating for Keimaro to continue. The boy's heart began to race with excitement as he slid his blade from its sheath, brandishing it into the silent air. He lowered his head, his dark hair coming over his eyes as he smiled. "It would be my pleasure, Lord Darius." He had felt the heat between them the entire walk to the castle. They both glared at each other but always smiled. Behind their facades, they both felt some sort of a strong fire that blazed within them, wanting to battle the other. Each wanted to see why the other was infamous.

The boy turned and saw General Mundo with a smile on his face, folding his arms as he stood by the king's side. Keimaro's eyes then flickered to Aika for a brief moment, and he could see the look of worry on the princess's face. He sucked in a deep breath and turned to Darius, admiring the prince's glittering steel. His golden breastplate shone brightly, and he was, without a doubt, completely ready for battle.

"Begin!"

The word echoed through the throne room, and steel clashed, exploding and sending sparks into the air. The two opponents had slammed against one another, their blades locked tightly, and their weapons shook in their struggle for dominance. Keimaro was surprised that Darius had taken the same rushing initiative that he had, charging the opponent straight on. He disengaged and went low, sweeping his leg outward and dragging it across the ground in an attempt to take out Darius's legs. But, the prince, who was accustomed to battle, leapt into the air after predicting the movements. His eyes met Keimaro's while he was in the air. Upon landing, he lunged forward with a yell, and his blade swept in a downward-cutting arc with beautiful form.

Keimaro spun away, allowing Darius's blade to hit the marble floor with a loud clang. His boots squeaked as he slid away, rising back to his feet. He grunted, lashing forward. He kicked off of the ground and leapt into the air, spinning multiple times to gain incredible momentum while slashing downward at Darius, hoping to land a powerful blow. Even if the prince parried the attack, it would still numb an arm from the strength of the strike.

Darius moved away in a single instant, rolling on the ground to evade the slash. He knew not to risk parrying the blow, and he stumbled to his feet, facing away from Keimaro and grinning widely. "This is it! Someone who is truly strong! It's wonderful!" he exclaimed. He turned and ran at Keimaro while laughing. He gripped his sword in a new way that Keimaro didn't recognize and lunged forward, his sword seeming much skinnier than it had before, like a needle.

Keimaro grunted as he tilted his head, the blade poking inches from his cheek. He felt a rush of wind hit his face, and his eyes widened. *What is this speed?* The blade kept coming in a barrage of blows that were all lunges, no more slashes. The attacks were so fast and offensive that Keimaro couldn't do anything except parry and dodge. He staggered backward, barely evading the flurry of blows that struck him. Small cuts began to form on his skin as part of his arms and legs were cut from the unpredictable storm of jabs.

This is bad. I can't do anything except dodge! he thought. Not to mention the fact that he was still backing up. Eventually he would hit a wall, and that would be the end of him. *Wait, no! The wall is where I will turn this around.*

Keimaro glanced over his shoulder and saw that he had been pushed almost across the entire room to the wall. The jabs kept coming, like a needle trying to poke holes in a pillow. He wasn't any practice dummy, and he sure as hell wasn't going to keep on the defensive. "Let's see what you've got, prince!" he murmured and kicked off of the ground. The action took the prince by surprise, and he watched as Keimaro placed one foot on the wall. The Royal Guard pushed off of the wall with incredible strength and flipped backward through the air, landing where he had left. His body swung, and his sword tore through the air, swinging with tremendous speed at Darius.

The prince staggered, not expecting the sudden blow. Keimaro turned his body sideways and kicked out twice, aiming once for Darius's diaphragm and the second for this throat. The prince moved out of range just barely, trying desperately to maintain his balance. Keimaro had to keep the pressure to ensure that Darius stayed on the defensive. If Darius were given even a chance to take control of the battle, it would be over for Keimaro. He had to put everything into his offense.

Keimaro spun his sword, twirling it in the air. He released the handle as he gripped it backward like a dagger and swiped it across the air rapidly, pressing Darius back. He blinked when the prince sidestepped to evade Keimaro's blow simply by getting out of range. Then Darius took a quick step forward and shot his needle-like sword outward in a fast jab. There was no time to react, and if the blade hit, he would die. In that moment of desperation, Keimaro's Shokugan activated. It was only a millisecond, used to rotate his body in a perfect spin so that the prince's blade shot past him. His irises changed back to their original dark color, and he found himself behind Darius.

The prince's eyes widened at what had just happened. He

gasped as his legs were taken out from underneath him in a swift moment. He grunted and hit the ground hard on his back, the wind driven from his lungs. He saw motion over his head as Keimaro flipped and spun over the prince, landing upon him. The boy's fist came crashing downward and stopped several inches from Darius's face, shaking furiously.

The king sat forward in his chair, intrigued by Keimaro's sudden turn-around. He clapped with an outburst of laughter. "Riku, you truly have shown me a sight that I haven't seen before." He didn't seem the least bit disappointed in the fact that his son had been defeated.

Keimaro was breathing heavily as he glared down at Darius, restraining himself from tearing the prince apart. He bit his lip and closed his eyes. Killing him now would do nothing. If anything, it would only set them back more. He had to wait until the Bounts were here before he decided to kill anyone. He slowly rose to his feet and extended a hand to the prince, offering to pull him up. "Are you okay, milord?" Every time he said the word *lord*, he felt as if he wanted to vomit.

"I'm all right, thank you," Darius said, allowing himself to be pulled to his feet as he gave Keimaro a small smile. "That was quite the performance. Never in all of my years have I seen someone with such remarkable talent and strikingly deadly blows as you. I wonder why your talented is being wasted in the castle guarding my sister against an invisible enemy rather than on the front lines massacring thousands of Spartans. But then again, I suppose these assassins must be quite strong if my father had to call me in." Darius reached around his neck and yanked off a gold chain. He held the chain up, letting a small locket dangle in the air. "As a token of my gratitude for sparing my life and for defeating me ... you were the first, so I must insist that you take this."

"Milord, I couldn't...."

"I insist," Darius said, placing the locket in Keimaro's hands and slowly closing the boy's fingers around it. "At any rate, I must go and bathe now. It's been a long ride, and I'm quite fatigued. I suspect there will be some sort of a ball, knowing you, father?"

"Yes, tonight!" the king said, rather excited.

"Perfect, I will see you all tonight then. Thank you for the battle, Riku," Darius said, giving a small nod to his squadron of soldiers as they began to file out of the throne room. Darius shot Keimaro a swift look over his shoulder along with a sly smile that stained his lips as he vanished through the doorway.

Keimaro watched the prince for a moment, his heart thumping as he wiped the sweat from his brow. There was a small chance that, in the millisecond he had activated the Shokugan, Darius had seen him. But the prince hadn't outright announced the discovery, so perhaps he hadn't noticed. *But that look he gave me sure was unsettling.*

The Royal Guard felt a tap on his shoulder as Judal and his fellow guards practically leapt onto him in a cheerful embrace with outbursts of laughter. "Where did you learn to do that?" his captain exclaimed, wrapping an arm around his shoulder. "Were you born in a circus or something? Those flips were insane! And the speed of your attacks were beyond belief! Are you going to teach me how to do that?"

"That was absolutely incredible!" one guard called out.

"You're the man, Riku!" a second said.

Keimaro's eyes widened at the praise that was being thrown at him. He couldn't help but feel warmth in his chest from these new comrades that surrounded him. He smiled. All of the soldiers suddenly straightened when the king cleared his throat. In unison, the guards dropped to their knees and bowed before their lord.

"Forgive us, milord! We spoke out of turn!" they all said at the same time.

The king burst out laughing and descended the steps of his golden throne to Keimaro. He tipped Keimaro's chin up and gave him a smile, as they looked each other in the eye. "You're something else if you were able to best my son. I truly do feel safe around you. My daughter informed me that you will be taking her to tonight's ball, is that correct?"

Keimaro's face turned bright red as he remembered Aladdin's story about how his eye had been cut for interacting with Aika. However, the king simply smiled when the boy nodded his head.

"Don't get too rowdy," the king said with a small smile. "You may take my daughter tonight. I trust you'll take care of her and keep her out of trouble. Take the rest of the day off to prepare yourself. Judal, escort my daughter to her room and make sure that she is ready for tonight's feast. Also arrange to set up your guards in a perimeter around the castle, just in case. We wouldn't want any disturbances on my son's first night home."

"Yes, milord," Judal said, pounding his chest in response as a formation of soldiers moved around Aika the very moment that she stepped off of her throne. "Yo, Riku," he called as they walked past. "I'll meet you up in the room, okay?"

"Sure thing," Keimaro said with a nod as he stood up from the ground and was suddenly confronted by the king.

The king simply grinned and touched his shoulder. "I'll see you later tonight then. I'll have some men get some attire for you for tonight's ball. You deserve a dance with my daughter after such a display of talent." He gave him a small nod before he began to leave the room along with another squadron of guards.

Keimaro stood there for a moment and exhaled. "That was something," he said to himself. Suddenly, he felt all of his hatred toward Faar being drained in a single instant. For once, he felt happy. A ball to look forward to with a princess that he'd come to love, a well-respected position in the Royal Guard, people who respected and treated him equally, everything seemed perfect. He almost completely forgot why he had even come to Bassada in the first place. But he knew, in the end, he couldn't escape his duty. He would have to assassinate the king still, despite his hospitality. However, for the boy, there was no time to sulk. In an instant, a group of tailors swept him away into another room to fit him for the night's ball. For once, Keimaro allowed his plan for revenge to be pushed away from his mind.

***

As Yata walked into the infirmary, he couldn't help but stare at the liveliness of the girl that sat back in the bed, propped up against her pillow. She looked at them as if they were foreign creatures. She blinked a few times to register the fact that she was seeing people. Her eyes reminded Yata of Keimaro's, except they glowed a constant red. Another person with the Shokugan; now this was something that one didn't typically see.

"Has she spoken yet?" Gavin asked Z, who shook his head.

"She doesn't seem to like talking."

"Maybe she's a mute," Buu cut in.

"I doubt it," Gavin muttered as they all stopped at the foot of her bed. "Hey, uh…." The soldier scratched his neck, quite unsure what to say in the awkward situation. "So, we were just wondering about how you got into that test lab underground. Do you remember anything?"

The girl said nothing.

"Guess she is a mute," Buu remarked.

"Shut up," Gavin sighed.

"What's your name?" Yata asked suddenly.

Everyone was silent as the girl looked up at Yata, brushing her long, black hair from her eyes. Her face seemed fuller, and her body had recovered a small amount from being fed over the past couple days. Nevertheless, she still looked extremely weak and skinny. "Eve."

"Eve?" Buu said. "Never heard of that name before. That

from the north?"

"And how did you come to get those eyes of yours?" Yata asked, giving her a reassuring nod. "Don't worry; we won't hurt you."

***

Eve felt overwhelmed with all of these men staring at her as if she were some type of specimen. She would've lifted her arm if she could to try and at least get up, but she truly didn't have the energy to do it. Not to mention the fact that she hardly remembered anything prior to being tested on by the government. *I suppose that's all they want to know anyway.*

She leaned back into the comfortable pillow and sighed with pleasure, not able to remember a time when she had been this comfortable or well-fed—not that she could remember much at all. The people who had performed tests on her had always taken it upon themselves to make her fast quite often or starve her simply to see what would happen. Perhaps it was that, or maybe they didn't want to spare food for mere test experiments.

And these eyes. Oh, she remembered how she had gotten them. The procedure was excruciating, and she remembered that she had been blind for several days. Someone had used an odd type of magic in order to make this all possible. "I got these eyes from transplants that they gave me."

"They? You mean the government?" the boy with flowing brown hair said.

"Yata, who else would it be?"

"Someone else," a voice echoed through the infirmary. Everyone turned to see a rather dashing blonde-haired boy walking into the room. He wore a fancy blue silk shirt with tight red pants. He tossed his hair as he walked forward, and Eve saw that one of his eyes was actually scarred with a long slash across it. "I have reason to believe that the government wasn't actually involved in this little underground project of theirs."

"Aladdin?" Yata said. "What do you mean?"

"I mean that I searched through their database of files, and I found no papers that regarded any underground experimentations at all. It seems as if the king isn't even aware of these test experiments occurring," Aladdin said. "That is why I believe that the Bount organization has something to do with this. Noah's whereabouts are unknown because, unlike Lena, he wasn't brought to the royal prison."

"What? He wasn't?"

"No," Aladdin said. "Whoever caught him is outside of the law. Even if he were executed, it would've been recorded. But there was nothing, not even a single mention that he had been captured in the first place. That means that another group is pulling a secretive side-job, and there's an undercover group in the government—a small handful of people who are secretly pulling behind-the-scene tests on humans. That's why I'm here, actually. Yata, Gavin, I wanted to ask both of you … who was that person that you saw underground? What was his name?"

Yata blinked a few times, deep in thought. It was difficult for him to remember such a specific name. It was some type of a general, wasn't it?

"General Mundo," Eve heard the soldier, Gavin, say. "I remember it was him. I served under him."

Aladdin smacked his forehead with a groan. "General Mundo is a spy? That's not good! Keimaro works extremely closely with General Mundo. If Mundo really is with the Bount organization, then he's going to be easily able to wipe Keimaro out and take the key."

"But he wouldn't risk that!" Yata exclaimed. "What if Keimaro didn't have the key on him? General Mundo would've killed Keimaro without being able to find out where the key was, if that was his objective all along. Which means…."

"They'll search his room first."

***

Yata and all of his companions burst from the infirmary, leaving Buu and Z behind as they sprinted for Keimaro's room.

"Crap! If Mundo knows the location of this mansion, then everything is going to go to hell! And if they have Noah, they might be able to extract the information using some type of magic. We have to assume that they know where Z's mansion is!" Aladdin exclaimed as they dashed down the hallway, throwing Keimaro's door open.

The room was completely trashed with everything knocked over and torn apart. The bed itself had been ripped open, and the mattress was tossed across the room. The pillows were slashed open with their stuffing pouring out onto the floor. Keimaro's cloak had been tossed to the ground, and his wardrobe had been ransacked. In the center of the room was Noah, who glanced at them over his shoulder. He wore the black cloak of the Bounts, and his eyes were empty, completely deprived of color and emotion.

"Noah?" Gavin blinked.

Yata's body immediately solidified, knowing what would happen next. A huge green fist that had been conjured out of the air rocketed forward and slammed into him, sending him flying across the hallway and ramming into the railing, almost falling off of the tower floor. He groaned, noticing he had completely bent the railing, which creaked when he got off of it.

"Noah! What the hell are you doing?" Aladdin yelled as he was smacked backward by a wall of blue energy conjured by Noah. The noble slammed into the ground and rolled, grunting.

"Guys, something's different about him," Gavin said, unsheathing his steel sword and brandishing it in front of him. He tensed up, taking battle positioning. "Look at his eyes!"

Noah walked out of Keimaro's room and flicked his wrist once more. In an instant, three things happened. A fist flew out and smashed into Yata once more, sending him flying off of the railing and out into open air, prepared to fall about fifty stories to the ground below. A blue rifle appeared in Noah's hand aimed at Aladdin. Noah fired, burying a conjured bullet into the noble's shoulder. A red blade materialized in Noah's other hand. In an instant, Noah's gun vanished, and he gripped the hilt of his sword with both hands, rushing at Gavin with his blade in the air.

Yata's heart was thumping rapidly as he clutched out at open air, not particularly fearing death but the pain that would follow when he smashed into the ground. Sure enough, when he hit the floor, the entire world seemed to spin in an abrupt turn, leaving ringing in his ears. "Ugh…," he muttered, leaning forward and rubbing his metallic head. "That freaking hurt, you four-eyed bastard," he growled and turned to see that many of the assassins were staring at him while others looked up at the burst of light appearing on the top floor as Noah engaged in battle.

"Evacuate the mansion!" Yata yelled to one of the assassins. "Spread the word, everyone!" he said, gripping his bat and turning to look up.

Noah had knocked Gavin to the side and leapt off of the large platform above. He fell down into open air, sweeping his hands outward. A conjured blue substance appeared in the air below him, creating some type of liquid. His body dropped into the liquid, slowing his fall. He slipped through layers of conjured fluid until he landed before Yata, slowly rising to his feet. The magical conjured substance vanished as soon as he was done using it. He adjusted his glasses with a single poke to the lenses and glanced at Yata.

This magic of his is really something. Being able to create anything that he wants out of thin air, Yata thought and smiled. His last fight against Yuri had been a loss. This time, he would go all out and show his opponent that he was not to be messed with.

"You really have pissed me off, four-eyes," Yata growled, his right arm changing from its original metal to diamond. "Maybe a good whack to the head will bring you to your senses,

Noah."

Noah raised an eyebrow and held out his hand, a massive green hammer materializing in his palm. He held his weapon outward and frowned. "You guys seem to know me. Who are you?"

Yata blinked a few times. *He doesn't remember me. What did those Bounts do to him?*

Noah grunted, dashing for the door to the mansion in a desperate attempt to flee. Yata intercepted him by swiftly stepping in his path. "I'll admit that your magic truly is something to be proud of, Noah, but my magic counters yours. You won't be able to hurt me when I'm in this form," he said, nodding to his diamond skin. "Now, I'm going to beat the crap out of you until you're ready to wake the hell up!"

Yata shot forward, swinging his metal bat at Noah. His bat slammed against Noah's hammer with a loud bang, echoing through the mansion as assassins evacuated around them. Whoever had sent Noah would surely arrive with backup soon. He had to finish this up quickly. If the Bounts were coming, they could wipe out all of these assassins around him in an instant. He rotated his body and swung with his diamond arm, launching a hard punch at Noah from the side.

Noah released his hammer, which vanished, and took a step back in response. He held up both of his hands so that a giant green wall appeared between Yata and him. Yata's diamond fist smashed into the wall and shattered it instantly, sending glittering green shards raining down around them. Noah flew back and hit the ground, sliding across the marble floor, grunting. He gripped his ribs, his bones aching from Yata's heavy blow. Even with the shield, the diamond was hard enough to smash through it and land a devastating blow.

Yata pumped his diamond arm, exhilarated with the heat of battle. A grin spread across his face as he straightened his back and clenched his fist tightly. This was only the beginning! It was about time he got some action. He began to advance when he saw a slight shimmer in the air in front of him. His heart thumped, and he raised his arms in defense, knowing that something was coming.

A man appeared from nowhere, teleporting in front of him with hardly even a sound. His spiked black hair came down over his red eyes, and Yata immediately recognized him. Tobimaru Hayashi. The Bount rotated his body, his black cloak flapping in the air as he drove a heavy kick into Yata's diaphragm. A burst of force emitted from the sole of his foot and ejected into Yata's stomach, sending the diamond body soaring through the air before slamming heavily into the ground.

Tobimaru slowly lowered his leg from the kick and brushed the hair from his eyes to glance at Yata as if the boy wasn't even worth his time. "You're still alive, huh?" he said with a scoff, his hands lowered at his side as he glanced around. "So, where's Keimaro? I have a fight to settle with him."

Yata rubbed his dented stomach and chuckled, pushing himself to his feet. "You sure are strong, Tobimaru," he snarled, swaying lightly as burning rage coursed through his veins. For once, he knew what it was like to be in Keimaro's shoes, completely filled with hatred. "Keimaro isn't here right now. But I'll stand in his place, if that's all right."

This is the guy who destroyed our city, killed our friends, and obliterated everything that I'd ever known. Sure, I hated the place, but that gives no one the right to take away the lives of everyone that I'd ever loved. Fourteen years of my life, wiped in a single hour. Yata's eyes began to morph into gems, his eyes gleaming like two sapphires. His entire body also transformed into glittering diamond to match his right arm, until he was a living statue of gem. "I'll kill you for what you did."

Tobimaru raised an eyebrow and gave a small smile, raising his hand. His blade unsheathed itself and floated in the air in front of him. The Bount grasped the hilt of his weapon, his eyes shining like two burning coals. "It seems that you have indeed changed over the years. This will be a memorable battle," he said and sighed, "but do you honestly think that you'll be able to handle me alone?"

"He's not alone," Buu said, suddenly appearing in front of Tobimaru, rotating his body into a rocketing punch. His gleaming brass knuckles flashed in the air as he swung out at Tobimaru, who tilted his head in a reactive dodge. The boy vanished and reappeared beside Yata, adjusting the metal on his fists with a small smile. "Don't forget that this is also my battle to fight," he growled, brushing the hair out of his eyes. "That was my village you screwed over four years ago, Bount. I'll see to it that you're killed. I've trained hard for these four years. I've cast away my own humanity to use this magic so that I could beat you terrorists to a pulp!"

Yata smirked, tapping his bat against his shoulder. "To think that we would be working together. Now that is something I never would've expected." He glanced over his shoulder and saw that Noah was staggering toward the door to flee. Yata was about to intercept him, but Tobimaru rushed forward with incredible speed and swiped his sword in an upward slash.

Yata simply allowed the sword to smash against his hardened skin. The diamond parried the blow for him with a loud clang as Tobimaru stood there, rather surprised. Yata swung a diamond fist at the Bount's stomach, but the slippery man quickly placed both of his hands on Yata's shoulders and propelled himself into the air, flipping over his glittering opponent.

Tobimaru landed behind him and continued forward at Buu, whirling his sword. Buu used his magic to teleport above the Bount in the middle of his slash and swung downward with a heavy kick at Tobimaru. The Bount blinked, raising his forearm to block the kick, grunting in response as a shock of pain burst through his arm. He turned to see that Yata was punching at him. Two opponents were truly overwhelming. Tobimaru swiftly spun away from the rocketing punch. He flicked his wrist and smiled.

Yata blinked as a wall of invisible force smashed into him and Buu, sending them flying across the large tower room. The diamond boy smashed into the floor, cracking the marble. He bounced like a skipping stone on water until he landed heavily on his back, grunting. He shook his head, slightly dazed, and looked at Buu.

"What the hell was that?" Buu groaned as he pushed himself from the ground into a sitting position, grasping his bleeding forehead. "His magic?"

"Telekinesis, that's his magic," Yata said, swaying as he stood back up. "Sure, it's a good offensive, but what can he do about diamonds?" the boy snarled, slamming his fist into the floor. The ground shook as diamond spikes burst from the marble floor in the direction that Yata was facing, moving in a straight line at Tobimaru.

Tobimaru began to move away from the line of fire, trying to avoid the attack. The path of the spikes followed him, curving. The Bount grunted as he leapt into the air as the final spike came upward, slashing at his legs. He exhaled deeply, satisfied with his evasion.

Then Buu appeared in the air above him with a wicked grin on his face, spinning his body. Tobimaru's eyes widened in surprise.

"Looks like you aren't going to be able to dodge this one, Hayashi bastard!" Buu yelled, performing a flip as he slammed the heel of his foot down into Tobimaru's back. There was a sickening crack as Tobimaru was sent flying to the ground, smashing into the earth and the spikes. There was an explosion upon impact, and dust flew in all directions from the force of Buu's attack.

"We got him!" Yata exclaimed.

The dust was swept away in an instant, and Tobimaru stood in the center of a cracked crater with blood splotching the corner of his mouth. His eyes were shining brighter than normal as a dark shadow loomed over his face. "The only thing that you've gotten," he glanced up and met Yata's eyes with an evil glare, "is me angry."

***

Keimaro adjusted his tie and coughed a few times, straightening his back as he stood with Judal. His captain was going to lead him into the ballroom. To be honest, the boy was quite nervous. His hands were shaking at his sides, and he felt abnormally hot in this suit. He brushed off his pants, even though there wasn't a single speck on them, and exhaled as he turned to face the captain outside of the open door to the ball. Fancy nobles and rich property owners were walking through the doorway, chatting together, and not a single one of them seemed nervous at all.

He looked into Captain Judal's eyes and smiled nervously. "Time to get this over with," he choked.

"Don't be such a party pooper, mate," Judal said, patting him on the shoulder with a chuckle. "You'll do great! Just do all the things that I told you to do! And you'll snatch the princess's heart like that!"

"Eh? Who said I want her heart! I mean, have you seen what they did to Aladdin?"

"Yeah, that's to scare off other nobles." Judal winked. "Aladdin had it coming to him. The way he pissed off the king was an atrocity to watch. But do you think the king would lay a hand on you? First, you would probably kill all of the men who tried. Second, you have the power to do whatever you want here! The king doesn't really have the power to control you because it would take an army to cut you down. You're too valuable to him, anyway. Just go out there and have fun, okay? I'll be right here if ya need me."

Keimaro nodded and chuckled, scratching the back of his neck. "You're right. Thanks, Judal. I owe you one," he said, high-fiving his roommate before he turned around to walk toward the door. Before he was allowed to step into the room, a short, scrawny man stopped him.

"Your name?" the petite man said, adjusting his tie, and

scanning his list swiftly over the small pair of glasses resting upon the bridge of his nose.

"Riku Hikari, but you won't find me on—"

"You aren't invited. Therefore, you are not allowed to pass."

"Wait, I work here, though! I mean—"

"Security!"

Keimaro sighed as two burly men began to step from inside of the doorway and block his path. He rolled his eyes, sliding his hands into his pants pockets. "You've got to be kidding me."

"Riku!" Aika's voice called, and the princess walked over to the doorway. Immediately the guards and the doorman dropped to their knees, as did some of the nobles who were standing behind Keimaro. "There you are!"

The princess was dressed in a long white gown that draped to the ground. The back was open, and her brunette hair was tied into an elegant bun. Her royal blue eyes beamed when she saw Keimaro, and she waved, her hands covered in the small white gloves that marked royalty. Diamond earrings dazzled from her ears while three gold necklaces curled around her slender neck as well. The amount of jewelry that she was wearing made her seem so much different than the girl he remembered from four years ago, but he wasn't complaining. He walked past the large guards, linking his arm with the princess. Keimaro bumped into the short doorman purposely, nearly knocking the man over. "Whoops," he laughed as he walked into the ball.

Keimaro's face felt extremely hot as eyes fell on him while he and the princess walked arm in arm. "I'm really not accustomed to this, princess," he muttered, his face flushed as his eyes darted about. "I've never really been to a festivity like this, and particularly my first being at such a huge event...."

"It's not that big of an event," Aika said, poking his ribs playfully. "And don't be so worried! You're red as a tomato right now. Just calm down! I'll lead you through every second of it," she said with a reassuring smile that made Keimaro feel even hotter than he already was while wearing his suit.

"I've never seen the infamous Riku so flustered before. Fearless in battle, yet shy as a cat when you're around my daughter," the king guffawed as he walked forward through the crowds of people with three guards surrounding him. "Ah, my beautiful girl," he said with a smile at Aika. "You look simply ravishing today."

"Thank you, father," Aika responded with a small giggle.

"Now, where is the man of the hour? My son?"

"Here, father," Darius said as he appeared at their side, wearing a tuxedo with a bright rose tucked into his coat pocket. His hair was curled in such a fashion that made him seem simply a model of perfection. The women were all watching him as he sauntered through the ball without any need of an escort. Even though Darius insisted on traveling alone, Keimaro knew that his father had arranged for soldiers to stay at a distance, constantly watching him. The prince had tucked one hand into his pocket and smiled when he saw Keimaro.

Keimaro and the prince shook hands swiftly, and Darius smiled. "Ah, so you'll be giving my sister a dance then? Well done. It's quite rare that my father would let my younger sister prance off with a young man such as yourself. But I trust you. I can see the sincerity in your eyes. As for my father, I'd like to have a small meeting with General Mundo quickly in private, if that's all right."

"Sure, that's fine. But, might I ask, what for?"

"Simply a business matter … you know, catching this Keimaro figure," Darius said with a smile. Aika shifted awkwardly. Darius looked at his sister for a moment but said nothing. He gave Keimaro a wink and disappeared into the crowds of people.

Keimaro's heart pounded as he turned to watch the prince

vanish from view into the groups of nobles. He could see the worry glistening in Aika's eyes after hearing what Darius had said, but he gave her a nod to reassure her that everything would be all right. Right now they just had to enjoy this night.

He inhaled deeply and felt Aika's gloved fingers gently lace through his. Before he knew it, the princess was pulling him to the dance floor, and all thoughts of the prince vanished from his mind. He had other things to worry about.

"Oh, gods," he muttered to himself, frightened at the mere thought of having to dance in front of all of these judgmental nobles around him. It was more frightening than having to face an army of soldiers. The sound of violins played loudly as a tune picked up, and soon nobles were leading partners to the dance floor as well.

Aika turned around to face Keimaro and gripped one of his hands, putting her other arm around his waist. Noblemen in the crowds who watched this event simply gaped in awe, incredulous that this commoner boy was given the chance to dance with such a pure, beautiful, intellectual being.

The nervous boy wasn't particularly positive about how to dance, but he had heard this tune before, and Judal had given him a quick crash course on how to dance to a few popular songs that were usually played at royal balls. He was a fast learner, but even for him it was difficult to master such fast movements. *Please, don't mess up!* Keimaro begged himself as the music began and the nobles moved all in unison, one with the music.

Keimaro gripped the princess's hand and placed his other hand on her waist as they began to move with the music, stepping to the side with every beat. He blinked when he noticed that he and the princess were moving as one, flowing like water. To be honest, it wasn't as hard as he had imagined it. It was simply listening to the music and moving accordingly. He could probably have winged this without even learning the steps—and, without a doubt, he had impressed Aika because she wore an expression of surprise and glee. Keimaro smiled, remembering the specific moment when he was supposed to twirl her. The moment came, and he reached up and twirled the princess elegantly, her dress spinning and her jewelry gleaming. She shined like a star out of all of the dancers as she spun about. When she slowed, Keimaro pulled her close to him and their eyes locked. Heat rose to his cheeks, and he gave her a bright grin, confident and happy with his performance in the dance. *Maybe this won't be so bad after all.*

***

Darius watched Riku as he danced with his younger sister, feeling no emotional attachment to the princess whatsoever. In fact, he didn't feel anything when he looked at his own father. All he wanted was the throne that he so deserved. He sighed as he leaned against the wall of the ballroom, watching the couple twirl about on the dance floor. "So, shall we begin, General?" he said with a nod to the man standing beside him.

"We shall," General Mundo said with a small smile. "The first step to our plan has begun."

***

As night fell, Yuri's gloomy eyes glared through the window of Aladdin's room out onto the fresh grass that gleamed underneath the moonlight. His hands were tightened around the hilt of a silver dagger, and his eyes were red with anger. Another day that Lena had been left to suffer and Keimaro had done nothing about it. He had to act.

The boy watched as nobles piled through the castle doors, disgusted with the fact that Keimaro was off partying rather than doing something about the situation at hand. Perhaps the idiot had forgotten about Lena. Yuri was truly wrong to have put his faith into Keimaro this whole time. He leapt out of the window and landed heavily on the grass below, beginning to walk forward without feeling a single bit of pain from the drop. It didn't matter how many enemies or soldiers there were. Even with Lena as weight, he could still escape. He would run off into the Forbidden Forest if he had to.

Yuri made his way around the side of the castle as Keimaro had instructed and located the doorway to the underground royal jail. It wasn't particularly heavily guarded from the outside so as not to draw any attention. But Yuri knew that there would be a lot of forces on the inside. Perhaps he should release all of the criminals in order to create enough chaos to escape with Lena unnoticed. Would that really work? The boy pulled his hood over his head, his white hair swaying before his turquoise eyes as he walked across the grassy courtyard toward the doorway.

The two guards standing on patrol took notice of Yuri and unsheathed their weapons, holding them out in defense as the dark figure continued forward. "Stop, in the name of the king!" one of the soldiers demanded. "What is your business here?"

Yuri's arm flickered, and two throwing knives hurled from his sleeves and buried themselves into the throats of both guards, silencing them. They collapsed in a heap on the grass, their blood staining the plants. Yuri didn't bother to touch the corpses and simply stepped over them, continuing onward to the jail. He grasped the doorknob and raised his eyebrow when he saw that it was locked. A small slide near the top of the door slid aside, and a pair of eyes replaced it.

"Who's there?" a man's voice growled.

Yuri responded by kicking the door with a tremendous amount of force, ripping it off of its hinges and crushing the man behind it in a swift moment. With a loud creak, the door slid down the stairs, the corpse underneath. The werewolf continued forward, stepping on the broken door, and moved into the darkness. Within moments, the shadows began to swallow him and he found himself in pitch-blackness. His hands were clenched at his sides as his eyes began to glow a beastly red. *I'm going to save her and kill all of these bastards that made her suffer. They'll all pay for this!*

"Now, now," a voice said from in front of Yuri. "That's not exactly the right thoughts to be having, is it?"

Yuri's eyes widened when an image flickered before him.

He hadn't seen this coming. How was it possible? A fist collided with his diaphragm and sent him rocketing through the air and back up the stairway from whence he came. He gasped, flying through the doorway and smashing into the courtyard, ripping dirt from the ground as he rolled head over heels at an uncontrollable speed. He jammed his feet into the ground as he tried to catch his foothold, but maintaining balance at such speeds was near impossible. He fell once more and landed heavily on his back, panting and gasping for breath. His eyes were wide with shock at what had just happened. *That was no ordinary punch. No human could throw me this far. That had to be a Bount! But what the hell are they doing here?*

***

Keimaro was enjoying himself and laughing with Aika as he twirled her once more on the dance floor. He dipped her finally, bringing her close to the ground. He held her tightly, and she blinked a few times at the advanced move. By now, the rest of the nobles had gathered around to watch the two dance. Though Keimaro had lacked confidence in his dancing prior to coming to this ball, he was already the star.

The ground rumbled, and Keimaro quickly pulled the princess back to her feet, glancing around at the castle. The glasses were rattling around them as thundering explosions echoed from outside. *What is this? An earthquake?* That was when Keimaro remembered. *Yuri.*

"Princess, get to safety immediately. I'll be right back. Make sure everyone stays inside!" Keimaro yelled, beginning to sprint through the crowds of nobles that separated at the sight of him. If this was Yuri, he would have to put on his mask in order to make sure that soldiers didn't see him protecting a rebel. That would blow his cover immediately. He broke into a sprint out of the door and ran past Judal, who glanced at him.

"Where the hell are you going? We need to stay and guard the princess! Let the rest of the guard handle it!" Judal yelled.

"I have a feeling something bad is going to happen if I

don't get out there!" Keimaro called over his shoulder as he dashed the hallways toward his room. He hoped that Judal wasn't following him. Thankfully, he didn't. What the hell was Yuri thinking? What was all this noise that he was making? The entire castle was shaking, leaving Keimaro with the uncomfortable feeling that something was happening beyond Yuri causing chaos. Someone out there was matching Yuri's power. A Bount.

Keimaro staggered into his room and slammed the door shut behind him, ripping off his tuxedo and tossing it onto his mattress. He reached under his bed, pulled out his cloak, and swiftly threw it over his body. Reaching into his cloak, he took out his mask. The boy exhaled as he looked through the eye-holes of the pale-white mask. He had to put this thing on again. He slid the mask over his face and grunted as it began to attach itself to his flesh, binding with his skin. He breathed, his voice completely altered now to become a deep metallic echo. He stepped outward and onto the windowsill of his room, where he admired the brilliant view once more. *Here we go.*

The boy leapt out of his window and out into open air, flipping through the free space. His black cloak flapped in the wind, and his hair blew back, his eyes squinting as he soared down the side of the tower, falling near the castle. He kicked outward and ejected a jet of flame behind him that sent him flying sideways diagonally through the air rather than simply straight down. As the Shokugan activated in his eyes, he began to feel an abnormal burn in his chest. He winced, grasping at his heart for a moment before the pain faded.

Looking over the grounds, he spotted Yuri battling a black-cloaked figure. A Bount. *Not just any ordinary Bount. It's him.* Keimaro's eyes widened when he saw the bald man cackle aloud, a familiar laugh that pierced his eardrums. *"Junko!"* he roared, releasing more flames behind him to propel himself forward.

***

Yuri panted, his ribs aching from Junko's blows. The bald man was extremely fast, and his magic controlled darkness to the point where even Yuri didn't know its limits. It was nighttime, and the Bount was at his strongest. Would he even stand a chance against this guy? He didn't have unlimited time. Soon, soldiers would come by and overwhelm them, and they would both probably be captured. That was not the best plan.

"Well, isn't this a tale of beauty and the beast!" Junko laughed hysterically, putting a finger to the bridge of his nose. "The werewolf is trying to save a starving beauty underneath the castle! My, my, Yuri! I've always seen you as the angry type, but recently you've been all calm and collected. Where's the fun in that?" He shrugged in an exaggerated fashion. "Come on, my big, burly beast! Show me the rage!"

"Don't piss me off, baldy," Yuri snarled, his teeth sharpening to daggers, his eyes red like two hot coals. "I'll rip you apart—"

"Then do it!" Junko urged him, still giggling. "Go on!"

"*Junko!*" a deep, echoing voice roared, and Yuri glanced up to see Keimaro coming downward at incredible speed—and it looked like he didn't intend to stop. Jets of flame emitted from the boy's feet as he slammed into Junko at full speed, obliterating the earth with a giant explosion. The two figures began to skip across the royal courtyard like skipping stones, bouncing off of the earth and smashing clumsily into the mansions of nobles. Massive chunks of debris fell to the earth as the ground began to rumble from the force of explosions. Any ordinary human would've died from such a fall.

Yuri watched as dozens of people began to run from their homes in the noble district, sprinting in the direction of the castle, where they hoped their king would offer refuge. Others ran in the direction of the city in an attempt to escape the battlefield entirely. Yuri stared for a moment at the destruction before racing after Keimaro and Junko to see the results of the explosion.

***

An endless ringing echoed in Keimaro's ears as he blinked a few times. Dust floated around him, and he could see pieces of debris everywhere. Flickering flames licked the ground, eating away at the courtyard's grass. Two shadowy figures were exchanging blows, their silhouettes the only thing that Keimaro could see. It was Yuri fighting Junko without a doubt. The boy began to roll onto his hands and knees, his bones aching. He had survived the huge fall, but even he questioned the logic behind that. He understood that he was a member of the Hayashi clan, so he would survive things that ordinary humans wouldn't. But the jump from the top of the castle to the bottom was farther than anything he had ever tried before, not to mention the fact that he had driven Junko through multiple mansions and destroyed most of the courtyard. What kind of an idiot enters a fight like that?

Keimaro pushed himself to his feet, swaying slightly. He watched as one of the silhouettes knocked the other to the ground with a swift punch. The shadow turned and began to walk in his direction. The boy's breath was heavy, echoing through his mask. He grasped the hilt of his sword and slid it from his sheath. His eyes widened when he saw that it was Junko who emerged from the clouds of dust. *How is this possible? He should have been extremely injured from my landing. How did he defeat Yuri?*

"Like this," Junko said, reading the young boy's mind and pointing over Keimaro's shoulder.

A burst of blood splattered onto Keimaro's chin and throat. His heart was pounding rapidly, and his breath became heavy, transforming into gasps of pain. A steel blade protruded from his stomach, skewering straight through his body as if he were nothing but a slab of meat. His eyes were wide with fear as he watched Junko, all of his energy draining as the blade slowly slid back out of his body. His legs gave out, and he collapsed onto his knees, his eyes dazed. *Who...?*

"Oh my, oh my!" Darius's cheerful voice said as the prince walked around Keimaro with a chuckle, tapping his sword to his shoulder. The blade was completely coated in Keimaro's blood.

"It seems that it didn't take as long as I thought it would to eliminate the infamous Keimaro Hayashi," he said, reaching down on the ground and grasping the golden locket that had dropped from his cloak. "Ah. Or should I say Riku Hikari?"

General Mundo stepped onto the other side of Keimaro from the smokescreen of dust. He drove his fist into the boy's face, and the mask shattered, leaving Keimaro in splintering pain as it crumpled to pieces on the grass. The boy fell onto his back, crimson liquid coating the ground beneath him. "It wasn't hard to make you come out of the shadows after all, Keimaro. I have been watching you for a while."

All of these guys work with the Bounts? Keimaro's eyes darted from Mundo to Junko to Darius. He never would've guessed that Darius would've been with the Bounts. As for General Mundo, he'd had his suspicions, but now it was too late. Mundo had been the one spying on him in the library. Mundo had been the one to set up this fight with Darius, to force Keimaro to use his Shokugan in front him. Everything was all planned out. And he had fallen right into the trap.

"Drag him to the ballroom," Darius said with a smile, reaching down to Keimaro and grasping the small chain that hung from around his neck. The key had been hidden in his shirt, but it was quickly yanked out from his neck. It dangled from the prince's hands in front of Keimaro. "So much conflict over such a small item, hmm? Junko, go get me the chest. It's time to end this and bring forth, finally, my age of darkness."

19. AN AGE OF DARKNESS

By the time Keimaro actually reached the ballroom, he was beginning to lose consciousness. His hands were covered in his own blood, and the nobles gasped in shock at the grotesque image as he was dragged before the king, who stood in complete disbelief. Keimaro was thrown forward and hit the floor with tremendous force, left in a daze. The marble floor was cold, and he didn't bother moving. He could hear Aika's muffled screams as she attempted to rush forward, but guards held her back.

"What is the meaning of this?" the king demanded.

"This is your infamous Keimaro Hayashi, milord. Why," General Mundo said, grabbing Keimaro by his hair and forcing his hair back for the king to see his face, "you can even see bits of the mask on his face. We caught him for you, as you ordered."

"Riku?" the king said, shocked. "But if he were Keimaro … he could've assassinated me this entire time. Why would he wait? You…," he said, looking at Darius as he sauntered through the crowds of nobles. "Darius?"

A knife hurled through the air, burying itself in the king's throat and slamming the old man to the ground. His choking sound was drowned out by the screams of terror from the noble audience. However, no one was allowed to leave the ballroom. The guards had made sure of that.

Darius walked over to his father's sapped body and reached down to look into the royal blue of his father's dying eyes. Within moments, the king was dead. The prince's face bore not a single sign of remorse, for it was completely devoid of emotion. He simply reached down and picked up the crown off of the fallen king's head. In a single moment, the entire ballroom silenced. Aika stood staring in absolute shock, her lips quivering at her father's corpse. Then she turned her attention to Keimaro, who was bleeding out in front of him. She rushed to him, shoving guards aside. Her father was gone ... but at least she might be able to save Keimaro.

General Mundo simply smiled and allowed Keimaro to be cradled in the princess's arms, taking a step back as he nodded to Darius.

"I am your new king," Darius boomed, placing the crown upon his head. "Those who oppose me as their ruler step forth now. My father is no longer capable of upholding his throne, nor is he worthy of this crown."

"And neither are you!" a noble yelled.

Darius raised an eyebrow in amusement at the comment and chuckled, nodding his head. He clicked his fingers, and guards grabbed the man and forced him onto his knees. The noble shook, terrified, as he stared at the ground, unable to meet Darius's cold gaze. The new king began to slowly pace with his hands behind his back. He stopped in front of the noble.

"Everyone else will now bow before the new king. *Bow.*" On command, all of the people in the room fell to their knees, bowing before their new king. Some were more reluctant than others. Some had to be forced onto their knees by guards. Darius unsheathed his sword with a swift motion and raised his blade over his head. "You see, this is the fate of those who oppose me." His blade slashed downward, tearing across the noble's chest. Blood spurted into the air as the man screamed in agony, doubling over onto the ground. Nobody moved forward to help him as he bled out on the marble floor—they feared for their own lives. In only moments, he was dead.

Darius slid his weapon back into his sheath and turned to his younger sister. "Go on, heal him. I know of your power, little sister," he said with a small smile. "You see, I know of everything. There isn't a secret that you can hide from me any longer."

Aika stared at her brother in disgust, reaching down to Keimaro's pale, frail body. She placed her hand gently over the bleeding wound, and her hand began to glow a bright white light. The flesh wove back together as if time itself were reversing. The blood was absorbed into the wound like a sponge as the skin kneaded into place. In only seconds, the wound was closed, and the color had returned to Keimaro's face.

"What have you done, Darius?" the princess screamed, turning to face her brother with tears in her eyes. "That was our father! He's done nothing but care for us our entire lives, and this is how you repay him? We have no reason to—"

"Power," Darius said. The single word silenced Aika, and the prince laughed. "Isn't that what it's been about all along? The only reason I decided to take up arms and fight for our empire is for power. I was granted the ability to command subordinate men to give their lives for whatever cause I chose, but that power wasn't enough! I will rule this continent and hold power over all. Haven't you known this all along, sister? There are those who are born to rule and those who are born to be ruled! Our father had his era of fun and games, but I am here to ensure that we dominate over everyone in this world. No one will be able to stand up to our empire with me as king! Any opposition will be crushed, whether it's outside or inside my empire!"

"Now you sound like the monster that I came here to kill…," Keimaro muttered weakly, slowly pushing himself into a sitting position. He chuckled with a shake of his head. "You know, I always found it weird. I don't care if all of you nobles look at me as a monster now, but only moments ago, you respected me. There is no difference between the Hayashi clan and ordinary humans. But, while I was posing as an 'ordinary human,' I noticed something odd. Your father didn't seem like he was the monster that I came to Bassada to kill. It was you— you led the Bakaara massacre. In fact, it was your idea to invade Bakaara all along, wasn't it?"

"You got me," Darius said with a sly grin, "and I'm happy to tell you that you'll feel the same pain that you felt before, soon."

"What?"

"I told you that I know everything."

Keimaro's eyes widened when he thought of Z's mansion. Darius knew about that, too? His hands were clenched into tight fists at his sides as he stared at the new king. What had become of them? "I'll kill you, you disgusting bastard," he snarled and watched as Junko walked back into the room with the chest gripped in his hands.

"Oh my, it looks like you're getting Kei all hyped without me!" Junko said as he set the chest down heavily onto the ground. All of the nobles stood back and watched in awe as Darius pulled out Keimaro's key and began to walk to the chest.

"Darius, stop it!" Yuri's voice yelled as three guards pulled the werewolf inside and forced him to kneel beside Keimaro. His face was covered in heavy bruises, and he gasped as he watched helplessly while the prince inserted the key into the chest and threw open the latch, lifting the lid. "You don't know what will happen if you do this. The world will be thrown into darkness! Humanity as we know it will perish! You won't have the power that you desire. All that will happen is corruption. You will die as well."

Darius reached down into the chest and pulled out a tiny silver whistle. He chuckled as he held it up into the air, glancing at Yuri and Keimaro over his shoulder. "I don't think you understand. This is my era. An age of darkness is coming, boys— the darkest storm that this world will ever see. You can either face the tempest and be engulfed by the shadows alone, or you can join me in the eye of the storm, where I will be your ruler." He raised the whistle to his lips and said, "Long live the king." Then he blew.

***

In that moment, the earth began to quake rapidly. The Forbidden Forest shook as the trees whipped back and forth. Monsters and beasts of all types raced from the forest line to stagger out onto the fields outside of Bassada. The earth split as a massive fault shot across the ground, opening a giant sinkhole that swallowed everything in its path. A roar split the air, mimicking an earthquake. A huge claw shot from the hole, squashing trees underneath its gigantic grasp, and the king of beasts began to haul itself out of the darkness of the forest. Large, bone-like structures flapped into the air with webbing that formed giant wings. Black scales that were stronger than steel covered the colossal beast, coating it in protective metal plates. Its eyes gleamed like two emeralds the size of boulders. They blinked a few times as the creature flapped its wings once, pushing the lower part of its body out of the abyss. It shook its graceful, monstrous head and snorted, smoke rising from its nostrils. Hind legs gained their foothold, smashing trees as the majestic beast stood upon the earth. The beast opened its mouth to reveal its sword-like teeth and released a jet of flame into the air, covering the sky in roaring fire.

The dragon had awakened.

***

"Now," Darius said, spreading his arms with a wicked grin as the castle began to shake furiously from the force of the dragon's roar. "Embrace your inevitable doom and accept me as your new king! Let's hear the world quake in fear!" With a thud, the dragon landed on top of the castle, ripping open the ceiling of the room with a single slash of its enormous claw. Debris rained down from the ceiling as nobles screamed and scattered, fleeing from the fierce beast.

Keimaro stared with widened eyes at the bright emerald gleam of the dragon's eyes as it snorted, prying apart the ceiling until there was nothing left but the open night sky. The boy's eyes flickered to a slight movement from the top of the dragon, and he saw a man stand up from the beast's mane before he leapt down, landing in front of Darius.

Kuro Hayashi.

The man had spiked black hair that was slicked back aside from a few strands that fell forward, casting shadows over his red eyes that truly resembled a demon's. He seemed ageless, ancient, and youthful all at once despite the fact that Keimaro knew that he was hundreds of years old. The man slid his hands into the pockets of his black cloak, which matched those worn by the Bounts. He gave Keimaro a smile, a small necklace swaying as he did so. "Ah, so it seems that you have succeeded in awakening me, Junko. Well done. And who is this boy that we have before me today?"

"He is—"

"Why are you asking who he is rather than who I am?" Darius demanded, stepping forward. "I am your king and therefore your ruler. I am the one who awakened you. Not Junko."

"Is that so?" the man said, glancing at Darius over his shoulder. He flicked his wrist, and Darius's entire body was practically torn apart. There was no blade, no magic, no nothing. Crimson blood simply splattered onto the floor, and the prince collapsed to his knees, shock registering onto his face. The new king stared at the man, his hands shaking and his face growing pale as a ghost.

Keimaro watched in shock. *How did he...?*

"You ... betrayed...." Darius coughed, his throat filling with his own blood as he glared up at the man with disbelief, his hand grasping a wound across his chest. "How dare...?"

The man swung his arm, and Darius's body writhed in a

335

barrage of invisible slashes before finally collapsing onto the ground in a heap, a pool of blood beginning to form around his unmoving corpse. The cloaked man's eyes opened slowly, lacking any remorse—and any emotion, for that matter. He had not a care in the world for the murder he had just committed.

He cracked his neck and sighed, stretching his arm into the air with a small smile. "So! You are a member of the Hayashi clan, no?" he said, kneeling in front of Keimaro. "My name is Kuro Hayashi, so I guess you could technically call me your ancestor, huh?" He chuckled, but Keimaro spat in his face, erasing the man's smile. He rose to his feet and wiped the spit off of his face with his hand. "The first couple of minutes of being reawakened, and this is the treatment I get, huh?" He looked at Keimaro with a raised eyebrow. "From the look in your eye, you understand pain. In fact, you understand me, no? How the gods took everything from you and killed—"

Keimaro rose up to face Kuro, his eyes shining red with rage. "The Bounts took my parents from me. No one else. In other words, *you* are responsible for their deaths," he said as he glanced over his shoulder at Yuri, who was still on his knees. He walked behind Yuri and touched the metal that cuffed his hands together. Keimaro's hand released a surge of fire into the cuffs, turning the metal bright red before it liquefied and splattered onto the ground.

Kuro watched with keen interest, raising his eyebrows with surprise at the flames that left Keimaro's hand. "It seems that we have quite the interesting specimen here, don't we, Junko? Someone else who is like me—or, rather, he is one-third of what I am."

Freed from the cuffs, Yuri moved to his feet, his spine writhing and stretching as his body sprouted white hair. His irises flashed bright red, and his body morphed into a werewolf in a mere instant, his claws sharp as knives. His snout elongated, and he snarled at the sight of Kuro, showing off his beastly fangs.

"And a werewolf," Kuro said with a smirk. "How vicious."

"Run," Keimaro said to Yuri. "I'll be right behind you."

Yuri looked at Keimaro for a moment with glistening eyes and grunted. He turned and dropped to all fours, looking at Aika and nodding. "Get on," he growled.

Keimaro met Aika's worried eyes and nodded, turning to face Kuro as the princess mounted the werewolf. They scampered out of the ballroom toward the courtyard where nobles and guards were yelling in confusion.

"So, speak your name. It is common curtsy. I gave you mine. It's your turn." Kuro called to Keimaro.

"Keimaro Hayashi."

"Ah," Kuro said with a smile, "and you are able to control fire, correct? How interesting. From the looks of your power, I would say that you received natural magic, like me. I didn't think that there was anyone in the world who was like me, yet I sense that I've come across someone with only a third of the power that I have. Say, where is the rest of the power? It must've been distributed through two others, correct?" Kuro raised his eyebrow and then laughed. "Oh, my. Don't tell me! That girl … the one who just scampered away with the dog. She has a third of the meteor's power, doesn't she? You know, I could use that power to take on the gods. Perhaps I should—"

"Don't you touch her!" Keimaro yelled, flames roaring in response and smashing against the outer walls of the room, shaking the entire structure. More rubble dropped from the ceiling, and Kuro clicked his tongue as he looked up at his dragon.

"Looks like you do have a soft spot for her then? Young love!" Kuro said, shaking his head with a sigh. "You see, that is where one finds an easy weakness. The heart is what weakens a human. Perhaps you've heard of this theory as well. I cut out my own heart so that I wouldn't have to deal with that particular weakness." He pointed to his chest where his heart would normally be as he began to walk around Keimaro slowly, his footsteps echoing on the marble floor. "What makes demons stronger than humans? It is their lack of compassion, their absence of social connection. What makes humans stronger than demons? It is their intelligence. Thus, I took two of the greatest weaknesses in humanity and demons and cast them away. I created a clan that derived from only the strengths of both demons and humans. But it seems that even you managed to use the human part of yourself to grasp at the weakness of love.

"Why would you welcome such a simplistic concept of attraction when it will bring you *nothing?*" Kuro boomed, his eyes suddenly flashing a demonic red. He circled Keimaro, who kept his head forward as he listened. "You believe that loving this woman will bring you happiness? You think that a simple idea such as love will change anything? Do you think it'll take away your loneliness? No, it will enhance it. But you know this already, don't you?" He grinned. "When she is gone, you will feel pain. All of your love will be transformed into hate, regret, and guilt. And you will be cast into the shadows of solitude once more, even deeper into the abyss than you were before. Love is a single path with no benefits at its end. There is only agony and solitude," Kuro said, stopping in front of Keimaro. "So, why risk it? Why form bonds with other humans when you are only going to be hurt in the end?"

"I don't know," Keimaro said with a straight face, as he looked Kuro solidly in the eye. "For me, it's because she reminds me of the past before my village was destroyed and my family was killed. She reminds me of the happiness that I used to feel four years ago before all of this. She makes me stronger and she gives me meaning. She gives me a reason to continue forward on this path."

"On what path? Revenge?"

"No. No, not revenge. The path to stopping evil. To stopping you," Keimaro said. "You said that love is a simple emotion. Well, Kuro, if you're such a perfect being, then how would you not understand that love is the most complex and inexplicable emotion that any human can feel?"

He paused, watching Kuro's eyes narrow before he

338

continued, "When I first saw the princess, I didn't even know what attracted me to her. I didn't know why the flow of her silky brunette hair appealed to me or why my heart thumped whenever I looked into her royal blue eyes. I can't explain the feelings that churn up within my stomach when I spend time with her every day. And I regret nothing. Aika makes me happy, and she has changed me for the better."

"You will end up in pain, and you will be alone when your bond is severed."

"No one lives forever," Keimaro said. "I know that you'd like to contradict that statement, but no one does. The bond will be severed eventually, but it will be worth it in the end. I would rather have formed the bond than never have made it at all. No bond lasts forever because no one lives forever. Not even you," he said, grasping the hilt of his sword and sliding it from his sheath with a loud scrape. Gleaming steel flashed into the midnight air. He whirled the blade and pointed it at Kuro.

"Go after the werewolf and the princess," Kuro said to Junko as he stepped forward with a chuckle. "Now this truly is something. I can see the fire in your eyes, Keimaro. I respect you. Your bravery is admirable, and your confidence is commendable. However, you made a single mistake. You threatened me," he said, clicking his fingers. His dragon snarled, taking position over Kuro. "Have you ever taken into consideration your own power? You continue to blabber on and on about how you will be able to defeat me and destroy evil. But do you really think you're strong enough to dream so big? I, the one who dominated the strongest dragon in this world. I, the first human being to slay the beast that left humans quaking in their boots. You believe you can threaten me, the strongest being in existence!" He pointed at Keimaro and grinned. "A god has been awakened. I will rule this world and make the Hayashi clan the dominant race that walks upon this earth. And no one will stop me, especially not a commoner boy created by my genes."

Keimaro's teeth gritted as Junko vanished to go after his friends. Aika wouldn't be able to defend herself, and Yuri couldn't take Junko on alone while defending Aika. He had to go after them. From the looks of things, something must've happened at Z's mansion as well. There was no backup coming, despite the fact that a giant dragon had just awoken from underneath the Forbidden Forest. He took several steps backward, ready to attempt his escape. *This doesn't look good,* he thought, his eyes on the dragon.

"Burn him," Kuro commanded.

Keimaro's eyes widened as the dragon roared, releasing a jet of golden flames at him. The radius covered the entire room in a sphere of fire that blazed before Kuro. Keimaro grunted, swinging his arms outward. The flames slid around him, leaving an air pocket of safety. As the flames died down, Keimaro had already begun to run, sprinting through the door.

The boy's heart pounded furiously as he released a jet of flame to increase his speed, forcing his legs to slam against the ground as he heard the roar of the dragon behind him. The castle shook furiously as the beast slammed its heavy claws down onto the structure, attempting to grasp the boy as he sprinted through the empty hallways. Keimaro finally broke out into the courtyard and couldn't help but stare as he saw absolute chaos.

Guards were slamming nobles to the ground in order to subdue them. They were beating them for discipline. Perhaps it was discipline—or perhaps it was simply revenge for the many times the nobles had undermined the guards. Now, in the absence of authority, the guards were simply seeking to ensure that everyone followed the rule of the new king, from the looks of it. That was Faar law. The subordinates of the king had to bow down to a new king even if they didn't agree with their leadership. The new king would be Kuro, without a doubt.

Keimaro stared in disbelief at the scorched grass and obliterated structures that resembled ruins of what had been mansions of the rich only that morning. Now there was simply flames and debris. The apple tree Keimaro had seen coming to the castle for the first time was now burning, its branches crumbling into ashes. Keimaro dashed past the tree as hot flames ate away at the bark. Corpses began to coat the ground as the nobles and guards fought each other in a chaotic brawl for dominance, but the boy knew that he had no time to deal with a troubled kingdom. He had to save his friends. That was when he remembered Lena, still suffering and locked up in her cell. Waiting for a savior.

The assassin ran to the side of the castle and sprinted through the open royal jail, dashing into complete darkness. The guards had left the criminals to rot in their cells. These men and women beat on their iron bars like madmen, screaming and yelling for Keimaro to release them as he ran past their cells. He didn't have time to save them all. Every time the earth shook, he knew that they were a moment closer to the castle collapsing on top of them. He couldn't leave Lena in such a dangerous place.

He quickly found her cell and saw that her head was bowed and her arms hung weak at her side. Her body looked limp, and fear surged through Keimaro's body. What if she was dead?

Keimaro's hand roared with heat as he swung it sideways, slicing through metal with ease. The bars dropped loudly to the ground, and Keimaro dashed into the cell, slicing the chains that bound Lena before grabbing her. Her eyes were open, and she blinked a few times, her face pale as a ghost.

"Huh? Kei?" she murmured, clearly in a daze. "You came!"

Keimaro stared at Lena for a moment, tears beginning to form in his eyes. Her face was purple from the many bruises that she had received. The once-fair skin that she had was now covered in lacerated cuts and slashes as a part of the torture she had endured. Her body was bony and skinny due to starvation and her own dried blood was splattered all over her clothes. Nevertheless, Lena cracked a tiny smile when she saw Keimaro. "Of course I did," Tears streamed freely down his cheeks as Lena buried her face into his shoulder, sobbing out of happiness. "It's over. I'm sorry. I'm so sorry. This is all my fault. I should've come sooner." Keimaro cried, hugging her tightly. They had hurt her so much. Her current state was much worse than he could've even imagined. And this was his fault.

"No, it's okay," Lena sniffed, her face still in Keimaro's shoulder. "The fact that you came is enough. I always had hope while sitting in this dark cell that someone would come and save me. I dreamed about it and now that it's happened, I can't complain," There was a loud rumbling as the ceiling shook, dust cascading from the ceiling. "What's that sound?" Lena asked, her voice fading. Her eyes closed slowly and she dozed off before she even heard his answer.

Keimaro picked Lena up into his arms, watching her rest. "That's the beginning of the end."

20. THE DARKEST DAYS

The city smoldered as if hell itself had taken over. Fires flickered on the rooftops of buildings, slowly devouring the structures as it spread. Civilians left their homes with their belongings packed into bags, screaming as they ran about, unsure of what to do. Guards had left their posts and were attempting to douse the flames, but the closer that Keimaro got to Z's mansion, the more deserted the areas were. He felt a surge of hope, but then he turned onto the last street and saw that the entire block had been lit aflame.

The building across the street from Z's mansion had been reduced to nothing but rubble. The tiled streets were cracked from the force of supernatural combat. Keimaro slowly lowered Lena onto the ground, pressing her unconscious body against a solidified, stable stone wall. "I'll be right back," Keimaro said, even though he knew Lena couldn't hear him.

He strode toward Z's mansion and gulped when he saw that the gate had literally been torn apart. Part of the walls around the mansion had been smashed and cracked, but what shocked Keimaro the most was the building itself.

The mansion was like a torch in the night. Roaring flames ate away at the foundation of the building. The entire structure creaked loudly as Keimaro stepped onto the burnt grass, and the mansion began to fall apart. The once-mystical castle was now crumbling rubble, leaving debris everywhere with tiny flames licking at the earth. Keimaro's widened eyes stared, and his lips quivered as he stared at the flickering fires. *This is just like the same fire. Four years ago.* Images of his burning home flashed into his mind. His mother. Mai. His father. Z's mansion collapsed, sending a wave of dust flying in all directions, engulfing Keimaro in its cloud. Keimaro's hair blew back from the force of the collapse, and he saw corpses lying on the ground—fellow assassins with pools of blood spreading around their bodies.

The Bakaara massacre....

Images of the corpses of his village people began to flash into his mind as he witnessed his comrades dead before his eyes. He even recognized one of them—a young girl lying on her back was the same one that Keimaro had seen in the arena fighting against Buu only days ago. Now she was dead. He also saw that girl, Mika, who had led him to his bath. Her eyes were fixated on the sky, her body sprawled in an unnatural position. "What happened here...?"

As the dust began to clear, Keimaro's eyes widened, and he stared with disbelief at what he saw. Ashes blew around in the air as silence dragged out. All sound was muffled in Keimaro's ears when he saw the dying body of his first and best friend, Yata. Blood was splattered across the ground, and his diamond form was generated around a large wound in his chest. He lay on his back, staring up at the sky, his face pale as a ghost.

"Yata...," Keimaro whispered, stumbling over to his friend and falling to his knees beside the body. "What happened?" he gasped, staring at the bleeding wound in his friend's chest. "Who did this? I'm getting you out of here, okay?"

"No," Yata groaned, closing his eyes in pain. His skin was changing rapidly between metal and flesh as if he were completely losing control over his own power. He coughed, and a white mist began to leave his lips, entering the air. "It's fine, Kei. It's fine...."

"No," Keimaro growled, holding his friend's wound in a futile attempt to stop the bleeding. "I won't let you die on me! Not after everything that we've been through! We came here to Bassada to stop these guys! The journey has just begun, right? We spent four years preparing for this. You can't leave me now!"

"Hey," Yata said, grasping Keimaro's wrist with a firm grip, using up the remains of his strength. He gave Keimaro the first real smile in what seemed like years. "It's okay. I believe that you'll finish what we started. Make sure Gavin stays out of trouble. And make sure you protect Aika, too," he said, sniffing. "It feels a bit early for me to go, doesn't it? There was a lot that I wanted to do. So, make sure you live on, okay? For me."

"Yata, I can't…," Keimaro whimpered, tears beginning to form in his eyes. "I can't do this. I'm so sorry. About that fight that we had. About everything. I trust you more than anyone else in the whole world, and … and you can't just go. We've been together the longest, and you're my first friend, my best friend. So please … don't…."

Yata reached up and touched his cheek gently. "It's okay, Kei. I know. I'll see you on the other side. Don't rush after me. Tell Aika that I'm sorry that I didn't get to see her. And tell that old idiot Gavin … to get stronger and to keep pushing forward. I see potential in him." He leaned back and fixed his eyes on the night sky. He smiled. "It reminds me of four years ago, ya know? A terrible memory. But a beautiful night." His eyes fixed onto the gleaming stars. And they never closed.

Keimaro shook Yata a few times, trying to shake the life back into his old friend. "Oi, Yata! You can't give up yet, you damn idiot!" he yelled, tears beginning to stream down his cheeks. "Weren't we going to see the world together? Wasn't that our dream? We promised…." He sobbed, burying his face into his best friend's bloody shirt. Squeezing his friend tightly, he whimpered. "Don't leave me here alone…," but there was no response except for silence. And just like that, it began to rain.

Gentle drops of fresh tears descended from the night sky, blanketing the city in water and dousing the flames that ate away at the buildings. Within minutes, the fire consuming Z's mansion fizzled out. Smoke rose into the air, and all that Keimaro could see was rubble, debris, and corpses sprawled across the grounds, surrounding the destruction of the building. A small sphere of white light left Yata's lips and drifted off into the air.

Keimaro brought his eyes up from Yata's shirt, the rain streaking down his face. The light reflected onto Keimaro's face before surging forward and seeping into his skin, fusing into his chest. A burning heat surged through his body, making it feel as though his insides were literally on fire. He gasped, grasping his head as images began to form in his mind. Then memories.

Yata?

***

Yata couldn't believe that Tobimaru had survived such a blow and walked away unscathed. In fact, he looked angrier than ever. Buu was unconscious at the Bount's feet, but Tobimaru didn't even seem interested in killing him. Instead, he whirled his sword and advanced on Yata, eager to finish off the job. The boy's arm morphed into a massive sharp blade of diamond that gleamed a bright, glittering turquoise as he pointed it at Tobimaru, his heart pounding. Never had he imagined that he would face off against Tobimaru alone. Was he truly ready for such a fight?

"Out of the way!" Aladdin's voice boomed. He punched outward, releasing a surge of bright lightning that streaked and crackled through the air. The lightning hissed, slamming Tobimaru in the chest and sending the Bount flying onto his back, sliding across the floor. "Yata, everyone else is evacuating. Something is happening. We should get out of here, too!" Aladdin grabbed Buu and began to drag the unconscious boy towards the teleportation pad.

With a rumbling roar, the entire mansion began to shake furiously. It felt as if the structure were going to collapse entirely. Yata grunted, falling onto his knees while trying to maintain balance. "What is this? An earthquake?"

"That...," Tobimaru chuckled, slowly pushing himself to his feet, "was a dragon, tin-man. The end of this world and its pitiful humans has finally come. Junko was able to get his hands on the key after all. Looks like your friend Keimaro had it all along. I figured he wouldn't leave it in such an obvious place as his room, but to be so cocky that he believed he could defend the key alone ... now, that is stupid enough to get the world destroyed. Kuro has awakened, and you are all doomed!"

"Not yet!" Gavin yelled, sprinting straight past Aladdin and Yata. In his hands was the gleaming Bloodthirster, which he gripped tightly. He was staggering, clearly being weakened the longer he held the weapon. He swung the blade with both hands at Tobimaru, who raised his own blade in defense.

"Gavin, you idiot!" Yata boomed while Aladdin dragged Buu onto the teleportation pad.

Gavin's eyes widened as Bloodthirster met the metal of Tobimaru's blade, shattering it into a million glittering pieces in a single swing. The soldier had the satisfaction of seeing Tobimaru stare incredulously at his shattered blade. He stood there powerlessly, watching as Gavin's blade slashed across his shoulder. Hayashi blood was spilled as the Bloodthirster cut deep, splattering crimson droplets onto the floor.

The soldier took several steps back, satisfied with his attack. "We're getting out of here!" he declared to Yata and Aladdin. "There's nothing else we can do if Kuro has awakened. We're all going to get killed if we stay." The soldier turned to run.

"You're not going anywhere!" a familiar voice snapped, and Hidan appeared behind Gavin, appearing out of thin air as he reached out, trying to grab the soldier's collar. Yata's fist cracked the Bount's face, sending the man sliding away.

"Go," Yata said, sucking in a deep breath as the mansion began to collapse from the fighting. Parts of the top floor fell and smashed heavily into the ground beside him, cracking the ground. "I'll hold them off."

"No, we're all going together," Gavin snapped, turning to

face Yata. "When I first met you, I understand, you didn't like me. But I've grown to respect you, Yata. You're extremely brave and, I dare say, an honorable man. There's no reason to throw everything away! We can fight them and kill them all together. There's three of us and two of—"

"That won't be enough to defeat them both," Yata said with a sigh. "Keimaro isn't here. We can't beat them!"

"Then let me stay!"

"Don't try and be the hero! It has to be me!" Yata yelled, his hands shaking at his side. "These guys were the ones who broke into my village four years ago and killed everyone I'd ever known. I have to stay back and fight them. I don't care if I die. At least you'll live to fight another day. Just promise me you won't be wimpy in the future," he said, walking toward Hidan and Tobimaru. "Aladdin, take him!"

Aladdin grabbed Gavin and began to yank him away from the scene, pulling the soldier toward the teleporter across the room. Gavin glanced back reluctantly and watched as his new friend began to encounter the two dangerous terrorists. He called out to Yata as tears glistened in the corners of his eyes. Yata was going to sacrifice himself. And, as Gavin was whisked away, he knew that he was powerless to stop Yata from his duty.

***

Yata was on the ground, his ears ringing from the blows that he had taken for what seemed like hours. His metallic skin was beginning to vanish as his body weakened, and the pain was no longer numb as it always had been. Now he felt excruciating pain from the Bounts' blows. And it was agonizing. He was on his knees in front of the mansion, weakened, hardly able to keep his eyes open. He saw that other assassins who hadn't been able to escape were lined up beside him as well. His heart was beating rapidly as Tobimaru and Hidan stood before the group of young assassins, their weapons bared. Yata was forced to kneel along with the other captured assassins.

Blood dripped from his lips, gathering at his chin before it fell to the ground. He looked past Tobimaru and saw Hidan walking to a young girl. Mai. His eyes met with the young girl's, and he gave her a small smile, despite his situation. Her dark eyes stared back at him as if in a daze.

"Mai!" Yata called out to the young girl, his throat filled with his own blood from a broken ribcage. "Tell Keimaro when you see him that I'm sorry, will you?"

"Keimaro?" Mai said with a tilt of her head. "Who's that?"

Yata's face paled when he heard the young girl's response. *She doesn't remember her own brother? What is going on?* He looked up and saw Tobimaru swing his sword across the bodies of Yata's defenseless comrades. Blood splattered across the ground, soaking into the earth as screams of agony echoed out. Yata closed his eyes, trying to drown out the sound of the assassins being killed, but their cries filled his head.

"My, my, what is going on here?" a familiar voice said. Yata's eyes opened to see Junko walking through a hole in the destroyed walls around them. The boy's eyes followed the Bount as he sauntered over to where Yata was kneeling, his hands behind his back in a gentleman-like fashion. The man smiled. "Ah, yes, I remember you. You were the boy in the Bakaara massacre. To think that you've lived four years without a home. Without a family. That's quite a feat, you know. Ah, you look like you're in pain," he said, tapping Yata on the chest. "Let me help you with that."

Pain bloomed in Yata's chest before he grew numb. Blood splattered onto his neck, and his eyes stared blankly at Junko, gasping. He looked down and saw that Junko had driven a dagger into his heart. Tears filled his eyes as he fell onto his back, metal beginning to solidify around his wound. He felt cold, as if he were being left alone underneath layers of snow. He smiled at the very thought of snow as the tears streaked his face.

The sounds of Tobimaru cutting down the rest of Yata's comrades were drowned out by his memories of enjoying winters in Bakaara. All of the children would come together and have giant snowball fights, tackling each other in the snow. He always won, of course. He felt a jolt as he remembered how Keimaro always watched them from a distance, knowing that if he had joined, he would have been targeted. Oh, how he wished that they could've been friends before all of this. That was something he would forever regret, that he had never had a chance to enjoy a normal friendship with his best friend.

***

After seeing Yata's memory, Keimaro's eyes opened to find that the rain had stopped. There was nothing but silence as he stared at Yata's unmoving body. The last time that they'd talked, they had fought. And all his friend had for him was pure intentions. He clenched his teeth, water mixed with tears still running down his cheeks. *I wish we could've had a normal friendship, too, Yata.* His hands were shaking at his sides, and he heard shuffling behind him but didn't bother to look.

Yuri had been thrown to the ground at the gate of Z's mansion. In his human form, the corners of his mouth were heavily bruised and blood splotched his cheek. He gritted his teeth, glaring up at Tobimaru, Hidan, and Junko. The three Bounts had ganged up on him and defeated him soundlessly. The werewolf glanced over his shoulder to see Keimaro kneeling at Yata's corpse. Yuri stared at his fallen comrade in shock, incapable of believing what had happened to the mansion and to Yata. He wasn't given much time to mourn because he was hauled to his feet and thrown to the ground beside Keimaro. The Bounts dragged Aika along and shoved her down beside Yuri.

"Oi, Hayashi boy," Junko said, tapping Keimaro on the shoulder and holding his bloodied dagger in his hand. "Stop crying. He's gone, all right? What you should be thinking about is how you will get him back. You see, if you help Kuro—"

"You're still trying to get me to join you?" Keimaro said, his voice deep and shaky. "You killed my best friend. My first friend. He was always there for me. He always gave me hope that we would be successful in avenging my family. He was more than just a friend; he was a brother to me. And you killed him…."

350

The boy sprang to his feet and swung around, slamming his fist into Junko's face with such speed that the other Bounts weren't able to react.

A crack sounded, and Junko spiraled through the air, landing several meters away with blood streaming from his broken nose. The Bount grunted as he twirled his dagger, chuckling nervously. "You've got guts, Kei. You always have, even back then in Bakaara. But you're foolish!"

"Am I?" Keimaro said, turning to face the Bounts. His eyes were glowing an ominous red, but they weren't filled with hatred. They were apathetic. "I've made up my mind, Junko. I'm going to tear you apart … and you're going to know what it's like to feel true pain." He began to make his way toward his opponents.

Tobimaru sighed, looking around for a weapon since Gavin had shattered his blade earlier. He wrenched a stray sword from the ground, pointing it at Keimaro. He frowned, looking at Keimaro in disbelief. "Is he suicidal?" he muttered to his partner. "What could he possibly—"

Keimaro swept his hand in the air, and flames roared to life —but this time, something was different. The flames morphed from their warm colors into a pitch-black, swirling around in the air at Hidan. The Bount swept away with a gust of wind and vanished before the flames were able to hit him. Still, the mere sight of this fire was enough to make Tobimaru stagger back in fear. The boy moved on to Junko, who was staring in awe.

Junko jabbed with his dagger at the boy, but Keimaro saw everything coming. He grabbed Junko by his wrist, twisting and snapping it like a twig. He ignored the Bount's cry of agony and yanked the man onto the ground, forcing Junko onto his stomach. "You've done nothing but make me suffer," he snarled, driving his foot down onto Junko's back, rapidly stomping on the man's squirming body. "I'm sick of losing the people that I love. I'm sick of everything!"

Tobimaru snapped to his senses and sprinted at Keimaro to save his comrade. His eyes widened when Keimaro, with unbelievable speed and power, drove a kick into his diaphragm. The man doubled over, grasping his stomach, the air forced from his lungs. *What?* he thought. *How is he able to read my movements so easily?* The Bount raised his hand, using his telekinesis to choke Keimaro with as much pressure as he could muster.

Keimaro glared at Tobimaru and swept his hand, sending black flames that forced the Bount to disengage, staggering away before the dark fire could engulf him. The boy heard Junko's whimpers of pain, and Keimaro drove his sword down into the Bount's leg, skewering his flesh and pinning him to the ground. Blood splattered across the earth as the bald man screamed out in agony. His eyes were wide with fear, never having experienced such pain before. Tears streaked down his cheeks and mucus ran out of his nose as he raised his hand in an attempt to cast magic, but Keimaro knew exactly what he was planning. He brought his boot crashing down on the man's second wrist, breaking that cleanly as well. "You look like you're in pain, Junko," he said, bringing his hand upward. Black flames began to coat his fingertips, and his eyes gleamed with malice as he brought his arm down. "Let me help you with that!"

His arm sank into flesh, cutting through Junko's back as if it were nothing. In silence, Keimaro yanked his hand from the flesh of the Bount's corpse, blood coating his skin as he staggered back. He swayed slightly, feeling everyone's eyes upon him. His heart was pounding, and he felt his stomach giving way. His fingers tingled with an unknown sensation surging through his veins. His vision blurred, and he stumbled over the corpse at his feet.

Tobimaru shifted nervously and gripped his sword in front of him tightly, not quite sure what to do. He extended his hand and grasped Keimaro's body with an invisible force, yanking the boy in his direction. Tobimaru's grip on his blade loosened as he slashed his sword sideways as Keimaro was dragged toward him.

Keimaro blinked as he felt the abnormal tugging, as if the air itself were yanking at him. He grunted as he found himself staggering toward Tobimaru, and then he saw that the Bount's sword was cutting at him. He raised his hand, hitting Tobimaru on the inside of the wrist in order to prevent the blade from reaching him. He swung his fist, catching the Bount in the cheek with a loud crack. Tobimaru took a step backward, his head snapping to the side forcefully. When he turned his head back to face Keimaro, his eyes were filled with a glowering hatred. He roared as he punched at Keimaro.

Keimaro's eyes widened as he was thrown backward as if a cannon had slammed into his stomach. He rocketed several feet into the air before he felt something invisible grasping at him again. He gasped as his trajectory was completely changed while in mid-air. Defying physics, he was dragged back toward Tobimaru with incredible speed. His face met the Bount's fist at full-force. The blow knocked Keimaro onto his back, and he slid past Tobimaru, groaning. Despite his audible response, the punch hadn't exactly hurt. Normally he would've at least had a bloody or broken nose from such a direct hit, but it felt as if the entire blow had been muted, numbed somehow.

Tobimaru turned to look at Keimaro and raised an eyebrow. "It seems you have benefitted from your friend's death."

Keimaro held out his hands and saw that, although they looked normal, they were solid steel, reminiscent of Yata's metallic powers. Was it possible that when the light had struck him in the chest, it had been similar to how the meteor's energy had transferred to him four years ago? It was quite possible. He looked at Yata's unmoving body and gulped. Even after death, Yata was still with him, helping him to the very end. He clenched his hand into a tight fist and was suddenly gusted off of the ground by Hidan's wind magic and was hurled across the entire courtyard, smashing into the dirt like a skipping stone.

***

Hidan appeared out of thin air beside his partner and whistled, brushing back his hair with a swift motion. "Wow, looks like he's even more frightening, huh? Black flames and increased stamina from his friend. You could say that we are in a bit of a predicament, Tobimaru."

"More than you know," Tobimaru said, rubbing his wrist as he twirled his sword and watched Keimaro, who was beginning to get up. "Our attacks don't do much damage to him anymore. He isn't like Yata. Yata was incapable of avoiding or blocking our attacks, so he was practically a punching bag. We just waited until his stamina drained out. However, Keimaro will be harder to hit, and his flames are the ultimate offensive."

"What's with the black flames, though?" Hidan muttered. "He killed Junko without any effort. Should we be worried?"

"Black flames are infamous and are typically used only by demons. The flames are called the Kuroi Homura. They are the fires that burn within the depths of hell," Tobimaru explained, watching as Keimaro slowly pushed himself to his feet. "They can burn through anything, even water. The only thing that can douse them is holy water. Other than that, the flames burn for eternity. But what intrigues me most about this is that the flames can be used only by pure demons. Keimaro and I are both half-human. How he's managing to use them doesn't make sense."

"It's because we have someone before us with quite some potential," Kuro's voice echoed. Kuro stepped from behind Keimaro as if appearing out of thin air. He tapped Keimaro's shoulder with a light chuckle before vanishing.

***

The boy saw nothing over his shoulder, but he was sure that he had heard Kuro's voice just behind him. He glanced to his right and saw Kuro walking forward with his hands folded behind his back. "What the hell do you want?" he snarled. "Did you come here to die like your friend?"

Kuro looked past Keimaro at his fallen comrade, Junko. He opened his mouth to speak, but no words came. Soon his sullen look was replaced with a small smile. "I suppose this is something that I had not anticipated. You have surprised me. You do have talent, Keimaro. As the creator of the Hayashi clan, I can assure you that what makes you stronger is your hatred. But, to think that your anger and hatred can reach such an extent that you can transcend your own humanity … now, that truly is something. What is it that triggered this?" His eyes scanned the area and locked onto the lines of dead bodies behind Yuri. "Ah. Friendship, bonds that were forcefully severed, I presume?" He began to walk forward and came between Tobimaru and Keimaro. "This magic is making you incredibly strong, I agree. We could use you."

"Use me?" Keimaro scoffed. "After all that you've done to me? You killed my family, destroyed my village, kidnapped my younger sister, and killed my best friend along with all of my other comrades. They are lying here as corpses before our eyes. How dare you offer me a position to work beside you to accomplish your sick, twisted desires!"

"My desires, actually, are the same as yours," Kuro said with a laugh. "You see, everything here is so simple. I left Junko with a simple set of instructions. Create a monster. Make the monster suffer to the point that he lost his reason to live. And he created a monster, you."

Keimaro cringed at the word. He gritted his teeth, glaring at Kuro.

"I wanted to transform a tranquil and peaceful life into a world of hell. You see, such a sudden twist of events, such forceful yanking of loved ones from one's life can cause traumatic changes. Simply from looking into your eyes, I can see the type of person that you were before all of this happened," Kuro said. "What happened to your family and your village—the Bakaara massacre, was it? That was what made you into a monster. A killer, one bound to revenge. However, we can give you back that life of tranquility. Everything that you've ever wanted can be given back to you. You see, that is the point of everything that we have done to you."

"You've tormented me in order to force me to join you so that I can get everything back?" Keimaro snarled.

"In order to open your eyes to the cruelty of the gods. Your family was doomed from the very beginning. Whatever Junko did to your family was going to happen either way. The Hayashi clan is doomed to be extinct. There is no way to exist in a world created by gods who want us dead. It is us or them, don't you see?" Kuro exclaimed, growing louder as he spoke. "The objective of the Bount organization is to destroy the gods and take our place on their throne to govern over this world. With the power of the gods, we can bring anyone that you want back to you. We can help you achieve anything that you desire. Anything that you've ever wanted will be given to you. You can see your mother again, your father. If you join us, your younger sister will be reunited with you immediately."

Mai.

Keimaro closed his eyes at the very thought of having everything that he had ever lost returned to him. Yata would return, his mother, his father, the people of his village. Everything could go back to normal. He wouldn't have to keep seeking revenge. Wasn't it the gods' fault that the Hayashi clan was to be executed? If the Faar Empire hadn't cooperated, they would've had some other force carry out their desires to burn down Bakaara. It was a hard decision. Join the people who had taken everything from him in order to get everything back, or fight against them because it was the right thing to do. His eyes opened.

"Well?" Kuro said.

"I'm afraid I'll have to decline," Keimaro said. "As much as I want my family back, I could never ally myself with someone that I hate so much. I would be itching to tear all of you apart every second that I spent with you." He pointed his finger at Kuro. "I don't care what everyone says about you. I don't care if you're the strongest being alive. I am going to be the one to kill you, and you will rue the day that you ever created a monster like me."

Kuro raised an eyebrow in amusement and guffawed, grabbing his belly as he laughed hysterically. "You're a stubborn one. Well, I cannot blame you. After all, I would feel the same way in your position. Though, you might decide to change your mind. Go on, I will give you this one chance at life. If the world doesn't eat you up by the next time we meet, I will do it myself. Meanwhile, I hope that you will think of the offer."

"What?" Tobimaru snapped. "You're going to let him go?"

"If I kill him, then Junko's intentions over these four years will have gone to waste," Kuro said with a smirk as he eyed Keimaro. "Besides, I do see that you have what it takes to follow in our footsteps. You are much like me. I want my revenge. That is why I am going to destroy humanity and cast the world in such a dark shadow that they will forget what sunlight ever looked like. You can reject this offer and run off with your band of assassins. However, an age of darkness is coming. Are you and your friends truly strong enough to stand against it?" He laughed, clicking his fingers as he began to walk away, motioning for Tobimaru and Hidan to follow.

"In the meantime, we will keep your younger sister alive. That is, until it is ensured that you will not accept the deal. Then her use will be expired. Until next time," Kuro said, stepping over the destroyed rubble of the wall that had surrounded Z's mansion. "I wonder what young Mai will think of her older brother's decision."

Keimaro's hand curled into a tight fist at his side, and his knuckles cracked. Without thinking, he launched himself forward at Kuro, his eyes crazed with mad hatred. He roared, swiping his hand as a line of hot flame moved with him. But Kuro was fast, countering and dodging his every movement. Keimaro released everything he had. He swung and slashed, punched and kicked, but nothing seemed to touch the Bount leader. Instead, Kuro stepped about, reading Keimaro's movements like a book—and he smiled the whole way through.

Keimaro ripped his sword from its sheath and slashed downward, flipping through the air and bringing it into the ground where Kuro had been only a moment earlier. Flames radiated across the singed grass, blackening it to a crisp. He dragged his blade across the dirt, whipping it forcefully out of the earth at Kuro, but the Bount made sudden movements that seemed to freeze even time itself.

Kuro touched Keimaro's wrist with hardly any force at all, and a spasm writhed through the boy's body, forcing him to drop his weapon. He stared in disbelief at the actions of his own hand before a punch slammed into his cheek. With a second's notice, he was tumbling. The world spun continuously as he was thrown across the courtyard, bashing through the remains of Z's outer wall and smashing into the neighboring buildings. It didn't seem like he could stop. He gasped, rolling through the wall of a house where he found himself on a wooden floor, the entire structure creaking loudly. He pressed his palms to the ground, his hands shaking furiously, his head throbbing. A ringing in his ear dragged out, irritating him.

"You see…." Kuro's voice was rather far away, but Keimaro could hear it clearly. The sounds of the debris crunching beneath Kuro's boots mixed with the ringing as the Bount spoke. "You have potential. Never the potential to defeat me, no, but you do have what it takes to be at my side." The man stood behind Keimaro, hovering over him with an evil grin printed on his face. "What do you say?"

"I say," Keimaro spat, blood dripping down his lips, "screw you."

"That's unfortunate," Kuro whispered, swiping his hand into Keimaro's stomach with a blow that sent him crashing through furniture and slamming against the wooden wall of the house. "I see that you can take quite the beating now. Your skin feels like steel. Am I hitting a piece of metal?" He chuckled. "You seem to have gotten stronger already from when I last saw you—and that was what, an hour or so ago? That is very remarkable. What happened? Someone close to you died?" Kuro walked over and grasped Keimaro by the collar of his shirt, slamming him roughly against the wall and peering into his eyes. "That is what makes you stronger. Pain, agony, suffering. The point of everything that we are doing is to make you stronger. I don't understand why you don't see that."

"That gives me all the more reason to hate you," Keimaro

snarled, glaring into Kuro's glowing red pupils. "Perish in hell, scum. I'll see you there in a couple of years."

Kuro opened his mouth angrily, but then he paused, and a wide grin spread across his lips. "You have chosen to suffer, have you not? Pain in life is unavoidable. However, you have isolated yourself from society to the point where you have become an alien to those around you. Isolation leads to pain, and pain leads to suffering. And suffering leads to hatred." He brought his lips to Keimaro's ear and whispered, "Do you hate me?"

Keimaro's eyes were wide when suddenly he was hit in the stomach with an enormous amount of force. He doubled over and was released, grasping his diaphragm. His eyes were watering uncontrollably as a roaring heat burst through his stomach. He felt sick, as if he were going to vomit. His chest and stomach writhed as if a fire blazed inside of him, burning out his insides. "What did you do...?" he snarled, his throat squeezing tight as he began to wheeze.

"You're quite an intrepid young boy," Kuro said, sighing as he slid his hands into the pockets of his torn black cloak, "but you aren't prudent and lack the ability to think before you act. You see, there are a few things that you don't yet understand. I merely unlocked your inner potential that has been dormant for all of these years. You will become stronger, but it takes responsibility and self-control to tame such angry fires that will roar within you. That heat that you feel right now in your chest, in your heart, is your rage. My offer still stands. It is understandable that you hate me and my organization, or even our cause. However, perhaps you should think about why you are angry. Pain is not a choice, but suffering is. You choose to suffer rather than press on with life and embrace what liberties and beauties exist in this twisted world. But I suppose that is what makes you and me one and the same. It has been years, and my hatred has grown over a long period of time. Just remember where your anger should be directed, and perhaps you will reconsider the offer. Otherwise, the next time that we meet, I will take from you everything that you love. You will be cast into such darkness and such suffering that you will be on your knees begging for me to offer you the position at my side once more. And when that happens, I will deny you. Do not make the mistake of defying me twice," he said simply before he turned to walk away.

Keimaro winced as he watched the Bount stalk into the distance. "Come back here...," he snarled, pushing himself onto his stomach. He felt weak, incapable of actually getting to his feet, but he wanted to catch the bastard nonetheless. "If you don't finish me off now, I swear to god, I'll rip you to shreds when we next meet!"

***

Tobimaru and Hidan were watching the scene from the courtyard while keeping their weapons trained on Aika and Yuri, making sure that they didn't move a muscle. Yuri was barely conscious, but Aika was shaking and staring at Keimaro, who was lying on the ground. As Kuro stepped over the debris of Z's outer wall, he clicked his fingers. In an instant, the building where Keimaro had been exploded, sending roaring flames soaring into the air. Wreckage flew outward in all directions with a shockwave of dust that swallowed the three Bounts up in an instant.

Aika gasped as she covered her eyes, the dust flying around her and engulfing her and Yuri. The strong breeze began to blow her hair back, and she shut her eyes as the roar of the explosion echoed in her ears. As the howling winds died down, she wiped her face with her sleeves and stared down at her torn, dirtied dress. Then she glanced up at the obliterated remains of the house. It was a simple wasteland of nothing, dirt blowing about. The entire building had been eradicated.

Aika's eyes searched for any sign of life, and she found Keimaro lying on the ground on his back, his cloak flapping in the silent air. Blood was smeared across his chest, and his eyes were closed. The princess's heart leapt a beat, and she pushed herself onto her feet, lifting up her dress as she ran over the debris, sprinting in Keimaro's direction.

"Kei!" she screamed before being grabbed by her forearm. Her eyes widened as she was yanked backward, staggering over pieces of crushed rubble. "Let me go!"

"You're trouble, aren't you?" Tobimaru said, shoving Aika back onto the ground, pointing the tip of his sword at the princess. "Learn your place, or I'll cut you in half," he warned, his eyes glowing.

Aika couldn't help but see the parallel between this man and Keimaro. Their eyes were filled with the same hatred. Still, underneath that mask of anger and pain, she saw a glimmer of humanity within. For this man, it was buried much deeper than it was for Keimaro.

"Out of the way!" Yuri boomed, suddenly in his werewolf form. His white fur was matted with blood as he flashed forward with incredible speed, slashing at Tobimaru with his claws. The Bount leapt into the air, avoiding the blow but unable to dodge a second uppercut that caught him in the jaw and sent him flipping through the air.

Tobimaru landed on his feet beside Hidan and grunted, twirling his sword as he examined the opponents. "So, you're putting up a fight then? I'll kill both of you if need be." He glared at the werewolf with bitter acrimony.

Kuro simply stood at a distance with his hands in his pockets, witnessing the events unfold before him. He raised an eyebrow when he saw the dust from the explosion beginning to swirl in the air as a dark aura filled the air. He exhaled deeply through his nostrils, and a grin began to spread across his face as he turned to the pile of rubble burying Keimaro. "It seems that his inner beast has awoken."

A crack split the air, and everyone turned their heads to the pile of rubble that covered Keimaro. A burst of howling flame tore through the debris, sending a beam of fire straight into the sky. Bits of rubble began to lift upward, floating several feet off of the ground, as if gravity itself had been reversed. A shockwave of dust flew outward in all directions as Keimaro slowly rose to his feet, swaying. His eyes were redder than the fire itself. His cloak had been partially burned apart from the extreme heat, and its ashes drifted off in the light winds. On his diaphragm was an insignia burned into his flesh, glowing wickedly and filling the air with its dark aura.

"You're not going to touch them," Keimaro growled, lowering his eyes, *"or I will personally see to it that you share Junko's fate."*

Tobimaru stared at the new person before him, incredulous. Such a dark aura resonating from him … was this the same Keimaro that he had seen only moments ago? He glanced back at Kuro over his shoulder with disgust.

Don't tell me that he awakened Keimaro's inner darkness with that mark, he thought. *That could result in our deaths—and those of his friends as well. What the hell is Kuro up to?*

"We are falling back," Kuro murmured.

"What the hell?" Tobimaru called to Kuro with a scoff. "At least capture the bastard! He'll work for us if you just use Danzo to—"

"To what?" a woman's voice called out.

"That voice…," Tobimaru muttered under his breath as he glanced to his right and saw a tan woman with gleaming blue eyes. She wore a long white cloak wrapped over her linen clothing, and she had three pistols holstered at each side as well as two swords cross-sheathed across her back. Her white hood was pulled over her head to shadow her face, but there was no mistaking her voice.

"Aoi," Tobimaru growled. "The Queen of the Seas. The Third Immortal. You were the woman who journeyed with Zylon and Kuro centuries ago. What's an old woman like you doing here?"

A man stood beside her with a young girl slung over his shoulder. He had a red bandana pulled around his brown hair, and his blue eyes gleamed with hysteria. He had a cleanly shaved face and was dressed in a buttoned-up blue coat over fine linens. His long, baggy pants were sewn from ragged white linen as well. A large red sash was tied around his torso, and a thick leather belt encircled his diaphragm. There were two holsters for pistols at his side and another two on his chest over his jacket. A blue cape draped down to the ground behind him, and a golden medallion with a skull insignia dangled from his neck. He revealed a small smile as he cocked a pistol using his thumb, pointing the barrel at Tobimaru and Hidan. "Don't forget me, mate. It ain't polite."

"Edward Jones, too," Hidan said, holding out his hand, where a red staff formed from the wind. He tapped the staff to his shoulder and sighed. "Oi, Tobimaru, don't get too hasty now. This is dangerous."

Kuro scoffed as he took a step forward to look at Aoi and smiled. "Aoi, my old friend, it's been a while. Too long, perhaps. I assume that you'll be helping Zylon and his band of fools to stop me, then? You won't take up this final offer to assist me?"

"As much as I would love to become a god," Aoi said, pulling back her hood to reveal flowing blonde hair. She tossed her hair playfully and gave a sly smile. "I don't think it would be much fun if I already had all of the power in the palm of my hand, aye? So, I suppose I'll help Zylon this once with his stupid affairs."

Kuro sighed and waved for Tobimaru and Hidan to follow him. "Then do so by fleeing. You will have an hour before Danzo activates the Chains of Memories. This is the only warning that I will give you," he said with a smile. "For old times' sake, hmm? After all, Aoi, I know how much you like your freedom. If I were you, I'd get out of this empire as soon as you can. And you, Keimaro," he said, turning to face the young man, "I expect you to ponder the offer I have made you. If you refuse, I will order your execution. I cannot have a member of the Hayashi clan rashly running loose in my new world."

"Kuro, stop this sick plan of yours," Aoi said as the Bounts began to walk away. "I don't want to have to result to violence and—"

"And what?" Kuro said, stopping to glance at the woman over his shoulder. "Fight me? Who do you think is currently the strongest being in this world? Do you truly believe that your armada of pirates will be able to defeat me? Or that your own personal strength will even make a tiny enough contribution in your efforts to actually stop me? I can sink your ships and kill all your men with a single glance. I can obliterate entire cities with a simple wave of my hand. Armies run at the sight of me walking alone down a battlefield. I am the perfect weapon. I am my own army. In fact, I'm invincible now that I have awakened with my dragon at my side. Make all the threats you want, woman," he said, continuing to walk away. "In the end, anyone who opposes me will feel the full wrath of my hatred."

"Stop!" Aoi commanded, drawing a pistol from her holster and pointing it at Kuro's back. She stepped forward slowly. Hidan and Tobimaru cringed at the sight of the weapon, but Kuro simply turned around, his look completely devoid of emotion. "You won't get away. Your plan from the very beginning has endangered everyone in the world. Don't you see how selfish it is?"

"This lady is a bit crazy…," Yuri muttered, transforming back into his human form. "Pointing a gun at Kuro Hayashi … that's a death sentence."

Keimaro watched with interest from a distance, taking a few steps off of the pile of rubble to get a closer look at this stranger who was threatening Kuro. Her bravery was commendable, but did she have the guts to follow through with pulling that trigger?

Kuro walked toward Aoi with his arms open and raised his eyebrows. "Go on then. Shoot me," he said, walking up to the woman and grabbing the end of the gun. He placed the barrel against his forehead and looked straight into Aoi's eyes. "Pull the trigger and put an end to this sick plan of mine then, if you're so sure that you want it all to end."

"Oi, Kuro…," Hidan murmured, "you—"

"Shut up," Kuro snapped and smiled at Aoi. "Go on; pull the trigger. Kill me. If you're going to do it, do it."

Aoi's eyes were wide with incredulity, her face pale with disbelief. Her hands were shaking, and the pistol rattled in Kuro's hands. Her finger twitched on the trigger, unsure whether or not she wanted to pull it. Sweat began to stream down her face, and she gulped, sighing as she lowered the weapon.

"As I thought," Kuro said, spinning around and sweeping her off her feet with a swift kick to the legs. The woman left the ground and flew parallel to the earth as Kuro brought his fist down toward her stomach, ready to tear out her insides with his bare hands. "That will be your downfall."

Keimaro was suddenly upon him with frightening speed, prying his sword from the debris in the ground. He held it tightly by the hilt as he slashed it upward at Kuro's throat with deadly accuracy.

The Bount leader tilted his head back as the blade cut through open air. He took several steps back with a scoff. "You fleas keep interfering," he muttered and glanced to see the other pirate's pistol trained on him.

Edward's eyes were trained on Kuro with his wrist completely still, the pistol not shaking at all. He was perfectly ready to shoot to kill. "I'm not weak like the Queen over here, mate." He pulled the trigger, and gunpowder erupted from the pistol in a loud explosion, sending a spiraling ball of lead flying at Kuro at blinding speed.

Kuro's hand shot up, and the bullet hit his palm, stopping in its tracks. "That's enough of that," he said. He turned away and began to walk with his fellow Bounts through the holes in Z's mansion's wall, making their way casually back to the castle. "I intend to see you soon, Keimaro," he called over his shoulder, flicking the bullet onto the ground.

Keimaro stared in disbelief at the Bounts and looked at the

bullet that rolled uselessly on the ground. He turned to Edward, recognizing the man. He had broken into Edward's house and taken refuge there after he had assassinated that politician. He turned to Aoi, who was lying on the ground. He held out his hand to her. She had spoken of working with Z, which meant that they had to be on the same side. "Are you all right?" he asked.

"Yeah," Aoi said with a brief nod to Edward. She sighed as she brushed off her white cloak. "Reckon he'd do that. I also thought I was strong enough to actually pull that trigger, not that it would've done much anyway." She sighed. Keimaro remembered that Tobimaru mentioned that she was the Third Immortal, so she was like Zylon and Kuro, ancient. But she looked to be thirty at the maximum. "At any rate, we need to get out of here. We found your friend taking quite the nap in dangerous territory. Lena, I believe Edward said. Did you leave her there, mate?"

"Yeah," Keimaro said, motioning to the destruction around them. "That was before all of this happened. It was safer to have her there than have her with me."

"Aye," Aoi said, glancing at Yuri with a smile. "Ah, if it isn't the werewolf. And how is your friend faring?"

"She seems all right," Yuri said, nodding to Aika. "Just a few scratches and bruises."

"Good, so the only one in poor condition is this girl that Edward is holding. But first, we need to get out of here," Aoi said. "We will get her fed and tended to once we are outside of the empire."

"Are we really in that much of a rush?" Yuri asked. "I mean, Lena needs medical attention. Aika should be able to heal her. If we just give her—"

"You realize that the Bounts still have Danzo, correct?" Aoi interrupted. "That means that if we don't get out of here in the next hour, we are all doomed."

"Why is that?" Yuri frowned. He wanted to get Lena help as soon as possible. But at the rate things were happening, that didn't seem too likely.

"Because Danzo is planning on activating the Chains of Memories."

"What do you mean by that?" Keimaro intervened.

"It's exactly what it sounds like. Danzo is a memory specialist with magical capabilities that no one seems to understand. It's too strong to be deemed artificial magic, but it takes too much of a toll on him when it is used to be natural," Aoi said. "Danzo is a member of the Bount organization, but you probably haven't seen him. He is a wise old man who has lived for several centuries. He typically uses his magic on a large scale, which leaves him at a weak stage for a long period of time."

"Then why don't we just cut him down while he's weak? That's one less Bount to worry about," Keimaro observed.

"If only it were that easy. You see, the reason that Danzo is a member of the Bount organization is because of his magic and wisdom. Members of the organization are able to fight on their own, but Danzo cannot fight. In fact, an ordinary soldier could probably kill him in a battle. However, his ability to manipulate others as if they are mere chess pieces is the reason he is dangerous. With his magic, he can enter someone's mind and change their memories entirely. He can make things that never happened, happen. He can make a person meet someone whom they have never met before," Aoi explained. "That's the issue of what is going on here. Kuro is the brute force in all of this, but the real mastermind behind their plan is going to be Danzo. When he unleashes the Chains of Memories, he will change the memories of every single human in the Faar Empire, and they will all work for Kuro permanently. In other words, the empire of Faar will be under Bount control, and the fate of mankind will be dominated by the largest army in the world."

Keimaro said nothing while the rest of his comrades began

. to panic.

"Sparta is already on the brink of destruction." Edward offered. "Faar will easily bring them down unless they have assistance. Even with us there, the Faar army stands at over a hundred million soldiers strong. The Spartans have only ten thousand at their maximum. We should—"

"We aren't running away, if that's what you're implying," Yuri growled at the pirate. "If the Spartans collapse, so does Athens. It'll be like dominoes. Once Sparta falls, everything in this world is going down with it. We need to stop them. You damned pirates just love running away, don't you?"

"Then what the hell do you propose we do, eh?" Edward snapped at the werewolf. "Mate, I don't want to risk my life for a damned lost cause! The chances of survival and victory are zero! Zero!"

Everyone began to argue, but their words were drowned out by Keimaro's mind as he stared forward through the ashes and destruction and locked his eyes onto Yata's peaceful body. He bit down on his lip, his hands balling into fists at his side. "*Enough*," he said, and everyone was silenced immediately. Keimaro stared forward, his heart throbbing. "It is not a lost cause." His voice broke the silence as he closed his eyes.

"When I joined you guys as an assassin, I thought of all of you as tools for my vengeance. I see now that I was foolish. I want to thank all of you for changing me," Keimaro said with a small smile as he looked at Aika. "I used to want to destroy this world, but right now ... right now I want to save it.

"Kuro has been awakened. A dragon along with him! The entire Faar Empire is about to be mind-controlled, and we've lost many comrades." He spoke softly, watching as a gentle breeze blew Yata's hair from his closed eyes. "But don't let that discourage you. This is still our world. This is still our fight! If we turn around now and run, we won't be escaping anything. We'll still perish. So now, it's a matter of whether we decide to die fighting or die running." Keimaro glanced at Edward. "I'm not exactly a fan of running, I might add."

The pirate raised an eyebrow and sighed. "Aye, I see what yer saying."

Aoi grinned, giving Keimaro a big slap on the back. "I like you already! Brave and fierce. You're exactly what we need to bring down Kuro, but there's a lot that we need to do before we head to take him down. Right now, we need to focus on fleeing the empire. Edward's house has a teleporter, similar to the one that was in Zylon's mansion. We'll port ourselves to Sparta where we'll discuss our next step. We're going to have to somehow find a way to slay Kuro's dragon. That is the first step to bringing down this tyrant." As the pirate spoke, she began to step over piles of rubble, making her way toward the cracked streets of Bassada. "Quickly, follow me! If we're going to get anything done, we need to get out of here before Danzo's chains are activated."

Keimaro watched as everyone began to follow Aoi, eager to get out of Bassada as soon as possible. But he didn't move. Aika noticed and turned to look at him with worried eyes. "Are you coming?" she asked with a sincere tilt of her head.

Keimaro looked at the princess for a moment, his lips quivering before he shook his head. "Yeah. Just go on without me. I'll be right there," he said as rain fell from the sky. What seemed like a light shower turned into a downpour, and Aika nodded, leaving without another word. Keimaro turned to Yata's body, which still lay in the mud. He looked peaceful.

Yata's blood was washed away with the rain, and he lay amongst dozens of lifeless teenage bodies that were punctured with wounds. The destroyed remains of Zylon's mansion were reduced to piles of charred wood and cracked stone debris, the rest of the ashes washed away. Keimaro walked to Yata's body and stood there, watching his old friend.

A part of him wasn't able to accept the fact that his best friend had died. Another part accepted reality. Before he knew it, tears were mixing with the streams of rain that streaked down his cheeks. His wet hair came down over his face. "Why wasn't I here for you like all of the times that you were for me?" he murmured, grinding his teeth. He tried desperately to hold back his sobbing. "In the end, I wasn't strong enough to stop all of them."

There was a moment of silence. The only sound was that of the rain.

Keimaro ran a hand through his wet hair, sighing. "You warned me about this. You told me so many times that maybe this path wasn't the right one. Vengeance. I always thought that when I killed Junko, I would feel fulfilled. But right now, I don't feel happy. I don't feel anything but this terrible pain in my chest. All of this time, I've been chasing the past." He bit his lip, and the rain finally stopped, the clouds beginning to part in the darkened skies. The moon's light shined through the opening and beamed down on Yata's body, bathing him in a bright glow. "And I never realized what I had until I finally lost it. I'm sorry, Yata.

"But now I realize what I have to do. Chasing the past isn't going to help. In order to have a future, I'll cast away the past. I have friends behind me now; I'm not alone. But I want to open up a bright future for myself. No, not just for myself, but Mai, Lena, Yuri, and all the others, too! I want to have a future of peace. In order to do that, I'm going to have to defeat Kuro," Keimaro said, extending his hand outward before him. His hand began to morph from skin into gleaming metal, and a small smile appeared on his face, tears still glistening in the corners of his eyes. "I know that you'll be watching me, Yata. So watch closely. I'll crush the Bount organization with this power, and I'll save this world."

***

Tobimaru and Hidan walked silently behind Kuro through the destroyed streets of Bassada. There were people in the streets, quaking in fear at the very sight of Kuro. Tobimaru knew who Kuro was, but he didn't exactly know what to do now that Junko was gone. Junko had been their original leader since Kuro

Brandon Chen

had been in his slumber. Now that Junko was dead, did that mean that Kuro was leading them? Realistically, even if Junko had survived, Kuro probably would still have ended up leading them. "Hey," Tobimaru called out to Kuro, who stopped in his tracks. "Why did we let Keimaro go? He's only going to become more dangerous. With those black flames, he already managed to kill Junko. It won't be long before he masters control over fire and metal. He'll become a more formidable opponent and a threat like that shouldn't be allowed to roam freely."

Kuro sighed, glancing over his shoulder at Tobimaru. "You're a member of the Hayashi clan, aren't you? Two survivors of the massacre ... that was something that I did not expect. You must've been recruited by Junko in my absence," he said with a sly smile. "Keimaro is growing strong; you're correct. In the future, if he continues the same way, then he will become a problem. But with only two-thirds of the meteor's power, he cannot defeat me. I have the full, harnessed natural energy of the meteor's strength. Someone who hasn't obtained all of the meteor's power cannot defeat me—and I suppose that you know the only way he can get the other third of the power."

Tobimaru said nothing. It was Aika's death. If Aika died, then the power would be transferred to whoever touched her next. In other words, Keimaro would have to sacrifice her in order to gain the strength to defeat Kuro. He scoffed. *So Kuro really isn't worried about anything. He believes that Keimaro won't kill Aika.*

"As he currently is, Keimaro doesn't have what it takes to sacrifice anything to obtain power," Kuro explained, beginning to walk away. "Soon he will begin to realize that he is too insignificant to make a difference in this world ... and he will succumb to the darkness that I have offered him."

ABOUT THE AUTHOR

Brandon Chen is a high school senior and a self-published author. He has been writing stories since about the age of twelve. After numerous revisions and re-writings, he finally published Book 1 of Age of Darkness in late November of 2014. It is a fantasy/adventure/action novel targeting a young adult audience. While he is still open-minded about career choices, Brandon intends to pursue a college degree at NYU while writing the Age of Darkness trilogy and other works. He lives in Connecticut with dozens of stories swirling around in his head daily.